T0028916

DEAD SPRINT

CAROLINE FARDIG

SEVERN RIVER
PUBLISHING

DEAD SPRINT

Severn River Publishing
www.SevernRiverBooks.com

ISBN: 978-1-64875-471-5 (Paperback)

ALSO BY CAROLINE FARDIG

Ellie Matthews Novels

Bitter Past

An Eye for an Eye

Dead Sprint

Parted by Death

Relative Harm

To find out more about Caroline Fardig and her books, visit

severnriverbooks.com/authors/caroline-fardig

To my running buddies, Maria, Elisbeth, Rebecca, and Ryan, who inspire me to keep training when I don't want to and who also help me figure out where to hide bodies in Hamilton County.

PROLOGUE

It was colder outside than she'd anticipated. Her breath plumed billowy clouds into the icy air, leaving a trail behind her. The addition of another layer of clothing would have been ideal, but by the time she had gone a half-mile, her body heat compensated for her lack of planning.

Night runs were her favorite, especially in the winter when a light blanket of snow covered the ground. The trail wound through the wintry woods and across wide expanses of prairie, quiet and calming. She could hear the rush of the nearby river, but she concentrated on listening to her breathing, as was her ritual. Her ice cleats gripped the ground beneath them, a perfect amount of traction to keep her pace quick.

She'd planned only to run a light three miles as a warm-up for tomorrow's race, but the tranquil trail beckoned her to keep going. She wasn't ready to give up the peace this particular run was inspiring in her. Tacking on an extra few miles to a workout was nothing to an old pro like her.

Slowing her pace to a jog to conserve energy for tomorrow, she continued on, focusing on the rhythmic *crunch, crunch, crunch* of the snow under her feet as she inhaled and exhaled in time. It took her a few breath cycles to notice a different rhythm creeping in. It was faster than hers, and growing louder.

She turned her head to glance back down the trail. Another runner was gaining on her. She thought she'd be alone out here. A flicker of anxiety shot through her. It was darker along this wooded part of the trail, her headlamp only illuminating a few feet in front of her. She brushed off her apprehension and kept going.

The runner passed her, waving and only offering a muffled, "Hey" through a cold-weather mask. She watched the person disappear around the next bend in the trail, her flow beginning to return as she relaxed.

Running, especially long-distance, afforded her the chance to unplug from life. To worry about nothing besides putting one foot in front of the other for miles on end. To turn off her always-humming brain and just be.

After another mile, she'd found the zone. She closed her eyes. She hadn't felt this free in a long time.

A rustling to her right broke her out of her too-short reverie. Frustrated, she opened her eyes in time to see a sudden blur of movement and experience a blinding blow to her right kneecap. Her leg gave out, the pain engulfing her as she stumbled and landed in the snow. She screeched in agony, only to have her cries cut off as something sharp slashed across her throat, cinching tight as someone dragged her off the trail. She fought back, kicking her feet and clawing at her throat to pry the wire away. It loosened for a moment, only long enough for her to gasp for a partial breath. Then a searing pain encircled her neck, slicing from all directions. Tighter and tighter, it dug into her flesh, burning and robbing her of all air. She struggled with all her might, but she couldn't get free. The world became hazy around her. The pain ebbed. She was in the zone again.

Free...peaceful...

Unplugged.

1

Earlier that evening

"Sorry I'm late. My meeting ran long."

Vic Manetti took my hand and pulled me through the doorway to his home. "It's okay. Good meeting?"

"It was a meeting."

He pressed a kiss against my lips. "Come on in and I'll introduce you to the club."

I dawdled behind him, removing my coat and purse and taking my time hanging them on the rack in the foyer. After the day I'd had, the thought of having to be polite and conversational with a group of strangers made me want to run away screaming.

Vic announced to the small crowd in his living room, "Everyone, this is Ellie Matthews. I'm sure I've told all of you about her."

Vic's guests, easily the seven most physically fit humans I'd ever seen in a room together, stopped what they were doing and turned toward me. They all grinned at me, every one of them trying to hide the fact that they were giving my body a quick scan to size me up. Runners are the worst.

One of the men snapped out of it. "Vic talks about you all the time, Ellie. Nice to finally meet you. I'm Mateo."

"Hi, Mateo."

The first woman to determine I was absolutely no threat to her tossed her long hair back over her shoulder and let out a giggle. "We've met before, but I don't know if you remember me. I'm Shawna. We ran into each other a few weeks ago on the Monon Trail in Carmel, but you weren't in much shape to talk."

"Right, hi," I said. When Vic and I went out running, he regularly saw people he knew and often stopped to chat. I was usually disheveled, out of breath, and unable to carry on a coherent conversation.

The rest of Vic's running club—Chris, Tracy, Jonathan, Rebecca, and Eve—chimed in to greet me.

I pasted on a smile. "Nice to meet you all."

Vic put his arm around me. "Since tomorrow's run is Ellie's first competitive race..." He paused while everyone gave me a way-too-enthusiastic round of applause. "I'm sure she'd love to hear any tips you guys have for staying focused, keeping up pacing, and most importantly, staying warm out there."

I hoped no one would actually pull me aside and talk running. I'd agreed to exercise with Vic to get myself into better shape. He'd somehow mistaken that to mean I wanted to become an Olympian. When he found out I'd been on the cross-country team for one measly year in high school, he immediately signed me up for a 10k and made it his mission to train me for it. I enjoyed the weight loss benefits of running, but I wasn't interested in the competitive side of it, nor did I care about focus or technique. But of course Vic's well-meaning friends didn't hesitate to bombard me with "tips."

"Go with layers. Layering is the key to a good cold-weather run. I have so little body fat, it's hard for me not to freeze out there," Eve said, her big doe eyes wide with sincerity.

Tracy asked me, "Do you listen to music while you run?"

"Always," I replied.

She turned up her nose. "Well, you shouldn't. You should be listening to your breathing, and your mind should be free from distractions."

I listened to music for the express purpose of distracting my cluttered mind. And also so I didn't have to hear my wheezy breathing.

Mateo said to Tracy, "Not everyone subscribes to that elitist theory, you know. If she's been training with music, then she should use it tomorrow." He turned to me. "It could throw off your stride if you're used to running in time to the beat. Plus, I don't know about you, but I get bored without my tunes."

I noticed a haughty glance pass between Tracy and Shawna.

Chris said, "I'm susceptible to exercised-induced asthma, so I like to wear a runner's mask. A mask makes all the difference when it's cold out."

Tracy evidently wasn't ready to let the music thing go. "Vic, I'm shocked you allow her to listen to music while you train her."

Before Vic could say anything, Mateo let out a bark of laughter. "*Allow* her? He's not the boss of her."

I caught Mateo's eye and nodded my appreciation for his snappy retort.

Shawna turned her attention to me. Her tone was super condescending. "Ellie, your first race will seem the longest. It's really important to be in the right frame of mind. Break down the mileage into segments and push yourself from one segment to the next. I never compete without writing out a race plan, even in short races like this one. Like my trainer always says, if you don't plan to win, you'd better plan on failing."

My only "plan" was to bundle up and jog it out. It was only a low-key trek through the woods, not the Boston freaking Marathon. And it would burn off enough calories that I could reward myself with a candy bar later in the day without feeling guilty about it. *That* was a win in my book.

Rebecca frowned. "Or she can just have fun with it and not worry about the competitive stuff."

With the same snooty attitude she'd had with me, Shawna turned to her and said, "Training is when we're allowed to have fun—in moderation, of course. Racing is serious. You could stand to be more serious about your own running, Rebecca. You might do better tomorrow if you can increase your focus and mindfulness. Your last few races haven't exactly been your best effort."

Rebecca's cheeks colored. "Not everything has to be a competition."

Snorting, Tracy said, "It's literally a competition."

Shawna gave Rebecca a fake smile and tossed her hair again. "What's the point of even getting up in the morning if you're not in it to win it?"

Rolling her eyes, Rebecca griped, "There's no way for anyone else to 'win it' with Shawna the Ultramarathoner around. I guess the rest of us should all go ahead and plan on failing."

Shawna thrust out her bottom lip, but other than that didn't seem too offended by Rebecca's comment. I wondered who she was trying to impress with the full-on sexy pout and all the hair tossing. Mateo was rolling his eyes along with Rebecca. Chris was secretly ogling Eve while he thought no one was watching. Jonathan's concerned gaze was focused on his wife, Rebecca. Vic was the only guy paying any attention to Shawna. Although I didn't blame her for trying to flirt with my handsome date, it definitely made me like her even less.

Jonathan changed the subject. "You know, there's a lot to be said for enjoying the scenery. I hear we're going to get another couple of inches of snow overnight. I love a fresh snow. Should make a beautiful backdrop for the race. Nature can be a pretty good remedy for when it gets boring out there."

Mateo said in a loud aside to me, "This is all bullshit. All you need to do is picture a big glass of wine waiting for you at the finish line. You'll run like the wind."

Vic's grip on my shoulder tightened. "Thanks for sharing your advice, guys. But none of us are going to run our best if we don't fuel up. Let's eat." As everyone else headed toward the kitchen, he backed me into the empty foyer and put his arms around my waist. "Sorry about that. They mean well. I probably shouldn't have encouraged them."

"It's fine, really." I leaned into him and lowered my voice. "What I want to know is, why did you stand there and let them pick at each other? I figured a lawman such as yourself would want to keep the peace." Vic was an FBI agent I'd met a couple of months ago while working a multiple homicide case for the Hamilton County Sheriff's Department.

He shrugged, a smile playing at his lips. "They always start bickering when someone brings up technique. I figured you'd get a kick out of it."

"And that is why I like you, Agent Manetti."

We joined his guests in the kitchen. The countertop was covered with dishes full of food. Healthy food. Everything was gluten free, vegan, or Paleo; not the typical fare you'd normally find at a potluck-style dinner in central Indiana. No casseroles crowned with tater tots or buttery dump cakes here. No "salads" with mayonnaise as the main ingredient or bacon-wrapped anything. Damn. I would have killed for some comfort food. At least I knew I'd be able to stomach the beef stew Vic and I had put in the slow cooker during our lunch break.

Eve handed me a plate with a square of something on it. "I bet you like pizza, right, Ellie?"

What was that supposed to mean? "Um...sure."

"Then you'll love my Paleo pizza. The crust is made of cauliflower! Dig in."

The flaccid object on my plate was most certainly not pizza. And I would eat cooked cauliflower when hell froze over.

"As good as this looks, I'm afraid I have to pass. I'm allergic to cauliflower."

Eve's jaw dropped. "That's *terrible*! How do you keep Paleo without cauliflower? I'd be so fat without a substitute for carbs."

The truth? I only kept Paleo while Vic was watching. The rest of the time, I simply tried to eat less and keep the junk food to an acceptable minimum. With all the running Vic was having me do, that was enough to shed most of the weight I'd put on over the past few months.

Chris joined us, his face stuck in a permanent smile. "Cauliflower isn't my favorite, so I often turn to turnips as a carb alternative. In fact, I brought a bowl of turnip mash you've got to try. I used to be quite heavy, and one of my biggest weaknesses was mashed potatoes. Once I found healthy replacements for the foods I binged on, the pounds melted away."

The next hour went much the same, with people pulling me aside to share their personal journeys and the gross food they'd brought. All in all, this dinner party wasn't a whole lot different than the AA meeting I'd attended earlier. Same addictive behavior; different monkey. Same boring stories of how they'd overcome a bad habit and were now so damn fabulous at being healthy. Even worse, Tracy and Shawna took their shirts off and began comparing sports bras in the middle of Vic's living room.

I had to get the hell out of here.

I beckoned Vic into the laundry room off his kitchen so we could speak in private. "Vic, I'm exhausted. I hate to cut out early, but—"

"No you don't. You've been ready to leave since you got here."

He didn't seem perturbed, so I didn't try to sugarcoat the truth. "You got me. These are not my people."

"I know, and that's okay." He gave me a kiss. "Although if you leave now, you'll miss Pictionary."

I snorted. "Pictionary with these competitive divas? It's going to be a bloodbath."

"Always is."

"Well, please don't let it get to that. The last thing I want is a phone call in the middle of the night for me to drive back over here to process a crime scene."

I didn't expect home to be much more pleasurable than Vic's dinner party. I'd had an argument with my sister earlier in the day, a far too common occurrence in the past couple of months.

To make things worse, when I pulled into my driveway, I learned Rachel had company. I took a moment to inhale and exhale a deep breath, hoping to control the mixed emotions swirling in me.

I peeked through the window on my way to the front door. Nick Baxter, my colleague from the sheriff's department, was on the floor of my living room, wrestling both my Golden Retriever and my three-year-old nephew. Rachel was sitting on the couch, laughing at the good-natured mayhem. My heart swelled. I hadn't seen a smile on her face in days.

During the last case I worked, Rachel had been abducted and held against her will. The psychopath our department had been chasing had taken her to get to me. Rachel had lingering post-traumatic stress, and I had lingering guilt. The two of us living under the same roof was at times too much of a reminder of the incident.

Baxter had taken it upon himself to be available when Rachel needed someone to talk to, having first-hand experience with family recovery after a kidnapping. On particularly bad days, she wouldn't speak to anyone but him. Although he wouldn't admit it, he also harbored serious guilt over Rachel being taken and held for as long as she had been. He'd been on the case as well, working tirelessly to get her back safely and working just as hard to keep me sane. After all we'd been through together, I hated that he and I had ended up leaving things strained between us.

When I went inside, Trixie and Nate immediately abandoned their wrestling match and ran to greet me. I patted Trixie's head and scooped Nate into my arms.

"How are you, big boy?"

"Good," Nate replied, grinning ear-to-ear. "Did you see me, Auntie Ellie? I had Detective Nick in a headlock!"

"Yes, I saw that. Nice work." I said to Rachel and Baxter, "Hi, guys."

Baxter gave me a half-hearted wave. "Hey."

Rachel's smile had vanished. "You're home early."

Tough crowd. I let out a nervous chuckle. "Yeah, I was afraid I'd lose it if one more person tried to pass off cauliflower and turnips as edible food."

Nate asked, "What's cauliflower and turnips?"

"Gross veggies I would never ever make you eat," I replied, tickling his belly. I said to Rachel, "Want me to put the boy to bed?"

"Bed? No!" Nate cried, slithering out of my arms and running toward his mom for protection.

She gave him a hug and a kiss. "Say goodnight to Detective Nick and go get ready for bed, kiddo."

Pouting, Nate went over and gave Baxter a high five.

Baxter smiled at him. "Goodnight, Nate. Sweet dreams, buddy."

As Nate dragged his feet on the way toward his bedroom, I said, "I guess I'll say goodnight, too."

Rachel didn't acknowledge me.

Baxter nodded in response, his eyes bearing the same wounded expression they always did when he looked at me.

2

"Manetti, why did I let you talk me into this?" I griped, bouncing from foot to foot to keep from freezing to death in the biting, cold wind. "And why do these races all start so damn early?"

Jonathan had been right about the forecast. It had snowed another couple of inches overnight, blanketing Strawtown Koteewi Park with a layer of pristine white. While pretty, the snow had brought cloud cover with it, and the temperature had tanked. I would have been happier with melting gray slush if it meant the chance for a few rays of sunshine.

Vic smiled and rubbed his hands up and down my arms. "You'll warm up once you start running, I promise. And the early starts help out your friends in local law enforcement. This particular one isn't such an issue since it's on a trail, but road races are scheduled early so there's less traffic to divert along the race route. Plus, the EMTs aren't as busy on Saturday mornings, so they can hang around here in case they're needed."

"I was looking for sympathy, not answers."

He laughed. "Fair enough. I think we can head to the starting line now."

We did a few final stretches, I put my earbuds in, and we were off. I tried to concentrate on not being cold, but nothing was working. I glanced at Vic, who was already in his zone, looking relaxed and happy to be here. I was pretty sure I was scowling with everything I had. But as we came up on the first mile, damned if I didn't warm right up and start feeling a lot better. I soldiered on, surprising myself by being able to make a bit of pleasant conversation.

The trail at Strawtown Koteewi Park wound through quiet stretches of woods and prairie in a rural area of northern Hamilton County. Three sides of the park were edged by the White River, which you could see at certain points along the trail. It was gorgeous in the snow, but for running purposes, my preference would have been full foliage and warm sunshine.

As we came up on the start of mile five, nearing the end, we noticed runners slowing a hundred yards ahead of us. A knot of people began to form on the right side of the trail, their attention directed toward the woods.

"I bet someone fell. I'll go see what I can do." Vic took off at a sprint toward the crowd.

How he could pick up the pace at this point was beyond me. But then again, he'd been sandbagging it this whole race in order to stay with me. He was probably excited to get to finally run at his usual speed. I, on the other hand, jumped at the opportunity to slow to a walk and catch my breath. Before I could get my breathing under control, I saw Vic begin waving at me to come on. Bummed that he caught me slacking, I started jogging again. But then I noticed something didn't seem right up there. I popped out my earbuds in time to hear Vic yelling my name. His voice sounded strained. With every ounce of strength I had left, I powered up the trail, stopping only when I got to the crowd of runners, who Vic had managed to push back from where they'd originally congregated.

"Please stay back. Don't step off the trail. I know you're all upset, but you need to keep going and clear this area. No photos or videos." Vic's voice was commanding as he held out his hands, his expression hard and unreadable. That was his cop face. Something was wrong. "Ellie, I need you over here."

I pushed my way through the runners making a feeble attempt to do as Vic had instructed. When I was able to get to the front of the crowd, I noticed trampled pink and red splotched snow at his feet and a woman lying a few yards behind him, partially blocked from view by a downed tree trunk. The only thing she was wearing was a dusting of snow, a stark contrast to the dark blood caked across her neck and chest.

Snapping to attention, I shut down the emotions stirring inside me, except the irritation I felt at the people who'd dragged their feet through what was clearly blood. I turned to the stragglers who were only pretending to disperse and barked, "Back up and move out, people! You are making a mess of my crime scene. Go!"

Vic muttered to me, "Have a little empathy, Ellie. Besides, this isn't your crime scene yet."

I retrieved my phone from a zipper compartment inside my jacket. "Give me two minutes and it will be." I dialed my friend Jayne Walsh's number. She gave a groggy hello, to which I replied, "Good morning, Sheriff. I hate to wake you with bad news, but a body has been found in Strawtown Koteewi Park. Definite foul play going on here."

Jayne slipped into her sheriff voice. "Where exactly in the park? And do you by chance have an ID?"

"On the northern trail loop. I'll drop you a pin." I said to Vic, "Any idea who the victim is?"

He stared at me, his eyes strained. "Shawna Meehan."

"Shawna from last night?" When I'd come onto the scene, I'd concentrated on the victim's mangled neck rather than her face.

He nodded.

I placed my hand on his arm. "I'm sorry, Vic." To Jayne, I replied, "Shawna Meehan. I personally saw her at seven last night, so TOD is within the last fourteen hours."

"Okay. Do you know her well?"

"No, only an acquaintance."

"Do you want this one?"

"Yes."

"Good. I'll get everything in motion. Do what you can to secure the area until we can get a deputy out there."

"Already on it. Vic's here, too."

She paused. "Okay."

I knew what she was thinking. Locals didn't like it when the Feds horned in on our investigations. Manetti had been assigned to lead our last homicide investigation when it veered into serial killer territory. While he wasn't bad as Feds went, all of us butted heads with him at one point or another over his bureaucratic practices. Plus, he was bossy as hell, even when he wasn't in charge.

"I got this, Jayne."

Her voice took on a motherly warmth. "You always do."

I ended the call as Vic finished shooing away the last of the looky-loos, except for two women, who had stayed put and were huddled together on the other side of the trail, their backs to the scene.

As Vic and I stood guarding the access point between the trail and the crime scene, I asked him quietly, "What's up with those two?"

His voice rough, he replied, "They found her. One of them stopped to tie her shoe, and her friend stayed with her. While the friend was waiting, she noticed the body and ran over to see if she could help."

I groaned and swore under my breath. Well-meaning people trying to help the victim were the biggest threat to a crime scene. They moved the body. They made new fingerprints and footprints and ruined existing ones. They wiped away DNA and trace and added their own. Sometimes they even went so far as to restage the scene if they felt the manner of death was embarrassing for the deceased.

"They were friends of Shawna's. Of course they were going to do anything they could for her," he said, frowning. "I guess I've never been around you when you're gearing up to work a death scene. It's a good thing you normally stay behind the tape and away from the public. You're not good with people, especially those in crisis."

I let his assessment slide, considering he was upset by the death of his friend.

Two EMTs came driving up the trail in a two-seater ATV pulling a trailer.

Vic flagged them down before they got to the clearing and instructed them to park there, keeping the trail bordering the crime scene clear. The more perimeter area the better, because where there was blood, there was always more blood. It was easier to block off a larger area than you needed rather than having to expand the scene later.

Vic said to the EMTs, "I'm Special Agent Vic Manetti, FBI." He gestured toward the downed log. "Body's over there. Not much you can do."

One of them replied, "We'll check it out."

While the EMTs checked for a pulse and went about their procedures with the victim, Vic went over to speak with the two women. I diverted several upcoming runners off the trail, away from the crime scene, letting them know to keep going and that there was nothing to see here.

Mid-conversation with one of the women, Vic jerked his head up and began striding toward me. He brushed past me, heading for the body.

"Whoa there, Manetti," I said, hurrying to get between him and my scene. While I didn't begrudge the EMTs having to do their jobs, they were doing enough additional damage. "I'm currently in charge of securing the scene, and only essential personnel get access. That doesn't include you."

"I want to look at something."

"Then do it from here."

His expression became hard. "You can't tell me what to do. I'm a Federal Agent. I outrank you."

I huffed. "Are we going to do this again? I know we don't work well together professionally, but at least respect me enough as a person to allow me to do the job entrusted to me by the Sheriff of this county."

"Come on, Ellie. The women said they noticed Shawna's knee had a good deal of blood on it, too."

"If they saw it, then so will Dr. Berg. He'll examine it and fully document it in his autopsy report."

He stared down at me, frowning.

"Vic, if the situation were reversed, would you let me traipse all over a federal scene? I don't think so."

Without another word, he stalked back over to where we'd been standing before. I joined him, the air between us thick with tension. I hadn't seen this side of him since we'd first met. I hadn't missed it.

As the EMTs were packing up and completing their report, a harried race official and a security guard came zooming up in another side-by-side ATV. They tried to insert themselves into the situation, asking all kinds of questions and demanding to see the body up close. I informed them that the Hamilton County Sheriff's Department—not the race officials or their rent-a-cops—held jurisdiction over the area and that they'd better not try to step a toe into the scene. When they pouted about being left out of the action, Vic asked them if they would find an alternate route for any runners still on the course and take charge of sealing off this portion of the trail from everyone except emergency personnel. That seemed to placate them enough that they left.

Moments later, two Hamilton County sheriff's deputies drove up in yet another ATV and approached us and the EMTs to introduce themselves. After Vic and I gave them a quick rundown of what had happened since we'd arrived on the scene, they excused us from our post and informed me that my team would be here shortly with my gear. After conferring with the EMTs, they cut off the trail at each end of the clearing with crime scene tape and staked a line of tape down the opposite side of the trail, giving the scene extra perimeter room. One of them stood guard at the tape while the other deputy went to speak to the two women who'd found Shawna. The EMTs left the scene.

That left Vic and me alone together.

I said, "I guess I'll see you later, then. Depending on how much we find here, I may be busy for a while."

"Or I could save you the trouble and tell you who killed Shawna."

My eyebrows shot up. "What? You know who killed her? How long have you been sitting on that information, and why didn't you share it with the deputies?"

"First responders don't need to worry about the investigation."

I regarded him for a moment. If I had to guess, I'd assume he was planning to use this angle to try to worm his way into the investigation. I could see him itching to take the lead on this case and be the one to avenge his friend's death. But that wasn't going to happen. The locals weren't going to simply hand over their case. And even if they did, the people in charge of the FBI's purse strings wouldn't want to waste resources on a non-Federal matter. The most Vic could hope for was the courtesy of being kept in the loop of our investigation, and even that wasn't a given.

When he offered nothing else, I prompted him, "So are you going to tell me who killed Shawna, or were you just being dramatic?"

His face twisting into a scowl, he said, "Her good-for-nothing boyfriend."

3

I had to fight the urge to blurt out, "No shit, Sherlock." When a woman met a violent end, it was nearly always the "good-for-nothing" significant other. That was always where the detectives started. Not exactly a brilliant revelation.

Instead, I said, "I take it you know him."

"Unfortunately."

Thanks to the abrupt halt of my run and the cold air, my joints were stiffening at an uncomfortable pace. Waiting with Vic in a tense, awkward silence for the cavalry to arrive didn't help matters, either. After a few minutes, three side-by-side ATVs pulled up, hauling two detectives, the coroner and his assistant, a criminalist, the sheriff, and a mountain of gear.

Jayne approached Vic and me first while the others gathered their things and began preparations to cross the tape. "Thank you both for being here and getting this area under control. Ellie, get suited up, and all of us will have a quick conference before we get started."

"Will do." I headed to the ATVs and said to the team, "Morning, everyone."

I got cheerful responses from my fellow criminalist, Amanda Carmack, the coroner, Dr. Everett Berg, and his assistant, Kenny Strange. I got luke-warm reactions from Detectives Jason Sterling and Nick Baxter.

Baxter handed me a duffel bag. "This is yours."

"Thanks."

I opened the bag, thrilled to find they'd brought me lined winter coveralls. I put them on and traded my running shoes, ice cleats, and gaiters for heavy boots, hoping it wouldn't be too long before the feeling returned to my icy toes. I cinched up the hood of my coveralls and put on a respirator mask. Much better.

Amanda handed me an insulated travel mug. "We thought you might need this."

Letting out a yelp, I grabbed it from her and ripped off my mask to take a drink. Hot coffee seared my tongue and throat. It felt wonderful. "You're the best. I've been freezing my ass off out here."

She murmured to me, "You should thank Nick. It was his idea."

"Okay everyone, gather up," Jayne called. The team—plus Vic—circled around the sheriff. "Agent Manetti and Ms. Matthews were on the scene shortly after the body of our victim, Shawna Meehan, was discovered by two runners who'd stopped along the trail. I'll let them bring us up to speed."

Before I had a chance to say anything, Vic took the floor. "I noticed a crowd forming on the trail ahead of me, so I went to find out what was going on." He pointed to the two runners still conferring with one of the deputies. "Those women found the victim while they'd paused for one of them to tie her shoelaces. When I spoke with them, they said they'd recognized the victim, Shawna Meehan, and rushed over to try to help her. They said she was originally lying on her left side with her back to the trail. They turned her face-up to check whether or not she was still alive. She wasn't, so they called 911 and had some of the other race participants run ahead to alert the race staff. I had them stay behind to give their statements and sent the crowd on their way. Ms. Matthews contacted Sheriff Walsh, and the two of us secured the area until the deputies arrived. The EMTs were here earlier. I believe they gave their report to the deputies and returned to their post at the finish line."

Jayne turned to me. "Ellie, anything to add?"

"Only that the scene isn't in great shape, as you can see. Before we could secure the area, a bunch of gawkers trampled the place. We may lose out on some evidence where the snow is so churned up and...bloody."

Vic frowned at me. "There wasn't much we could do about it."

I didn't give him or anyone else the satisfaction of a reply, especially since I saw a few of my colleagues take notice of the negative vibe he was radiating at me.

Jayne said, "Ellie, you mentioned you'd seen the victim last night."

Vic cut in again. "Shawna attended a party at my home last night. She left around seven P.M. She mentioned she was heading out here to finish up a couple of things."

I frowned. "She did?"

"You were standing right next to her when she said it. She was in charge of pre-registration and got in some late entries. She had to bring some more bibs out here to have the extra race packets ready for people to pick up at the registration tent this morning."

"Oh." That must have been around the time I started tuning everyone out.

Vic shook his head, not even bothering to hide his disgust.

Baxter's brow furrowed. "If she came to the park to drop some things at the registration tent near the starting line, what's she doing all the way out here?"

Vic shrugged. "If I had to make a guess, I'd say she was warming up for today's race. Shawna loved her night runs." His voice got tight when he uttered her name. He was taking this harder than I'd expected.

Jason Sterling asked, "Who all knew she'd be out here?"

Vic paused a moment before replying, "Everyone at the party."

Sterling smirked at me. "Except Matthews, who was evidently off in la-la land."

I glared at him. Sterling never passed up the chance to take a jab at me.

Baxter said to Vic, "We'll need a guest list."

Vic nodded, his expression troubled.

Jayne said, "If there's nothing else, sign in with the deputy and let's get this show on the road. Essentials only behind the tape."

Vic grumbled something, but went and stood off to the side with Jayne.

After we'd signed the crime scene entry log and began donning our protective gloves and booties, Sterling asked me, "You and the G-man in a snit?"

"You could say that. He tried to pull rank on me so he could nose around the scene before you all got here. He didn't like being told no by a lowly criminalist."

Sterling snickered. "Maybe it's that he's not used to being told no by Ellie Matthews."

"Watch it, Sterling," Baxter barked.

I leaned down to pick up my field kit so no one could see the blush I felt rising on my cheeks.

Amanda tried to smooth things over. "I'm sure emotions were running high since he knew the victim, right?"

I straightened up. "Right. In fact, he knows practically everyone involved in the race. Which is why he also didn't appreciate my lack of empathy toward the gawkers gathered around making trouble. He all but called me a frigid bitch."

Sterling said, "But you are a frigid bitch."

I gave him a fake smile. "Takes one to know one."

"Knock it off, you two," Baxter grumbled. "We've got work to do."

4

I put a waterproof tarp under my field kit and got out the camera to take some overall shots of the area, plus my voice recorder for notes, while the detectives watched Dr. Berg perform his field examination. Amanda obtained shoe prints from the two women who'd found the body, in case we happened to need them for comparison. Since the body had snow on it, any shoeprints the killer made out here would likely be buried, but it never hurt to be thorough.

Dr. Berg stood and changed his gloves. "Ellie, you're welcome to get in here and take some photographs before we remove the deceased."

"Thanks, Doc," I replied.

I could see the detectives chomping at the bit to start investigating, but I needed the photos showing the area around the body as undisturbed as possible. The snow was a mess on the side of the body closest to the trail, between the women who found Shawna, the EMTs, and Dr. Berg and Kenny all adding their foot and knee prints. On the other side, the snow was pristine, except for where it had mixed with Shawna's blood.

Based on the amount of blood I'd seen at first glance, I knew the injuries Shawna sustained had been gruesome. I hadn't paid a great deal of attention to the body before now, because it wasn't necessary until it was time to do my job. Plus, it would have been hypocritical for me to barge into the belly of the crime scene while I was telling everyone else they had to stay out.

The victim's rosy skin had turned a translucent milky blue, with her face darker and more purple. Her long, dark hair lay matted and frozen with blood and snow. The skin of her slender neck had been sliced through all around. I assumed the killer had used a garrote, a simple but deadly weapon made of nothing more than thin wire wound between two handles. As Vic had said, her right knee was busted, a big bruise formed around an angry wound. The only thing that seemed normal about her was that her eyes were closed, although that wasn't always the norm for a strangling victim. I switched on my voice recorder and murmured my observations while taking photos of the full body, then close-ups of the wounds.

When I was done, I nodded to Dr. Berg.

He said, "The weather has affected my ability to precisely determine the time of death, but I'm putting the window between roughly seven and eleven o'clock last night. I've noted some petechial hemorrhaging, so I think the preliminary cause of death is asphyxiation as a result of ligature strangulation by garrote. Blood loss from the ligature lacerations may have been a factor as well. I hope to be able to determine what type of wire was used during the autopsy." He gestured to her knee. "Our victim also sustained sharp force trauma to her right patella, possibly from a crowbar based on the shape of the wound. I would assume that injury occurred first, the blow incapacitating her long enough for the killer to begin the strangulation. There are a few scrapes and minor defensive wounds on her hands, but nothing to suggest a lengthy struggle. Her clothes were removed postmortem." He pointed to her shoulders, which were smeared haphazardly with blood. "Void patterns and blood swipes on her skin below the laceration suggest the victim was wearing clothing—at least above the waist—when she sustained her injuries. I'll examine the body for evidence of sexual assault during the autopsy." Dr. Berg turned to his assistant, Kenny. "I suppose we're ready for transport."

Kenny nodded, and the two men headed toward the trailer to get their equipment.

Sterling and Baxter approached the body and crouched down next to it.

Sterling said, "Is that her windpipe I'm seeing?"

"Yes, but can we not talk about it?" Baxter said, the color fading from his face.

"I'm just trying to help you out, man. Heave up your breakfast so we can get down to business. You know you want to."

"Jason..." Amanda warned, frowning at him.

The two of them had been dating for a while, and she was doing her best to smooth out Sterling's rough edges. I didn't think he'd ever lose his smart mouth, but the compassionate side of him tended to show more often these days. However, when there was the added stress of a big case to solve, all bets were off.

Sterling leaned down to get a closer look at the wound. "Might've been the killer's first rodeo. Looks like it took a couple of tries to get the job done." He pointed out two different ligature marks on the victim's neck. "I bet this one hurt like a bitch if she was still conscious, but it didn't do the damage. Now this other one...the killer got right. It sliced through all the way around, like a hot knife through butter."

"I'll be back," Baxter choked out, running for the woods.

Sterling chuckled. "There it is." He waited until Baxter returned before continuing, "Based on the false start, I think either the vic put up a fight and the killer had to regroup, or the killer needs to practice his garroting skills.

I snorted. "You think the killer ought to go out and *practice* garroting people to improve his game?"

"You know what I mean. To me, this job seems amateurish. The killer decided he needed to kneecap the vic first, before he went for the throat. This chick was, what, a buck ten at most? I don't feel like she would have been that hard to subdue."

I replied, "True, she had no body fat whatsoever, but she was an ultra-marathoner. She could outrun practically anyone alive was probably as strong as an ox."

Baxter cleared his throat. "In that case, she would need more subduing than the average victim. The killer knew that, so he prepared for it. That makes it seem not quite so amateurish."

We halted our conversation as Dr. Berg and Kenny came back. As much as we joked around and did whatever was necessary to harden ourselves against the gruesomeness at death scenes, the time when our victim was removed from the scene was one of reverence and quiet. The four of us backed away as Dr. Berg and Kenny lifted Shawna's body to the body bag on their gurney. I glanced over at Vic. He was standing alone, watching with clear pain on his face.

I went over to him. "You doing okay?"

Ignoring my question, he asked, "What did the coroner say?"

"You know I can't tell you that."

He turned his troubled eyes on me. "You didn't seem to have a problem bending the rules when your sister was the victim."

My temper flared, but I managed to keep my voice steady. "That was different. Her life was at stake."

He said nothing.

I sighed. "Go home, Vic. There's nothing you can do here."

Vic continued to stare ahead, his expression stony as he watched the gurney being loaded onto the trailer for transport to the morgue.

"I'll call you later," I muttered, leaving him alone.

I removed my latex gloves and headed to the ATV for another hit of coffee, thankful that my colleagues had thought to pack thermal glove liners to go under our examination gloves. I hadn't processed an outdoor scene in weather this cold in years. Amanda had, though, which was probably why she remembered to bring along the extra layers.

As Kenny was securing the gurney to the trailer, Dr. Berg approached me. "How is your sister, Ellie?"

My heart ached. Violence like this reminded me how much she and I had both gone through. "It's still tough for her."

He patted me on the shoulder. "Keep your chin up. Healing takes time."

"I know. I wish I could do more for her. She's not as open with me as she was before."

"That's perfectly normal. Don't forget you're a quasi-parental figure to her. Any rebelling she feels like doing is going to come straight at you."

The idea gave me a bit of comfort. "I never thought of it that way."

"Does she have someone she feels as though she can confide in?"

My gaze landed on Baxter, who had gone over to speak with one of the women who'd found Shawna. When she began to cry, he stopped questioning her immediately so he could hand her a tissue. Then he waited for her to dry her eyes and compose herself as if he had all the time in the world.

I smiled. "She does. Nick has been wonderful with her. He gets through to her on the days no one else can."

"He's a good man."

I nodded. "I know."

He regarded me for a moment and raised an eyebrow. "Do you?"

"What is that supposed to mean?"

Dr. Berg turned his attention to Vic, who had pulled Sterling aside to argue about something, then he stared pointedly at Baxter, who had his hand on the crying woman's shoulder, consoling her. "I'm sure you'll figure it out eventually."

As Dr. Berg hopped into the ATV next to Kenny and left with Shawna's body, my eyes wandered again toward Baxter. He was now speaking to the other runner who'd been first on the scene, exhibiting the same patience and kindness he had with her friend.

Amanda appeared next to me. "I guess it's time to roll up our sleeves, so to speak. Although before we get too up close and personal with that snow, we need Tyvek."

"You are absolutely right."

While warm, the coveralls we were wearing weren't made for protection against biological fluids, and that pink snow was full of them. At some crime scenes, hazmat suits were not necessary. This was not one of those scenes. Plus the Tyvek material would help keep us warm out here. These suits were borderline unbearable in the summer heat, but in the winter they were a lifesaver. After we put on the white suits, she dug through one of the bags and came up with two handheld whisk brooms.

Handing me one, she said, "Who'd have thought we'd get paid to play in the snow?"

I laughed. "You are way too perky today."

"To be fair, I didn't just run six miles in the snow."

"I only managed four. My official ranking for my first race is going to be 'did not finish.' Not exactly what I was going for."

She shrugged. "There's always next time."

I shivered, but not from the cold gust of air that hit us. Until last night, Shawna Meehan had thought there was going to be a next time for a lot of things. I hadn't allowed myself to dwell on the bigger picture surrounding her death. But I couldn't help thinking back to Sterling's question about who knew she was going to be out here last night. Unless the detectives found someone else who ran into Shawna after she left Vic's house, the members of his run club were the last to see her alive, and quite possibly the only ones who knew where she'd be.

I put my worries aside and slipped on some new gloves as I followed Amanda to where the body had been. We photographed the area, then sectioned it off into small quadrants. We each took a quadrant and began sweeping away the snow, inch by inch. After each quadrant we searched, Amanda and I both stopped to note what we had (or had not) found in each area.

Not too long later, the women who'd found Shawna's body were dismissed and given a ride by one of the deputies. As soon as he returned with the ATV, Jayne let us know she was heading to the station. Vic left with her but didn't bother saying goodbye to me. Baxter and Sterling took to the woods encircling the scene to look for anything the killer might have discarded.

Amanda and I had worked our way through four of our twelve quadrants. All I'd come up with was a sickening amount of bloody snow. I gathered a sample to send to the state lab for analysis, although I was convinced the blood had to have belonged to the victim. The blood would be diluted, but they could still work with it. While I had my materials out, I collected another sample from the more trampled area. I bagged and tagged both samples and filled out a request form for DNA analysis.

Amanda gasped.

"What is it?" I asked, peering her way.

"I need the camera. This may be huge."

I retrieved the camera for her and stood back to watch her work. There was an end of a wooden dowel about an inch in diameter sticking out of the snow. It was smeared with a dark substance that looked a lot like blood. My stomach clenched.

Amanda took a photo of her find, then set an evidence marker next to it and took another photo. She looked up at me, eyes wide. "Can you grab a smaller brush?"

"On it." I hurried to my kit to retrieve a smaller brush while she called the detectives over.

I handed Amanda the brush. Baxter, Sterling, and I waited impatiently while she carefully cleared the snow away from the six-inch section of dowel, revealing a thin silver wire wrapped around the center. She kept brushing, down the length of the wire, finally locating the other end of it, which was twisted around a second piece of dowel.

"I didn't think we'd be this lucky," she breathed, staring down at her find.

Sterling couldn't wipe the grin from his face. "Good job, babe," he murmured.

While Amanda took more close-ups of the garrote, I went to my kit to get a large manila envelope to hold the weapon. I figured the thicker material of the envelope would stand up better than a paper bag to any melting snow left on the item. On the evidence tag, I noted the standard information: case number, item number, today's date, Amanda's name, and a brief description of the evidence contained inside. Crouching down next to Amanda, I opened the envelope, and she lifted the garrote from the ground and placed it inside. I also handed her a piece of red evidence tape and a marker.

I said, "You found it. You do the honors."

Eyes sparkling, she sealed the envelope with the tape and scrawled her initials across it in a few places. That practice provided an easy way to prove evidence hadn't been opened and tampered with. There was no way on earth to reaffix the sticky, intentionally rippable red tape exactly the way you'd found it and line up the initials. Low-tech, but effective.

Baxter said, "You think you can get prints off it?"

I shrugged. "Depends. I'm willing to bet the killer had gloves on last night, for the simple reason it was cold as shit. So if he didn't think to wear gloves while he was making the garrote *and* didn't manage to smudge those fingerprints while doing the deed, maybe we can find something. Lifting prints is going to be tricky anyway between the untreated wood and the fact that it's been in the wet snow for twelve hours. We'll do what we can. We might have a better chance finding touch DNA."

A frown was his only reply.

Sterling said, "Let me see the camera."

Amanda handed it to him, and he shuffled through the photos she'd taken of the garrote. He paused on one that was a close-up of where the wire attached to one of the handles.

"What are you thinking?" Baxter asked.

"I had a lengthy and boring discussion with the G-man about who he's already decided the killer is. For his money, it's our vic's loser boyfriend."

"Isn't it always?" Amanda asked.

"It is, which is why I initially wasn't impressed with Special Agent Know-It-All's not-so-groundbreaking theory. But this time there's a kicker."

Baxter said, "What's that?"

He showed Baxter the photo on the camera's screen. "The garrote was made with a guitar string."

"How do you know it's a guitar string?"

Sterling showed the screen to all of us in turn, pointing in the photo to a tiny brass cylinder on the end of the wire. "Because of that. The little ring is what holds the string in place under the bridge of a guitar."

I said, "So? Guitar strings are strong, cheap, and easy to find. What makes the use of one of them significant in this case?"

Sterling replied, "According to your boyfriend, the vic's boyfriend is a guitarist."

My eyebrows shot up. "Oh. That's kind of damning."

Sterling nodded. "Damn right it is."

"And to be clear, Manetti is not my boyfriend."

Baxter, Sterling, and Amanda stared at me, but none of them uttered a response.

Sterling said to Baxter, "Let's go pick up the boyfriend."

5

"How dumb is the boyfriend to leave behind a murder weapon made from a guitar string when it's a known fact that he's a guitarist? Isn't that like shouting, 'I did it!'?" I said, returning to my quadrant and continuing my search.

Amanda nodded. "It seems pretty stupid to me."

"But by taking every last piece of her clothing, he's coming off *not* stupid about removing potential evidence. Why leave the one thing that could tie him to a homicide and clean up everything else? And why follow her all the way out here to kill her? Why not kill her at her home or coming out of work or...anywhere but here."

"Are you saying it might not be the boyfriend? Surely you don't think it could have been some random person off the street."

"Well, I mean, you can't rule out the fact that this could have been a random act. Not yet, anyway. But then again, who hangs out on a deserted trail in the snow on a Friday night with a garrote in his pocket?"

She chuckled. "Can't argue with that logic. It's someone she knows. Considering how she was left, this looks like a sex thing. For that reason alone, my money is on the boyfriend."

We kept digging, brushing snow away layer by painstaking layer. Even with the added inner thermal gloves, my fingers were frozen. The Tyvek suit had helped my overall chilliness, but still all I could think about was sitting by a fire with an enormous mug of hot chocolate. At least I wasn't daydreaming about what kind of alcohol would work best to warm me up, which was a big step in the right direction for me.

When we got to our final quadrant each, Amanda let out a squeal. "I found a phone."

I looked over at her, smiling. "You're two for two today."

She took some photos of the android smartphone in the snow, added an evidence marker, and took more photos. She gently shook the snow off the phone and took it over to the tarp to let it dry before processing it for fingerprints.

When she came back my way, she said, "He took the clothes but left the phone. Why?"

I used this opportunity to stand and stretch, rubbing my hands together to try to get some warmth back in them. "I suppose the killer could have thought the police might try to locate her cell signal. If he'd taken it, it could have led them straight to him."

"True. But if you're bright enough to put that together, you probably wouldn't have run off without the murder weapon. Plus, don't forget about the other weapon used on the victim—the crowbar Dr. Berg said had caused the damage to her knee. We haven't found anything like that yet."

"You're right. This wasn't a quick pop-and-drop. It was planned. The killer came prepared, and he spent the time to remove her clothes afterward. Even though the garrote and the phone ended up seemingly discarded, it wasn't a rush job."

We finished checking our final quadrants and changed our gloves. Amanda went to dust for fingerprints on the phone while I went for more coffee. I used my few minutes of downtime to sit in the ATV and rest my weary legs. After she'd finished with the phone, she took it to the deputies and put them on the task of getting it to our cyber investigators. A phone could afford us a wealth of information, from the victim's movements up to her death to certain kinds of financial information to whom she contacted last. If we were lucky, we might even find a text or email argument containing a threat.

Amanda came my way and took a long swig from her water bottle. "I got a couple of smudgy prints off the phone, but they all seem like they're from everyday use. But we won't know until we get them back to the lab." She wrinkled her nose as she looked past me to survey the trampled pink snow near the trail. "Ugh. Now for the real mess. This is nightmare fuel."

So many people had tracked across it, the snow had even been beat down to the ground in places. The area in question was about fifteen feet long by four feet deep.

"I know. If it had been me instead of Vic coming up first on those gawkers, there would have been even more blood. How could you not notice you were churning up bloody snow under your feet?"

She smiled. "When there's a dead naked lady ten feet away."

"Okay, maybe in that case. If we're going to go with the theory that the killer incapacitated our victim by kneecapping her as she was running down the trail, it stands to reason that she might have been killed there before being dragged over behind the log."

"No doubt there was some kind of bloodshed in that area." She shook her head. "I hate contaminated crime scenes. Even if we find something, there's a good chance it's going to be unusable."

"Agreed. My students are always appalled when I tell them that some forensic work will be a blatant exercise in futility and go against all common sense, but still be a mandatory part of the job."

My "real" job was teaching criminalistics courses at Ashmore College. I'd been full-time with the crime scene unit years ago, until I'd had a case hit too close to home and switched careers. Jayne had always been on me to return. When I'd become involved in a case several months ago, she'd managed to talk me into consulting with the department on their high-profile investigations.

Amanda frowned. "Yeah, and the one time you don't follow protocol to the letter, you get your ass handed to you in court by a defense lawyer."

I chuckled. "You're not a full-fledged criminalist until a nasty lawyer has twisted your words and made you come off like an idiot on the stand. Welcome to the club."

"I definitely learned my lesson. That said, seeing as how this area is wrecked already, do you think we can use the big brooms?"

"I thought you'd never ask."

Processing this area as meticulously as the area under the body wasn't necessary. There were hundreds of footprints, and we couldn't assume any trace materials we might find had been left by the killer. At this point, I was only looking for clothing items belonging to the victim and the crowbar.

Amanda opened a large duffle bag and got out two long handles and two angle broom heads. The broom part wasn't much bigger than our whisk brooms had been, but at least with the handle we didn't have to stoop over like we had been for hours.

We screwed the heads into the handles and started sweeping again. This packed snow wasn't nearly as easy to move as the untouched snow had been. After removing the snow from the area as best we could, we netted exactly nothing, but at least the physical labor got my blood flowing again.

Amanda glanced around the small clearing, her quick mind onto a new idea. "We've processed the two areas where we believe the violence occurred. The guys searched several feet into the woods. Again, this is going to be absolutely no fun, but I think we need to sweep the whole clearing."

I wanted nothing more than to leave this frigid hellscape, but she was right. We could miss something if we didn't search the whole place. And I liked the way she was taking charge. Although I was an outside consultant, I was the lead criminalist on all homicide cases. However, I thought it was good for her to develop her skills at running a scene, so I'd been purposely slow at giving orders so she might jump in with her thoughts of what to tackle next. She hadn't disappointed.

"I agree."

With new broom heads, we started near the edge of the woods, sweeping snow into the brush and out of our way. After we'd cleared about a quarter of the clearing, which in total was roughly twenty feet by thirty feet, I was sweating, an oddly welcome feeling that was bringing feeling back to my extremities. But I was also starving.

"Any chance you have some food in your bag of tricks?" I asked Amanda.

She stopped sweeping to lean on her broom. "I brought a couple of granola bars. Will that do it for you?"

"It will. Thanks."

I headed over to the ATV and discarded my gloves, putting my own personal gloves back on while I ate a granola bar and checked my messages.

I had a text from Rachel: *How did your race go? Are you still good to watch Nate tonight?*

I blew out a breath. I had no idea how long I'd be working today. It depended on how long it took to clear the area to finish our search, how much more evidence we found that would have to be processed at the lab, and how many meetings I had to attend at the station and the morgue. I didn't mind the long hours. My concern was how my last-minute change of plans was going to affect Rachel. Her text seemed upbeat enough. Even though she'd been unhappy with me yesterday over the petty argument we'd had, she seemed to be over it now. That was our new normal. Her mood swings, while unpredictable, at least didn't last long.

I texted back, *Didn't make it to the finish line. But I did catch a homicide investigation.* Feeling bad about possibly ruining her plans with her friends tonight, I added, *I'm sorry, but I probably won't be home for a while. Can you ask David to watch Nate?*

I hoped our stepfather could watch Nate in my place, because I didn't want Rachel to have to miss out on her plans. Tonight would only be her second time to venture out on the town with her girlfriends since the incident. For weeks, she'd stayed holed up inside our house, refusing to even go out into our backyard to play with Nate. She missed several days of classes at the start of the semester before she was able to pull herself together enough to rejoin society. I didn't blame her. The media had hounded her for interviews, and her fellow Ashmore College students had crawled out of the woodwork, hoping to achieve some sort of status or sick satisfaction by trying to befriend her. It was more pressure than a twenty-one-year-old full-time college student and single mom should have to endure.

Her response was *I'll ask him.* She didn't add a middle finger or angry face emoji, so I assumed she wasn't too upset with me.

"I found something," Amanda called.

I chucked my gloves and phone and put back on my thermals and a new set of latex exam gloves. Hurrying over to her, I asked, "Something good?"

She was crouched over a mostly empty Pepsi bottle. "What do you think? Left by the killer or random litter?"

I crouched down next to her. "There's no snow under it. Turn it over."

She took a quick photo, then turned the bottle over. It was smeared with mud on the underside. She took another photo. "Definitely litter. I found a good couple of inches of snow under the garrote and the phone, which makes sense since there was already a layer of snow down before the time of death window. It snowed Thursday afternoon, right?"

"That's right."

"I'll make a note that we found this bottle, but I'm not bagging it."

"Works for me."

We kept sweeping and found a few more food wrappers, but they were all much the same as the Pepsi bottle—on the ground under all the snow and caked with mud and leaves. Anything dropped last night should have been pristine, encased between two layers of fairly fresh snow.

Once we'd gone over the clearing with a fine-toothed comb, so to speak, Amanda and I stood back to survey our handiwork. I didn't know about her, but my back was killing me. And I was hungry for some actual food. Another granola bar was not going to cut it for me.

She sighed. "So we've ended up with a whopping two pieces of evidence?"

"Four, actually. The phone, which the cyber guys should be working on already, the garrote, and two blood samples."

"And we won't be getting any clothing later from the coroner, so...this could be the easiest homicide ever. At least for us. Maybe for the detectives, too, if Agent Manetti's hunch about the boyfriend is correct."

I shrugged. "Could be."

"Something still bugging you?"

Shaking my head, I replied, "I'm probably trying to read something into this because our last case was so nuts. Chances are, this is a straightforward incident of domestic violence. Let's finish up. I'm so ready to be indoors."

Amanda and I measured the area and completed a rough sketch of the scene, which we'd have to turn into a finished sketch using the lab's computer. It was more difficult to accurately measure an outdoor area verses an indoor area. But since this scene was contained in a small clearing, it was easier than most. Double-checking that we hadn't left any stone unturned, we signed out with the deputies and drove away, on to our next task at the lab.

6

Upon arriving at the sheriff's station in Noblesville, Amanda and I checked our meager evidence in with the evidence clerk. The blood samples would be sent to the state lab for DNA testing. We then took the garrote to our lab for examination.

It was never particularly warm in the lab, but today it felt downright toasty after the several hours we'd spent outdoors. Amanda and I traded our jumpsuits for lab coats and put on new gloves and masks before removing the garrote from its packaging and setting it on a clean piece of butcher paper on a workstation. We both stood back to study it for a while.

She said, "Pulling prints from the handles will be tricky. We've got a porous surface here—untreated wood—which has been wet and is still holding onto some moisture. I'm going to say...Oil Red O. What do you think?"

I nodded. "I think that's a good start."

Baxter came into the lab. I could tell from his slouched posture that things weren't going his way. "I'd love to hear some good news."

Amanda replied, "We just got back, so at the moment we have no news. Sorry."

He sighed. "Did you find anything else?"

"The victim's phone. Cyber should be working on it now."

"They're done with it. Not much help, I'm afraid. Is that all that was out there?"

I said, "I took samples of the blood we found. But given the amount and placement of it, I'm pretty confident it's going to be the victim's, which also falls under the category of no news. Plus, we won't get the results back from DNA for weeks, so it's not like it could help you now anyway."

He nodded. "Great."

"Did you find the boyfriend?"

"We did."

"And?"

"And we did our best to question him, but we didn't get very far. He's currently sleeping off whatever it was that he drank for breakfast."

I made a face. "Ooh."

"Yeah. Anyway, I came by mainly to let you know the pre-autopsy meeting is going to start soon, so you'll need to get to the morgue."

When he and I were on better terms, it was a given that we'd go over together. Now I guessed I had to ask. "Um...can I catch a ride with you? I don't have my car."

He hesitated long enough that I thought he might say no. "Sure. Let's go."

We walked to his SUV in silence. Although I wished there were something I could say to smooth over his hurt feelings, I stood behind the decision I'd made not to get romantically involved with him. Baxter was too good a cop and too good a person to let the strain between us affect an investigation. At the scene and in the lab, we'd been able to converse normally about the case, and I knew we'd continue to do so. But the spaces in between were painfully awkward.

Neither of us spoke on the short drive to the coroner's office. But when he put the SUV in park, he turned to me and asked, "What's your take on this case? What does your gut say?"

"Honestly, my gut is confused."

"Same here."

I trusted Baxter's gut. If he felt like something was off, something was off.

I let out a breath. "While it would be nice to have an open-and-shut case we could wrap up before dinner, I'm relieved to hear I'm not the only one who thinks this isn't as straightforward as it seems. I thought I was being overly analytical because of our last case."

"I'm sure Shawna Meehan's family won't mind if we get overly analytical in order to bring her killer to justice."

In one sentence, Nick Baxter summed up the reason why he was one of the best investigators around. He cared about the victims and their families more than any law enforcement official I'd ever met.

I smiled. "You're absolutely right, as usual."

He regarded me for a moment, but then looked away. "Tell me what you don't like about the evidence."

"It's too neat. Too perfect."

Nodding, he said, "Give me specifics. What are your red flags?"

"The garrote, mostly. It was made out of a guitar string, and the boyfriend is a guitarist. Too on the nose. Red flag. It was left right there next to the victim, begging to be found, even though the killer went to a lot of trouble to remove and cart away every stitch of clothing on her. Red flag."

"Those were my red flags, too."

"What does Sterling say?"

"He says I'm nuts. He sees the guitar string garrote as a 'use what you have' last-minute weapon, so he doesn't think the murder was particularly well planned. The victim had a restraining order against the guy only six months ago, but evidently they'd kissed and made up since then. Sterling thinks that's another smoking gun. He also thinks the fact that she was found naked points to a sex thing, which again brings it around to the boyfriend. He's ready to lock the guy up."

"But you're not."

"No. I don't know if the guy could have pulled off this murder. For starters, he's a drunk—" His face fell. "Sorry. I mean, um, he's clearly got a problem with alcohol, so..." He trailed off with an apologetic grimace.

"No offense taken." I smiled. "Are you trying to say you think he might not have even been able to stumble out to the crime scene?"

"He sure as hell couldn't stumble out there in the condition he's in now."

"I see your point. But that's where drunks can be slippery. He could be a functioning alcoholic with fairly decent stretches of lucidity between black-outs. If so, that might account for our red flags. He could go from doing dumb stuff like forgetting the murder weapon to being really careful about removing and picking up all the clothes." I shrugged. "Him being a drunk may be a simple explanation as to why this whole thing is so damn fishy."

Baxter's shoulders slumped. "So does that mean you're on Sterling's side?"

I let out a bark of laughter. "Make no mistake—I *never* on Sterling's side. I'm just saying we drunks can be wild cards, that's all."

His expression softened. "How are you doing with...everything?"

"Pretty good. Some days are easier than others. The meetings are not exactly my scene, but sometimes they help." I paused, then said quietly, "I haven't had a drink since I promised you I wouldn't."

His smile lit up his boyish face. "That's great to hear. I'm proud of you."

I felt my cheeks heating. "Thanks."

He glanced away. "Um...we should probably get inside."

"Right."

Baxter and I headed into the coroner's office and stopped outside the morgue to put on the requisite protection—gowns, masks, and gloves. We then joined Sterling, Dr. Berg, and the District Attorney, Wade McAlister, who were congregated around Shawna Meehan's still body on an autopsy table.

As per usual, the morgue was as quiet as a tomb. A place of reverence, at Dr. Berg's insistence. However, when the hot-tempered DA got anxious about how many leads the detectives had and inevitably started berating them, the vibe in here could turn on a dime. Since they already had a suspect in custody this time, I hoped DA McAlister would keep a lid on his griping.

Dr. Berg said, "The autopsy for Shawna Meehan will begin at eight o'clock tomorrow morning. As I mentioned to most of you at the scene, the preliminary cause of death is asphyxiation as a result of ligature strangulation by garrote, likely exacerbated by blood loss from the same wounds." He pulled aside the sheet to reveal Shawna's right knee. "Non-mortal major wounds include this sharp force trauma to the victim's right patella. I will verify the type and size of weapon used during autopsy." He covered her leg and removed the sheet from her hands. "There is also some minor defensive edema on the hands, a fractured finger, and two broken fingernails. I've noticed no evidence of trauma to the victim's external genitalia. However, given the state in which she was found, I'll still be performing vaginal, oral, and anal examinations and collecting a full set of samples for a sexual assault kit during the autopsy." He covered the body from head to toe. "Does anyone have questions for me at this time?"

None of us spoke up.

Dr. Berg nodded. "Very well. Which of you detectives will be attending the autopsy tomorrow morning?"

Baxter said, "I will."

"I'll see you then. Goodbye, all."

We murmured our goodbyes to Dr. Berg and headed out to remove our gowns.

The DA might not have had any questions for Dr. Berg, but he had plenty for the rest of us.

He wheeled on Sterling. "Are you sure about this suspect? There's not enough evidence yet to arraign him. You've only got seventy-two hours to make something stick before we have to cut him loose."

Sterling replied, "We're waiting on a warrant to search his apartment. I'm hoping to find the vic's clothing there, or at least something of his with her blood on it. That'll be all we need to put this guy away."

The DA frowned. "Find something, because I don't want a repeat of last time."

Baxter clenched his jaw. "There won't be a repeat of last time."

DA McAlister turned his attention to me. "Speaking of evidence, why is it that there wasn't more evidence collected for this case? Did you go over the whole scene, or was it too chilly for you to stay out there long enough to do a thorough job?"

Sterling of course thought it was hilarious that the DA had turned his wrath onto me and had to cover up a smile. Baxter watched with a frown.

I took a moment to settle myself before replying. "Yes, we went over the entire scene as we would with any investigation. There was no evidence to be found. The victim was stripped naked, so there's no clothing to process. The body was outside in the elements for the better part of twelve hours, so finding trace was pretty much out the window. We found the murder weapon, the victim's cell, and I took samples of the two areas where she shed blood. There was nothing else out there to collect."

"You'd better find me some prints on that murder weapon, then."

"Whether or not the killer left behind viable fingerprints is not something I can control. If he did, I'll find them."

"Well, do something, because I've even got the FBI breathing down my neck with this one. Evidently this girl was some agent's old flame, and he's hell-bent on making sure her abusive new boyfriend's ass is nailed to the wall."

My stomach felt like it was free falling. "Who called you from the FBI?"

"Manetti. The agent who worked with us on the Eye for an Eye Killer task force. He said one of his agents is all hopped up about this homicide. He offered his help and said he wanted to be kept in the loop."

Baxter's frown had deepened, as had Sterling's smirk. I couldn't look at either of them.

"I need to make a call," I muttered as I hurried out the door.

7

Outside, around the corner of the building, I dialed Vic's number. I didn't expect him to answer, so I was mentally rehearsing the speech I planned to leave on his voicemail.

"Manetti."

Taken by surprise, I hesitated, but only for a moment. "Did you use your FBI influence and lie to the Hamilton County District Attorney in order to gain confidential police information for personal reasons?"

He growled, "I deserved a briefing on the case, and both you and your friend the sheriff refused to give it to me."

"So you pulled a good ol' boy with the DA."

"I want Shawna's killer behind bars today, and I'll do whatever I need to do to make that happen."

"Including making accusations based on jealousy and personal bias, evidently. When were you going to tell me you and Shawna used to be a thing?"

He huffed out a breath. "I didn't want it to cloud your head while you processed the scene."

"Oh."

"And I'm not jealous of her idiot murderer boyfriend."

I was glad he wasn't there to see me roll my eyes. "Clearly."

His tone got defensive. "I'm allowed to have had a life before dating you."

My jaw dropped. "You think I'm mad because I don't like it that you used to date Shawna? I don't care about that. I'm mad because you're meddling with my job."

He was silent for a moment. "I'm sorry. I only want to get Shawna the justice she deserves."

"I do, too. So does everyone on this case. You know us. You've worked with us. Why don't you trust us to do this?"

"I... Look, Ellie, I think we should talk about this in person."

"Well, I'm kind of tied up right now. I don't know how long I'll be."

"Call me when you get done. Day or night."

"Okay."

I ended the call, less angry but still disappointed that Vic had gone around Jayne and hassled the DA. He normally wasn't like that.

I trudged over to Baxter's SUV and got in the passenger side. He had it warmed up, a welcome feeling after my chilly phone call.

After we'd driven a few blocks, he asked, "You doing okay?"

I didn't think it was fair to speak to Baxter about my relationship issues with Vic. "I'm good. I'm starving, though. What are the odds you'd be willing to stop—"

"Already way ahead of you," he said, turning into the nearest fast-food restaurant and pulling into the drive-thru lane. "You want your usual?"

"No fries this time."

He feigned shock. "Ellie Matthews is passing on junk food during an investigation? Has hell frozen over?"

"Very nearly. If you must know, I'm trying to be healthier all around. Between all the alcohol I drank and then the chocolate I used to replace the alcohol, I put on a little extra holiday weight. Fries are a no-go for now— that is, unless things get super stressful. Then I'll reevaluate my priorities."

"Fair enough."

After getting our orders, we gobbled down most of our food on the way to the station. There was no time to waste during the first forty-eight hours of an investigation, and that included time spent eating and sleeping. Once the pre-autopsy meeting at the morgue concluded, the next item on the agenda was always a meeting with the sheriff to go over next steps for the investigation.

Baxter and I headed for the conference room once we got to the station. Sterling was already there, staring at the crime scene photos and paperwork scattered on the table in front of him.

"You two get lost on the way back?" he asked, not looking up from the report he was reading.

"We stopped for food," Baxter replied.

"Matthews finds out there's trouble in paradise and immediately goes out on a dinner date with another guy?" He shook his head. "I wouldn't get caught up in that hot mess if I were you, Nicky."

Baxter opened his mouth to let Sterling have it, but I jumped in before he could speak. "First, nothing about this is your business. And second..." I drew a blank, so I said the first thing that came to mind. "Go to hell."

Sterling laughed, but at least he shut up.

A few moments later, Amanda and Jayne entered the room and sat down.

Jayne said, "What have you all got for me?"

Sterling went first. "The suspect, Skyler Marx, is in holding. Baxter and I spoke with him around noon, but he wasn't too responsive. We're letting him sleep off his bender, so he should be ready for a full interrogation shortly. We've got a warrant to search his apartment for the clothing Shawna Meehan was wearing at the time of her death and for any clothing or personal items of his that might have her blood on them."

"Good. Amanda and Ellie, a forensic report?"

Amanda's eyes were trained on the table. She seemed embarrassed. "While Ellie was at the coroner's office, I processed the murder weapon. I looked at it under a magnifier and with an alternate light source first but could find no discernable fingerprints. I swabbed what I thought might have been a smudged partial and sent it to DNA." She looked at me, her expression defeated. "I treated the wooden handles with Oil Red O, like we discussed, which should have reacted to the lipids in any latent prints. Nothing showed up except a few smudges. The phone was the same. I found two usable prints, but they were both Shawna Meehan's. I've got nothing. I'm sorry."

I said to her, "We didn't expect to find much, especially since both of those items sat in the snow all night. Don't beat yourself up."

She gave me a half-hearted smile, but I knew she was still upset.

Jayne said, "Ellie's right. Sometimes the evidence doesn't cooperate. We manage. Detective Baxter, can you bring us up to speed on what you learned at the morgue?"

Baxter replied, "Not a lot of new developments there. Dr. Berg thinks sharp force trauma to the victim's kneecap caused her to become incapacitated so the killer could strangle her with the garrote. She has some defensive bruising, a broken finger, and some broken nails. He's going to do a rape kit at autopsy, which is tomorrow morning at ten. I'm attending."

"Did DA McAlister have anything to add?"

Baxter shifted in his seat. "Well, he mentioned that Agent Manetti had called him to offer his services and to request to be looped in on our investigation."

She flicked an irritated glance in my direction. "And I suppose Wade was happy to oblige. He seemed to have hit it off with Manetti after the investigation last time."

Baxter nodded. "It sounded like the DA didn't mind sharing."

Sterling chuckled. "Yeah. He shared the fact that Manetti used to sleep with the victim and has quite a vendetta against the new boyfriend."

Amanda's eyes grew wide. I fumed silently.

Jayne shook her head. "This is getting a little personal. That said, Ellie, I think it would be best if you bowed out of the investigation."

My jaw dropped. "What? Me? *I* didn't sleep with her."

"But you're seeing the victim's ex, who is trying his damnedest to squeeze information out of us. It's pressure you don't need."

"I'm not an idiot. I'm not going to randomly blurt something out to him."

"I know, but you understand how it looks. You're done. Go."

I stared at Jayne, barely able to process what was happening. "What about my second examination of the evidence to back up Amanda?"

"I'll call Beck in to do that."

If Amanda hadn't been able to find any fingerprints on our evidence, there was no way in hell Beck would be of any help. Beck Durant, the lead criminalist, was a waste of oxygen. One of the reasons I consulted for the department was because he was so inept. The only reason he still had a job here was because his mommy was one of the county court judges with friends in high places.

Once Jayne made up her mind, there was no changing it. I stood and grabbed my purse. "Okay. See you guys."

I left the room and marched down the hallway with my head held as high as I could manage. I'd never been pulled off a case before like this. Vic had once excused me from the task force we'd been on together, but it hadn't been done in front of a bunch of my colleagues.

As I got to the front door of the station, I realized I couldn't even get home. I could walk, seeing as how home wasn't too far, but I was exhausted. I arranged for an Uber and stood at the door, waiting.

"I didn't mean to get you kicked off the case."

I turned to find Baxter standing behind me. "I know." But he sure as hell meant to throw Vic under the bus.

"Need a ride home?" he offered.

"I'm Ubering."

"Let me take you home."

"You've done enough."

His expression darkened. He held up his hands and backed away from me. "See you around, then."

8

I found my sister sitting on her bed, zipping up some high-heeled boots over her skinny jeans.

She looked up at me, confused. "I thought you'd be out working all night."

"Change of plans. Now I can watch Nate." I looked around. "Where is he? It's too quiet in here."

"David took him to a movie. You're off the hook for tonight. Go out with Vic."

"Eh. Some alone time wouldn't hurt me." I took in the distressed jeans and silky camisole she was wearing, accented by sparkly earrings and an armful of bracelets. Her hair and makeup were stunning. "You look gorgeous, Rach."

She wrinkled her nose. "Is it too much?"

"Not at all."

Rachel had been slouching around in oversized hoodies and yoga pants for weeks, her long hair stuffed under a knitted beanie. She'd gone through six cans of dry shampoo and only showered when it was a dire emergency. I was happy to see her making an effort again with her appearance. Her self-confidence had taken a big hit.

"I saw on the news there was a body found during your race. Is that your case?"

I leaned against the doorframe, scowling to myself. "It *was*."

"You're salty tonight. Are you going to tell me about it or bottle it up like you do?"

I smiled. The old Rachel was in there. The trick was to get her to stay out for more than a few hours at a time. "Are you sure you want to hear about my issues?"

She shrugged. "It's a hell of a lot more fun than dwelling on mine."

I went over and collapsed on the bed next to her. "Good, because I have to vent to someone or I'm going to explode."

"What's up?"

"Jayne took me off the case because Vic is being an asshole."

She shook her head. "What?"

I never gave Rachel specifics about my cases, but I figured it was okay to share this, considering it was straight-up relationship and office drama. "Vic used to date the victim, Shawna Meehan. Now he's dating me, so it could be a conflict of interest for me to process the evidence in her case."

"But didn't you spend all day working on it?"

"Yes, but I didn't find out about their relationship until about an hour ago."

She made a face. "And I'm betting you didn't find out from Vic."

"Bingo. And not only that, he's trying to butt into our—their—investigation, throwing around his big FBI badge. He tried to get info out of me, Sterling, Jayne, and even the DA. It's not his jurisdiction. Not his business."

"Tell him to knock it off."

"I did, and he threw a temper tantrum."

She smiled. "You know what the punishment is for throwing a temper tantrum."

I laughed. "You think five minutes in our time out chair is all he needs?"

"He's older than Nate. He may need more like ten or fifteen minutes to fully reflect on his actions."

"I'm so glad I came to you. Problem solved."

She glanced at the clock and hopped up. "I'd love to stay and fix the rest of your many problems, but I have to go."

Chuckling, I stood and hugged her. "Have fun."

With Rachel and Nate gone, the house was quiet. I had my faithful Golden Retriever, Trixie, by my side, but she wasn't much on conversation. Restless, I went rummaging through the kitchen. I wasn't hungry, but needed something to take the edge off. A few months ago, I would have been searching for a bottle. Now...well, now I wasn't exactly in search of a bottle, because my brain knew better, but my idle hands had an agenda of their own. I found the remnants of Nate's Christmas candy that had been pushed to the back of one of our cabinets. Surely he'd forgotten about it and wouldn't notice if I took some.

I grabbed a full-sized chocolate bar and a handful of mini candy canes and took them to the couch with me. I sat staring at the blank TV screen as I began the binge, each candy cane I ate adding layer upon layer of gluey sugar to my teeth until my molars stuck together. My stomach burned. I was pretty sure I'd managed to give myself an ulcer over the last several months, but hadn't bothered to see a doctor about it. I went and retrieved an antacid out of the medicine cabinet so I could continue my pity party. As I was tearing into the candy bar, there was a knock at my door. Pissed about being interrupted, I took my time shuffling to the door.

Vic stood there, unable to look me in the eye. "I heard you got let go from working the case. I'm sorry, Ellie."

"You should be, because it's your fault." I took a big bite of the candy bar.

He frowned. "The circumstances dictated your dismissal, not—" Finally looking at me, he made a face and said, "What are you eating?"

"My feelings," I mumbled around a mouthful of chocolate.

"Give me that."

I pulled my candy bar out of his reach. "No. Get your own."

"Look, Ellie, I want us to work this out. Can I come in?"

"You know the rule."

Rachel and I were not the best at choosing romantic partners, so we'd made a rule a long time ago that we didn't bring men into the house. It was for our safety, both physical and emotional. Nick Baxter was the one and only exception to our "no men in the house" rule. Since I'd met him, he'd had my back, regardless of the state of our relationship. He'd saved my life on more than one occasion. To be fair, Vic had saved my life, too, but the jury was still out on him otherwise.

Vic glanced toward my driveway. "Rachel's car is gone, and I don't hear Nate. You're alone, right?"

"Ooh. Using your Special Agent powers, I see."

He ignored my jab. "Does the rule apply if they're not here?"

I blew out a breath. "I guess not." I stood aside so he could come in.

Trixie greeted him with a big doggy smile and a wildly wagging tail. Not much of a watchdog. She'd be best friends with anyone who'd pet her head.

Vic sat at one end of my couch. I took the other end.

He eyed the empty candy cane wrappers on my coffee table but chose to keep his comments to himself. "I'm sorry for the way I acted toward you today. I should have been up front with you about my former relationship with Shawna. And I shouldn't have tried to obtain case information from you."

"You think?"

"I'm trying to apologize, here. You're not making it easy."

Vic Manetti did not apologize often, mostly because he always thought he was right about everything. I should probably take it while I could get it.

"I'll behave. Keep apologizing."

His expression softened, and he reached for my hand. "When I saw Shawna there, I...kind of lost it. She'd been dating that guy, Skyler Marx, before she and I got together. He'd cheated on her, and when she called him on it, he hit her. She went to the police, and he started intimidating her to get her to back down. I helped her get a restraining order against him, and one thing led to another between us. I don't think she was ever really into me, aside from the fact that she saw me as her protector. We'd only been together for a few months when Marx managed to get to her and convince her he'd turned over a new leaf. She bought into his bullshit and went back to him. The guy is a real piece of work, but for some reason she loved him. And now this."

"Wow. No wonder you think he's guilty. He's a sociopath."

"Exactly."

I squeezed his hand. "I wish you could have articulated that this morning, but I get now why you were so upset. Vic, you can't blame yourself for her death."

His jaw clenched, and I saw his eyes glistening with tears. I never thought I'd see that in a million years. "I can, and I do."

I scooted toward him and put my arms around him. "I've been there. You can't shoulder this responsibility. It'll eat you alive, trust me."

He pulled back. "This is different than with Rachel. She was still alive. You had hope."

I cast my eyes down. "I was talking about my mom."

Vic knew about how my mother had met her violent end. He didn't know about the guilt I continued to carry regarding her murder.

He asked gently, "What about your mother's death could possibly have been your fault? I thought you'd left home after high school and had little contact with her."

"I did. But when Rachel got pregnant, I took her away from our mother. The place they were living looked like a crack house, and I knew Mom had been prostituting herself for drugs while Rachel was under that roof. Because of that, I told her she'd never see either of us again, and she'd never lay eyes on her grandchild. She was in with some terrible people. If she hadn't been murdered, she probably would have died from an OD anyway."

"For that reason alone, you can't blame yourself. She made her own choices."

I said quietly, "So did Shawna."

"Yet you said you blame yourself anyway. So can I."

"The purpose of my illustration was so that you'd do what I say, not what I do."

He smiled. "When do I ever do what you say?"

I snorted. "Never. I guess I wasted my breath."

Leaning over to kiss me, he said, "Not at all. I needed to talk to someone. Thank you for being my someone."

I smiled. "No problem."

9

I went about my life, hearing nothing more about Shawna Meehan's case other than what I could glean from the news media like any random civilian. Despite his best efforts, Vic had been shut out, too. After Shawna's boyfriend, Skyler Marx, had been held for a little over forty-eight hours, his hotshot lawyer had gotten him out, citing lack of evidence. The timing of his triumphant release from custody seemed a little contrived, given the fact that reporters from all the local TV stations just happened to be hanging around at the county jail, ready and waiting to go "live at five" for their evening newscasts. The cocky lawyer made sure to express that there were no hard feelings against the Hamilton County Sheriff's Department and that he wouldn't be filing a countersuit for his client's unlawful detention. To me, that only made his client seem guiltier.

Evidently Sterling hadn't found what he'd been looking for at the suspect's apartment and therefore couldn't tie him to the scene. I was sure he and Baxter (assuming Baxter had changed his mind about Skyler Marx's guilt, as I had) were scrambling to find another angle. I had to admit I was disappointed I wasn't allowed to scramble with them.

In the midst of the investigation, Valentine's Day had rolled around. It wasn't my favorite holiday, with all the touchy-feely crap everywhere you looked and the public professions of undying love (that we all knew wouldn't last through the week) going on around campus. But this year I didn't mind it so much. Rachel had been in a wonderful mood for the last couple of days. Vic, although still working through his grief, was much more attentive than usual. I didn't know whether it was because he'd had one of those "life is short" revelations or the fact that we'd bonded over our discussion the other night.

As I was watching the tail end of the news and getting ready for my date with Vic that evening, Rachel came into my bedroom. Even though her hair was only partially curled, she looked just as stunning as she had when she'd gone out on the town with her girlfriends. "Can I borrow your curling iron? Mine has been on its last leg for a while, and it finally gave up."

"Sure. I didn't realize you were going out tonight. Is David watching Nate?"

"Yep. We're dropping him off on the way."

"Are you and your friends doing a Galentine's thing?"

She blushed. "No, I have a date."

My breath caught in my throat. The last time Rachel had a date, she ended up a prisoner of a madman. I tried to calm down, telling myself that the odds of that happening again were astronomical. After all, she was twenty-one years old. She was an adult and a mother and could make her own decisions. But I couldn't keep my mouth shut.

"Who is it?" My voice sounded strained.

"Sis, I know where you're going with this, but trust me. This one is fine."

That's what she thought last time. "Who is it? Do I know him?"

"Yes. But this is so new, I don't want you to get all weird about it before I know if it's going anywhere."

"Why would I get all weird about it?" I demanded. My hands were shaking.

Rachel rolled her eyes. "You're being super weird *right now*."

"Give me a reason not to be."

"David met him, and he approves. He said I should go for it."

"David married our mother. Does he really have the best relationship advice to give?"

She laughed. "You're terrible. Now go have a nice dinner with Vic and please don't worry about me." She grabbed my curling iron and hurried to her room.

Don't worry about her? That was all I was going to do tonight. The last thing I wanted to do was hinder her from getting back out there and dating, but would it have killed her to tell me who this damn guy was? She said I knew him. I knew a lot of people, many of them criminals. If we were talking college boys at Ashmore, that narrowed it down to several hundred, plus a handful of men on the staff who weren't too ridiculously old for her. She'd already dated a sleazy dorm director. I couldn't imagine what loser she'd come up with next.

I heard Vic ring the doorbell as I was slipping on my heels. But when I went to the door, it wasn't Vic standing there.

"Hey," Baxter said, his eyes giving me a quick once-over before locking with mine. "You, uh...you look... Wow."

I felt heat crawl up my neck and flood my cheeks, unsettled by the fact that my insides were fluttering with abandon. "Oh...thank you," I murmured.

He didn't say anything, just kept his eyes on me, like he had something to tell me but couldn't get the words out. Not to brag, but I did look damn good. Thanks to Vic's strict exercise regimen, my new red dress fit me in all the right places, and I'd given extra effort to my hair and makeup for this evening.

I invited him into the house and tried to lighten our conversation. "Are you here to tell me we caught a new case? I mean, I'll go, but I hate to think the hour of my life I spent getting ready will be wasted on a dead guy." I forced out a laugh.

"No." He shook his head. "No new case. But speaking of cases, I, uh...I wanted to tell you I took myself off the Shawna Meehan case."

My jaw dropped. "What? Why?"

It was then that I noticed how haggard he looked. "I don't believe Skyler Marx is guilty, and Sterling wouldn't hear of it. We butted heads pretty bad."

"If you of all people can't get along with Sterling, he's out of options for partners."

He laughed. "We're still partners. Our argument didn't get that far out of hand, but I didn't want my name associated with the witch hunt he's been on trying to put an innocent man behind bars."

"Please don't think that I'm taking Sterling's side again, but from what I hear, this guy is anything but innocent. Maybe he didn't kill Shawna, but he did beat her up once upon a time."

"Sounds like you've been talking to Manetti."

Shrugging, I replied, "We've discussed it."

His eyes grew strained. "I suppose that means you two are on better terms again."

I nodded. "We're going out tonight. He should be here any minute."

"Well, I won't keep you."

When he didn't make a move to leave, I said, "Was there something else you came here for?"

"To pick up Rachel."

My heart thudded. I could barely put together a sentence. "Rachel. Pick her up? You?"

"Yeah."

"Oh, *hell* no." I opened the door and planted my hand in the middle of his chest, shoving him backward and outside onto my front porch.

"What's your problem, Ellie?" he demanded, frowning at me.

"My problem? My problem is you taking my baby sister out."

"Why? I come over here all the time. Tonight we're getting food out instead of having pizza delivered. What's the big deal?"

I raised my voice. "The big deal is that you shouldn't use your role as her confidante to get in her pants!"

His eyebrows shot up. "Excuse me?"

"And furthermore, you are way too old for her. Ten years is a huge difference."

He stared at me. I wondered if he would fire back with the fact that Vic was nearly ten years older than me, but he didn't. "What the hell are you talking about? Why do you suddenly think I'm being inappropriate with your sister?"

"You guys are going out on Valentine's Day. Come on."

"It's Valentine's Day?"

I rolled my eyes. "Baxter, seriously. You don't know what the date is today?"

"I've only slept four hours of the past forty-eight. I don't know whether I'm coming or going."

"Then why aren't you home getting some rest instead of creeping on my sister?" By this time I was shaking, as much from anger as the cold.

He took off his jacket and held it out to me. "Here. You've got to be freezing."

I stomped my foot out of frustration. "Damn it, Baxter. I'm trying to yell at you, and you interrupt to do something nice for me. Knock it off!"

He put his jacket back on and wiped a hand down his face. "I honestly don't understand what's going on with you. I'm not trying to take your sister out on a date."

"Does she know that?" I snapped.

His brow furrowed. "Yes."

I sighed, getting the sinking feeling that this situation was going to turn out far worse than I'd imagined. "I don't think she does, Nick. She told me earlier that she had a date but wouldn't tell me his name because she thought I'd get weird about it."

His face turned ashen. "What did I do?" he said as much to himself as to me.

"What exactly did you say to her when you made plans for tonight?"

"Well...Monday is the day Rachel and I usually get together to talk, except for last week, when I had to work, which is why we got together on Friday instead. She was complaining last time that she was getting tired of pizza, so I suggested we go out and get some dinner. She said..." He closed his eyes. "Shit."

"She said 'shit'?"

Shaking his head, he replied, "She said, 'It's a date.' I said, 'Yeah, pick you up at six.'"

"Shit."

"Yeah."

I could tell he was beating himself up about this. "It was a simple misunderstanding. It could have happened to anyone."

"Except with how fragile Rachel is, I should have been more on top of it."

"Look, I'll go talk to her and smooth things over."

Shaking his head, he said, "No, this is my mistake. I'll handle it, and then we'll move on. I won't let this affect our relationship. She and I have come too far."

Most people would have taken the easy way out. Hell, I would have if our situations had been reversed. But not Baxter. It wasn't who he was.

I put my hand on his arm. "Nick, I'm sorry for coming at you like I did. I should have known you'd be no less than a gentleman with Rachel." I blinked back the tears that suddenly filled my eyes. "Please know it wasn't you I was objecting to. It was the situation. She'd be...she'd be lucky to go out with someone who's even half the man you are."

He covered my hand with his. "Do you really mean that?"

"Of course I do."

"Then why won't you—" He stopped short as headlights swung across us. Dropping his hand from mine and taking a step back from me, he said quietly, "Looks like your date's here. Happy Valentine's Day, Ellie."

The lump in my throat wouldn't allow me to reply. I opened the door and let him inside, then grabbed my coat from beside the door and hurried out to Vic's car.

Vic was getting out of his vehicle when I got there. "I was planning to do the gentlemanly thing and come to the door to get you."

I let myself into the passenger side. Clearing my throat, I grumbled, "That's an antiquated practice. Just like celebrating Valentine's Day. Let's go."

He grinned. "Fair enough. You look nice."

Nice. I mustered a smile. "Thanks."

As Vic backed out of my driveway and turned onto the slushy street, I stared out the window, unable to get the way Baxter had looked at me tonight out of my head.

10

The next morning over breakfast, Rachel was quiet. I didn't ask about what had happened the previous night, and she didn't offer anything. Nate, however, talked up a storm about Detective Nick taking him and Mommy bowling for Valentine's Day. I assumed that after their chat they'd decided to take Nate along with them as a buffer. Rachel finally couldn't stand it any longer and dumped her barely touched cereal into the sink, then left the kitchen. My heart ached for her, but I could do nothing to help. She'd have to get over this on her own. Our twenty-minute drive to Ashmore was more of the same, with Nate in the back seat telling us all about how it was his turn to be the line leader today at daycare and Rachel off in her own little world.

I had early back-to-back classes this morning, so I had to set my life drama aside and focus on my teaching. However, halfway into my second lecture on the process of matching cartridge casings to firearms, Deputy Carlos Martinez walked through the back door of my classroom and waved to get my attention. He jerked his thumb toward the door. Shit. Now what?

I said to my class, "I have to step out for a moment. Please read the next section in your textbooks about the history of IBIS, the Integrated Ballistic Identification System."

I hurried out into the hallway, where I met the deputy. "Hey, Martinez. What's up? Is someone hurt?"

Martinez replied, "No—at least not anyone you know, I don't think. The sheriff sent me here to speak to you. She tried calling, but couldn't reach you. I was in the neighborhood."

"What does she need?"

"She wants you to work a case. I'm here to pick you up."

I frowned. I felt guilty leaving my job to go consult for the department, but crime didn't follow set hours. It often occurred at night when I was available, but not always. Luckily, I'd recently been assigned a teaching assistant. I had a packed schedule this semester, having to add extra classes because of the overabundance of students wanting to study forensics all of a sudden. Everyone and his brother wanted to take criminalistics classes from the criminalist who broke the Eye for an Eye Killer case.

I had a feeling I already knew the answer to my question, but I asked it anyway. "What kind of case?"

"Another homicide."

"Damn. Is it related to the Shawna Meehan case?"

He nodded.

After taking that in, I said, "Okay. Give me a few minutes to speak with my TA about taking over my classes today. I don't suppose you'd want to talk to my class about law enforcement while I take care of business, would you?"

He shrugged. "Sure. I'll tell them about the stoner who took a piss on my shoes yesterday." Chuckling, he entered my classroom. Nothing bothered Martinez. Not pissy shoes or speaking in front of a room full of know-it-all college students.

I hurried to my office and made arrangements for my TA to teach the classes I'd miss for the rest of the day. I tried not to think about what I'd be walking into. You never knew with a death scene. Plus, if this one had something to do with Shawna's case, Jayne had to have a compelling reason that I be put back on the team. I wondered if Baxter would be back on this one as well. I didn't see Jayne allowing him to stand on the sidelines if things seemed to be escalating.

It was bitter cold again this morning, so I grabbed all the extra clothing

I could dig up around my office and stuffed it into a bag to take with me. I returned to my classroom, where I was met with a wave of raucous laughter as I came through the door. Sure enough, Martinez was regaling them with a ridiculous but true tale. This one was about him getting dispatched to deal with a flock of sheep that was blocking Highway 37 up in Strawtown. He helped a farmer herd the animals back into their pasture, only to get head-butted in the nuts by one of the rams.

I walked to the front of the classroom and said, "Thank you, Deputy Martinez, for your time. Class is dismissed for the day."

As Martinez escorted me to his waiting cruiser, I asked, "Where are we headed?"

"Woodland Gardens at Central Park."

The scene was mere blocks away from campus, in a lovely and well-maintained community park. I shivered. This area should have been one of the safest places in the county.

On the short drive over, Martinez told me the story of his stoner arrest from yesterday. I was grateful for the distraction. On top of the apprehension I always felt on the way to a crime scene, I didn't know if I was prepared to work with Baxter so soon after our decidedly unprofessional conversation last night.

We came up on several news vans already lining up by the west entrance to the park. Shawna Meehan's murder had been the biggest story in weeks. The media had reported little else all weekend, and now there was even more fuel for their sadistic fire. I ducked down in my seat so as not to be seen. When I'd been at the center of the last investigation, my face had been plastered all over the news. I refused to give interviews, in part because of the personal nature of the investigation and also because I hated being in the spotlight. It was a decision that to some degree backfired, because it only seemed to make the reporters more tenacious in trying to get to me. I'd had to change my phone number and email address in an effort to evade them.

"Thanks for the ride," I said as we rolled up to a line of law enforcement vehicles clogging Central Park Drive West.

"Anytime," Martinez replied.

I got out of the cruiser and made my way down the street and onto the greenway, heading toward the path leading into Woodland Gardens. The entrance to the small wooded park had already been taped off. So far, the only officials here were a few deputies who'd likely been the first responders, plus Jayne, Chief Deputy Sheriff Rick Esparza, and Sterling and Baxter, who'd just crossed the tape and disappeared into the park. The crime scene unit's SUV and the coroner's van were nowhere in sight. No surprise, because unlike the others, they had equipment to pack before making the twenty-minute drive from Noblesville to Carmel.

Jayne was up ahead speaking to Chief Esparza, her second in command. She saw me and waved, then walked over to meet me. "Thanks for coming, Ellie. I know it's not easy to scramble to get someone to cover for you at the last minute."

"It worked out. Martinez babysat my kids while I did the scrambling."

She smiled. "I'm sure they were very entertained."

"They were."

"I know you weren't particularly happy with me over the last case, but we need you going forward. Another woman has been found dead, and we believe her death is connected to Shawna Meehan's."

"Am I going to be allowed to see this one through? You sure Manetti hasn't slept with this victim, too?"

Frowning, she said, "Come on, Ellie. You know that me taking you off the Meehan case was nothing personal."

I conceded, "I know. But I don't have to like it."

Her expression softened. "You wouldn't be you if you did. Beck and Amanda are en route, but you'll be the lead. They're bringing your gear. Sit tight." She returned to where she'd been standing with Chief Esparza.

My phone rang. I dug in my purse to find it. Vic's name showed on the Caller ID. I blew out a breath. He'd better not try to pull any more of his jackassery with me.

"Hey," I said.

Vic's deep voice was hesitant. "Hey...I heard there's been another homicide."

"Yes..."

"Are you on it?"

"Lead."

"That's good."

I dreaded where this conversation was going. "Vic, please don't—"

"I'm not calling to pump you for information. I'm giving you a heads-up. Given certain circumstances surrounding the two recent homicides, the FBI is going to assist with your investigation."

I groaned and cursed under my breath.

He chuckled. "I know. Nobody wants this, but it's happening. Because of my former relationship with Shawna, I won't be the official liaison, but they are allowing me to be a part of the task force."

"Are you sure that's a good idea?"

"What, you're not excited about getting to work with me again?"

Not in the slightest. We'd end up in a fight in no time.

Instead, I said, "I mean that you've got a lot to process about Shawna's death, and jumping into a related investigation is not going to do you any favors."

"I can lock it down when I need to." He was already defensive.

Here we go again.

11

The crime scene unit's SUV came pulling up, Beck Durant at the wheel. He nearly rear-ended Jayne's SUV as he tried to park. I saw Amanda berating him from the passenger's seat and chuckled to myself. I was happy she didn't shrink from him, given the fact that he was technically her superior. I hoped one day she would manage to knock him from his spot and achieve lead criminalist herself. But with his family connections, it might be impossible for her to climb any higher on the ladder here. That could be dangerous for the department, because someone with her skills could easily find a lead criminalist position elsewhere. I didn't want to lose her on the team, especially since we'd become friends, but I'd be first in line to write her a glowing letter of recommendation.

As usual, Beck gave me a condescending sneer as he exited the vehicle. "Oh, joy. You're here."

I didn't shrink, either. "And I'm the lead, so don't even think about giving me any lip."

He brushed past me and grumbled something about being pushed aside and his mother hearing about this. I followed him to the rear hatch, where Amanda was beginning to get herself suited up.

"Hey, Amanda," I said.

She smiled. "Hi. I'm glad you're back. Can you believe another one so soon?"

She handed me a set of coveralls, and I began layering up with the extra clothing I'd brought.

"This isn't good. What's the tie to Shawna Meehan?"

She lowered her voice. "Jason told me there was a photo of Shawna posted on a runner's forum yesterday. It evidently went viral overnight. The post threatened more violence soon, then another young woman was found this morning by a parks department worker, dead and naked."

I shook my head. "If it's the same killer, then that's getting into serial territory. When it was just the one, it could have been a relatively straight-forward sex crime. If we can find evidence of a tie between the two, who knows?"

Beck heaved his kit out of the back of the SUV. "You'd probably find out faster if you two would quit gossiping and get to the scene." He marched off toward the park.

I rolled my eyes. "Why did he have to tag along?"

Amanda shrugged. "The sheriff said all hands on deck."

"Damn."

"Yep."

I zipped up my coveralls and pulled the hood up over the knitted beanie I'd brought with me. "Don't worry. I'll stake off an area for him to search far away from the actual crime scene. Then the two of us can do our thing unhindered."

"Sounds like a plan."

We shouldered our gear and caught up with Beck. The three of us signed the entry log and headed into Woodland Gardens. It was beautiful— a small patch of woods with a trail wide enough for at least two of us to walk comfortably side-by-side, even with our clunky kits. Metal stakes noted different species of plant life, and wooden benches sat at intervals along the trail. It was a great area to practice trail running—in fact, Vic and I had come out here one time when we'd first started training together. But when Amanda and I came upon a stretch of tape denoting the inner perimeter of the crime scene, the place suddenly seemed bleak and oppressive.

Sterling and Baxter were standing well into the woods, I assumed so as to not make any more footprints around the body, which lay in the center of the trail. Like Amanda had said, the victim was naked. Again.

The woman was lying on her left side, facing down the trail. The whole scene was a chilling déjà vu scenario. Although not covered with snow, this victim's skin reminded me of Shawna's. Stripped of all clothing, she looked so cold. So still and alone. The striking difference was the mess of blood reaching out around the body. This scene hadn't been prettied up by a few inches of new-fallen snow. This scene was bitter, hard reality; grisly and stark in its unadulterated evil form.

Sterling looked up. "About time you all got here."

"Good morning to you, too," I said, making a point not to make eye contact with Baxter. He did the same.

Amanda smiled at Sterling but didn't take his bait. "You know we had to spend time packing our gear. Plus we're not allowed to have cool sirens and flashing lights like you, so we had to drive the speed limit all the way here like common folk."

He winked at her when he thought no one was watching.

Beck got out the camera and started to barge into the scene.

I caught his arm. "Hold up. It hasn't snowed since yesterday afternoon, so there may be shoeprints to be had, if the parks department worker didn't walk all over them when he found the victim. We all need to use the woods as our point of entry and exit, at least until the photos have been taken and we get a close look at the snow by the body."

Beck frowned at me. "I hate it when you're here."

"What a coincidence. I hate it when *you're* here."

Sterling snickered. "Ladies, ladies. You're both pretty."

Ignoring Sterling, I said to Beck, "Can I see the camera for a minute?"

He eyed me skeptically but handed it over.

"Thanks." I immediately gave it to Amanda. "You shoot it."

"Hey!" Beck complained. "I wanted to shoot it."

I said, "You suck at photography, and you always miss evidence. So, no."

Beck stomped back down the trail several yards and threw himself onto one of the benches to pout. I walked into the woods to speak to Baxter and Sterling as they watched Amanda shoot the scene. Baxter and I would have to talk to each other eventually. Might as well rip off the Band-Aid.

I said to them, "Hey, I should probably warn you—the Feds are stepping in."

Baxter frowned while Sterling let out a string of curses.

I nodded. "That's pretty much what I said, too. Sorry to be the bearer of bad news, but I heard it straight from the horse's mouth. Manetti is on the task force, but they have someone else tapped to be the liaison."

Sterling griped, "That sucks even more. Manetti might be an asshole, but at least we know he won't let bureaucratic red tape stop him from getting his man. What if we get some strait-laced pencil pusher who won't let us do what we need to do to catch this guy?" Keeping up his tirade, he glanced at his watch. "When's the coroner going to get here? I need a TOD, and I need this body moved so you all can get in there and find some evidence as to who this woman is."

Amanda, who I thought had only been half-listening as she took photos of the scene, said, "It's not a guarantee that we'll find something to tell us who she is."

"Maybe he left her phone like last time."

She said, " 'Like last time'? Sounds like you've made up your mind that the same person killed both women."

Sterling replied, "You were at both scenes. What you do think?"

She shrugged. "Between the threat you mentioned and the way the body was left, I'd say it's a good possibility." Pausing, she took a long look through the camera's viewfinder. "Or it may be a no-brainer, considering the wound on this woman's knee looks just like the one on Shawna Meehan's knee."

The rest of us trooped through the woods to get a closer look. Sure enough, this injury was eerily similar to Shawna's—a bloody wound with a big bruise around it.

"Exactly. This is why I need to pick up Skyler Marx ASAP, before he decides to run," Sterling said, frustration evident in his voice.

Amanda asked, "You still think it was him?"

Sterling said, "Yes."

Baxter said, "No."

As Sterling glared at his partner, I said to him, "I want him to be guilty as much as you do, but isn't his lawyer going to cry harassment this time?"

"This is a new case. We can harass anyone we want."

Baxter rolled his eyes. "Until we have an ID on this victim, we can't go accusing anyone of anything. However, since we think the two homicides are connected, there are plenty of persons of interest in Shawna Meehan's case we can talk to and further narrow down a suspect list based on alibis for our Jane Doe's TOD."

Sterling conceded, "We do have several possible leads we can run down. Lots of people knew Shawna Meehan was going to be at Strawtown Koteewi Park that night."

Amanda asked, "How many people?"

Sterling said, "The eight others at Manetti's party, plus a race official she was planning to meet out at the park. So, nine."

Her jaw dropped. "Shawna was supposed to meet someone out there that night? Did she?"

Baxter shook his head. "No, he texted her at the last minute and said he got stuck at work. We interviewed him, and he said he had to pick up an extra shift when a coworker went home sick. He's devastated over the fact that Shawna was out there all alone. He'd planned to go on that run with her."

"If he had, she might still be alive." I frowned. "I suppose that brings the suspect list back to Manetti's friends, then."

Baxter flicked his eyes away from me. "And Manetti."

12

Manetti as a potential suspect—I hadn't considered that before. Of course it was a ludicrous idea, but they still had to follow protocol and check him out. I was pretty sure the FBI would think twice about letting him be on the task force if they got wind the detectives had him lumped in with their other persons of interest, though.

Sterling said to me, "And *you*. What's your alibi for around eight forty-five on Friday?"

I thought for a moment. "Um...he is." I pointed to Baxter.

Baxter said, "That's right. I was at her house that night."

Sterling's eyebrows shot up. "What were you doing at Matthews' house at night, Nicky?"

His eyes widening, Baxter rushed to explain, "I was with her sister."

A slow grin spread across Sterling's face. "Oh, this keeps getting better and better. Tell me more."

I tried not to cringe as poor Baxter got needled by his asshole of a partner. I hated to jump in, because it could make things even worse. Sterling was a pro at twisting people's words. He was a force to be reckoned with during an interrogation. Suspects didn't know what hit them when they got locked in a room with Jason Sterling.

Baxter's cheeks tinged pink. "I mean, I was there—as a friend—trying to help her work through everything she's been dealing with since the kidnapping."

Sterling turned to me, clearly disappointed. "Is this true? He's not in fact chatting up your baby sister?"

After last night, I was way too raw for this conversation. "There's nothing going on between him and Rachel. Quit being an ass."

Before he could fire back a retort, Dr. Berg and Kenny Strange came walking up the trail with a gurney.

"Good morning, everyone," Dr. Berg said, his expression solemn.

We all greeted him and Kenny and gave them their space to work. The detectives headed toward the park entrance while Amanda and I started unpacking and readying the items we would soon need from our kits.

Smarmy smile all over his face, Beck wandered over and held out his phone for the two of us to see. "Check this out. You know the photo you were talking about earlier? One of my guild buddies screengrabbed it before it got taken down and sent it to me."

Amanda and I gasped at the same time. You might not have known who the subject of the photo was—or even that it wasn't a lame attempt at an artsy nudie pic—if you hadn't been at Shawna Meehan's crime scene. But the shot was definitely of Shawna after she'd been killed and stripped. It showed her from the back, lying on her left side in the snow, in the same position as our new victim. Judging from the lack of snow covering Shawna's body and the fact that the photo had been taken at night, she'd been newly dead at the time. The caption below the photo read, "Fallen Beauty in Strawtown Koteewi Park. More to come soon."

Amanda and I exchanged a horrified glance.

Beck said, "Creepy, right?" He was such a disgusting little goblin.

I said, "You need to delete that and tell your friend to do the same. And you all need to quit sharing it."

"Like hell. This is murder memorabilia."

"Murder memorabilia is stuff from closed cases, dumbass. This photo is new evidence from an active homicide investigation. You should know better."

"You should stay out of my business." He stalked off again.

Amanda and I returned our attention to readying our kits, but not long after, Dr. Berg called us over and contacted the detectives to return for his field exam observations. Jayne, Chief Esparza, and a man I didn't recognize came back with them.

Jayne said, "Everyone, I'd like to introduce Special Agent Steven Griffin. The Bureau has offered his service to oversee a task force to investigate our two recent homicides due to their violent nature and connection. In the interest of time, I'll let you introduce yourselves later." Neither she nor the chief looked happy about being pushed aside by the Feds.

Special Agent Griffin gave a curt nod. For many reasons, I was glad it wouldn't be Vic overseeing us, but I couldn't help think that Sterling had been right. At least Vic was the devil we knew.

We all gathered at the edge of the crime scene tape for Dr. Berg to begin.

After clearing his throat, he said, "The victim sustained multiple sharp force injuries to the torso, most likely from a knife. I can be more specific as to the size and shape of the blade after autopsy. Based on the amount of blood lost, I'd say the cause of death is exsanguination. I'll determine upon further examination if either of her lungs were punctured, but it's clear-cut that she died here from the attack. She has several defensive wounds on her arms, so I'd say she at least tried to put up a good fight. There's also evidence of sharp force trauma to her right patella." He frowned. "Upon first glance, I believe this wound looks quite similar to the type of wound I found on Shawna Meehan's right patella. I'll compare them when I perform the autopsy. It's likely that this injury occurred first in an effort to slow down and incapacitate the victim. The victim's clothes were removed postmortem, evidenced by void and swipe patterns I've noted in the blood across the upper body."

Sterling said, "Anything there to ID her?"

"Aside from a non-descript infinity symbol tattoo on her wrist, no."

Sterling scowled, but offered no comment.

Dr. Berg continued, "Rigor is fixed, so based on that and body temp, I'm placing the time of death window between four and eight P.M. yesterday. Again, it's a wider window than I'd like to give you, but with the cold conditions it's difficult to narrow it down any more and be accurate."

Baxter said, "No problem, Doc. We can work with that."

Dr. Berg nodded. "We'll begin transport unless anyone needs another look."

Agent Griffin stepped forward. "I'll take a closer look, if you don't mind."

The rest of us waited while the agent took his time surveying the body and the scene, snapping a couple of photos on his phone. Points to him for not stepping outside the footprints Dr. Berg and Kenny made. When he was finished, Dr. Berg and Kenny lifted the victim into a body bag and zipped it up, then wheeled the gurney out of the scene and down the trail.

Sterling turned to Amanda and me. "Get to digging, ladies. Find me something I can use."

"We'll do what we can," Amanda replied.

I asked him, "Do we know how far the parks and rec worker walked into the scene?"

"When we talked to him, he said he got about five feet away and saw all the blood. He's evidently not good with blood so he didn't want to get any closer."

"Good man." I called behind me, "Beck, can you go find the parks and rec worker and take some shoe impressions? I want to be able to rule his prints out."

Beck brightened up a bit. Taking shoe impressions wasn't difficult, nor did it take much thought. Maybe he'd actually be happy doing the monkey work as long as it wasn't demanding. "On it."

Agent Griffin pulled the detectives aside to confer with them, leaving Amanda and me to our task.

She was staring at the sickening amount of blood in the snow. "We need our Tyvek suits again."

"You're right." I yelled down the trail, "Hey, Beck! Can you bring us back some Tyvek suits, please?"

He gave me a thumbs-up as he kept walking.

I got out the camera and a stack of evidence markers. I also took out a voice recorder, which I turned on and put in the breast pocket of my coveralls, so I'd have an audio account of our investigation. Amanda would stop to take written notes periodically, but I found it much easier to verbalize what I was doing. Usually we discussed what we were doing while we were working, so I didn't have to do a lot of muttering to myself. Even though we used different methods to record our findings, we'd both have to spend time typing out our notes back at the lab. At least my hand wouldn't be cramping out here from the incessant writing.

I said, "Shoeprints first. They'll be the first to deteriorate."

Amanda grabbed two cans of spray paint and a flashlight and followed me along the edge of the woods to search for footprints. "The victim seemed pretty tiny. I'm betting she had little feet." She pointed to some footprints much larger than mine. "Those probably aren't hers, so there's a chance they belong to the killer."

"You're right." I glanced on down the trail. "Is that some more of them going farther into the park?"

She studied the ground, walking ahead of me through the brush. "I think so. And a line of similar prints coming from the other direction." She sprayed arrows next to the prints, orange ones versus blue ones to show which direction the person had been traveling in each of the two paths. She continued walking, tracing the paths several yards until she got to a tree. Gesturing at it, she said, "They stop here, behind this tree. It's wide enough to be a good hiding place. Plenty of deep prints and kicked up snow, like someone spent some time here."

I followed her tracks, studying the prints. "Any you see good enough to cast? This snow is wetter than I'd like. The prints aren't crisp. They're mushy."

"True. Wait a sec." She crouched down and shined the flashlight on one of the impressions. "Here's one that's not bad." She sprayed a wide orange circle around the print.

I came over and crouched next to her. The print was fairly decent. The tread pattern was visible, and it was deep enough to make a good cast, but not too deep to mush into the ground underneath. The brand name stamped onto the bottom of the sole was large enough to be visible as well —Brahma.

"Check out the brand of boot," I said.

Amanda groaned. "Brahma. Available at every Walmart in a thousand-mile radius."

"Don't forget Amazon."

"Oh, right. So there's zero chance of tracing the boot purchase. Why don't the bad guys make it easier on us by wearing custom-made shoes?"

"Killers are so insensitive."

I began taking photos of the shoeprint from different angles. I then set down an evidence marker and a scale and took more shots.

We crossed the path where there were no visible shoeprints and walked down the other side to study the trail from the opposite angle. From this direction, it was easier to see the prints near the blood.

"Ooh!" she exclaimed, pointing a few feet away. "Big bloody boot print."

"Perfect. The only person leaving big bloody boot prints should be the killer."

We got as close as we dared, both of us having to step around rivulets of blood and messy snow. Amanda sprayed another circle of orange paint around this print, and I photographed it several times without and with an evidence marker and scale, excitement bubbling up inside me. Not only was it some great evidence, but the print itself was perfect for casting. I then walked several yards away to get some wide-angle shots of the whole scene now that the shoeprint paths were marked.

"Did I hear you say 'big bloody boot print'?" called Sterling, his voice hopeful as he approached us.

Amanda smiled at him. "You did."

"What size?"

"Don't know yet."

"Can you take a minute and figure it out?"

I walked toward the prints and surveyed them. "Not with a lot of accuracy out here. It would be best to—"

He cut me off. "Ballpark it. Nine? Sixteen?"

I leaned over the print to study the scale. "Around thirteen inches, so...roughly a thirteen, maybe fourteen. A big shoe, so probably a tall guy."

"Like Manetti."

Behind him, I saw Agent Griffin's head pop up from his conversation with Baxter.

Straightening up, I rolled my eyes. "Yeah, like Manetti."

"I wonder if he has an alibi for the time of death window."

"He was with me after six. We drove downtown to St. Elmo's for dinner. You can GPS check his car and both our phones if you don't believe me."

"Oddly enough, I do. I'll go find out where he was before then. He's stuck at the entrance to the park, pouting again because he's still not essential enough to get past the tape." He chuckled to himself as he walked away. Baxter and Griffin followed him out.

Amanda shook her head. "You know I'm trying with him. Homicides always make him extra cranky."

"I know. Let's cast these prints before they melt. Do you see any more viable ones?

"None that are better than the two we found. Let's do this."

We dug in our gear and found a can of snow impression wax, two bags of dental stone mix, and two casting frames. I readied the dental stone as Amanda sprayed each footprint with three light coats of red snow impression wax, sealing the prints from damage and melting that might occur when we poured on the casting material. She then placed a metal frame around each footprint, taking photographs and making notes as she completed each step. I was excited to see the department was now using a new brand of dental stone mix, this one an all-in-one kit. The dental stone powder was premeasured for one cast and even came with water. All I had to do was break the water pouch inside and shake the bag until the powder and water became thoroughly incorporated. I mixed up two bags and buried them in the snow for a while to cool them down, which would lessen the chance for melting around the print when the dental stone mixture made with warmish water hit the frozen snow. Once I was ready to cast the prints, Amanda continued to photograph and document our progress.

We left the two impressions to cure and returned to our kits to change our gloves. Beck had just returned with our Tyvek suits. Behind him came the detectives and our new special agent friend. They walked up to the tape and surveyed our progress.

Griffin turned to Amanda, Beck, and me. "I hear you've found some shoeprints."

I replied, "Yes, and they're good ones. Now that we've got our protective suits, we'll start processing the area where the attack occurred."

"Good. I'm hoping the killer left us a couple of Easter eggs under the body like last time. Especially since this scene at first glance looks like a carbon copy of the other one. I'm assuming you heard about the photo of the other scene. The body was originally placed identically to this one."

Amanda leveled a glare at Beck. "Yes, Beck showed it to us earlier. His gamers guild buddy sent him a screenshot of it, which unfortunately he did not hesitate to share."

Beck whined, "Stop tattling, Amanda. And it was my *Star Wars* guild buddy."

Sterling turned around to stare Beck down. "Delete that photo. Now. And tell your nerd friends to quit sending it around."

"No. You're not the boss of me."

Sterling started striding toward Beck. "Becky, you sick son of a bitch, give me your phone. I'm going to delete that shit myself."

Beck backed away. "You can't do that."

Agent Griffin stepped between them, smiling. "Fellas, I'm sure there's a compromise to be had, here. Mr. Durant, might I see your phone to determine if the photo you received is indeed the one in question?"

Beck grudgingly got out his phone, pulled up the photo, and handed his phone to the agent.

Griffin took a long look at the photo, nodding as if in deep contemplation. Then he suddenly chucked the phone far into the woods.

Amanda and I shared a glance, eyes wide in gleeful shock at the agent's ballsy move.

Griffin was matter-of-fact as he addressed Beck, whose jaw was nearly on the ground. "As an employee of the Hamilton County Sheriff's Department, you should have deleted that photo the moment you received it and done your part to stop the rampant sharing of it. You're excused from the task force. Get out of here."

Taken by surprise, all Beck could do was sputter and flap his arms.

Griffin began walking away.

Beck suddenly choked out, "You can't do this. You're not even with the department. My mother won't stand for this."

Griffin wheeled around, his mouth set in a grim line. "Your *mother*? I don't give a shit who your mother is, pal. Get out of my crime scene, or I'll show you out myself. A friendly warning—you don't want that."

Griffin wasn't nearly as tall or physically formidable an agent as Manetti, but there was something about him that screamed *don't cross me.*

Beck evidently got that vibe, too, because he obeyed, schlepping back down the trail with his head bowed.

Amanda murmured to me, "No offense to Manetti, but I think I'm going to actually enjoy this Fed overseeing us."

"Same."

13

Amanda and I put on our white Tyvek suits and changed booties and gloves. The detectives and agent were milling around the perimeter of the scene, muttering to each other. While the two of us were sectioning the struggle area into quadrants, the agent took a call on his phone.

"Griffin." After a pause, he said, "Let me put you on speaker." After tapping his phone's screen he said, "Can you please repeat that, Agent Manetti?"

We all stopped what we were doing to listen to Vic.

"I think the victim's name might be Angela Meadows. I went through the missing persons cases filed in the surrounding counties during the past few days and found hers. She was reported missing last night. The Carmel city police filed an initial report. Ms. Meadows is thirty-six years old, so they'd planned to wait the customary forty-eight hours before launching an official investigation into her disappearance. As far as I can tell, the photo on her driver's license matches the photo of the victim you sent me from the scene. Of course that's not a positive ID, but considering her apartment is only two blocks from here, we've got a good starting point."

Griffin replied, "Good work, Agent. Run down the person who filed the missing persons report and get all the information you can about Angela Meadows. We'll need to find a friend or relative to ID her ASAP."

"Will do," Vic replied.

Griffin ended the call and turned to the detectives. "I want a warrant to search Angela Meadows' apartment. I want her vehicle located and searched. I want a list of her family, friends, and coworkers, and I want that list compared to Shawna Meehan's list. Find the connection between the two of them."

Baxter nodded. "We'll take care of it."

The agent turned to Amanda and me. "When you're done processing the scene, contact me. I want a full rundown of what you find out here." He took off at a jog out of the park before we even had a chance to respond.

She and I went back to marking our quadrants, but we were both still paying attention to the detectives' conversation.

Sterling said to Baxter, "Send the grunt work to someone at the station. I looked at Marx's paperwork from his stay in county. His list of personal effects includes a pair of size thirteen boots. I'm going to go get him."

Baxter held out a hand. "No, you're not." As Sterling took a breath to start his argument, Baxter continued, "I'll go talk to him. You're not going to get anywhere with him or his lawyer, but maybe I can."

Sterling conceded, "You're probably right."

"I am right."

"Fine. I'll write up the warrants. But you'd better bring me Marx on a platter."

The corner of Baxter's mouth pulled up. "All of him? That would have to be one big ass platter."

I ducked my head to cover a smile. Baxter's jokes were terrible, but I'd missed them. During the last case, the two of us were so gutted over Rachel there was no room for joking around. After that, he was never in a joking mood around me.

Sterling grumbled something and started walking. Baxter followed him out.

Amanda said, "Now that everyone has finally left us alone, we can get down to the dirty work." She handed me a whisk broom. "Are you getting a sense of déjà vu, too?"

As I took the broom from her and surveyed the quadrants of bloody snow, it hit me again. "Totally."

She stared at the mess in front of us. "This is gross. I can handle blood, but something about it mixing with the snow is turning my stomach today."

"I see your point. The snow helps it spread so much farther than it normally would. I feel like the whole place is contaminated."

"All the more reason to get this over with. And don't forget this snow was already here. Unless the killer buried something intentionally, any evidence to be had should be on top. So if the snow isn't disturbed—like most of the area outside our primary attack area—we shouldn't have to dig through it like last time, right?"

"Right."

I started my examination by taking a sample of the bloodiest part of the snow, which should have the most concentrated blood in it. Again, no doubt it had come from the victim, but it was still a necessary part of the evidence collection. We had sixteen quadrants this time, a larger area than before, so we each had eight sections to process. We swept away snow and chipped at ice particles with our brooms. Amanda had been right—unless the killer had purposely buried something he intended to leave behind, we weren't going to find anything.

But then, on quadrant six of eight, after brushing away the first inch of snow, I found a gray strap sticking up. I gently brushed back more snow and found that the strap was to an Apple Watch.

"Bingo," I said, straightening up to go get the camera.

Amanda halted her search to peer into my quadrant. "If that's hers, which I'm betting it is, we should be able to track her movements getting out here. Oh, and the time. This alone could pinpoint her TOD, like Shawna Meehan's phone did."

"Which raises the same question again—with the wealth of information contained on a smart device, why would the killer leave both for us to find so neatly under his victims? I mean, at least launch them into the woods and make us work to find them."

"Like Agent Griffin?" she said, chuckling.

"Yes. You know, at some point, he's going to have to allow Beck back out here to retrieve his phone."

"True." She thought for a moment. "I'm not sure about the killer's intentional placement of the devices, but better to be able to track the victims' movements leading up to their deaths than the killer's movements afterward. If he'd taken the phone and the watch and decided to ditch them somewhere, there'd be a trail to follow. There's a possibility someone might have seen him do the ditching, or a surveillance camera might have caught his vehicle driving by. And unless he busted the devices all to crap, either one could be tracked and found, and then we'd still be able to determine the victims' pre-murder movements *plus* his post-murder ones."

I returned with the camera and snapped a few photos of the watch. "Leaving them at the scenes was the simplest and safest option, then. I can get behind that." I placed a scale and an evidence marker next to the watch and took more photos.

Amanda continued to sweep the snow from her quadrant while I went back to the kit to get the tools I needed to collect and process the watch. I changed my gloves and lifted the watch from the snow. I doubted it would work until it warmed to above freezing, if at all without some technical coaxing, but I pressed the button on the side anyway. Nothing happened, so I walked it over to the clean piece of butcher paper I'd placed on our tarp, laid the watch down, and covered it with a tiny pop-up tent to protect it from the elements while it dried. I'd come back later to dust it for fingerprints.

We continued to comb through the remaining quadrants, but found nothing more.

"I guess the killer didn't feel the need to leave the murder weapon behind this time," I said, standing and flexing my cramped legs.

"Maybe it was his favorite kitchen knife, so he took it back home."

"Yuck."

She smiled. "From a practical standpoint, the guitar string on the garrote would be bent and unusable after being wound around those dowels. It was essentially trash, so he had no problem leaving it behind."

Or he planted it there because he wanted the police to be too busy looking at Shawna's guitar-playing ex to bother tracking down any more leads, which was what had happened. This killer was starting to look awfully calculating all of a sudden. According to Baxter, Skyler Marx couldn't calculate a first grade math problem. There was something bigger brewing here. With Amanda being firmly in Sterling's camp, I decided not to bring up my theory. There was no reason for the two of us to argue over the possibilities, especially since we didn't have to do the investigating. One of the things I loved about working on the forensic side was that our findings were always proven by science. No gray areas. Investigative work was all gray areas.

I replied a non-committal, "Yeah." I brushed the snow from my knees. "I need to see if the watch is dry so I can dust it."

"I'll clean up here."

I headed over to the kit and changed my gloves, then got out a flashlight, a magnifier, and the fingerprint dusting kit. Kneeling again in the snow, I switched on the flashlight and studied the watch with the magnifier. There seemed to be a couple of partial latent fingerprints on the screen, most likely from the end of the victim's finger as she touched the tiny icons to open apps. I wasn't expecting to net much from this, but maybe I'd get lucky.

I brushed black fingerprint powder over the gray strap and aluminum case and used gray fingerprint powder on the dark watch face. I got the flashlight and magnifier out and took another look. I found a decent thumbprint on the strap, but it was probably where the victim would hold the watch in place while she secured the strap to her wrist. I smoothed a tape lift over the fingerprint and pulled it up slowly. It was a good print. I then tape-lifted the two partials I'd seen on the watch face. One came up decently, the other not so much, as it was smudged. It wouldn't matter. I fully believed these prints belonged to our victim. I filled out the requisite information on the back of the lift cards. Then I placed them in an envelope, sealed it with red evidence tape, and marked my initials across it.

Glancing over at our shoeprints, I called to Amanda, "It's probably time to pick up the casts."

"Ah. The moment of truth."

She seemed apprehensive. I understood. Snow casting was a one-time shot. Plus, there was no guarantee any type of shoeprint would come up perfectly, even if you did everything right. It wasn't out of the ordinary for damage to occur as a cast was removed from the ground. I'd had one break in half because it got jostled around on the way to the lab. But it wasn't as if all casts were destined to crumble into a million pieces and be unusable. If all else failed, we had a dozen photographs that could be used to obtain the information we needed. The cast was simply better evidence.

We retrieved the camera and two cardboard boxes and went to the first impression.

Amanda said, "You're welcome to do the honors."

It seemed to me that she needed some confidence in this area, and confidence only came with experience. "Maybe we can each do one. Will you find the photos that correspond with this cast?"

I knelt down in the snow beside the initial print we found, the worse of the two. I purposely left the bloody print for Amanda, hoping the better print would be more likely to give her a better outcome. Before lifting the cast, I took a marker and labeled the back with the date, my initials, and the case number. Amanda rattled off the photo numbers that corresponded to this impression, which I also jotted down on the back of the cast. I then dug my fingers into the snow under the edge of the cast. Unlike trying to unmold a cast from gloppy mud, it didn't take much effort to lift the cast away from the increasingly slushy snow. The sun had come out, and the snow was beginning to melt.

These casts would have to dry at the lab for at least twenty-four hours before we could pack them up to send to the state lab. However, if we were careful with them, we could measure the shoeprint and try to pinpoint the size. At the state lab, they could get into much more sophisticated examinations, including tread wear, which could ultimately tie a specific shoe to a specific wearer. For the purposes of the current investigation, the shoe size would suffice.

For the second cast, Amanda went through the same routine I had. She came up with a perfect cast. The relief showed all over her face. We then boxed up the casts, filled out evidence tags for the boxes, sealed them, and set them aside.

Surveying the scene, Amanda asked, "Does this mean we're done?"

"Except the rough sketch of the area. We need to do that and get Agent Griffin back out here, but then we're good to pack it in."

14

——————

While waiting for Griffin to arrive, we measured the area we had processed and documented our findings. I would have of course preferred to measure and draw out a room with four walls. The boundaries of this scene were more difficult to determine than our previous outdoor scene. Here, the only defining structural markers were nondescript trees. So, we had to hunt for manmade markers and semi-permanent benches nearby and measure from them. For additional accuracy, we used our measuring wheel to measure the exact distance from the crime scene tape all the way to the entrance to the park. Once all the long-distance measuring was done, we did the measuring within the actual scene, showing the distance between where the body was found and where all the shoeprints were found.

While Amanda completed the rough sketch, I collected our tools and packed our kits to go back to the lab. She had taken her warm glove liners off to draw the sketch, and I could tell by the way she rubbed her writing hand that it had to be aching from clasping a pen for so long in the cold. I'd gotten used to the intermittent aches and pains in my knees and lower back from all the outdoor running Vic had been making me do. But after laboring out in the snow and frigid temperatures a second time in only a few days, my body felt more like eightyish than thirtyish. At least this time we had a little more to show for our trouble—seven pieces of evidence counting the fingerprints I pulled from the watch. It was a good thing we didn't have a lot to process, because once the warrants came through for Angela Meadows' apartment and vehicle, we'd be called back out to help complete the searches.

Griffin returned, with Sterling trailing a few feet behind him.

Skipping straight to the point, Griffin said, "Walk me through the homicide."

Amanda seemed taken aback. We didn't normally do this at the scene. We usually presented our findings at a meeting with the team later in the day.

I said, "The trail leading up to the scene had so many sets of different footprints, we concentrated on examining the area around and beyond where the attack occurred. We found only one set of shoeprints beyond the attack area, which we believe belong to the killer. Let me show you."

I led the way through the woods beside the trail. Amanda, Griffin, and Sterling followed along.

Gesturing to the ground, I said, "The prints next to the orange arrows head in a path toward that tree ahead." I kept walking, coming around the back side of the tree. "Based on the mashed snow here, we think our killer spent some time behind this tree before attacking the victim. That circled print is one we casted. The red is wax, not blood." Heading across the trail and into the woods on the other side, I pointed at the other prints. "The blue arrows show the path he took to return to the attack area. The print circled in orange is another one we casted. This print had blood in it— same size and tread pattern as all the other prints. Because of that, we're pretty confident the killer wears roughly a size thirteen shoe."

Amanda took over from here. "Those staked-out quadrants encompass the area where the attack occurred and the victim was found. The only item we managed to uncover from that area was an Apple Watch. It was dead, but we're hoping Cyber can revive it. We got two partials and one full fingerprint from it, but based on their locations, they look like they were made by the wearer during normal use. It's of note that we found the watch buried under an inch of snow. It had stopped snowing before the attack occurred, so any evidence to be had should have been on top of the snow unless someone made it a point to bury it. We did not find any weapons in the attack area this time. And considering none of the other snow in the area looks like it's been disturbed, aside from the two footprint paths, we don't believe there were any other items buried out here."

Griffin grazed a glance across the scene, nodding. "Okay." He turned and marched back toward the park entrance without another word.

Amanda and I turned to each other and shrugged, then went to gather our gear.

She said to Sterling, "We're done. Scene's all yours."

He shouldered Beck's kit, which Beck had left behind when he got banished from the scene. "I'm done with it. I came out here to get you two. We got the warrants for Angela Meadows' apartment and vehicle. We're supposed to head straight there."

Today had been decidedly warmer than Saturday, but I was still numb after being outside all this time. I hoped the heat was turned up in her apartment. Even with the Tyvek suit, I was frozen.

After muscling our gear into the back of the crime scene unit's SUV, we filled out a chain of custody form showing we entrusted our evidence to a deputy to take to the station. We then shed our two layers of jumpsuits and other protective clothing and changed into all clean pieces so as not to cross-contaminate the next scene. Sterling waited impatiently, drumming his fingers on the hood of the vehicle behind our back hatch.

Even though I knew he'd balk, I asked, "Can we get food on the way? I'm starving."

"No. Besides, you could stand to miss a meal, Matthews."

Amanda gasped. "Jason!"

He snorted. "What? She knows it."

I rolled my eyes, but offered no rebuttal. He wasn't wrong. I still had a few pounds to go.

Indignant on my behalf, Amanda crossed her arms and glared at him.

He said in a nicer tone, "We don't have the time."

She zipped up her clean jumpsuit and slammed the hatch. "You should have said that in the first place."

I chuckled to myself as Amanda and I got in the SUV and made the short drive to Angela Meadows' apartment complex. "Thanks for having my back."

"Ugh," she groaned. "Some days it's all I can do not to wring his neck. Good thing I like him."

"He likes you, too. Otherwise he'd make no effort at all. Please don't make trouble between the two of you because of me. Whatever he dishes out, I can take."

"I know, but it would be nice if he could be nice to my friends."

"Honestly, I wouldn't know how to handle him being nice to me."

I was surprised to see Baxter sitting in his SUV in the lot at the apartment complex. Amanda pulled into a spot next to it, and Sterling pulled in next to us.

The moment the four of us exited our vehicles, Sterling descended on Baxter. "Did you pick up our boy?"

"No, because he's not our boy."

"Damn it, Baxter, if you're going to beat this dead horse again—"

Baxter said over Sterling's tirade, "Marx has an airtight alibi for last night."

Sterling's shoulders slumped. "Are you sure?"

"He left the jail at five-thirty. His lawyer drove him straight to a bar, where his buddies were throwing him a party to celebrate his release. He was on stage with his band from seven to nine, and they shut the place down at two A.M. I spoke to the bartender, who said he had to deal with 'those no-talent assclowns' all evening. He said he'd love to see the guy locked up, but Marx was definitely at that bar from the time he was released until well after our victim was reported missing."

Frowning, Sterling said, "Well, shit. If he didn't kill this woman, then who did?"

I said, "Wait, back up a second. Marx found out he lost his girlfriend Saturday, and Monday he's out partying? Anyone besides me have a problem with that?"

Baxter shook his head. "You wouldn't if you'd talked to him. He didn't have much of a reaction at all about her passing. And he wasn't even angry over the fact that she'd been brutally murdered. He didn't seem to care."

"Oh. Well, that sounds consistent with what Manetti told me about him."

Sterling shook his head. "I still like Marx for Shawna Meehan's murder.

But if he couldn't have done this one, we've got nothing and no leads. Right now, we need to find out everything we can about Angela Meadows, and fast. Let's divide this up. Amanda and I will take her vehicle, and you guys take the apartment."

That was hardly dividing things up, considering the square footage of an apartment versus a vehicle. And I'd assumed I'd be working with Amanda and Sterling, not alone with Baxter. Based on the look on Baxter's face, he thought much the same thing.

We got our kits out of the SUV and parted ways. Baxter and I headed into the apartment building to meet the super. She already had Angela's apartment open and was standing in the hallway speaking to a deputy stationed at the door.

While Baxter introduced himself to the super and began questioning her regarding her tenant, I went inside the apartment and set down my gear. I studied the door and the casing, paying particular attention to the area around the lock for signs of tampering. I saw none. If the interior seemed to show signs of struggle, I would fingerprint those areas, but if not, there was no need.

I surveyed the living and kitchen area, snapping a few photos here and there, but nothing leaped out at me as being out of place. In fact, this place was as neat as a pin. There were no indicators that the occupant had left in a rush, or more importantly, that someone else had been in here uninvited. There was no mess anywhere—not even any dirty dishes in the sink—that might point to our victim making a quick exit before having a chance to tidy up. As I entered the single bedroom, I found a purse on the bed, so I photographed it and looked inside. According to the driver's license and credit cards in the wallet, this was Angela Meadows' purse. I also found the latest model iPhone in the purse.

"Is that her purse?"

I jumped at the sound of Baxter's voice. "Yes. Her phone's in it. Cash, too. Nothing seems to have been taken."

He cleared his throat. "I didn't mean to startle you. Find anything that could tell us why she was at the park?"

I shook my head. "Nothing yet."

"Okay." He left the room to go look around in the living room.

The two of us had done fine working together today in public, but now that we were alone the vibe between us was uncomfortable at best.

I kept on, opening the closet only to find clothing hanging neatly from the rod, extra sheets and towels stacked on the shelf above, and shoes matched in two perfect rows on the floor. There were several pairs of expensive running shoes, brands non-runners generally didn't shell out the money for. In the middle of the row of athletic shoes, there was an empty spot where one of the pairs was missing. And once I paid attention to the different styles of clothing, I noticed a section of exercise outfits, ranging from thermal to skimpy, to fit any season. I walked over to the dresser and opened a few of the drawers. Lots of colorful sports bras, as I expected.

"Hey, Nick," I called.

He appeared in the doorway moments later. "Yeah?"

"I think I know what Angela Meadows was doing in the park last night, and why she had her smart watch with her but left her purse, phone, and car here."

His eyes landed on the open closet. "She was out running, like Shawna Meehan."

"Yes. That could be your link."

He nodded and got out his phone, then disappeared into the living room to make a call.

I bagged and tagged her phone, hoping it might afford us some information on her personal life.

After closing the drawers and closet, I stuck my head in the bathroom. It was even tidier than the rest of the place, if that was possible. There were no toiletries or makeup items scattered across the counter. The towels were folded neatly on their racks rather than lying in damp mounds on the floor. Judging from the way she kept house, Angela Meadows would have been appalled at being associated with the disgusting scene this morning. This was one of the most spotless homes I'd ever processed.

My sister and I could stand to take a page out of Angela Meadows' book. I'd always had an irrational fear of my untidy house being a crime scene at some point and someone like me having to go in and wade through the mess to process the place. With a three-year-old and a hairy dog in the house, it wasn't easy to keep the place clean. It also didn't help that Rachel and I had lived our childhoods in squalor and had zero drive to keep a neat home ingrained in us by our parents. Add the fact that she was a full-time student and I had two jobs, and we were doomed to be slobs. With everything going on in our lives right now, though, the state of our house was the least of our worries.

I returned to the living room, where I found Baxter flipping through a stack of mail he'd found on a small desk.

He looked up. "I don't suppose you found the murder weapon after I left the scene, did you?"

"No. We only ended up with some blood to test, an Apple Watch with a few fingerprints that probably belong to Angela, and the two shoeprints."

"I get leaving the watch. It would be like leaving the victim's phone at the first scene—no trail. It shows thought, like removing the murder weapon. What do you make of him leaving the garrote behind the first time?"

"Amanda and I were discussing that earlier. You're probably way ahead of me on this one, but I can't help thinking the killer intentionally left the murder weapon made out of a guitar string in order to implicate Skyler Marx and drive any potential attention away from himself."

He smiled. Not a big smile, but a genuine one. "As usual, we're on the same investigative page. Yet another reason I don't think Skyler Marx is our guy."

I could feel the tension between us ebbing away as we got deeper into our discussion. I wanted to believe we could get back to where we'd been before he'd told me he cared about me and I told him he'd be better off without me. I knew from experience that anything we would try to start would only end with me doing something stupid that would ruin both our personal and professional relationships. So, I'd pushed him away, taking up with Vic as added insurance I wouldn't break down and change my mind. What I didn't take into consideration was how much it would hurt Baxter to see me with another man. But the outcome only proved my original point that I suck at relationships, because I managed to ruin our friendship without even getting any romance out of it.

I shook off what I was thinking. "So who hates Marx enough to frame him for murder?"

He shrugged. "I don't know. Everyone? The guy's an asshat."

"I'd say Shawna's friends and family should have the biggest issues with him. But at the same time, I'd hope none of them would kill her in order to get back at him for what he did to her. It would be counterproductive."

"That was confusing, but I get your point. Keep thinking about it. I could really use your insight on this one, especially since Sterling and I aren't seeing eye-to-eye."

The fact that Baxter had always given credence to my opinions and hunches during our investigations, not to mention that he always introduced me as his partner, meant a lot to me. Normally, the detectives didn't consult with the criminalists about our gut reactions to the case itself; we were there mainly to provide physical proof that they'd captured the right suspect. Baxter was a different breed of investigator, though. He wanted justice served, and he wasn't above using any resource available to see it done.

He continued, "As for Shawna's friends, I'm not counting them out. They make up the bulk of who knew where she was going the night she was killed. I was hoping since you're at least an acquaintance of most of them..." Pausing, he looked down and seemed uncomfortable again. Then he said quietly, "Personal stuff aside, I was hoping you'd consider working some extra hours with me...like before. I could use your eye for detail while I interview Shawna's friends, and seeing a friendly face might put them at ease. Plus, Sterling and I need to work our hunches separately or we're going to be at each other's throats and get nothing done."

I blurted out, "I'd love to. Anything for—" I caught myself. "The department."

He studied me for a few moments, long enough that I felt heat start creeping onto my cheeks. I fought it, clenching my jaw in an effort to keep control over myself.

He finally said, "Good. Thanks." There was something in his eyes, but I couldn't read it.

And just like that, it was uncomfortable again.

15

Baxter and I wrapped up our search of Angela Meadows' apartment in silence. When we got to the parking lot, I saw that Amanda and Sterling had left without us. Great. That meant a twenty-minute drive to the station alone with Baxter, with nothing to do except continue to ignore each other or force some conversation, neither of which sounded like fun. I couldn't even have him drop me at the college to pick up my car, because Rachel would need it to get home this afternoon.

The only conversation that occurred on the way was when Baxter called Sterling on speaker to ask him what he and Amanda had found in Angela Meadows' vehicle. They had come up empty-handed. Evidently her car was even more pristine than her home, without so much as a bit of loose change in the cup holder.

After he ended the call, we returned to deafening silence. What had been uncomfortable earlier had crossed the line into excruciating. When we reached the station, I threw a quick "thanks" over my shoulder and hurried ahead of him to the evidence room. I checked the phone in and asked the evidence clerk to alert the cyber guys that they had a phone to process. I continued on to the lab. Amanda was standing over a worktable, removing the shoeprint impressions from their boxes so they could continue to dry.

"Sorry I deserted you back at the apartment complex, but Jason was antsy about us getting out of there," she said.

I eyed her suspiciously. "He wanted to stop and get something to eat without me, didn't he?"

She stripped off her gloves and beckoned me to follow her into the lab's adjacent office. "Yes, but to make it up to you, we brought you a peace offering." She handed me a brown paper bag from a local hamburger place.

I opened the bag and breathed in the greasy aroma. "You are the absolute best."

"To be fair, Jason bought it."

"Only because you made him, I'm sure."

"True."

I snickered. "I bet he loved that."

Smiling, she said, "Oh, he cursed your name all the way back to the station."

"I don't doubt it. I'm going to go enjoy this, but I promise I'll be quick."

"Don't hurry on my account. It's not like we have a lot of evidence to process."

I headed toward the breakroom, showing great restraint by not digging into the fries on the way. It was mid-afternoon, and I'd had nothing to eat or drink since early this morning. Breakfast seemed like a lifetime ago, and I was beyond starving. After giving my hands a thorough scrubbing in scalding hot water, I bought myself a soft drink and sat down to eat my ridiculously late lunch. The cheeseburger and fries were heaven. I was only partway through them when Vic walked in and gave me a kiss on the cheek.

"Hey," I said, wondering if there was any way I could avoid a lecture on the dangers of carbs and high fructose corn syrup.

"Amanda told me I'd find you here." He frowned as his eyes landed on the spread in front of me. "None of those foods are on your diet." Right on cue.

"Maybe not, but it's all I have."

"That's no excuse. Let's run out and get you something else."

I shook my head. "No time. I need to get to the lab."

"Also not an excuse."

"Did you come here to shame me or talk to me?"

He smiled. "Can't I do both?"

"Not if you want to be able to walk out of here."

Chuckling, he sat down next to me. "Let's talk, then. I'd be remiss if I didn't warn you of the dangers of running alone around here right now. If you decide to take a run later, I want you to come find me so I can go with you."

I smiled. No way in hell I was going to waste an hour running if I barely had five minutes to throw down my lunch, but I wasn't going to tell him that. And while I let him believe I went running on my own on a regular basis, I'd only actually done it once. Instead, I joked, "So you can protect me, tough guy?"

"I'm not being misogynistic. I imagine the killer has been following our investigation and knows you're a part of it. I hate to say it, but out running alone you'd be the perfect target." He shrugged. "Same could be said for me. Hazard of the job."

Suddenly my food didn't seem quite as appetizing as before. I set my cheeseburger aside. "Let's talk about something else besides what great candidates we both are to meet a violent end."

He reached over and squeezed my hand. "I didn't mean to be so morbid. Tell me about what you did today."

I hesitated. "Wait. You're for sure on the task force? Officially?"

His cheerful expression faded. "Really, Ellie? You think I'd come in here without clearance?"

Yes. "It's part of my job to protect the evidence, no matter who asks."

"I'm officially on the task force."

"Okay."

I brought him up to speed on what Amanda and I had found at the crime scene and also what we'd found, or more accurately hadn't found, at Angela Meadows' home and in her vehicle.

Frowning, he said, "Too bad we don't have more physical evidence, but at least I was able to find Angela Meadows' connection to Shawna. They went to the same high school and were on several sports teams together. According to Shawna's sister, the two of them had remained in touch and would occasionally travel together to out-of-town races."

I nodded. "Then I guess the only question is, who's got beef with both of them?"

"I'm working to establish a connection between Angela Meadows and Skyler Marx."

"You know he has an alibi for last night, right?"

"I'm not buying it. Detective Baxter only talked to one bartender, who was probably too drunk to be a credible witness."

Snorting, I said, "Oh, okay. I didn't realize they'd changed your agency to the Federal Bureau of *Assumption*."

He glared at me. "Marx is guilty."

"I get that you want him to be guilty. I do. But you're going to get yourself kicked off this task force if you're showing bias because of what you know about his past with your ex. We're investigating Angela Meadows' homicide, not Shawna's."

He clenched his jaw. "They go hand in hand."

"They *seem* to go hand in hand. But you know full well that investigating a case without a suspect in mind will allow you to see the bigger picture. You're trying to make the evidence fit the suspect, not the other way around. I feel like I shouldn't have to point this out to you."

"Then don't. Stay in your lane." His voice had an edge to it I didn't appreciate. This was exactly why I didn't want to date anyone I had to work with.

"Fine." I got up and dumped the rest of my food in the trash, my appetite gone. I left him there and returned to the lab.

I found Amanda in the office, sitting at our AFIS computer, the one we used to examine fingerprints and run them through the Automated Fingerprint Identification System database. She was working on the fingerprints we'd found this morning. "That was quick," she said.

"Yeah. Manetti came in and harassed me about this case, so I didn't waste any time getting back here."

Her eyebrows shot up. "Are you two at it already? You haven't even had to do any actual work together yet."

"I know. That's what I'm worried about. This is not going to end well." I changed the subject. "Did you get to study the shoeprints?"

"I did. They're all yours."

I washed my hands and put on gloves, got a fresh lab coat from the closet, and headed into the lab to the table where the two shoeprint casts were drying. I positioned a lighted bench magnifier over one of the casts. They were both of the same left boot, and both casts measured thirteen and a quarter inches. I got out the table we used for determining shoe size ranges based on lengths of various types of shoe soles. My estimation was a size thirteen or thirteen and a half. That information would be close enough to weed out a few suspects, but I was no expert on shoes. In order for the shoeprint to be valid evidence in a trial, someone at the state lab would have to determine the exact model and size of the shoe. They could even determine an individual wear pattern that could further tie it to the wearer.

I called to Amanda, "Did you come up with thirteen to thirteen and a half for the size?"

"Yes," she replied. "And I emailed photos and a request for analysis to the shoe guys."

"Awesome."

My work with the shoeprints was done. The next task would be completing a second examination of the fingerprints Amanda was working on. While I was waiting for her to finish, Baxter knocked on the open door of the office.

"You want to ride over to the morgue with me?" he asked.

After our ride from Carmel to the station in Noblesville, I wasn't convinced it wouldn't be more fun to walk the short distance in the frigid cold. I was surprised he even offered. "Sure."

I must have hesitated for too long before replying, because a slight frown creased Baxter's face. "You don't have to. You're welcome to catch a ride with Sterling instead."

Hoping to defuse this conversation before it became like our last one, I went for the joke. "I'm sure as hell not riding anywhere with Sterling. He's mean and won't stop for food." I winked at Amanda, who snickered to herself.

A smile pulled at the corner of Baxter's mouth. "That's why I never want to ride anywhere with him, either. Come on."

16

I ditched my lab coat and followed him out of the station and to his vehicle. Although we didn't say much on the way over, at least we weren't openly at odds. I wasn't looking forward to this meeting, not that I ever did. Walking into the morgue without a decent amount of evidence and no clear suspect was a recipe for disaster. The DA was not going to be pleased.

We suited up and made some small talk with Dr. Berg while we waited for everyone else to arrive. Sure enough, DA McAlister was already angry when he walked in.

He zeroed in on Baxter and me. "This is a nightmare. Due to your overwhelming lack of competence, we've got a second homicide on our hands. Way to go."

"Wade," Dr. Berg said, his tone a warning.

The DA ignored him. "I told you before that I didn't want a repeat of last time, and now we have a repeat of last time, including the damn Feds barging in. I want this guy caught today."

"Enough!" Dr. Berg bellowed. "Not in here."

DA McAlister stared at him in shock, but at least he shut up. Sterling and Agent Griffin entered the room, both nodding their hellos. I assumed they'd heard the raised voices from outside.

Dr. Berg cleared his throat. "Good afternoon. The autopsy for Angela

Meadows will be tomorrow morning at eight o'clock. Who will be in attendance?"

Baxter and Griffin said at the same time, "I will."

"Very good. The preliminary cause of death is indeed exsanguination from seven sharp force wounds to the torso. I will cast the wounds during autopsy to ascertain the type and size of weapon that was used." He turned back the sheet and pulled up the victim's right arm, which had a couple of nasty gashes across it. He did the same for her left arm, which had only some bruising. "There are defensive wounds on her forearms, but no other contusions on the body. I've found no evidence of trauma to the external genitalia. As with the Shawna Meehan case, I'll perform the proper examinations and collect the needed samples for a sexual assault kit." He spread out the sheet to cover the body once more. "Can I answer any questions at this time?"

Griffin asked, "Were you able to pinpoint that TOD any better?"

Dr. Berg shook his head. "Unfortunately, no. The cold and snow play havoc with the state of the body."

I asked Griffin, "Was Cyber not able to get the watch to turn on? Its GPS information should pinpoint it nearly to the minute."

"The last report I got was that they're still working on it." He added under his breath, "Whatever that means." I imagined if Cyber couldn't work some kind of sorcery on that watch and get it running soon, they were going to get an earful from Griffin.

Dr. Berg said, "Any other questions I can answer?" When no one spoke, he said, "Have a good evening."

Sterling and Griffin flew out of the room in a rush, ripping off their protective wear as they went. Baxter, the DA, and I followed.

As we were removing our gowns and discarding them, DA McAlister decided to take the opportunity to pick at me some more. "You managed to find even less evidence than last time."

I replied, "No, we logged four items into evidence last time and seven this time, counting fingerprints and DNA samples. That's more, not less. Check your math."

"Don't get smart with me. The victim's watch with her fingerprints on it and a vial full of her blood are useless to me, and a couple of footprints are not going to sway a jury to convict. Maybe we should have Agent Griffin send his forensic team out to find what you missed."

Baxter cut in, "DA McAlister, our team is as thorough as any around. If she says that was all the evidence, then—"

The DA wheeled on Baxter. "Was I talking to you, Detective?"

Baxter didn't back down. "No, but you're berating a member of my team."

DA McAlister's tone dripped with disdain. "You chuckleheads better get your shit together. I'm not taking anyone to court if I can't nail him to the wall." He turned on his heel and marched out the door.

I rolled my eyes. "I don't know how he manages it, but he gets crabbier every time I see him."

" 'Crabby' is too kind a word for that man," Baxter said around a clenched jaw.

"Well, I guess if he was all sunshine and roses, he'd be a horrible DA. Thanks for defending my work, though. I honestly do feel bad about the lack of evidence I was able to get for you."

He held the door open for me. "Don't apologize. We're up against someone smart who has clearly planned his kills. Luckily, we're smarter. We'll figure this out, with or without evidence."

I smiled. Baxter's positive attitude had been absent for a while, thanks to me. It bolstered my spirits to see it again.

As we got into his SUV, I said, "Hey, I never heard—did Dr. Berg find evidence of rape during Shawna Meehan's autopsy?"

"No. Nothing. No semen or spermicide from a condom, and not even any traces of saliva. The guy didn't touch her. At least, not with mouth or his..." Baxter flushed. He has never been able to talk about sex with me.

I fought back a grin. "I get it. At least we're not dealing with a case of necrophilia here."

"Right. I'm going to go out on a limb and say we're going to get the same news about Angela Meadows."

"So why take the panties off a corpse unless you're going to get kinky with it?"

He made a face. "No clue."

"I get removing your victim's outerwear if you'd got cut or punched during the struggle and were afraid you'd leave your own blood behind. But everything? Why go to the trouble if you're not planning to seal the deal? It's an extra wasted step."

"To a sane person, yes. But not to a nutjob like this. He has a reason. Maybe he's trying to inflict shame for something they did to him or something he perceives they did to him."

"You can't shame the dead."

"True, but you can shame their memory."

"Which, again, doesn't affect them in the slightest. Got any *good* theories, Detective?"

He frowned. "Not if all you're going to do is bash them."

I chuckled. "I'm sorry. Please, tell me more."

"The clothes could be trophies."

"Now we're getting somewhere. I like that idea. Clothing trophies are better than body part trophies, at least."

Wincing, he said, "Too soon."

I wrinkled my nose. "Yeah, I realized that right after I said it."

"Call me unfeeling, but it's a hell of a lot easier to work a case when you don't know the victim."

"And no one's life depends on you figuring out the truth."

"That, too."

We locked eyes for a moment, then I said, "Speaking of my sister...I'm sure it was incredibly difficult for you to have to let her down last night. But you made a little boy's night by taking him and his mom bowling. Thank you."

"No need to thank me. Rachel took it well enough, except..." He sighed. "She tried to play it off like it was nothing, but I know she was upset. She was quiet the whole night."

"Same this morning." When his brow furrowed with worry, I added, "I'm sure once she gets over the embarrassment, she'll be fine."

"I hope so. I'd hate to think I caused her a setback."

"I told you not to beat yourself up over this, Nick. She told me she wasn't sure this thing with you was even going to go anywhere. If it's any consolation, I don't think she had her hopes up too high."

"That still doesn't make me feel better about it."

"Give it time. Besides, you're not her type. Not even close. I'm sure on some level she knew that."

He gave me a confused look. "Not her type? Who doesn't like nice, smart guys?"

I grinned. "Especially humble ones."

He laughed. "You know what I mean."

"Based on her track record, Rachel doesn't. She only dates losers."

"That's her big sister talking. I'm sure she's had some decent boyfriends."

"Decent looking, maybe, but not decent human beings. It's like she's hardwired to seek out the worst possible guy she can find, the dumber the better. Nate can already read better than his biological father."

"Now you're just making stuff up."

I shrugged. "He's sitting in Marion County lockup for grand theft auto, resisting arrest, and aggravated battery of a police officer if you'd like to test him. I'm sure he has nothing better to do."

"Sounds like a great guy."

"And that's why he doesn't know he's Nate's dad."

From the set of his jaw, I could tell Baxter didn't like what I'd just said. Sure, men had a right to know they'd fathered a child. But in my mind, what Rachel's ex had done to her forfeited all of his rights. When she'd mentioned to him that there was a possibility she might be pregnant, he slugged her and took off before she had the chance to confirm her suspicions with a pregnancy test. That finally opened her eyes to who he really was. She happened to run into him a few weeks later and told him her pregnancy scare had been a false alarm. He said that was a good thing, because he would have made her get an abortion. Definitely not the kind of person you'd want to help you co-parent a child.

I said, "It may not seem fair, but there are extenuating circumstances."

"I wasn't passing judgment."

"Not verbally, at least."

He shrugged. "Okay, fine. As a man, I take offense at stuff like that."

"Well, this guy isn't a man, he's a piece of shit. He sold drugs to our mother. He tried to get Rachel hooked on drugs, and he hit her more than once. He was twenty-five while they were together, and she was only seventeen. That makes him a statutory rapist as well, so there you go. Can you imagine having to hand our sweet little Nate over to someone like that for even a minute?"

"I withdraw my former objection."

"I thought you might."

17

Baxter started heading south out of Noblesville instead of taking us back to the station. "I hope you were serious when you said you wouldn't mind doing some interviews with me."

"I was. Does that mean we're doing one now?"

He nodded. "I figure we can knock one out before our next meeting. My goal for tonight is to run down all of Manetti's party guests again and find out where they were last night. You game?"

"Sure."

"Chris Bruner's work is just down the road. It'll be easier to catch him here rather than having to drive up to his house in Cicero. What do you make of him? He didn't have a solid alibi for the time Shawna Meehan was killed, but he didn't have a motive, either. The only thing that struck me as odd about him is that he seems way too happy."

I snickered. "True. I don't know much about him except that he has an unholy obsession with exercise and turnips."

He gave me a questioning glance.

"The guy loves his turnips. He wouldn't shut up about them at Manetti's party."

"Does he grow them?"

Shaking my head, I said, "I don't think so. He just eats them."

"Oh."

Chris worked in the office side of a manufacturing plant south of town. Even with Baxter's badge, we weren't allowed to run amok through the place. The front desk attendant called Chris to come down to meet us.

While we were waiting, Baxter checked his phone. "Good news. I just got a text saying that Cyber managed to get the watch working. TOD is right around six forty-five."

"That'll be so much easier to pin down than the four to eight window. To be honest, I wasn't looking forward to having to coax four hours' worth of alibis out of six different people."

Chris approached us. "Ellie Matthews," he said, smiling as ever, even though clearly confused. "I didn't expect to see you at my work."

I shook hands with him. "I'm afraid it's not a social call, Chris. This is Detective Nick Baxter of the Hamilton County Sheriff's Department."

Chris's smile faded as he shook Baxter's hand. "I already spoke to someone from your department regarding Shawna's death..."

Baxter replied, "I know, but there's been another development in our investigation. Do you know an Angela Meadows?"

"Yes, she's a fellow running enthusiast. I often see her at races. Shawna introduced me to her, in fact."

"Would you call Ms. Meadows an acquaintance or a friend?"

"A friend, I suppose."

I asked, "Do you ever go running with her?"

"Sort of. If we see each other out and about, we might share each other's company for a few miles. We never make any formal plans."

"Where do you see her 'out and about,' exactly?"

Chris thought for a moment. "Carmel, mostly, on the days I run the Monon Greenway."

"Ever see her at Central Park?"

"Sometimes." His brow furrowed. "Why are you asking about Angela? Is she in some sort of trouble?"

Baxter said, "Before we get into that, I need to know where you were last night between six-thirty and seven."

Chris stared as us for a few seconds, until it almost got uncomfortable. He blinked once and said, "At a Weight Watchers meeting."

"I'll need an address."

Chris reached into his pocket and took out his phone. Forcing out a laugh, he said, "Not much of a Valentine's Day, huh?"

His fingers were shaking as he pulled up a map app and showed the information on his phone to Baxter. Baxter took a photo of Chris's screen with his phone.

Pasting on a dead-eyed smile, Chris said, "Is that all you need from me? I should be getting back to the desk."

Baxter regarded him for a moment. "How about your shoe size?"

"My...shoe size?"

I said, "It's just a general protocol thing for this case."

"Okay...I wear a thirteen."

Baxter replied. "Thank you. That's all for now. We'll be in touch."

"Goodbye, Detective. Ellie." Chris turned on his heel and strode away, disappearing into the stairwell instead of waiting for the elevator.

I said, "He's lying."

Baxter nodded. "Big time."

"And he was in such a hurry to get away from us, he forgot all about getting the scoop on his friend Angela."

"Right again."

We exited the building and headed toward Baxter's vehicle.

The way Chris had reacted didn't sit well with me. "He's rattled. You want to wait and follow him when he leaves work?"

Baxter chuckled. "While I appreciate your investigative enthusiasm, we should be getting back for the meeting."

Shrugging, I said, "Eh, the time's not set in stone."

"Let's not give old Agent Steve a reason to put us on his shit list just yet."

I let out a snicker. "Okay, I see your point. But I'm putting Chris Bruner on *our* shit list."

"Good. He's even a match for our boot print size. I'll have one of the deputies run down his alibi and dig into his background while we're in the meeting."

As we were getting into Baxter's SUV, my phone rang. I glanced at the screen. It was my AA sponsor. I made a face and declined the call.

"Something wrong?" Baxter asked.

"No, it's just my sponsor. I'll deal with it later."

"I'll be happy to wait while you take the call. Aren't you supposed to check in regularly?"

I hesitated. "Yes, and I do...but I always let her phone calls go to voice-mail and then text her a response. I don't really like her."

"Then you should ask for a new sponsor."

I sighed. "Probably. I mean, she's a nice enough person, so I hate to complain about her. I just don't like talking to her. Or rather, listening to her. She'll ask me how I'm doing, then interrupt me and launch into some boring ass story about herself. I don't have that kind of time."

"Ellie." From his tone, I could tell some sort of lecture was imminent.

"Nick," I replied, heavy on the sarcasm.

He went on, undeterred. "If you won't make time for a talk with your sponsor, will you make time to go to a meeting later?"

"We have five more people to track down tonight. I'm not bailing on you after I told you I'd help."

"Taking care of yourself is not bailing. There's time. I'll even go with you if you want."

The fact that he would do that for me made my heart want to burst. No one else had ever offered to go along. That said, the last thing I wanted was for Baxter to actually attend a meeting with me. While meetings were a necessity to my continued sobriety, they sometimes struck a nerve and made me feel like a pathetic, struggling addict again. I didn't want him to see me that way.

I lowered my eyes. "It means a lot to me that you would go to a meeting with me, but... I'll go on my own. I'll find a meeting later tonight. I promise."

"Okay."

When we got to the conference room, the task force was already assembled. Agent Griffin, Jayne, Chief Esparza, Sterling, Amanda, and Vic were all seated around the table. The moment Baxter and I were settled, Agent Griffin began his meeting.

"Let's get cracking on this, shall we? The victim, Angela Meadows, was killed yesterday evening. Cyber has the victim's watch working, and according to the GPS information they pulled, our victim reached the crime scene last night at roughly six forty-five P.M." He scrawled "TOD 6:45 PM 2/14" on the whiteboard behind him and circled it twice. "We will proceed with that as our time of death. Preliminary cause of death is exsanguination by way of seven stab wounds." He wrote "7 STAB WOUNDS" and underlined it three times. "As in the Shawna Meehan homicide, this victim's knee was injured, likely in an attempt to slow her down and make her easier to kill. The victim was also found in a similar position to that of Shawna Meehan, unclothed and lying on her side." He wrote "KNEECAPPED" and "CLOTHING REMOVED." Turning to me, he said, "Ms. Matthews, do you want to elaborate on the scene?"

I hated going first. Opening my file, I said, "Yes. The area of struggle was fairly large this time, and we managed to pull a couple of shoeprints from it that we believe belong to the killer. Best guess, the boots he—or she—was wearing are a men's size thirteen, so we're dealing with a person over six feet. That could help narrow down our suspect list. Aside from the watch you mentioned, there was no other physical evidence left behind."

Not bothering to acknowledge my report aside from writing "MEN'S 13 SHOE" and "6+ FEET TALL" on the board, Griffin went on to the next. "Chief Esparza, where are we with canvassing the homes in the adjacent neighborhood?"

Esparza replied, "Our deputies have contacted all but two of the homeowners whose backyards overlook Woodland Gardens. Unfortunately, several of them weren't home that evening. But of those who were, none of them said they noticed any commotion outside."

Frowning, Griffin said, "Detectives, your report?"

Sterling bored us all with his account of obtaining warrants for Angela Meadows' vehicle and apartment, compiling a list of her friends and family to be compared with Shawna's list, and his plans to start interviewing potential matches. Baxter did largely the same thing, informing everyone of Skyler Marx's tight alibi and his plans for interviewing Manetti's party guests for their alibis regarding the time of the new homicide.

Baxter ended with, "If you don't have any objections, I want to partner up with Ellie for these interviews. Since she's acquainted with them, I'm hoping her presence will help put people at ease so they'll open up."

Griffin looked from Baxter to me and nodded in approval. "Getting the dream team back together for another case? I like it. No reason not to use an extra set of eyes and ears. Ms. Matthews, do you mind putting in some additional hours assisting Detective Baxter?"

I nodded. "I'd be happy to."

Vic, who'd been actively frowning throughout the meeting, especially when his party guests were mentioned, was up next. "I spent the morning verifying our victim's identity and tracking down more information on her disappearance. Angela Meadows worked as a home health nurse, so fortunately her fingerprints were in CODIS. I had Dr. Berg collect her prints and one of our guys verify them ahead of contacting her next of kin. I interviewed her boss, who'd filed the missing persons report. When she didn't show up last night at eight P.M. for her shift, he and her coworkers tried calling her, but of course couldn't get her. One of them drove over and checked her apartment. Her boss said it wasn't like her to miss work without letting him know, which was why he was so proactive in reporting her disappearance." He hesitated for a moment, his frown deepening. "I've been working this afternoon to find out what kind of connection Angela Meadows had with Shawna Meehan. So far, I've learned that they were high school teammates who remained friends into adulthood. They've made trips together lately to out of town races. Given that, it stands to reason that Angela would be at least acquainted with Skyler Marx, but so far I don't have a better link than that they simply both knew Shawna. I feel like there's more, so I'll continue to dig into it."

I resisted the urge to roll my eyes, although I did sneak a peek at Baxter. From the set of his jaw, I assumed he was thinking the same thing I was. We were going to get nowhere as long as certain members of the task force refused to let go of Skyler Marx as the prime suspect for a crime he couldn't physically have committed.

Griffin nodded. "Since you knew Shawna Meehan well, I want you to collaborate with Detective Sterling comparing his lists of our victims' acquaintances."

When Griffin mentioned Vic knowing Shawna, I noticed my colleagues casting glances at me, evidently waiting for some type of reaction on my part. No one seemed to understand that it didn't bother me that they'd gone out. I mean, the fact that he'd been attracted to her made me question his standards a little. But considering my past lovers, I was certainly in no position to judge him for it.

Griffin went on, "I've got a team over at the field office combing through Angela Meadows' financials, BMV files, and background records. So far, nothing has popped, but it's still early. We should know a lot more tomorrow. Sheriff, anything to add?"

Jayne, who usually ran this meeting and oversaw major investigations, had again been shoved to the side by the Feds. She took it in stride, though. "Scheduling of man hours will be similar to our last big case. Investigators and criminalists will take the day and evening shifts. Mandatory eight-hour sleep breaks. Mandatory one-hour lunch and dinner breaks. More if you need. The chief and I will handle the night shift so someone from the task force will always be on duty." She addressed Griffin and Vic. "Agents, Hamilton County wishes to be fully cooperative with our friends at the Bureau. Our entire department is at your disposal."

Griffin said, "Thank you, Sheriff. I believe the rest of you have your marching orders."

As everyone got up to leave, Vic said to me, "Ellie, can I speak to you for a moment?"

Figuring he was going to apologize for earlier, I said, "Sure." When Baxter gave me a questioning glance and tapped his watch, I said to him, "Meet you at your desk in five."

Once everyone else had vacated the conference room, Vic shut the door and turned to me. He was closed off. No expression whatsoever. "I want to talk to you about interviewing the members of my run club."

I already didn't like where this was going. "So talk."

"Please don't be rude to them. They're grieving."

"I don't intend to be rude to them. But I'm also not going to coddle the living at the expense of the dead. My duty is to Angela Meadows." I looked him square in the eye. "So is yours."

"I've been at this a lot longer than you have. I know what my duty is."

I slung my bag over my shoulder. "Are you done? I have to go."

"I'm done."

"Do you have nothing else to say to me? Maybe something like 'sorry for being a dick earlier'?"

His expression grew dark. "I'm not going to apologize for speaking my mind."

I gave him a fake smile. "Okay, then. Good night, Agent Manetti."

18

I met Baxter at his desk. "Our first stop better be for food."

He smiled as he stood and put on his jacket. "It's like you read my mind."

We'd managed to shake off our earlier awkwardness, but another vibe was becoming apparent. From the deafening silence between us as we headed to his vehicle and got inside, I knew there was a burning question he wanted to ask me.

"You want to know what Manetti wanted?" I said.

"No," he replied, eyes wide with innocence.

"Liar."

"Okay, fine. You got me. I can see the steam coming out of your ears, so I'm assuming it wasn't a good talk."

"He warned me not to be rude to his friends when we go talk to them."

Baxter couldn't keep a straight face. "Now why on earth would he say a thing like that to you of all people?"

I reached over and smacked him on the arm. "He can't do stuff like this. If what he'd said actually swayed me to treat any of our persons of interest differently, that's tampering with an investigation."

"Not that I'm agreeing with the guy, but it's not tampering if a superior requests that you conduct your interviews with a certain amount of care."

I gaped at him. "I know you did *not* just call him my superior."

He shrugged. "Multi-agency task force hierarchy sucks. I'm sorry to have to be the one to inform you, but criminalists aren't at the top. Neither are detectives."

"But he's being a big ass," I whined.

"You say that like it's a surprise to you."

I glared at him in response, which only made him chuckle all the way to the fast food sub place he'd chosen. It was difficult to stay angry when Baxter had one of his infectious good moods going. While we ate and also on the drive down to Fishers for our first interview, we talked like the old days, only making sure to avoid touchy subjects like Rachel and Vic.

We had to wind around on a twisty road just north of Geist Reservoir to find Jonathan and Rebecca Caldwell's home. It was a lovely place with a backdrop of inky darkness. I imagined their view of the water was stunning in the daytime.

Rebecca answered the door, holding an adorable little girl about a year younger than Nate on her hip. She blinked when she saw me, looking from me to Baxter with confusion.

I said, "Hi, Rebecca. Remember me? I'm Ellie Matthews."

"Of course. We met at Vic's." She glanced again at Baxter.

"This is Detective Nick Baxter. We're here hoping to speak to you and Jonathan for a moment regarding an active investigation. It shouldn't take long."

The color drained from her face. She called, "Jonathan! Can you come down here, please?" To Baxter and me, she said, "Come on in."

Baxter said, "If you don't mind, Mrs. Caldwell, we'd like to speak to you and your husband one at a time."

She nodded, eyes wide. "Sure." She bellowed, "Jonathan!"

Her little girl began crying. I felt for Rebecca. Kids seemed to sense when you were worked up, and for some inexplicable reason always felt the need to melt down right along with you. Rebecca ushered the girl into the nearby living room and sat her down with some toys.

Jonathan trotted down the stairs, his face stuck in a frown. "Where's the fire, Bec?"

Baxter moved his jacket aside so his badge was visible.

Jonathan noticed it right away. "Oh. There it is," he muttered under his breath. He registered my presence, every bit as confused as his wife had been. "Ellie, what are you doing here?"

"Detective Baxter and I need to speak to you and Rebecca about a case we're investigating. Separately."

He opened a nearby door, which led to a study. "Um...is it about Shawna? Because I spoke to another detective a few days ago." He led us inside and sat behind the desk, offering us the two chairs that faced him. We sat down.

"Not exactly. We're here to speak to you about a woman named Angela Meadows." Baxter pulled a BMV photo of Angela out of his jacket pocket and showed it to Jonathan.

"I recognize her from a few races we've run. She's always up there with Shawna on the winners' podium." He let out a chuckle. "My wife always just misses medaling when those two are around."

I nodded. "She said something to that effect at Vic's party, as I recall."

"Well, you met Shawna. She can be a bit much sometimes." He shook his head. "Sorry. I shouldn't speak ill of the dead."

Baxter said, "No worries." A wail could be heard from the other room. "We'll get down to business and get out of your hair. Where were you last night between six-thirty and seven o'clock?"

Without missing a beat, he said, "We were here. Emmalyn gets squirmy at restaurants, so instead of going out to celebrate Valentine's Day, we stayed in and had our own little party."

My heart ached. The Caldwells seemed like decent people, and it was a shame neither of them had an alibi for either murder. I'd glanced at their file on the way over here and saw that they'd been at home on the night Shawna died as well. I hated the fact that they were in potential trouble for being homebodies who enjoyed quiet family time.

I asked, "Did you have food delivered or anything like that? Can anyone besides you and Rebecca attest for the fact that you were both here during that time?"

He shook his head. "I picked up a pizza on the way home from work. I got here just before five-thirty. By six-thirty we were sitting down to watch Emmalyn's favorite Disney movie for the hundredth time."

I tried. "Okay. One more thing...do you know anything about Angela Meadows aside from the fact that she's a fast runner?"

He shook his head. "No. I've never even spoken to her. Sorry." He hesitated for a moment, then recognition dawned on his face. "Is she the woman who was found in Central Park today? I heard the tail end of the news report on the radio as I was driving home this evening."

I nodded. "She is."

He stared at me. "And you think Rebecca and I could have had something to do with her death?"

"We're not accusing anyone of anything. We're simply following protocol."

His expression went dark. "Were you following protocol when you let that scumbag Skyler Marx go free? He was out of jail, what, an hour or two before this other woman was killed? Seems to me like you should be accusing him of something, not us."

Baxter said, "Sounds like you know Marx pretty well. How?"

Clearing his throat, Jonathan replied, "Not well. I'd see him with Shawna on occasion."

"Do you know if he was close to Angela?"

"No, but it stands to reason that they at least knew each other through Shawna."

Baxter nodded. "I'd have to agree with that. And what size shoe do you wear?"

Jonathan stared at us. "What?"

"What is your shoe size?"

"Twelve. Why in the world would you need to know—"

Cutting in, Baxter said, "Thank you, Mr. Caldwell. Would you mind sending your wife in here now?"

Jonathan stood, his face flushed with anger. "I'll get her."

Once he was out of earshot, Baxter said to me, "Look at you, not being rude at all. You were even trying to help him out with his alibi."

I frowned. "I have my moments."

"What did you hear Rebecca Caldwell say at Manetti's party about the victims?"

"Something to the effect of 'no one could ever hope to win a race with Shawna around.' "

"Hmm."

"Hmm, nothing. Angela's killer wears a big shoe. Rebecca doesn't really fit the bill."

"Her husband certainly does."

We abruptly ended our conversation when we heard footsteps on the hardwood floor behind us. Rebecca hurried in, seeming even more unnerved than before. She took the seat her husband had vacated, eyes wide and breathing hard.

I said, "Rebecca, I realize our presence in your home is disconcerting. I'm sorry for that. But we have to do our due diligence by speaking to everyone who might have information we could use."

"I understand," she breathed.

"Could you tell us where you and your husband were between six-thirty and seven P.M. yesterday?"

"Here. The three of us spent the evening at home." Her eyes filled with tears. "Can you tell me what's going on?"

Baxter got out Angela's photo and showed it to Rebecca. "This is Angela Meadows. She was killed last night in Central Park."

Rebecca put a shaking hand over her mouth. "First Shawna and now her?"

"Yes. Can you tell us how you know Angela?"

"Only from racing. Shawna introduced me to her. They were friends."

"Were you friends with Angela?"

She shook her head. "No. One conversation with her was enough for me. She and Shawna are—or were, I suppose, two peas in a pod."

"How so?"

She turned to me. "Well, you remember how Shawna got smug with me at Vic's party?"

I nodded.

"My first and only impression of Angela was even worse than that. I placed third in a race after the two of them. During the medal ceremony, they proceeded to tell me everything that was wrong with my running style —from stride to attitude—and why I'd never come in first."

She frowned as she spoke, but I noticed that she had visibly relaxed. Time for the empathy card.

I said, "Wow. Serious bitches, then. They ruined your medal ceremony."

Out of the corner of my eye, I saw Baxter wipe a hand across his mouth to cover a smile.

Shrugging, she said, "I mean, yeah. It's not like they didn't have the clout to back it up, but who does that?"

I thought fast, hoping there were more people Rebecca might want to throw under the bus. "Well, Tracy tried to berate me the night I met her. Mateo had to step in and defend me."

"Tracy comes off harsh, but she means well enough. She's hardcore and thinks everyone else should be, too. Plus she's got a girl crush on Shawna, so she always takes her side during one of our 'discussions.' She's much easier to take when she's not trying to impress Shawna."

I'd noticed Tracy and Shawna being fairly chummy that night, but hadn't thought much about it until now.

Baxter said, "Girl crush? As in romantic or hero worship?"

Rebecca replied, "Hero worship. Tracy is a serious gym rat, but she's trying to branch out into ultramarathoning like Shawna. The extra weight she carries from muscle mass has been a stumbling block, but she refuses to give up lifting. You can't really do both well. Tracy's having trouble accepting that there's a sport out there where she can't excel."

He pressed, "Do you think that makes her jealous of what Shawna can do?"

"In a way, I guess."

"Did Tracy know Angela?"

"Yes."

"Has she ever showed any kind of jealousy or rivalry toward her?"

Rebecca's eyes widened and she held out her hands. "Wait. I am in no way insinuating Tracy had anything against Shawna or Angela, if that's what you're getting at."

I said, "We're trying to figure out who might have wanted to hurt both of them, so we need you to be as candid as possible. Any parallels we can draw between the two of them will be helpful. Your husband mentioned

Skyler Marx. Do you know much about him or know if he and Angela had any kind of connection?"

She stood, her expression suddenly becoming blank and unreadable. "I don't really know him. I can't...I can't do this." She hurried out, leaving us alone in the room.

Baxter turned to me and murmured, "That got awkward fast."

I nodded, wondering what had gone on inside Rebecca's head. "I guess that means we're done here."

We called our goodbyes to the Caldwells, who didn't bother to see us to the door.

Once we were back on the road, Baxter said, "They're hiding something. Mrs. Caldwell especially."

"Or we freaked her out and she simply couldn't handle the stress. It's not every day that a detective barges into your house and all but accuses you of having a reason to off someone."

He shrugged. "She shouldn't be freaked out if she has nothing to hide. Don't forget—they have no alibi for either murder."

"I'm sure if it were me that I'd be in a similar situation. I spend most evenings at home with my family. If you hadn't been at my house Friday night, I'd be in the same boat as they are. They shouldn't be punished for being homebodies. They're a nice couple who like to spend time at home with their kid."

"Or they're a killer couple, trying to cover up their secret life."

I frowned at him. "Did you hear how ridiculous that sounded?"

A smile pulled at the corner of his mouth. "It might be out there, but stranger things have happened."

"Oh, come on. If you're going to kill someone—two someones, in this case, both murders at least marginally premeditated—why would you not have your alibi in place? Or at least why not make something up to send us on a wild goose chase to buy yourself time to go on the lam? Lack of alibi can show you're not trying to hide anything."

"Lack of alibi can show lack of planning. Maybe they're new to the murder biz."

I stared at him for a moment, trying to wrap my mind around the Caldwells being stone cold killers.

He snickered. "I can practically hear the gears turning in your head. You're not seeing it, huh?"

"Not at all."

"I don't know that I'm seeing it either, but something is going on with them."

19

We tried Eve's apartment, but she wasn't home. Baxter put Vic on the task of running her down while we went to visit Mateo. At his home, a new construction in one of the more expensive subdivisions in Carmel, a woman in her mid-twenties answered the door. She was gorgeous, wearing a stunner of a short blue dress and black stilettos that made my feet hurt just looking at them. As Baxter introduced us and told her we'd like to speak Mateo, she grew pale under her expertly applied makeup and shrank from the doorframe.

"Mateo isn't here right now," she said, her voice wavering.

Baxter replied, "And you are?"

She cleared her throat. "His wife."

My eyebrows shot up before I could catch myself.

Baxter asked, "What's your name, ma'am?"

"Jennifer Padilla."

"Mrs. Padilla, could you tell us where we might find your husband? We'd like to speak to him tonight."

She flicked her eyes away from us. "I don't know where he is."

Baxter gave her his card. "Please have him call us at his earliest convenience. Oh, since I have you here, could you tell me where Mr. Padilla was last night between six-thirty and seven?"

"Here," she blurted out. "He was here. With me."

"Thank you. You have a nice evening."

As we were walking away, Baxter was already shooting Vic a text to have him track down Mateo as well.

"What do you make of that?" he asked me as we got into his vehicle.

"She was kind of squirrely, but the part I couldn't get past was the fact that Mateo has a wife. I wasn't trying to profile him or anything, but he struck me as being gay on first impression. Clearly I made a bad assumption, but I don't recall him wearing a wedding band or breathing a word about a wife."

"Maybe you should call Manetti and get the lowdown on these people. It might be helpful."

I muttered, "I'd prefer not to talk to him right now, if it's all the same to you."

Baxter didn't offer a response.

I went on, "Plus, what about keeping an open mind? That's why we're doing these interviews instead of him."

"Fine. We'll do the interviews, and then we'll get the lowdown."

Vic had found out that Eve was teaching a pound class, whatever that was, at a boutique fitness center in Carmel tonight. We walked into one of the exercise classrooms to find a couple dozen spandex-clad women dancing and beating bright green sticks together.

Eve didn't look too thrilled to be interrupted while teaching, but we didn't have the time to wait forty-five minutes for her class to end. However, once I introduced Baxter and told her what we were here for, she became the same perky person she'd been when I'd met her.

She leveled a sweet smile at Baxter. "It's nice to meet you, Detective." Then she turned to me and gushed, "And it's great to see you again, Ellie. I'd love it if you'd stop by one of my classes sometime to work out with me. It would be so beneficial for you." She eyed my torso. "While running is great cardio, it obviously isn't doing a ton for your core. We should get you into one of our Hot Pilates classes."

I forced a smile. "Thanks for the offer. We need to speak to you about where you were last night between six-thirty and seven."

"I was here. We offered a special pound class for singles last night from six to seven. Sort of an anti-Valentine's Day." Giggling, she said, "I guess you wouldn't have had any need of that. You're lucky to have snagged Vic."

"Yes. So very lucky."

Baxter said to her, "I know you've gone over this with Detective Sterling, but do you mind if we chat about where you went Friday night after your run club party ended?"

"Sure. I came here." Giggling again, she rolled her eyes. "I'm *always* here. I only meant to stop by to pick up my paycheck, but I couldn't help joining in on my friend Britney's plyo class. I left here around nine-thirty."

"And who can we speak to in order to verify that?"

"Britney's around here somewhere. She teaches the next class in this room. You can also speak to the owner of the gym, Gus. He was here both nights."

Baxter smiled. "Thank you, Ms. Shelton. One more question. Do you know Angela Meadows?"

Her perma-smile turned a little fake. "Not well."

"Can you tell us anything about her?"

"She's Shawna's snooty friend. I try to keep my distance when those two are together." Finally letting go of her smile, she added, "They get kind of judgmental."

I feigned shock. "*They're* judgmental? Toward *you*? How awful for you to have to endure that."

Baxter shot me a look.

Eve didn't catch my sarcasm. She sighed. "It is. Someone else's body image is something you don't mess with. It's not kind or helpful."

I nodded. "It is certainly not, Eve."

Baxter cut in. "Do you know of anyone who'd have a reason to want to harm either Shawna or Angela?"

"No. I mean, they aren't exactly all sweetness and light, and plenty of people are jealous of all their racing wins. But that's not a reason to want to hurt someone." Her face fell. "Wait. Did something happen to Angela, too?"

"She was found dead this morning."

Eve's shoulders slumped, her eyes filling with tears. "And here I am speaking badly about her. I'm sorry. I take it all back."

Baxter smiled at her kindly. "Don't beat yourself up. We need your candor. If you think of anything that might help us catch the person or persons who killed both women, please give us a call anytime." He handed her his card.

She smiled again, at the same time managing to turn her full lips into a pout. "I'll be sure to do that, Detective Baxter. I hope you don't think I'm a bad person."

I had to turn my head so she didn't see my disgust.

Baxter, of course, played it up, even placing his hand on her arm. "Of course I don't think that. We appreciate your help, Ms. Shelton."

"Please call me Eve."

"Good night, Eve."

Once we were out of earshot, I said in a mimicking whine, "Oh, Detective Baxter. I hope you don't think I'm a bad person."

"She was nice." Before I could dispute that, he added with a boyish grin, "Did you not think it was hilarious when she said 'pound class for singles'?"

I walked ahead of him so he wouldn't see the grin pulling at the corner of my mouth. "Grow up, Baxter."

Before we left the building, we spoke to Britney, who confirmed Eve's alibi for Shawna's murder, and found the owner, Gus, who verified that Eve was here at the gym on both nights in question.

As we climbed into his SUV, Baxter said, "Considering our two strike-outs with home visits and the fact that Rebecca said Tracy is a big-time gym rat, why don't we try looking for her at her gym first?"

"You know where she works out?"

He nodded. "Sterling found her there the first time. Plus, we may be able to kill two birds with one stone. James Lorenz, the person who was supposed to meet Shawna Meehan at the park Friday night, works there."

I frowned. "Should that coincidence be a red flag?"

He shook his head. "I don't think so. In fact, it's also Skyler Marx's gym of choice."

"Skyler Marx is in this mix? That's a little much."

"Not if you consider that Marx introduced Shawna to both James Lorenz and Tracy Greer, and Tracy invited her to be a part of the run club."

"Oh."

We pulled up to the gym, Rip Barbell Club, which was housed in a nondescript cinderblock building in an older section of Noblesville.

I stared at the place. "Okay, I don't get it. What's the draw?"

Baxter said, "According to Manetti, anyone in the area who's serious about training is a member here. The place is cheap and hardcore, and they're known for not getting in your business, even if you're lifting more than you should or you're juicing or whatever."

"If that's the case, are you saying my girl Eve isn't serious about training?"

"Eve looks like she focuses more on her glamour muscles."

I cocked my head to the side. "Really? Does that mean you were you checking her out, Detective?"

He shrugged. "Maybe."

A flicker of jealousy burned the inside of my chest. I couldn't say anything that wouldn't come out passive aggressive, so I kept my mouth shut as we hopped out of his SUV and headed for the door.

20

Baxter said, "After hearing about Tracy Greer's alleged 'girl crush' on Shawna, I want to delve into her alibi for that murder. She told Sterling she arrived here at the gym at eight-twenty and stayed until ten. But I want to hear it from the horse's mouth."

I let out a snort of laughter. "Oddly enough, she does look a bit like a horse."

He frowned. "That's not very nice."

"See for yourself. She's over there at the chin-up bar."

He peered through the window. His eyebrows shot up. "Oh. You weren't exaggerating."

"Not even a little."

He smiled and held the door open for me. After he badged our way past the young woman at the front desk, we wound through the gym equipment to get to Tracy, who dropped down from the bar as she saw us approach.

"I know you," she said, sizing me up like she had the moment I'd walked into Vic's house the other night.

"I'm Ellie Matthews. We met at your run club party Friday."

She turned up her nose. "Right. Vic's girlfriend."

"I'm not his girlfriend," I said, blurting out my automatic response.

Her eyes narrowed. "Then is he fair game?"

I had to stifle a grin. "Uh...yes. Have at him. He likes it when women ask him out."

After my two disagreements today with Vic, I didn't feel bad about purposely sending Tracy his way. He had mentioned to me that Tracy would on occasion try to make an advance on him. He'd never been interested in her, so he'd shut her down every time. Things would get uncomfortable between the two of them for a while, but she always seemed to bounce back. Now that I thought about it, me being Vic's plus one might have been the reason Tracy was so cold toward me that night.

Baxter introduced himself and showed her his badge. After they shook hands, he said, "Is there somewhere we could talk that would be more private?"

She shrugged. "I'm fine here. I have nothing to hide."

Baxter said, "Okay, then. Can you tell me where you were last night between six-thirty and seven?"

She picked up a heavy-looking black ball and turned to me. "Hey princess, why don't we toss the old medicine ball around while we talk?"

"Hard pass," I replied.

"I know Vic's *supposedly* working on cardio with you, but you could really use some muscle definition."

What was with these bitches and their fitness shaming?

I stared her down. "You throw that thing anywhere in my general direction, and my partner will arrest you. Now answer the damn question."

She sneered at me and set down the ball. "Fine. I was at work. A couple of nights a week, I work at Ashley Sporting Goods on Eighty-Second. For the discount. My boss, Wayne, was there with me."

Baxter took down the information. "What about Friday night after the run club party?"

Her expression turned stony. "You mean when Shawna died? You think I killed Shawna? She was my friend."

"We're re-interviewing everyone who knew where Shawna was going that night."

"Why? Skyler did it. You guys had him. How did you manage to screw it up?"

Baxter and I both stared at her.

I asked, "Why do you think Skyler Marx killed Shawna?"

"Because he's a drunk asshole."

Baxter said, "Can you be more specific? Did you ever see him abuse her?"

"No, but when she'd come around with black eyes and bruised ribs, it wasn't too hard to guess what was going on."

"How often did that happen?"

"Every couple of months, at least."

"When was the last time you noticed her being injured like that?"

She thought for a moment. "Two weeks ago."

Baxter and I shared a worried glance.

He said, "Did she ever talk to you about it?"

"No. Even when I'd bring it up, she insisted everything was fine and that their relationship was solid."

I asked, "Any chance it was someone else beating her up?"

She looked at me like I was stupid. "Why would it be anyone besides him?"

"No one can corner the market on abuse."

Baxter said, "Let's get back to the question. Friday night. Where were you?"

Tracy leveled a smug smile at me. "I was the last to leave Vic's place. After everyone was gone, we had an intimate discussion on the proper technique for goblet squats. He's got perfect form."

His tone dry, Baxter said, "I'm sure he does. We're only interested in knowing what you did *after* you left his house."

"I came straight here. Feel free to check it out with the staff. I swiped my ID card at the door, and I even paid my monthly dues that night. Talk to James. He took my credit card payment. I left you all kinds of paper trails."

I said, "Technically, those are electronic trails."

"Shut up, nerd," she snapped.

I held up my hands. "Whoa, hey. Let's not get all 'roid ragey, here."

Baxter cut in. "Tell us about Angela Meadows."

"She's an idiot."

He let out a sigh. Even his patience was wearing thin with this one. "Tell us something about Angela Meadows that might pertain to Shawna Meehan."

"They'd been friends since high school, but they weren't super close. Shawna wasn't super close with anyone, though. She was all about training. Amazing work ethic."

As much as I wasn't a huge fan of Shawna's, the more I heard about her personal life, the more I felt sorry for her. She pushed everyone away, and for what? So she could win races that didn't matter? She had the best team of investigators in the county working on her case, but because she had no close friends, no one could seem to come up with any information about her that might point to who would want to kill her. Aside from her degenerate boyfriend, of course.

I asked, "Who knows both Shawna and Angela and might have had something against them? Maybe someone jealous of their physical abilities or...even a guy who might have dated both of them at some point."

"Everyone is jealous of their physical abilities. They're the runners to beat in this area."

"Do you think there's anyone out there who would want to win a local race so badly that they'd actually kill their competition?"

She again looked at me like I was stupid. "If you don't win because of your own strength and hard work, it's not a win."

"So that's a no, then."

"Yeah," she replied, heavy on the sarcasm.

Baxter said, "I think we have what we need. Do you know if James Lorenz is working here today?"

"He is." She scanned the room for a moment, then pointed at a muscular man coming out of a nearby hallway carrying a stack of towels. "Right there."

We approached James Lorenz. His pockmarked, boyish face and unruly hair didn't match his imposing and expertly sculpted physique.

Baxter said, "Mr. Lorenz, we've spoken before. I'm Detective Nick Baxter and this is Ellie Matthews with the Hamilton County Sheriff's Department. We'd like to speak to you about Tracy Greer."

James set the towels down on a nearby bench. Lowering his voice, he said, "She's right over there. Is this private?"

"No. She said we should speak to you regarding her whereabouts on Friday evening."

"Oh. What do you need to know from me?"

"We'd like confirmation she entered the gym when she said she did and also verification that she paid her monthly gym dues that night."

He nodded. "Follow me." We followed him to the front desk, where he got onto a computer and opened up an application. After a few clicks, he tilted the screen for us to see. "This is our key card swipe log. Looks like she got here at eight twenty-two and left at ten oh-five."

I asked, "Why do you have people swipe on the way out?"

"It's not a requirement; it's more of a service that we provide to our members. We send them weekly, monthly, and yearly reports logging their workout time."

Baxter said, "And her membership payment?"

James opened up a different application. In a few moments, he pointed to the screen. "There we go. She paid her dues by credit card on Friday, February the eleventh at eight thirty-five P.M. I—I took her payment." He looked like he was going to cry.

I said in as kind a voice as possible, "Thank you for the information, James. I know you've already spoken to the detectives about where you were that night, but could you walk us through it one more time?"

His massive shoulders slumped. "I was stuck here. My shift should have ended at seven-thirty. My coworker who was supposed to relieve me was here and ready to go, getting in a workout before his shift started. I had my keys in hand, on my way out the door, and he suddenly started throwing up everywhere. He could barely stand, so I sent him home and told him I'd cover for him. I texted Shawna and told her I wouldn't be able to meet her." He drew in a shaky breath.

The guy had to be harboring some serious guilt about not meeting Shawna out at the park that night. His mere presence could have scared the killer into changing his plans. However, if someone really wanted Shawna dead, they would have tried again at some point. If that had been the case, at least this poor guy wouldn't have had to blame himself forever. The universe seemed to love to sucker punch people sometimes.

I said, "James, no one is responsible for Shawna's death besides her killer. I know it's easy to beat yourself up over it, but it'll make you crazy if you don't make peace with it. I hope you can do that."

He gave me a faint smile. "Thank you for saying that, but I can't imagine ever being at peace with what happened."

"It takes a lot of time. Maybe us bringing who did this to her to justice will help a little."

He stared out the window, not seeming to be focusing on anything.

Baxter said, "If you don't mind, we'd like to ask you one other thing. Do you know Angela Meadows?"

James turned his attention back to us. "By reputation only. She's a top runner around here."

I said, "So we've heard. Do you have any idea why someone would want to hurt both her and Shawna?"

"I don't know much about Angela." He shook his head. "Wait. Did something happen to her, too?"

"She was killed last night."

James wiped a shaking hand down his face.

Baxter said, "Thanks for your time, Mr. Lorenz."

As we left James there, still on the verge of tears, Baxter said to me, "You know, you were a little rude to Tracy Greer. Manetti won't be pleased."

I scoffed, "Who cares? She's awful."

"She's also got tiny feet and two rock-solid alibis."

"*If* we verify last night's with her boss. And for my money, anyone could wear size thirteens with enough pairs of socks. You can go bigger, but you can't go smaller. Those big boots could have even been worn over someone's regular shoes, like galoshes."

He smiled. "I suppose...but you know that's not likely, right?"

Shrugging, I replied, "This killer is crafty, leaving certain things for us to find and taking other things. I wouldn't put anything past him. Or her."

He got out his phone. "We'll get to Tracy's alibi first thing tomorrow. Manetti just sent us Mateo Padilla's location." Frowning, he added, "He's at a wine bar in Fishers. Are you okay with going there? If not, I'll go alone."

I could do this. I'd been to restaurants with bars lately. I'd watched people at nearby tables drink alcohol of all kinds. As long as it wasn't within reach, I was good.

I hoped.

"I told you I'm in this."

21

Baxter and I weren't dressed well enough to go to this place. The men all sported tailored suits and the ladies were cinched into designer dresses. But the snooty maître d' managed to look past our fashion failure when Baxter shoved his badge in his face.

I murmured to Baxter, "That thing's like an automatic membership card to anywhere on the planet."

He grinned. "And a more valuable piece of bling than any in the room."

That was accurate, even considering the exorbitant amount of money the bars' patrons must have dropped on their jewelry. These ladies were absolutely dripping with diamonds. Any one of the men's watches was easily worth more than my car.

I spotted Mateo across the room, striding our way. He met us before we could get too far and steered us toward three stools at the end of the tall mahogany bar. Luckily, this was a classy establishment that didn't decorate the back bar with their alcohol inventory. Instead of partially used bottles staring me in the face, there was weird art.

While Baxter reintroduced himself to Mateo, I studied him. He was sweating, and the temperature in here was anything but warm. He was hiding something, and after scanning the room, I had a decent idea what it was.

I smiled. "Hi, Mateo. Here alone?"

"Entertaining a client," he replied, his tone clipped.

I pointed to a handsome man sitting alone in a booth on the far side of the room. He was toying with the olive pick from his martini glass and watching us with wide, frightened eyes. "Is that him?"

Mateo gave a quick glance over his shoulder. "Yeah, that's him. Now what's this about?"

Baxter said, "We're re-interviewing everyone who knew where Shawna was going after she left your run club party Friday night. Can you tell me again what you did after you left Vic Manetti's home?"

"I went straight home and stayed there the rest of the night. The police verified it through my security system."

"And what about last night between six-thirty and seven?"

Mateo kept his eyes trained on us, unblinking. "I took my wife on a mini vacation for Valentine's Day. We stayed the night downtown at the Conrad."

Baxter caught my eye. "Sounds like a nice evening. Not to mention another easy alibi for us to run down. Thanks."

"Alibi?" Mateo choked out.

Ignoring his question, Baxter went on, "How well do you know Angela Meadows?"

Mateo shook his head. "I don't know her."

I said, "Are you sure? I feel like you should."

"I don't think so." His voice cracked as he was speaking. He cleared his throat and loosened his tie.

"She's a friend of Shawna's. Another overachieving runner."

He shrugged. "Oh, that girl. I guess I know who she is. That's all. What does she have to do with any of this? And why do I need an alibi for last night?"

"Angela was killed last night."

His eyes bulged out. "It wasn't me."

I smiled. "I'm sure it wasn't. And as soon as we verify your alibis, you should be home free. We have to follow procedure for everyone. I'm sure you understand."

He nodded, pulling at his tie again.

Baxter said, "I think we have everything we need. You have a nice evening, Mr. Padilla."

Mateo practically ran from us.

Baxter chuckled as we headed for the door. "I'm not seeing that guy as a cold-blooded killer."

"And not that it matters for my galoshes theory, but he doesn't have particularly large feet."

"And that. So the question is, what did he do that made him feel the need to start squirming just now?"

I said, "I think it has something to do with his 'client.' Did you spot him across the room?"

"I did."

"Anything strike you about him?"

He raised one eyebrow. "What, that he's Padilla's *date* instead of his client?"

"Exactly. A business client being entertained at a place like this would have been more angry than frightened when his meal ticket for the evening started being questioned by the cops. That guy cared about what was happening to Mateo."

"Bingo. Now we get to do the surveillance work you wanted."

I brightened. "Ooh, yay. Does that mean we get snacks?"

He chuckled. "Yes, we can have snacks."

"Leave that to me. I'll be right back."

I jogged down the sidewalk to The Well, one of my favorite coffee-houses in the area. After buying us some coffees and giant muffins, I met Baxter at his vehicle.

He took a sip of his drink. "Thanks. You know how to do surveillance right."

"I know. And I'm sure I'm lots more fun than Sterling, too. How do you stand being cooped up in a car with him?"

Grinning, he said, "Some days it's all I can do not to punch him in the face."

"If it ever comes to that, you call me immediately."

"So you can talk me down?"

I snorted. "Hell no. So I can watch."

Baxter leaned his head back and laughed. I hadn't heard this kind of laughter out of him since our first case together. If things could stay like this between us, I'd be perfectly happy. But of course this was me we were talking about.

My phone rang. It was Vic. I bit off a chunk of my blueberry muffin, debating whether or not I actually wanted to pick up.

Nothing got past Baxter, who'd sneaked a look over my shoulder. Gone was the joking mood. "I realize you two have got some stuff going on right now, but we do need to speak to him about the case."

I put the call on speaker and answered. "Hey. You're on speaker with Baxter and me."

Vic waited a beat before saying, "Oh. Okay. I wanted to know if you'd found Mateo."

"Yeah, we did."

"Good."

Silence hung in the air between us. Surely he hadn't called to ask a dumb question.

Baxter said, "We want to talk to you about the people in your run club. Maybe get some insider information now that we've spoken to all of them."

Vic said, "What do you want to know?"

I detected an edge to his voice. It was getting a little tiring how he felt the need to protect these people. Granted, they were his friends, but they were also potential suspects in two homicide investigations. He had to pull his act together or he was going to compromise this investigation for all of us.

Baxter started firing questions at him. "How did your run club form? Who started it? How did everyone come to be members? Were any of them connected in the past?"

Vic paused for so long I glanced at the phone to find out if the call had dropped. They he said quietly, "My ex-wife started the club."

My jaw nearly hit the floor.

Baxter put one hand on my shoulder and used the other one to cover up the speaker on my phone. He murmured, "Did he not tell you he had a wife?"

I shook my head. Baxter gave my shoulder a squeeze, then removed his hand and let go of my phone.

Vic began, "Ellie..."

Keeping a tight lid on my temper, I said, "Just tell your story. You and I will deal with the other thing later."

Vic sighed. "It started ten years ago. None of the original members are still in the club except me. Rebecca and Jonathan joined first out of this group. They were invited by someone who dropped out a couple of years ago. Rebecca had been a student in one of Eve's spin classes, so she invited Eve. Jonathan used to work with Chris, so there's that connection. I invited Tracy. A club member who ended up moving away invited Mateo. Tracy invited Shawna about a year ago, but it ended up that Chris also knew her from before."

Baxter looked at me and frowned. "From before? What's their history?"

Vic replied, "Nothing too exciting. They had the same trainer."

"What about Shawna's history with Tracy?"

"They met through Skyler Marx."

I said, "We know. He seems to have a connection to a surprising number of persons of interest in this case. What's up with that?"

"It's true, he does. These people were his friends before they were Shawna's friends." Vic paused for a moment, and his tone softened. "You have to know something about Shawna. She didn't make friends easily, and she didn't keep friends, either. Before she met Marx, she essentially had no one, except Angela, I suppose. The only good thing Marx ever did for her was to introduce her to a few of his friends, who wound up becoming her support system after he beat her up."

"Speaking of that, Tracy told us about Shawna having black eyes and broken ribs fairly recently. Know anything about that?"

He let out a grumble under his breath. "I wouldn't have been able to tell about broken ribs, but she hadn't had a black eye lately that I knew about. At least I hope she hadn't."

"Maybe she's a good makeup artist."

"I think she'd have come to me if Marx had started abusing her again."

I thought for a moment. "But would she, though? She dumped you for him, so she might not want to admit to you of all people that she made a bad decision. Tracy said she called her out over it, but Shawna still wouldn't 'fess up. If she wouldn't tell a friend who specifically asked, she probably wouldn't tell a former boyfriend who didn't. Plus, you'd have slapped another restraining order on her guy, or worse, paid him a not-so-friendly visit—either of which would have only resulted in getting her beat some more. If she valued her safety, she most likely hid it from you with all she was worth."

After another long pause, he admitted, "You're right."

"I know I am. I watched my mother get caught in the same cycle time and time again."

Since we'd been talking to Vic, I'd fallen down on our surveillance job. Luckily, Baxter hadn't. He tapped my arm and jerked his head toward the wine bar. Mateo and his "client" exited the place and headed into the parking lot.

Baxter said to Vic, "What's the story with Mateo? He has a wife, but..."

Mateo suddenly placed his hand on the back of his "client's" head and drew him in for a lusty kiss.

"What?" Vic prompted when Baxter didn't finish his thought.

Baxter shook his head. "Never mind. Answered my own question." After covering up the mic again, he murmured to me, "You called it."

I nodded, wondering if this new development would have any bearing on our investigation. Regardless, we had to treat this situation with sensitivity. Investigation or not, it wasn't our business to out Mateo. However, either he or his wife had lied to us about his alibi for last night, and that had to be resolved.

My head struggling to keep everything we'd learned straight, I turned to Baxter. "That should be enough information for now, right?"

He smiled. "Yeah, for now. Thanks, Manetti."

"Sure. Ell—"

I hit the end call button.

Mateo and his date had parted ways and were now pulling out of the parking lot. Baxter put his SUV into gear and began following Mateo's car.

He glanced over at me. "I think you might have hung up on your boy while he was trying to say something to you."

I folded my arms. "I was done talking."

"You two need to either make up or break up. Or at the very least put a moratorium on picking fights with each other until this case is over."

I frowned. "Or maybe he should bow out of the investigation like he should have in the first place."

"You and I both know that's not going to happen. It's up to you to be the bigger person here."

I didn't want to talk about this, especially with Baxter, so I said, "Have you noticed that men seem to like Shawna a lot more than women do? Tracy and Mateo being the exceptions."

He gave me a disappointed frown but went with the new conversation. "Yes, I have. From what we've heard, she seemed to target women more often than men in her constant competitiveness. Same with Angela Meadows."

"And yet we believe two of the men involved have lied to us about their alibis."

"It'll be interesting to see how it all shakes out once we've verified where everyone was during the two murders."

We continued following Mateo, who drove straight to his home.

Baxter rolled past the house and kept driving. "Well, that was anticlimactic. It's getting late, and you promised you'd go to a meeting. Where can I drop you?"

I thought for a moment. "Um...there's a decent one here in Carmel at eleven. I can Uber home."

"Works for me."

Decent was an overstatement. The first fifteen minutes was nothing more than a gripefest. If I heard one more stick insect of a woman complain about gaining weight from "idle hands" during her recovery period, I was going to scream. Was I fighting the same exact issue? Yes. But I had bigger hindrances to my continued sobriety than stressing over an extra pound or two of fat.

My phone buzzed in my pocket. We weren't supposed to use our phones during meetings, but between being involved in two active homicide investigations and dealing with family issues, I wasn't about to let a call or text go unanswered, rules or not. I gave the group leader an apologetic smile and excused myself.

It was a text from Vic asking to see me tonight. He offered to pick me up after my meeting. I frowned, realizing Baxter, the only person who knew I was here, had intervened. I considered blowing him off, but I remembered what Baxter had said about making up or breaking up. The investigation came first.

Unsure of what I was going to say to Vic when I saw him later, I trudged back to my chair. Finally, someone besides the vapid rich bitches had taken the floor. This guy was quite their opposite, not terribly clean and wearing unpurposely tattered jeans. Despite his messy appearance, he was more emotionally put together than the rest of us combined. He told his story, of his fall from grace to clawing his way back to sobriety. He'd lost his job, his home, his family, and his friends. And bit by bit, he'd worked tirelessly to restore what he'd ruined. However, he didn't take any credit for getting his life back together. He said his relationships had been mended because of the unconditional love he received from the wonderful people in his life. That without his people, he'd be dead, or at least want to be. The one thing he wanted everyone to learn from his story was that none of us are above needing—or offering—forgiveness.

If that wasn't a sign, I didn't know what was.

After the meeting ended, I found Vic outside waiting for me, leaning against his car as if he didn't have the strength hold himself upright. The man looked spent.

I walked over and stood facing him. "Hey."

He couldn't seem to look me in the eye. "Ellie, I don't even know where to start."

"Then I will. How long were you married?"

"Seven years."

I nodded slowly. "That's a long time, Vic."

"It is. I should have said something. I should have told you about Shawna, too."

"You think?" I shook my head. "I've kicked men to the curb for far less than this." When his face clouded over even farther, I reached for his hand.

"But...I'm trying not to be that girl so much anymore. Especially with those pesky twelve steps I'm supposed to adhere to now."

He met my eyes. "So this isn't it?"

I shrugged. "I like being with you. That is, when you're not being a shit."

Gripping my hand tight, he said, "I'm sorry. For everything."

"I'm sorry, too. I should have been more understanding. I know this thing is eating you alive."

He nodded. "I don't know how to turn off my feelings this time. I've never had this deep a personal investment in a case before. Except for our last case."

"It sucks, doesn't it?" I studied him for a moment. "What was your personal investment in our last case?"

"I didn't want to have to face you if we failed to get your sister back."

"Why, because you were afraid I would have scratched your eyes out?"

A ghost of a smile pulled at one side of his mouth. "No, because I was attracted to you from the start and wanted to have a chance at taking you out on a date. I figured you'd never speak to me again if I didn't deliver."

I grinned at him. "You're not wrong about that."

"I honestly don't understand how you kept it together."

I shook my head. "I didn't. I drank, I wrecked my Christmas tree, and I repeatedly verbally abused my boss, who evidently was having inappropriate thoughts about me."

"You managed to clear your head when it mattered. I'm not there yet."

I reached up and cradled his cheek in my hand. "I bet you're closer than you think. The fact that you care so deeply can be a good thing. Maybe all you need to do is shift your focus. Rather than fixating on revenge, make it your goal to honor Shawna's memory by getting her the justice she deserves."

His expression turned hopeful. "That might actually work. When did you get so insightful?"

"It's the meeting. I'm sure I'll be back to my normal cynical self in an hour or so. Before that happens, let's discuss why you never bothered to tell me you were married."

Shrugging, he said, "I tend not to talk about my ex unless I have to. It's embarrassing. She left me. She said I was all about the job."

"It took her seven years to figure that out? It took me seven minutes. And there's nothing wrong with being all about the job. You *are* the job. So am I. So are all the people on our team. That's what makes us good at what we do."

"It also makes us terrible at relationships."

I let out a mirthless laugh. "Well, no one can be good at everything. Even after I quit the job and became a mild-mannered college professor, my love life didn't improve. I think we're doomed."

"That's a real downer."

Now that I'd forced him to talk about his past, I figured I'd be a hypocrite if I didn't do the same. Plenty of people knew about my hookup with Sterling, and I'd rather Vic not find out from someone else before I admitted it to him.

"It is, and I've got even worse news. In the spirit of full disclosure...I should probably tell you I had sex with Sterling in a men's restroom once. And pretty much everyone knows about it."

He winced. "Maybe let's table the full disclosure for right now. My head may explode if I think about that one for too long."

Full disclosure or not, I wasn't ever planning to mention the fact that Baxter and I had shared a kiss a few months ago. It hadn't gone any further physically, plus no one knew it had happened besides Baxter and me, and he'd never say anything. There were about a million other facets to my relationship with Baxter that not even I understood. Telling Vic about any of them would only serve to make him skeptical of our partnership and quite likely jealous of the time we spent together, if he wasn't already. Nothing could happen between Baxter and me. Ever. Our partnership was too important.

"Yeah, I'd say that's more than enough truth for one evening."

22

I slept well, likely out of sheer exhaustion. Rachel, on the other hand, didn't seem to have gotten a good night's sleep. The dark circles under her eyes and short temper were telltale signs she'd had inadequate rest. I hoped she wasn't still upset over the misunderstanding with Baxter.

I took over getting Nate ready for daycare when she started snapping at him to quit dawdling and get dressed.

He said to me as I was combing his hair, "You missed dinner last night, Auntie Ellie. Mommy made spaghetti."

I gave him a hug. "I'm sorry, kiddo. Detective Nick and I have to catch a bad guy. I probably won't be home much for the next few days."

He pouted. "I won't see Detective Nick, either?"

"Nope. Sorry, buddy."

"Do you think Mommy will be happy soon?"

My heart seized. I honestly didn't know the answer to that. "I'm sure she will be." Eventually.

I spent the first couple of hours of my workday in the lab office alone, typing up my notes from processing yesterday's scene. Baxter was attending

Angela Meadows' autopsy. Amanda and Beck had been called out to process a scene in Westfield, the robbery of a convenience store early this morning. While still technically a member of our task force, Amanda was close to finishing her work on the two cases, so she would be returning to her normal duties and normal hours. If more evidence came in, she'd of course drop everything to work on it. If I hadn't agreed to help Baxter with the investigation side, I would have been able to get back to my normal life sooner as well. But if I were honest, I enjoyed the work so much I wasn't in any hurry to give it up.

Baxter knocked on the open door to the lab office. "Good morning."

I sat back in my chair. "Hey. Did you have fun at the autopsy?"

He chuckled. "Don't I always? Big news—Dr. Berg found saliva on the victim."

I wiggled my eyebrows. "So the killer did in fact get kinky with a corpse."

"It would seem so."

"Gross. Where?"

"Only on and around her lips and on her cheeks and neck."

" 'Only'? You believe the location of *where you put your mouth on a corpse* makes a difference in how big a freak you are?"

He shrugged. "In the grand scheme of deviant behavior, yes."

I shuddered. "Agree to disagree."

"Maybe the killer was trying to resuscitate her."

"After stabbing her seven times? Doubt it. And that doesn't account for the cheek and neck saliva. I bet he licked her. He's a corpse licker."

He grimaced. "Could you please not say that?"

"What, corpse licker?"

"Yes. And besides, he could have kissed and/or licked her before he killed her."

Shaking my head, I said, "I doubt that, too. Based on the footprints, he was hiding behind a tree so he could do a sneak attack. No time for foreplay."

He seemed to ponder that for a moment. "True. As much as I hate to encourage your disgusting theory, it's much more likely that the saliva transfer occurred post-mortem."

"So why make out with dead Angela but not dead Shawna?"

"That's the million-dollar question."

"Well, one good thing about working with the Feds is that they can get DNA results back fast. If Manetti can work his same magic again, we'll know who our killer is in three days."

"*If* he's in CODIS. That may be a big if on this one, considering none of our current suspects have priors."

"That's a good point...can a person go from zero to corpse-licking-serial-killer in one step?"

He shook his head. "Maybe. I don't know."

I grinned. "You know, the Feds haven't given this killer a stupid nickname yet. I think we'd be remiss if we didn't suggest 'The Corpse Licker.'"

Rolling his eyes, he said, "You should absolutely bring that up during the meeting." He glanced at his watch. "Which should be starting in a few minutes."

Vic appeared in the doorway, haggard but smiling. His smile had been the only thing I'd liked about him when I'd first met him. I hadn't seen a real smile out of him for days. "Hey."

"Hey, yourself," I replied, giving him a mock stern look. "I hope those dark circles under your eyes don't mean you stayed up working on the case, Agent."

"Left over from a rotten week, I promise."

As he backed out of the office, Baxter said, "I'll see you in there."

Vic came toward me and took my hand, only to pull me up from my chair and into a tight embrace. "I slept better last night than I have all week. What you said got through. I'm going to work on focusing my energy in a positive direction."

Since we were alone, I gave him a lingering kiss. "Good."

"That doesn't mean I'm going to be any less than my normal badass self, though."

I grinned. "You better not. You make such a sexy G-man."

The task force assembled in the conference room for our meeting, nearly everyone looking worse for wear. Jayne and the chief had been up all night, and if I had to guess, Sterling wasn't abiding by the mandatory eight-hour sleep break. He had dark circles under his eyes and a lot of information compiled in several thick folders stacked in front of him.

Agent Griffin said, "Good morning everyone. We have a new development in the case. Another crime scene photo, this time of Angela Meadows, was posted on the Internet early this morning on a different runner's forum." He pulled a photo out of a folder in front of him and sent it around the table. "Same general idea as before. This caption reads, 'Dying for Love in Woodland Gardens. Who could be next?' "

Baxter slid the photo to me. This shot wasn't artsy like the one of Shawna Meehan, which had been taken at such an angle as to hide the bloody mess that had been made. But then again, there had been so much blood at Angela Meadows' scene, there was no way to angle any shot that could have hidden the carnage. I managed not to shudder at the image and passed it off to Jayne.

Sterling said, "Do we think he'll wait three days again between kills?"

Griffin shook his head. "I don't know. We can't assume anything at this point, but we do need to keep working as hard as we can, as fast as we can. Getting away with two murders may embolden our killer. While that could be dangerous, it could also lead to him becoming cocky and making a mistake. I've got a team at the Bureau working on determining the origin of this new post."

Sterling muttered, "Better not be another dead end."

I shot Baxter a questioning glance and mouthed, "Dead end?"

As Agent Griffin went on about how awesome his guys were at tracking cyber footprints, Baxter texted me, *The photo of Shawna Meehan was posted from a computer at the Kirklin Public Library. Old library, no cameras anywhere. Old librarian, doesn't remember anyone suspicious coming or going that evening. Total dead end.*

I nodded. Another smart move by the killer. Kirklin, Indiana was a tiny community in Clinton County, just northwest of Hamilton County. The killer had done his homework, again, finding a place where he'd be completely invisible and anonymous while he carried out his sick plans.

Griffin went on, "Let me bring you up to speed on the autopsy Dr. Berg preformed this morning. His preliminary findings have not changed. However, he managed to determine that the knife used to kill Angela Meadows had a six-inch blade, which, as those of you who were at the death scene know, did a lot of damage. He also found that the killer used an overwhelming amount of force with each swing of the knife. There is extensive bruising around each wound and even an imprint of the hand guard of the knife on the victim's skin. The killer intended to inflict some pain and was strong enough to do it. Also, Dr. Berg found a significant amount of saliva on the victim's mouth, cheeks, and neck, which he believed came from her attacker. I'm having the Bureau put a rush on the DNA analysis."

Baxter caught my eye, his mouth pulling up in one corner as he nodded in Agent Griffin's direction. I had to clench my jaw to keep from snickering at him trying to goad me into sharing my gross nickname for the killer with the rest of the group. The only person who might actually find it funny would be Sterling, so I kept it to myself.

Jayne and Chief Esparza discussed how they'd run financials and background checks on Rebecca, Jonathan, and Chris, since none of them had solid alibis for either murder and the men met the shoe size criteria. The three were squeaky clean, except Chris had had some credit issues a few years ago. That was too far in the past to warrant worry in the present, so we were still in the same holding pattern with the three of them—they could be guilty, or not.

Agent Griffin said, "Detective Sterling, your report?"

Sterling cleared his throat. A lot of times, he droned on and on at these meetings, giving us the full blow-by-blow of investigative events rather than the highlights. I hoped Griffin would spur him along. We were burning daylight.

Sterling said, "Angela Meadows's family lives elsewhere, and they all had alibis for the night she was killed. Her friends have been harder to run down, since she had more of a life than Shawna Meehan. She often went out for drinks with her coworkers. I'm in the process of looking into all of them. Her boss said there were a couple of family members of her home health patients who'd threatened her within the last month when she entered their homes to do her job. I'll be following up on those leads as well. I'm also planning to cross-reference patients at the physical rehab facility where Shawna Meehan worked as a nutritionist. It's possible that Shawna might have crossed paths with some of Angela's home health clients. It's a long shot, but another possible connection. Also, according to her coworkers, Angela had been dating a guy named Joel Goldman for a couple of years, but broke it off four months ago. He's also on my list to run down today."

Griffin nodded. "You've certainly dug into your research, Detective. Agent Manetti, your report?"

A slight furrow to his brow, Vic said, "I've been working with Detective Sterling on the information he presented, although he neglected to mention it."

Sterling said nothing. I thought I detected a bit of a frown on Griffin's face.

Vic went on, "I spoke to Shawna Meehan's trainer this morning and found out that he'd been home alone during her murder. He didn't seem to know she was going out to the park that night alone. In fact, he said he would have advised against it because of the remote location, simply for the possibility of injury with no one around for miles to help. He has a solid alibi for Angela Meadows' murder and said that he'd never met Angela. He does have a tie to one of our persons of interest, Chris Bruner, who was another of his clients. He refuses to work with Chris anymore because of a disagreement over a payment a few years ago, which corresponds time-wise with Sheriff Walsh's note that Chris had had credit issues a while back."

Griffin scribbled on the legal pad in front of him. "Not really a red flag for Chris Bruner, but I'll make a note of it. Detective Baxter and Ms. Matthews?"

Baxter spoke for both of us. He gave a report of our interviews with Shawna's friends and outlined our plan to verify their alibis and dig further into who both women might have come in contact with lately.

Griffin stared us down, unimpressed. "That's it? A couple of months ago you two solved a thirteen-year-old homicide *and* located a serial killer who didn't intend to be found in well under seventy-two hours. It's been four and a half days since Shawna Meehan was killed, and you've got barely a handful of unlikely suspects with no priors and essentially no motives. What's the matter? Not enough urgency to this case for you?"

As Baxter and I sat there horrified that he'd throw Rachel's kidnapping in our faces, everyone at the table leveled glares at Griffin and began to open their mouths to protest on our behalf.

Vic managed to speak first, his tone a terse warning to his fellow agent. "*Steve.*"

Griffin's nostrils flared, but he backed off, sort of. He addressed the table. "I want a suspect in custody today."

Maybe he wasn't going to be easier to work for than Vic.

He went on, "And to help you with this, Agent Manetti and I have put together a profile on our killer. He's male and around the victims' ages, likely in his early thirties. He knew both women and may have had a romantic relationship with one or both of them, possibly even a sexual relationship with Angela Meadows. Based on his shoe size, he's over six feet tall. Due to the significant force exhibited on the wounds of both victims—the extensive bruising around Angela Meadows' stab wounds and the extent of Shawna Meehan's neck injury from the garrote—he's strong. He's also likely fast and agile, as he was able to subdue and overpower both victims, who were known for their speed. He was close enough to these women to have knowledge or access to their schedules, or at least patient enough to observe them and learn their movements. We believe he most likely endured some sort of childhood trauma pertaining to a female figure in his life, probably his mother. He's either religious and judgmental or misogynistic, leaving his victims stripped to teach them a lesson or make a show of what he believed to be their sins or transgressions. He's intelligent, having chosen to leave behind certain pieces of evidence but taking others. He's arrogant and attention-seeking, bragging about his kills by posting photos of them online. And most importantly, he's violent. When you go to question or take into custody someone you believe to be a viable suspect, please do so with extreme caution and some form of backup. Any questions?"

No one said anything. Agent Griffin ran this task force much differently than Vic had with our last one. Sure, Vic had bossed us around like Griffin, but that was where the similarities stopped. On the last case, we'd all collaborated during these meetings and bounced our ideas off each other, a lot of times figuring out the answers to the problems that had been stumping us individually. With Griffin, there was none of that. These meetings were more informational than helpful—an email would have sufficed and saved all kinds of time. As far as I could tell, his presence wasn't doing much of anything to aid our investigation.

Griffin stood. "Get back to work, then."

23

Baxter and I spent the rest of our morning compiling the alibis various deputies had verified for us on our possible suspects. We made a quick trip to the sporting goods store where Tracy worked nights to finish tracking down the last alibi we needed.

Back at the station in the conference room/task force command center, Baxter handed me two files to put in our "no longer a suspect" pile. "Eve checks out and Tracy checks out. Both of them were exactly where they said they were for both TODs."

We'd not had any news on the Caldwells, which meant they were both stuck in our "still a possible suspect" pile. I stared at their files, hating the thought of them still being on the radar. "Did you subpoena the Caldwells' phone records?"

He leaned back in his chair. "Yes, but I don't like either of them for murder. Their financials are perfect, and neither of them have had so much as a speeding ticket. If we don't find anything in their phone records, I'm ready to put them with the non-suspects and move on."

"Same." I sighed. "Is it just me, or is this the biggest bunch of boring ass people you've ever seen? No hot messes, no shady weirdos, no crazy-eyed freaks, no comic relief. Everyone's too normal, aside from most of them being way too obsessed with physical fitness. Worst of all, neither victim was interesting enough to kill in the first place."

Baxter laughed. "That's why it's taking so much longer than last time and getting Agent Steve's panties in a twist. We've yet to come across anyone who seems to have the backbone or the desire to wipe another person off the planet. Skyler Marx is about as close to a hot mess as we've got, but he didn't kill Angela. I don't know how we're going to manage to catch a viable suspect by the end of the day to appease the boss."

"What's Griffin going to do if we don't? Remove us from the investigation? That's already happened to both of us in one fashion or another. It won't hurt my feelings."

"Oh, come on. You know you want to be there when we crack this case."

"Fine. Maybe a little." I huffed, opening Mateo's file to peruse the information we'd gotten back on his Valentine's Day stay at the Conrad Hotel. "Looks like Mateo was definitely at the Conrad during Angela's murder. It says here that he checked in at six-thirty, so there was no way he could have been in Carmel killing Angela at six forty-five. The front desk staffer said he checked in alone. Indisputable alibi, but that makes the fact that his wife lied to us about where he was make even less sense."

"I say we go back to their house and ask her."

"Maybe we should ask him first. The last thing I'd want to do is unintentionally out him to his wife."

"Good point." He opened Chris's file. "Speaking of liars, Chris Bruner was not at a Weight Watchers meeting Monday night. He'd been there the prior three Mondays, but not this past one. I've subpoenaed his phone records. After we talk to Padilla, we'll pay him a visit and try to force a real alibi out of him."

At Vic's party, my first impression of both of these men had been positive. But now they'd both lied—or had someone lie for them—to me and to an officer of the law. What could be so important to keep quiet that they'd risk being cast as a murder suspect? And were they so dumb that they thought we wouldn't figure it out?

Jayne knocked on the door and stood lounging against the doorframe. "Does the 'dream team' have a hot lead on a suspect for tonight's arbitrary deadline?" she asked, an amused twinkle in her eye.

I let out a sigh. "At this pace, it's not looking too promising."

"You two keep doing what you're doing. Don't let Griffin get in your head, and especially don't let him goad you into shouldering the burden of this investigation alone." Smiling, she added, "Besides, he's not giving the rest of us on the task force enough credit. I've got deputies working on obtaining and scrubbing through any security footage to be had in the area surrounding Central Park. No luck yet on finding anyone lurking about, but the day is young. And phone records for the Caldwells and Chris Bruner are ready whenever you are."

Baxter replied, "Thanks, Sheriff."

I smiled. Jayne always knew what to say to bolster our spirits when cases got tough. With the Feds stepping in way too often lately, I missed having her overseeing our investigations.

Her expression turned stern. "Have you two taken your mandatory lunch break yet?"

I shook my head.

"If you haven't left this room by two, I will have you escorted out."

"Yes, ma'am."

We did as we were told, deciding to treat ourselves to lunch in downtown Indianapolis since we had to make the trip anyway to speak to Mateo Padilla at work. While Baxter drove, I began the tedious task of studying Rebecca and Jonathan Caldwell's phone records. Most of their cell calls were to each other. Using my phone, a quick Internet search netted me the owners of several recurring numbers: their daughter's daycare, Rebecca's hair and nail salons, their financial advisor, two pizza places, and an amazing Ethiopian restaurant near their home that Vic had taken me to last week. There were plenty of out of area calls, several of which were from known scam numbers. I assumed the more frequent out of area numbers belonged to family members, but I'd need to verify that when I was back at the station with access to the department's cell number databases. There were also a handful of local numbers I'd have to check as well.

After stopping for a late lunch, we headed to Mateo's office building, which was located on Monument Circle in the heart of downtown. When Baxter and I introduced ourselves to Mateo's assistant and asked if we could speak with him, I thought the poor woman's eyes were going to pop out of her head. She scurried into his office, and we only had to wait a moment before he appeared at the door and invited us inside.

Mateo smiled, but it didn't reach his eyes, which were guarded. "Hello again." Closing the door behind us, he said, "Is there something else I can help you with?"

Baxter said, "We checked with the Conrad. Your alibi is good for Monday night."

Mateo reached to loosen his tie like he had last night when he'd gotten nervous. "Good."

"But I'm sure by this point you've spoken to your wife..."

Mateo nodded. "She, um... I'm sorry about the conflicting stories. She said she accidentally mixed cold medicine with alcohol and got confused."

Frowning, I replied, "She was battling a cold *and* a fairly serious drug interaction last night? I'm going to have to call bullshit on that. She was dressed for a night out—gorgeous dress; killer heels. Plus she was completely coherent. Try again."

His eyes grew wide, but he gave us a quick answer. "She's easily confused on a good day. Not the brightest bulb, I'm afraid."

Baxter shook his head. "Come on, man. She covered for you to the cops. Don't throw her under the bus."

"I'm not—"

I cut in, "Mateo, we know you're stepping out on your wife. It's not our place to get in the middle of that, which is why we came to you instead of her to find out why she lied to us. Did she not know where you were Monday night, or did she not want *us* to know where you were?"

Mateo's jaw dropped. He couldn't seem to get any words out.

I went on, "You understand that we can't simply look the other way when we get conflicting accounts of an alibi for a person of interest in a homicide investigation, right? Even though your alibi checks out, we can't neglect getting to the bottom of why your wife tried to cover for you."

"You've got this all wrong. I'm not cheating on Jennifer," Mateo choked out.

Baxter said, "We saw you kiss the guy you were with last night."

Mateo seemed to crumple in front of us. He dropped into the nearest chair and put his head in his hands. "Is this going in your report?"

I replied, "Not if you start answering our questions. And no judgment here, but don't you think you owe it to yourself and to your wife to tell her the truth about who you are?"

He mumbled, "She knows I'm gay."

Baxter prompted him, "So she covered for you because...?"

"Because..." He heaved out a long sigh. "She doesn't want the authorities to find out I'm gay."

I could see the wheels turning in Baxter's head. He had this figured out, and I was pretty sure I did, too.

He asked, "And why is that?"

Mateo looked up at us, a pleading expression on his face. "If I tell you everything, can I trust you not to put it in my file or in any of your reports? And especially not share it with any Federal agencies?" He gave me a wary glace. "Or with any Federal agents?"

Baxter said, "Your green card marriage is the least of our worries. The INS won't hear about it from us."

Mateo breathed a sigh of relief. "Thank you. Jennifer knew I was at the Conrad with my boyfriend Thomas on Monday night. When you questioned her, she thought it would be best if she didn't bring up the hotel at all, in case Thomas and I hadn't been discreet around the staff. She tried to get in touch with me to let me know what she'd told you, but I had my phone turned off all evening. That's the real reason we didn't have our stories straight. I'm sorry we couldn't have been truthful with you from the beginning."

I smiled. "It's okay. But can you try to do something about your green card situation? Something legal?"

"I am. I'm going through the process of becoming an American citizen. I only need to stay married a few more months, and then the charade can be over. I hate it that I have to lie and Jennifer has to lie for me so I can live in this country. It's my home—I grew up here; I just wasn't born here. When I graduated from college and was told I would have to go back to Colombia, I panicked. Jennifer is my best friend, and she offered to marry me so I could stay."

Baxter turned to me. "I'm satisfied. You good?"

"I'm good." To Mateo, I said, "Let me know when you pass your citizenship test. We'll go out and celebrate."

He smiled, this time happily. "Absolutely."

24

Thanks to a wreck that snarled traffic on our drive back to Noblesville, Baxter and I had just enough time to make it to Chris's office before five o'clock.

Chris, too, didn't seem terribly happy to have us bother him yet again. Forcing a smile, he said, "Hello. Back so soon?"

Baxter replied, "I'm afraid we're going to need to talk about your alibi for Monday night. You weren't at a Weight Watchers meeting. We checked."

Chris sucked in a breath. "Did I say Weight Watchers? I meant...the gym. I went to my gym."

Baxter regarded him for a moment. "You sure about that?"

Clearing his throat, Chris said, "Yes."

"We need the address for your gym, then."

Chris obediently pulled out his phone, and again, his hands were shaking. Another lie. What was he hiding?

Baxter took a photo of Chris's screen showing the name and address of his gym. "We'll verify that. Anything else you want to tell us?"

Chris shook his head. "No." He managed to keep his face neutral, but the fact that his voice went up an octave gave him away.

"Thanks for your time again," I said.

Chris nearly ran for the stairwell this time.

Baxter rolled his eyes. "This is getting old. What do you say we follow him this time?"

"Ooh, another surveillance mission. Do we get snacks again?"

"You just ate lunch a couple of hours ago."

I scoffed, "So?"

"We'll grab something on the way back to the station."

While we waited in Baxter's SUV for Chris to finish up work and leave for the day, Baxter called Chris's gym. After a short conversation with the person on the other end of the line, he reported, "Not only was Chris not at the gym Monday night, the manager said he just got a frantic phone call from Chris begging him to cover for him if the cops called."

My jaw dropped. "Honestly, I'm ready to cross Chris off our list for being too stupid to pull off two murders."

"I'm right there with you."

We sat there for a good thirty minutes, wondering if Chris had figured out we'd stuck around to follow him and was trying to wait us out. Out of sheer boredom, we made small talk and ran through every topic of conversation under the sun, until Baxter threw me a curve out of the blue.

He asked, "Is it true you and Rachel are both named after characters from the TV shows your mom was watching while she was in labor?"

I rolled my eyes. "Yes. I'm named after Ellie Ewing on *Dallas*, and Rachel is for Rachel Green from *Friends*. My mother didn't have a lot of imagination, nor did she ever make any kind of future plans. In fact, she didn't have a single thing ready for a baby when she brought Rachel home from the hospital. No diapers, no crib, no clothes. Nothing. She gave me a whopping twenty dollars and told me to run to the store and buy whatever it was that babies needed. I was nine years old. What did I know?" I slapped my hand over my mouth. "Sorry. You asked a simple question, and I dumped my Mommy issues on you."

"It's okay," he said with a sincere smile. "Rachel told me that story, too. About how you got punished for spending the money on a stuffed animal for her."

I sighed. "It was worth it. Especially considering it was the only new toy the poor girl ever had until David came into the picture a few years later."

"It was worth it to her, too. She says she still has it."

I nodded. I knew that. The white bunny I'd bought her, which was now gray and threadbare, sat on the dresser in her bedroom.

He placed his hand on my arm, but then must have thought better of it. Quickly removing his hand, he said, "I didn't mean to upset you."

It was then that I realized I had tears in my eyes. Wiping them away with the back of my hand, I said, "It's fine. I just—I really thought getting Rachel away from our mother would solve all of her problems. I thought I'd saved her." I shook my head. "I shouldn't have been so quick to pat myself on the back. What happened to her as a result of being around me is way worse than anything our mother could have done to her."

This time he reached over and grabbed me by both shoulders, turned me to face him, and didn't let go. "Don't you ever say that, Ellie. What happened to Rachel was not your fault. I know you've blamed yourself this whole time, but it has to stop."

I frowned. "I'll stop blaming myself when you do."

His jaw clenched. "I don't—"

"Yes, you do. You are gutted over the fact that this was your case and you didn't find her sooner."

His grip tightened. "Shouldn't I be? It was my job to find her, and every minute I let go by was another minute she had to endure hell. And then, when I try to make up for it by being there for her during her recovery, I somehow manage to make her think I'm interested in a romantic relationship with her. That's the real crime." He let go of me and leaned back, his expression darkening. "You didn't hesitate to make that clear."

Before thinking, I fired back, "And I also apologized for being a raging jealous bitch about it. But for the record, my original objection was valid. When a grown-ass man in his thirties tries to mentor an impressionable twenty-one-year old college student, romance of any kind should never factor into the equation."

"I agree, which is why I wasn't trying to romance her. You do know that, right?"

"I do now."

He seemed to be in the mood to argue, which wasn't like him. "And why the high horse about the ten-year age difference? Manetti's got ten years on you."

"Ten years isn't a big deal when both people are full-fledged adults."

He abandoned his argument and studied me for a moment. "Wait. Did you say 'jealous'?"

"No." I had. I'd slipped, but hoped he hadn't noticed. He noticed everything.

"You did."

I cleared my throat. "Well, I misspoke."

He didn't say anything more, but I wasn't sure I'd convinced him. I could only hope he wouldn't bring it up again.

After descending into an awkward silence, we thankfully didn't have to wait much longer for Chris to exit the building and take off at a run for his vehicle. After squealing out of the parking lot, Chris barreled up Highway 37, weaving in and out of traffic as he went. Baxter had to haul ass to keep up with him. Chris finally slowed down to make the turn into to the Kentucky Fried Chicken off 141st and rolled to a stop in front of the drive thru menu.

After pulling into a space in the parking lot across the access road so we could observe Chris unnoticed, Baxter blew out a breath. "Wow. From the way he drove over here, I thought he was on a mission to do something much more dastardly than grab a chicken dinner. I could have ticketed the shit out of him for all the traffic violations he committed."

I thought for a moment, then my heart sank. "Uh oh... I'm pretty sure he's here to eat his feelings. I bet you he buys a vat of mashed potatoes and inhales them before he leaves the parking lot."

"That's oddly specific."

"He told me at Vic's party all about his lifelong struggle with his weight. One of his binge foods was always mashed potatoes. If he's here, he's stressed."

"Well, two of his friends were murdered this week. That's pretty stressful."

"Yes, but it doesn't account for the fact that he lied to us about his alibi. Twice."

We watched Chris drive up to the window and pay for his food. I got Baxter's binoculars out of his glove box and watched the cashier hand Chris a giant Styrofoam bucket and a plastic spork. My hunch was right. Chris pulled into a parking space under a floodlight and removed the lid from the container. Steam plumed up. Licking his lips, he stared at the food, his expression wavering back and forth between excitement and despair.

I frowned and handed the binoculars to Baxter. "I don't think I can watch this."

Baxter snickered. "What? Watch a grown man go to town on a pint of mashed potatoes?"

"No, watch him fall off the wagon."

"It's mashed potatoes, not heroin."

"Look at his face."

Baxter peered through the binoculars. "I'll give you the fact that he does seem to be having a particularly euphoric moment going on."

Feeling Chris's pain from all the way over here, I said, "Mashed potatoes might as well be heroin to him. I have to do something."

"He'll know we're watching him. You'll give up our cover."

"It's either that or my integrity."

He smiled. "Do what you have to do."

I hopped out of the SUV and headed across the street, picking my way across the slush piles. Chris was so involved with his mashed potatoes that he didn't notice me until I rapped on his window.

He let out a yelp and fumbled his container enough that a splotch of gravy shot out onto his shirt. When he saw it was me, he tensed even more. He rolled down his window, breathing hard. "What are...what are you doing here?" he asked, trying hide his contraband in the passenger seat.

I cast a meaningful glance at the container. "I was in the neighborhood and thought you could use some support, one addict to another."

"What? Oh, that?" He gestured toward the seat next to him. "It's not what you think. I...I'm bringing some dinner to a neighbor who's fallen ill."

"Chris, I saw you eating the mashed potatoes."

"You saw wrong."

I gave him the disappointed look I normally reserved for Nate when he misbehaved. "You've lied to me three times in two days. What's up?"

He started to flush. First his neck turned red, and then it crept up his cheeks. Sweat popped out on his upper lip and brow. Wiping a hand down his face, he said, "Lied? Three times?"

"Yes."

His eyes darting around, he demanded, "Wait. Are you following me?"

I turned and waved to get Baxter's attention and beckoned him to join us. As he came our way, I said to Chris, "As a matter of fact, I am."

"You can't do that."

"Sure I can." When Baxter appeared at my side, I said, "We checked out your second attempt at an alibi for Monday night. You weren't at the gym, and the manager told us you asked him to cover for you."

His voice cracking, Chris cried, "What? Uh... You must have spoken to the wrong person. I was at the gym. Really. I have no life." Giggling like a crazy person, he added, "Where else would I have been?"

Baxter shrugged. "I don't know. Maybe at Central Park...killing Angela Meadows."

Chris's jaw dropped, and he started gasping for air. "No! No. I didn't... I never... *No.*"

"I'm done with the lies, Mr. Bruner. If you don't tell us the truth about where you were that night, I'm taking you in for formal questioning."

Chris hung his head and began to weep. "I was here."

Baxter and I shot each other a glance.

I said, "Here, like here in the parking lot or inside?"

He jerked his thumb toward the restaurant, unable to speak.

I reached through the window and placed my hand on his shoulder. "Chris, I understand that you're ashamed of the truth, but surely it's preferable to being a suspect in a homicide of one of your friends."

"Barely," he choked out.

"We'll give you a moment to pull yourself together, and then we all need to go inside and speak to the staff. If one of them can verify that you were here that night, we'll leave you alone."

As I was stepping back from the vehicle, Chris reached out and caught my hand. His face registered panic. "Please don't tell Vic."

"I would never gossip to him about this, if that's what you're getting at. But he's on the task force with us, so he's privy to the information. I can't do anything about that."

"I don't want this getting back to anyone in the club."

"I can promise you that Vic won't share any of this with them. Your alibi is confidential."

He breathed a sigh of relief.

I said, "Not for nothing, but they're kind of a judgmental bunch. Why not find a new club?"

Wiping his eyes, he said, "They might be judgmental, but they hold me accountable. I need that."

Baxter and I walked Chris into the restaurant and asked to speak to the manager. After figuring out which of her employees was working the register Monday night, she introduced us to a pimply-faced teenager.

His eyes lit up when he saw Chris. "You're the dude who sat in the corner and slammed four family-sized potatoes and gravy on Valentine's Day. That was epic. You deserve a T-shirt or your picture on the wall or something."

Chris started tearing up again, so I steered him outside to his vehicle while Baxter finished interviewing the kid. Once I had Chris settled into his seat, I saw Baxter exit the restaurant and give me a thumbs up.

I said to Chris, "Good news. You're off the hook."

He blew out a long breath and lowered his head to rest on the steering wheel.

"If you don't mind me asking, why the bingeing? Were you close to Shawna and Angela?"

Raising back up, he said, "Yes, I was fairly close with both of them. But... there's more." He sighed. "I had also asked Eve if she'd like to go out with me on Valentine's Day. She turned me down. It was a tough blow. I've liked her for quite a while and had finally gotten the courage to ask her out."

"If I recall correctly, she was working that night. Maybe that was the reason she said no."

He shook his head. "She made it clear that she wasn't interested in me romantically."

"Oh. That sucks. I'm sorry." I reached into my jacket pocket and retrieved a pen and a business card with my official Hamilton County criminalist information on it. I wrote my cell number on the back. "I hope you won't need this, but if you feel like gorging yourself again instead of dealing with your problems, call me. We'll talk."

"I'll do that."

I gestured toward the container of mashed potatoes still sitting in his passenger seat. "Want me to get rid of that for you?"

He handed it to me and let out a rueful laugh. "Please."

"I'll see you around."

"Thank you, Ellie."

I hurried back to Baxter's vehicle and got inside. Waving the bucket in his face, I asked, "Want some?"

"Hard pass." He smiled. "You did a good thing."

"I know."

Chuckling, he said, "The worker said Bruner was already at the restaurant when he went on shift at six P.M. and didn't leave until right before he took his break at eight."

"Good. I didn't want it to be him."

25

Baxter and I picked up some tacos on the way back to the station. We only had thirty minutes until we had to endure yet another meeting with Griffin, who I was sure would be less than impressed that we now had even fewer possible suspects than we started with this morning. As Baxter and I sat in the breakroom eating, I spotted Vic through the window, walking this way with a plastic container in hand. If I had to guess, I'd bet he was here early to bring me some Paleo-friendly food. If I wanted to keep the food I'd planned on eating and avoid another lecture, I had to think fast. I swept my arm across the table, pushing my stuff in with Baxter's.

Baxter gave me a strange look. "What the hell are you—"

I cut him off. "Shh. Be cool."

As Vic walked through the door, I grabbed my cup of coffee and lounged back in my chair as if I were only in here having a conversation with Baxter while he ate his dinner.

Vic smiled. "Hey."

"Hey. What's up?" I said.

Mouth full of taco, Baxter only gave Vic a head nod.

Vic laid the container on the table in front of me. "I brought you a salad. Thought you might be hungry."

I smiled. "I am. Thank you."

Although loaded with vegetables and grilled chicken, this salad was not going to sustain me physically or emotionally until my shift ended at midnight. I started eating it, trying not to stare longingly at my tacos, which I knew were getting soggier every moment they sat there not being eaten.

Vic eyed the mess of food in front of Baxter. "You know, Detective, you might be young now, but all that garbage you're eating is going to catch up with you one day. Right, Ellie?"

I took a big bite of salad so I didn't have to answer.

Baxter nodded. "I see your point. But Ellie and I have nearly a decade before we're as old as you and have to start worrying about stuff like that."

If Vic had taken offense to Baxter's jab at our ten-year age difference, he didn't let on. "She's getting a handle on it early. It wouldn't hurt you to do the same."

Vic was barking up the wrong tree. Baxter was a fit guy. Although he didn't make a big deal out of it, he exercised regularly, and he only ate fast food when he was busy and stressed working a big case. It was kind of our thing that we ate terrible food together to blow off steam while we were stuck working long hours.

I could see Baxter fighting a grin. "Yeah, she's really got a handle on eating healthy, all right." Baxter finished the last bite of his dinner and wiped his mouth. "I see the error of my ways. In fact, I think I'll get rid of the rest of this and go find some fruit or something."

Fighting to keep the horror I felt from showing on my face, I watched helplessly as Baxter scooped up his empty wrappers and the rest of my dinner and made a big show of tossing it all in the trash can.

He caught my eye as he headed out the door. "You enjoy that salad."

I had to clench my jaw to keep from calling him a bad name.

Vic stood. "I need to go, too. I'll see you at the meeting."

Mustering a smile, I said, "Thanks for bringing me dinner."

"No problem." He walked to the door but then stopped short and turned. "By the way, did you tell Tracy we'd broken up?"

Busted. "Oh...um...not in so many words, but I might have given her the impression you were available."

He gave me a disappointed frown. "I assume that's why she called me up this afternoon and asked me out on a date."

"Yeah...that would be why." Now that he and I had kissed and made up, my little joke didn't seem so funny. I sighed. "I'm sorry. I was mad at you, and Tracy was giving me nothing but attitude during my interview with her. I made a poor choice."

"Yes, you did. She was angry with me when I told her I wouldn't go out with her."

"I bet she's even more angry with me. Now if we need more information from her, it'll be harder to get. That's on me."

"It is. But when I talked to her, I made sure to leave you out of it. It was time I let her know, regardless of my current or future relationship status, that I'm not interested in being more than friends with her. I needed to make it clear, especially considering she's tied up in this case. She hung up on me."

Wincing, I said, "Ouch. You didn't need any more drama this week. I'm really sorry."

"It's okay. I'll see you in there." He gave me a half-smile, but I could tell he was still unhappy with me.

After that uncomfortable exchange, I needed those tacos more than ever. Once Vic was out of sight, I ran to the trash can, hoping I might be lucky enough to pluck out a wrapped-up taco that hadn't been contaminated by the rest of the garbage.

"What are you doing, Matthews?"

Elbow-deep in the trash can, I jumped, turning to find Sterling smirking at me as he entered the breakroom. I sure as hell wasn't going to tell him the truth. He'd never let me live it down. "I dropped my pen in here."

He made a face. "Then get a new one. Don't dig through the trash like a hobo."

Scowling, I went to the sink to wash my hands. I couldn't stomach any more of the salad, so I stuck it in the refrigerator and got out of there as quickly as I could.

I found Baxter at his desk. "I can't believe you trashed my dinner. Not cool."

He spun around in his chair and leaned back in it, grinning. "But you ended up with such a better dinner. You didn't need that 'garbage food.' I did you a favor."

I growled at him in response.

He chuckled. "Why don't you just tell him you need a break from the restrictive diet? At least until the case is over."

Vic had been great about helping me get my health back. Yes, he went a little overboard on the diet for my taste, but that was Vic. He didn't half-ass anything.

"We're in a decent place right now. I don't want to rock the boat."

"If you're in a decent place, he should be willing to cut you some slack."

"It's complicated."

"It's complicated because you're making it complicated. I know you, Ellie. You need an outlet for the stress and fatigue. I'd much rather see you stress eat than—" He stopped himself.

"You can say it."

His expression and tone softened. "I mean, I hate to watch you cover up something about yourself to please someone else."

I nodded. It felt all kinds of wrong getting relationship advice from him, but he made a good point.

He added quietly, "You know you never have to be someone you're not when you're with me."

My throat got tight. "I know," I murmured.

Before things got too awkward, he changed the subject. "It's going to be a long night. I'll get you some more tacos later to replace the others."

"Now you're talking."

The meeting went as badly as I'd imagined. Griffin already seemed pissed when we all walked into the conference room. His frown deepened when he had to admit that his FBI Cyber team hadn't netted any usable information about the photo of Angela that had been posted this morning. It had been uploaded through the free Wi-Fi at a local coffeehouse, so the shared IP address couldn't point to one user. No luck on getting the staff to pinpoint who might have done the posting, either. According to the baristas, the upload occurred during their morning rush, when the place was always overrun with laptop users. The coffeehouse had surveillance cameras, but they were live feed only and weren't set up to record. Mainly for remote use by the owner, the cameras were there to make sure his workers weren't slacking and the lines weren't getting too long. Another dead end on the killer's virtual boasting.

The rest of the task force had no breakthroughs to share. Sterling and Vic had managed to vet all of Angela's coworkers, ex-boyfriends, and any threats she'd gotten from clients' family members. All they had left to run down were a few of her close friends. Jayne and the chief had taken their sleep break between the two meetings, so they didn't have much to report. While they were away, though, they had put a couple of deputies on the task of comparing patients at both Angela's and Shawna's places of work. They'd found no duplication of names, so that lead was toast. The security footage from the area surrounding Central Park also gave us no help. The available footage was trained on only one of the entrances, which was unused by any vehicles in the four hours prior to and after the murder. As cold as it was, the meager amount of people entering or leaving the park on foot from that entrance were bundled up so much that their faces didn't show. As Baxter gave our report, the mood of the room got bleaker and bleaker. The leads were drying up, and we were no closer to figuring out who was responsible than we had ever been.

Griffin's expression went dark. He slammed the file he was holding down onto the table. "What are we doing here, huh? Do I need to bring in a team of agents to clean up this mess and solve these cases?"

Chief Esparza, who was normally a laid-back guy, had finally had enough. Through gritted teeth, he said, "We have not one, but two fancy Federal agents working alongside us, and I don't see that either of you are adding anything to the investigation. If anything, Agent Griffin, your bad attitude and time-wasting meetings are what's hindering this team from getting out there and doing what needs to be done."

I flicked my eyes in Vic's direction. He had a cap on his temper, but barely. Yesterday, he would have had something to say about the chief's outburst. I was proud of him for being able to keep his cool.

Griffin, not so much. "Fine. If that's the way you all feel, then this time-wasting meeting is over." He stormed out of the room like a baby.

Calm as ever, Jayne took over. "Okay, so we have some of Angela Meadows' friends left to speak to. And the only persons of interest left for Shawna Meehan's case are the Caldwells?"

We all murmured in agreement.

"And there's nothing else we're missing?"

I'd been batting around a thought in the back of my head for a while now, and although I knew it wouldn't be a popular idea, it was probably time I shared it.

I said, "No one is going to like this, but I'm going to say it anyway. We need Skyler Marx's help."

As I'd expected, my idea was met with groans and disagreement from practically everyone at the table.

Sterling's objection was of course the most colorful. "That's a load of horseshit, Matthews. That assclown wouldn't help us if his miserable life depended on it. And I'd eat a dick before I'd take his help."

Jayne frowned at him. "Detective, that's quite enough."

I said, "I get that it won't be easy, but we need to speak to someone who actually knew Shawna Meehan."

When Vic opened his mouth to interject, I added, "Someone who knew the *real* Shawna Meehan, not the perfect Workout Barbie she wanted everyone to think she was. We need to hear about the Shawna Meehan who would go crawling back to her boyfriend after he beat her. We've run down all of her family, coworkers, and so-called friends, and not one of them can give us an accurate picture of what the woman did outside of working, exercising, and dating Marx. She wasn't tight with her family. She barely spoke to her coworkers during work hours and never spent time with them outside the office. The only interests she had were occasionally helping organize races and being a part of Manetti's run club. And according to most of them, the only reason she deigned to be a part of the club was to lord her physical prowess over everyone else. We need to know why the world's most boring woman was interesting enough to kill."

Vic frowned. "She's not the world's most boring woman. She spent a lot of time training, which didn't afford her much of a social life outside of dating Marx. And yes, she could be aloof. But once you got to know her, she was open and kind."

One by one, each person around the table turned his or her eyes toward me. This was really getting old. I'd had enough.

I snapped, "Why do you all stare at me every time he talks about her?"

Everyone immediately looked away, except Vic, who said grudgingly, "I agree that we need to speak to Marx."

Sterling grimaced, but conceded as well. "Maybe it wouldn't be the worst thing to interview him again. Anyone wanna flip for who has to deal with the prick?"

Baxter cut in. "Neither of you should speak to Skyler Marx. Ever. I'll handle it."

"You think you'll be able to get something out of him that we can't?" Sterling demanded.

Baxter gave me a sidelong glance. "I have an idea."

* * *

After the meeting wrapped up, I followed Baxter to his desk. "What exactly is this idea of yours going to entail? Because I have a bad feeling about it."

He said, "Marx's band has a gig later tonight. You're going to go and chat him up in between sets. Let him think you're a groupie."

"Me?"

"Yeah."

I nodded slowly, trying to imagine myself playing the part of a ditzy groupie. It wasn't a pretty picture. "Is the band any good?"

He laughed. "I didn't expect that to be your primary concern."

"Oh, it's not. I'd just hate to have to prostitute myself to terrible music."

His face fell. "I promise I won't let it get that far."

My eyebrows shot up. "You're going in, too? If he sees us together, he'll never talk to me."

"We'll sit at separate tables. He's no Einstein. He'll never figure it out. Besides, you don't think I'd send you anywhere alone, do you?"

I smiled. "No, I know you wouldn't."

* * *

In the lab office, after I'd eaten the replacement tacos Baxter had run out to get me, I spent some time speaking with my TA over Zoom to go over the lesson plans I wanted him to teach the next couple of days. We were going to need to wrap up this case soon. The powers that be at Ashmore College had been incredibly cooperative with the sheriff's department in letting me miss classes to consult, but there would eventually come a point when they'd feel they'd been lenient enough. I felt like that point was fast approaching. If something didn't shake out soon, I'd have to remove myself from the task force and go back to work.

I returned a couple of emails to answer students' questions on an upcoming term paper, and then my mind turned to decidedly less academic matters. I didn't know how long I'd been staring into space when a knock at the door startled me nearly out of my chair.

Baxter grinned at me from the doorway. "Thinking up yet another brilliant plan to help us crack the case?"

I wrinkled my nose. "No, I was thinking my plan about pumping Marx for information maybe isn't so brilliant, especially since I somehow got drafted to run point on it. If you must know, I'm trying to decide what I should wear."

He chuckled. "That's fair. It's part of the game."

"I need some inspiration. What kind of bar is it? Hipster? Country? Sports? Biker?"

"Dive."

"Ooh, the best kind. The mere fact that I have all my teeth automatically puts me in the top ten percent of women who'll be there."

"Is that all it takes?"

"Don't forget this is Indiana, where our love for basketball is second only to our love for meth."

He leaned against the doorframe. "Good point. At the risk of sounding sexist, I'd recommend playing to your audience instead of the venue. You'll need to wear something that will get a douchey rock-n-roller's attention. Something a little edgier than a turtleneck sweater."

Glancing down at my clothes, I feigned offense. "You pig. Are you saying that my conservative college professor attire is not going to do it for Skyler Marx?"

He shrugged. "Again, at the risk of sounding sexist...not a chance."

I drove home and ransacked my closet, managing to find an old Metallica T-shirt from my college days. It was a size too small now, but in a good way for my purposes tonight. After releasing my hair from the tight ponytail I'd put it in this morning, I put a few curls in it and fluffed it as best I could. I went heavy on the eye makeup, having to dig into the bowels of my vanity for eyeliner I rarely used. I rounded out the look with the most distressed jeans I owned and high-heeled black boots, but I didn't have the right jewelry. I went to Rachel's door and knocked.

"Come in," she called.

I walked into her room. "Can I borrow your black leather cuff? And some big earrings?"

Rachel looked up from her textbook, only to gawk at me. "What the hell are you wearing? And did you use all the eyeliner we both own?"

"It's a long story. We're trying to get some information out of a guy who's being uncooperative. He won't talk to any of the detectives or the Feds on the case, so I got drafted to...charm it out of him."

She bent over and belly laughed. Even at my expense, her laughter was a welcome sound. I went to her dresser and started pawing through her jewelry while she yukked it up. I took what I wanted and put it on, then turned to face her, waiting until she'd wiped her streaming eyes and quieted down to intermittent giggles.

"I'm glad I could give you a good laugh, there, sis."

She said in between snickers, "I'm sorry. I just can't... You don't look like you."

"Good, because I need to look like a groupie."

"You could definitely pass for a groupie. A slutty one."

"Mission accomplished." I winked at her. "Don't wait up."

She suddenly became serious. "Is this guy dangerous?"

I wouldn't lie to her, but I didn't want to worry her. "He's no Boy Scout, but I can handle myself."

"Ellie..." She began breathing heavily.

I went and sat next to her on the bed, taking her hands. "Please don't worry. Nick will be there with me. I'll be fine."

She nodded, although I noticed her eyes had again filled with tears, this time not the good kind. I hated what her ordeal had done to her. How it had made her panic over her safety as well as mine. To a lesser extent, it had done the same to me. But I had no other choice but to push my personal problems out of my head in order to do my job.

I gave her a tight hug and a few more murmured assurances before hurrying back to the station. After experiencing Rachel's rollercoaster of real, raw emotion, I suddenly felt ridiculous in these dress-up clothes. I sure as hell wasn't setting foot in the station like this. No one would ever let me live it down. I texted Baxter and told him to meet me in the parking lot.

He said nothing as he approached me, and I couldn't see his face in the dark. I hoped he of all people didn't think I looked stupid.

"I'm not sure about this, Nick. Rachel took one look at me and laughed. Do you think I'll get Marx's attention dressed like this, or will he laugh, too?"

Now that he was right in front of me, I could see his expression. It reminded me of the way he'd looked at me when he appeared at my door on Valentine's Day. "Uh…" He cleared his throat and ripped his eyes away from me. "Yeah, that'll do it. Trust me, he's not going to laugh." He got into his SUV. After silently waiting for me to do the same, he focused his full attention on backing out of his parking space and pulling onto the street.

It took a few minutes for the vibe inside the vehicle to return to normal. I was nervous enough as it was, worrying about whether or not I could pull this off.

I let out a pent-up breath. "Tell me again what exactly we need to get out of Skyler Marx."

"We want to know what connections Shawna and Angela had besides running races together. We want to know if he ever hung out with them or had any interaction with Angela but without Shawna. Also ask him if Shawna ever complained about Angela or shared any gossip about her. And if you can get him to really open up, ask him if Shawna ever talked to him about someone threatening her or if she was afraid of anyone. Besides him, of course."

"Oh, no sweat. Get some guy I just met to tell me all the personal details about his dead girlfriend and one random friend of hers. That shouldn't be hard at all."

"You're our only hope."

"Stop that. I'm nervous enough as it is."

He smiled. "I'm kidding. All I mean is that this is a long shot, and anything you can get out of him will be helpful."

"Okay." I gave him a mock frown. "But next time, you get to be the chatty ho."

"I've already been the chatty ho. Remember Linda Beasley?"

We'd run into a real cougar during the last case. She'd taken an immediate liking to Baxter, not that I blamed her. I'd gotten a good laugh out of watching him squirm away from her advances.

"This is so not the same thing. She took one look at you and got flirty and talkative, knowing full well you were a cop. You had to do nothing but sit there and look pretty. I, on the other hand, have to cupcake a total douchebag and get him to spill his guts to me without him figuring out I'm working with the cops."

He chuckled. "You think I'm pretty?"

"That's your takeaway?"

"Again, I'm kidding. I have faith in you. Besides, I'm sure it won't take long for you to have him under your spell."

I sneaked a glance at him. His eyes were on the road, but the slightest smile was tugging at his lips. Good thing it was dark in his vehicle so he couldn't see me blushing.

Baxter grew serious. "I know we've been joking around about this whole thing, but I do want to discuss the venue with you. I know you did fine at that prissy wine bar last night. But if it's going to be a problem for you to walk into a real bar, we're not doing this."

"I can walk into a real bar and be fine. I can watch people drink in front of me and be fine." I rubbed my forehead. "The only thing I'm worried about is if things actually do go well and he buys me a drink. I don't want a glass of alcohol within easy reach, and it'll look suspicious when I don't touch it."

"I thought of that. Tell him up front you can't drink because you're in court-appointed rehab after assaulting your last boyfriend. It should get you off the hook, plus it'll give you some street cred."

I drawled, "Aww, and it'll give us something in common. How sweet."

"That, too."

"I can work with that. Good idea."

He grinned. "I'm full of good ideas."

"You're certainly full of something."

26

I sat in Baxter's SUV, mentally preparing myself to do this job while he readied our communication equipment. I'd interviewed people before, and I'd even pretended to be less official than I was while doing it. This was different, though. I had to essentially pick this guy up, or close to it. While getting a date never proved to be too much of a problem for me, I didn't always land every guy I set my sights on. And having to do it in front of Baxter was going to make it all the more difficult.

"Earpiece," he said, holding a tiny flesh-colored nub in his open palm, which I took from him and placed in my ear. He studied me for a moment and then handed over a small clip-on mic and receiver pack. "I don't know where in the world you're going to hide this. Good luck."

While he turned his head the other direction, I reached up my shirt and clipped the mic inside the front of my bra, then snaked the cord though the cup and down my side. I plugged the cord into the receiver, which I stuck in my front jeans pocket. It could pass well enough for a phone with a bulky case.

"Done." I held out my arms.

He gave me a quick glance. "Can't see it."

"As long as no one gets handsy with me, I should be fine."

Baxter's face twisted into a scowl. "Anyone lays a finger on you, and I'm pulling the plug."

"Calm down, Dad. I got this. Dealing with terrible men is a specialty of mine."

"And keeping people safe is a specialty of mine. Don't test me."

I eyed him. "You're having second thoughts."

He hung his head. "This seemed like a good idea at first, but now..."

I didn't give him the chance to back out. Wrenching open the passenger door, I hopped out and ran for the entrance to the bar.

His voice filled my ear. "Ellie..."

"Game face, Detective. This is happening."

The word "dive" didn't begin to cover how gross this place was. The soles of my boots stuck to the floor as I snaked my way through the too-close tables to find an empty stool at the bar. I had to hand it to Skyler's band, Table 13. Dumb name, but they had a decent sound and had managed to pack the place. Or maybe the crowd was here for two-dollar shot night.

I ordered a can of Red Bull so the bartender wouldn't bug me, and so I didn't have to drink out of any of the glasses I assumed he hadn't bothered to wash properly. Out of the corner of my eye, I noticed Baxter walk through the door. He didn't hide the disdain on his face as he swept the room and headed for an empty table near the back.

"This place is a shit hole," he said.

I covered my mouth with my hand as discreetly as I could. "No kidding. At least the band is good."

"Good is a stretch. They're okay."

He was being contrary. The band was good, and Skyler was great. He knew his way around a guitar. If I had to guess, the other jokers in his band were holding him back. He could hold his own in a much better band. And he definitely looked the part of a rocker. He was handsome and ripped, and from the way he played to the crowd, he knew it. As far as looks went, I could see why Shawna had been interested in him.

Baxter added, "Ellie, I want to make something clear—if at any time you're uncomfortable, say the word and we'll end this."

Speaking of uncomfortable, it dawned on me that my spot at the bar maybe wasn't the best place I could have chosen to sit. Dozens of bottles of alcohol stared at me from the shelves lining the back bar, only feet away. I swiveled my bar stool so they were out of my line of sight.

"I got this, Nick. And don't get all protective and come barging in before I get what we came here for. I'll decide if I'm in over my head."

He paused. I knew he wouldn't like my terms. "Okay."

"Hey, no more conversation. People are going to think I'm a nutjob if I sit here and talk to myself."

"As you wish."

I felt bad for cutting him off. I'd much rather spend an evening making pleasant conversation with Baxter than sitting here alone, trying to pretend to be into the music on the off chance Skyler would happen to notice me. But I had to get in the zone, otherwise this plan was not going to work.

After about twenty minutes, the band finished their set and exited the stage.

"Go time," Baxter said in my ear.

I didn't reply. I was already off my barstool and making a beeline toward the stage so I could ambush Skyler before another slutty groupie could get her claws in him. I reached him as he was stepping down onto the floor.

I smiled, looking up at him through my lashes. "Hey. You guys were great up there."

"Thanks," he said, brushing past me.

I followed him. "You're Skyler, right?"

No response.

"I'm Ellie."

Over his shoulder, he gave me a bored, "Hi."

Clearly it was not going to be love at first sight. I had to speak his language. "Can I buy you a drink?"

The corner of his mouth twisted into a smirk. "Sure." Bellying up to the bar, he called to the bartender, "Four shots of tequila."

I offered to buy him *a* drink, not *four* drinks. What an ass. A horrid thought struck me, and I tensed. What if he meant there to be two shots for him and two for me? Given the fact that he was a major alcoholic, I was hoping they were all for him. Either way, it was a waste of eight perfectly good dollars. I'd better get some information out of this loser.

"How long have you been with the band?" I asked, sidling up close to him.

"Three years."

"Obviously you've been playing guitar longer than that. You're really amazing."

"Yeah, I've been playing since high school."

He wasn't giving me much to work with. Plus, there was no good segue between "your band is good" and "tell me about your dead girlfriend."

"At least you did something productive with your teen years." I let out a flirty laugh. "I spent mine shoplifting and picking locks."

I heard Baxter stifle a snicker. He'd taken great delight in hearing about all my teenage exploits, especially how I'd been arrested once by a beat cop named Jayne Walsh. She'd managed to scare the delinquency right out of me. I owed that woman my life.

Skyler simply stared at me, unimpressed.

Before I could think of anything else to say, the bartender came back and set four brimming shot glasses in front of Skyler. He picked them up and nodded to me. "Thanks for the drink, Emily."

While I paid the bartender, Skyler walked away and set the shots down in front of some skank at a nearby table. Damn, I was too late. He must have had her on the hook before I got here.

Baxter was full-on laughing now, so much he could hardly choke out, "Ouch. Harsh rejection, there, *Emily*."

"Shut up," I muttered through gritted teeth as I watched Skyler and his lady friend slam two shots each. "I'll figure something out."

"Do it fast. You're losing him."

I hissed, "And you're not helping. Get out of my head!"

Before I could come up with a new game plan, a man appeared next to me and said, "Hi, I'm Mike. I saw you from across the bar and wanted to—"

I held up a hand without even looking at him. "Not interested."

"That wasn't a pickup line. I'm trying to apologize for my friend Skyler. He can be a real asshole."

I turned to face him. The guy was around Skyler's age, and mine, thirty-ish. He was equally as built as Skyler and had a nice smile, although overall decidedly less attractive. My guess was that he was the wingman in the relationship, which should suit my purposes well. Skyler's overeager friend could know a lot of his personal business.

I gave Mike my brightest smile. "You're apologizing for your friend's bad behavior? I don't know that I've ever heard a guy do that before." I held out my hand. "I'm Ellie." I panicked when I realized I hadn't come up with a fake name, so I used my stepdad's last name. "Ellie Collins. And you're Mike...?"

As we shook hands, he said, "Hopkins. I feel like I should buy you a drink to make it up to you. What'll you have?"

I'd caught a whiff of those four shots of tequila earlier and had had a hard time pushing the aroma out of my head. "Just a Red Bull."

Baxter murmured, "Mike Hopkins...I know that name. Oh, yeah. That's the guy James Lorenz had to cover a shift for at work the night Shawna Meehan was killed. The guy who went home sick."

I struggled to keep my face passive. Another tie to that gym we visited last night? This was getting way beyond a coincidence in my mind.

Mike called to the bartender, "Two Red Bulls." Turning back to me he said, " 'Just a Red Bull,' huh? You on the wagon, too?"

At first impression, Mike seemed too nice to be interested in a woman who'd supposedly beaten up her boyfriend. I thought fast to come up with a better cover for why I was teetotalling this evening—one that wouldn't involve me bonding with my mark over alcoholism. "No, I'm...still hung over from last night."

He nodded. "I've been there. A couple of weeks ago, actually. I'm newly sober. Thirteen days."

Ouch. The first two weeks sober had been a particularly difficult time for me. Although a bar wasn't the smartest place to hang out in his delicate state, good for him for getting this far. I respected him for that, but I needed to focus on getting the information I needed so I could get out of here.

Changing the subject, I said, "I get the feeling you've had to apologize for Skyler before."

Chuckling, he said, "Only a couple hundred times."

"Have you been friends for a while?"

"Oh, yeah. Best bros since middle school."

"Wow. It's so cool that you've stuck together all this time. I bet you've been through a lot."

"I could tell you some stories."

I laid my hand on his arm. "Then tell me. I'd love to hear your stories, Mike. The crazier the better."

Mike paid for our drinks and beckoned me over to a table near the one where Skyler and his underage-looking date were making out. I grabbed a chair where I could sit with my back to them. Playing it cool with Skyler was my only option at the moment.

I listened as Mike launched into some lame tale about Skyler talking him into going cow tipping the night of their high school graduation. I pretended to listen with rapt attention while trying to come up with a way to bring him into this decade. Baxter couldn't seem to keep his snide comments to himself, which was starting to wear thin. But when Mike began talking about how he'd been the one to have to save Skyler from getting caught by the farmer they'd pissed off, I figured out how to get exactly what I wanted out of him. I also figured out that he wasn't even as bright as Skyler.

I said, "You saved the day. I bet you're the level-headed one, right? Skyler gets into trouble and you clean up the mess. Sounds to me like he couldn't get along without you."

Mike smiled, bashful all of a sudden. "Aw, yeah, you could say that."

The band had gone back to the stage and started their next set, so I scooted toward him so I could be heard. "I'm sure he's really been leaning on you this week. I'm impressed he was able to resume his normal life so soon after all he's been through."

He nodded, taking a big gulp of his Red Bull. "The guy has had a rough week, all right."

"But then again, with a friend like you on his side, maybe that's where he found the courage."

Mike's face lit up. "You're so right, Ellie. Other people don't..." He shook his head. "No one else gets our relationship. His other friends say I follow him around like a puppy, but they're wrong. I have his back. That's what friends do. Skyler would do the same for me."

I hated to break it to him, but self-centered Skyler didn't strike me as the type to help anyone, including his "best bro."

"Absolutely. Were you the one who threw him the epic 'get out of jail' party I heard so much about?"

He visibly puffed up. "I was. It was all my idea."

"Nothing like a rager to help him forget about his dead girlfriend."

He made a face. "Honestly, he wasn't too torn up about Shawna. Things weren't going so great between them. He was going to dump her before long, anyway."

I flicked my eyes toward Baxter, who had perked up. This didn't sound so good.

I prompted him, "So...they weren't getting along? Were they fighting?"

"Not really. He was..." He chuckled. "Aw, you gotta know Skyler. He got tired of her and was ready to move on."

"I get that. When it's not working, it's just not working, right? You cut your losses and move on to the next."

"That's exactly what I told him. Kick her to the curb. She was taking up way too much of his time, anyway, plus she was possessive as hell. I was as tired of her as he was."

A warning bell went off inside my head.

Baxter said, "Go with that."

I smiled at Mike. "If she was starting to get possessive, their relationship was toast already. You gave him great advice. Did she horn in while you guys were trying to bro down?"

"Only all the time. She'd call him and demand to know where he was and who he was with. She didn't like me."

I gave him a mock punch on the arm. "How could anyone not like you?"

He waved a hand. "Ah, it was a competitive thing for the most part. She was a big running junkie and thought she was pretty hot shit. She didn't like it when I'd give her a run for her money during a race."

Baxter said, "Find out if he knows Angela."

I feigned interest. "You race competitively?" Making a big show of giving Mike's body a once-over, I added, "I can tell you work out."

"You did *not* just say that," Baxter groaned.

While I was looking, I noticed Mike had rather large feet. I had all but given up on the boot print being some kind of smoking gun—nearly all of the men linked to this investigation were big guys with big feet. But it was another box to tick for the sake of the investigation, and Griffin loved it when we were thorough.

Mike fell for my line and smiled from ear to ear. "I do. Skyler and me, we train together every day. He's been my guinea pig while I've been working on my personal training certification. Plus, I'm the assistant manager at a gym, so I lift during my breaks for fun."

I reached over and squeezed Mike's bicep. He flexed, and I oohed and aahed over it. Baxter made a gagging noise in my ear. He was not making this easy for me. I was going to have to kick his ass later.

"Feels like you lift for more than just fun. What gym? I might have to stop by sometime and let you work me out."

Baxter jeered, "That's what she said."

Mike replied, "Yeah. Anytime. I have a key, so I can even get you in after hours if you want. The gym is called Rip Barbell Club."

I said, "I'll check it out. So what kind of races do you run?"

"Usually marathons and halfs. Sometimes 10ks."

"All of those are a long way."

"Nah, it's easy if you train."

That was absolutely not true, but I didn't argue. "So, have you, like, won any races around here? Are you famous?"

His expression went dark, and he shook his head. "No. Not yet, anyway. I'm faster out of the gate than Shawna ever was, but she always found a way to beat me in the end. And then she'd be a total bitch about it and rub it in my face."

"She sounds like a hot mess. Did she even have any friends?"

"Barely. No one liked her." He let out a snide laugh. "They may never catch who killed her. Too many haters."

I was beginning to think that was true. Besides Skyler, she wasn't terribly close with anyone because of her snooty attitude. She did have a lot of haters, but on the flip side, no one seemed to care enough about her to go to the trouble of murdering her. Unless we managed to stumble on someone she'd royally pissed off, all we had were a few lukewarm leads.

I put my hand on Mike's shoulder and leaned toward him. "At the risk of sounding like a terrible person...it seems to me like Shawna had it coming."

The slow smile that crept across his face sent a chill down my spine. His eyes went flat and dark. Maybe I was sitting next to our hottest lead yet.

"I know, right? Couldn't have worked out better for me. There's nothing like getting rid of your competition."

Baxter demanded, "Does he have crazy eyes right now? Nod if he does."

Mike seemed perfectly sane and in control, except the vibe he was exuding had turned from warm and friendly to cold and eerily sadistic. Granted, he could be overly aggressive from struggling to keep his alcoholism in check, but this was a little much. I kept still, because I was afraid Baxter would barge in and shut this down before I was finished. I wanted nothing more than to get the hell out of here, but at the same time, I didn't want to have to seek Mike out again for more information. He was starting to freak me out.

I gathered my courage and nudged his shoulder with mine. "You are so bad, but I like it. With Shawna gone, nothing is standing in your way. You'll have a room full of medals at home in no time."

He shrugged, nostrils flaring. "The competition is still pretty fierce."

Using one of the lines I'd thought up to intentionally insert a key part of both murders (one that wasn't made public) into the conversation, I said, "Is there someone out there who needs a good kneecapping? I know my way around a crowbar. Ask my last boyfriend."

I watched his expression carefully as he draped an arm across the back of my chair and leaned in. If "kneecapping" and "crowbar" struck a nerve, he didn't show it. The corner of his mouth curved up. "You'd do that for me?"

Baxter said, "Is he actually considering your proposition or are you guys just flirting?"

I wasn't sure. I held Mike's still-cold gaze and murmured, "Hell, yeah. Give me a name."

A shadow fell across our table. I looked up to find Skyler Marx, four shots in hand, looking at me like I was a piece of meat and he hadn't eaten for days.

"Wanna join me for a drink, sweetheart?" he asked, his voice low and smooth.

I felt Mike's arm tense behind me. Interesting.

I didn't move from my place beside Mike. Giving Skyler a flirty smile, I asked with mock innocence, "Why? Did your little friend have to leave? Did she have to be home by curfew?"

Mike burst out laughing, his demeanor returning to what it had been earlier. While I was happy to be rid of freaky Mike, it wasn't easy for me to relax knowing he could slip in and out of his "normal" character at the drop of a hat. Big red flag on this guy.

He grasped my shoulder and drew me toward him. Giving me a kiss on my temple, he said, "Good one, babe."

Baxter's voice sounded strained. "You don't have to take this. Get up and walk away."

Skyler turned to Mike. He was smiling, but his eyes were flashing. "You trying to steal my girl, buddy?"

"*Your* girl?" Mike fired back. "Bro, you had your shot with her, and you blew it."

"We didn't have the time to make a connection earlier. Now I have the time. Besides, we all know I was her first choice. Get lost, Mikey."

Mike's grip tightened on my shoulder. For a moment, I thought he was going to get angry, but instead he started whining. "Come on, man. You get plenty of tail. Let me have this one."

It was a dumbass jamboree in here. Although I wasn't thrilled about being the pawn between two morons debating the rule of dibs, I actually felt sorry for Mike. It couldn't have been easy playing second fiddle to a dick like Skyler.

Skyler wasn't about to give in. As if Mike weren't even there, he pulled up a chair on my other side and set two shots on the table in front of me. "Let's have a drink."

The two little glasses of clear liquid held my rapt attention. This time Skyler wasn't drinking tequila—this was vodka, my former drink of choice. Everything else became hazy as I focused on those two drinks meant for me. I gathered my strength and shook it off. I could do this. I could sit here with vodka in reach. No problem. I breathed through my mouth so I couldn't smell the alcohol. No big deal.

Mike said, "She's not drinking tonight. You'd know that if you'd actually taken the time to get to know her."

Skyler rolled his eyes. "You think you could piss off and go be a wet blanket somewhere else? You suck when you're sober." He picked up one of the shot glasses and shoved it into my hand, sloshing the liquid in it everywhere. "Emily likes to party. Don't you, Em?"

While I tried not to come unglued over the fact that my hand was now drenched in vodka, Baxter said, "Get up. Now. It's over."

Mike growled at his friend. "Her name's *Ellie*."

Knowing I had only a finite amount of time before I lost my shit, I cut in, "Come on, you guys. Let's all drink to new friendships."

I clinked my glass against Mike's Red Bull and then against the glass in Skyler's hand. It took every ounce of willpower I had, but as the two men had their heads tipped back to down their drinks, I tossed mine over my shoulder, where it splattered harmlessly onto the floor behind me. I slammed the glass down onto the table, allowing myself a moment to celebrate my victory. While I was busy patting myself on the back, Skyler swooped in and planted a wet, vodka-flavored kiss on my lips.

I sat there, stunned. Before I could stop myself, I ran my tongue across my bottom lip, savoring the sharp tang I'd craved for sixty-one long days. My eyes went straight for the other shot waiting for me. My desire to drink it blotted out everything else. It was all I could think about. In the back of my mind, I registered shouting and sudden movement around me, but my attention was focused solely on that glass.

I reached for it.

27

My mind flashed back to the last time I'd had a drink in my hands. I was standing in my kitchen, at wit's end over my sister's disappearance. I could see the bottle of vodka as clear as day. But then I remembered what had stopped me from taking that drink; what had kept me on the wagon all this time. The drink in front of me suddenly didn't look so appetizing. I flicked the top of the shot glass and toppled it onto the table. The vodka spilled out, no longer a threat. Smiling, I turned toward Baxter to see if he'd witnessed my triumph, but he wasn't at his table.

"Ellie."

I whipped my head the other direction to find him standing next to me, his hand outstretched. I grasped it and launched myself into his arms. Clinging to him, I blurted out, "I didn't drink it. I wanted to so badly, but I didn't."

He held me tight. "I know. I didn't doubt you for a second. Let's get you out of here."

Once he let go of me, my euphoria subsided and reality came crashing back. The bar was in chaos around us. Skyler and Mike were in a knock-down drag-out fight. The other bar patrons, evidently not wanting to be left out of the fun, began shoving and hassling each other. Baxter steered me toward the exit as fast as he could. He didn't slow his pace or let go of me until he'd ushered me into his vehicle.

He climbed behind the wheel and let out a tired sigh. "I don't know if I should be impressed or appalled that you managed to cause a bar brawl."

I laid my head against the headrest. I'd zoned out the moment I tasted that vodka on my lips. I'd been hoping the scene in there wasn't my fault, but subconsciously I knew it was. Every time I thought I had my life put together, my white trash side inevitably came slithering out.

"I'm sorry. I certainly didn't go in there with the intention of inciting a riot." I wrinkled my nose and looked over at him. "And not to shift the blame, but shouldn't you have tried to do something to break it up before it got out of hand?"

He snorted. "I wasn't about to get between two juiceheads slugging it out. I'd have got my ass handed to me."

I smiled. "True." I couldn't get my smile to stay put.

Baxter reached over and took my hand. "Hey, are you okay? A lot of things happened there at the end that I know you can't be too happy about."

I shook my head. "Yeah, about that. I, um...I can still...taste it. The vodka from Skyler's mouth."

With a grimace, he let go of my hand and dug around in the console between us. "I may have some gum..." Finding nothing, he turned and grabbed a bag from the seat behind him and peered inside. "The best I can do is some old fries from my lunch yesterday. I'll warn you—they weren't even good when they were fresh."

In spite of myself, I started laughing. "I'm not quite at rock bottom, so I think I'll pass on your day-old backseat fries."

"Oh, wait." He reached into the bag and drew out a packet of ketchup. "How about this?"

The vodka taste wasn't going to go away on its own, and I was afraid it would gnaw at me if I didn't get rid of it fast. "Okay. I'm not above slamming a ketchup packet." I took it from him and emptied the ketchup into my mouth. I made a face as I swallowed. At least it covered the vodka. "That was awful, but thank you."

He tried to hide the fact that he had to work to control his gag reflex. "Don't mention it."

"I'm fine with never mentioning any of this to anyone. When we write this report, it's going to have to be vague. The full story will give Manetti an aneurism and cause Sterling to piss himself laughing. I don't want to have to deal with either one."

"Yeah, but you know I recorded the whole thing, right?"

I'd been too nervous to register what Baxter had been doing with the surveillance equipment before I left his vehicle. I buried my face in my hands. "Shit."

After starting his vehicle and leaving the parking lot, Baxter changed the subject, sort of. "On the bright side, you managed to get a lot of information out of Marx's buddy. We hadn't considered friends of his as persons of interest, but this guy seems to have a decent amount of motive to have killed Shawna Meehan. Maybe even Angela Meadows, if she was someone he perceived as a threat as well."

"I'm not a hundred percent sold on Mike's motive being to kill people who can run faster than him. On the other hand, I didn't like the way he went dark when he was talking about knocking out his competition."

"I wondered if he wasn't also referring to the fact that he was essentially competing with Shawna for Marx's time. If that's the case, which I think it is, then you've got relationship jealousy, which is always a great motive for murder."

I frowned. "Oh, yeah. He did get pretty weird about all that. It's sad that their bromance is so one-sided."

"I wouldn't feel too bad for him. Once we start digging into his life, I'm betting we're going to find plenty of reasons to think he's not the nice guy he pretended to be tonight."

"And let's not forget he was the one who went home sick from work Friday night, causing James Lorenz to have to cover for him, causing Shawna Meehan to be out alone and get murdered. Now we find out he's got beef with Shawna? The more I think about it, the more I worry everything could be connected."

"I wondered that, too. Once I figured out who he was, I shot a text to the sheriff and asked her to run background on him. I haven't heard back yet."

As we headed to the station, I tried to push the events of this evening out of my mind, but they kept playing in my head as if on a loop. I wished I could revive the feeling of victory I'd had when I decided not to take that drink. But my brain chose instead to dwell on how badly I'd craved it in the first place. How I'd come so close to falling off the wagon. How much hold one tiny glass of liquid still had over my life. When there was no alcohol around, it was fairly easy to not think about it. But when it was available and literally at my fingertips, it was harder than I'd imagined to say no. I felt like I was back in the early days of my sobriety, my entire being focused minute by minute on fending off the urge to drink. It wasn't that I wanted a drink right now, because I didn't. What engulfed me was the realization that I wasn't in nearly as much control of myself as I'd thought I was. I stared straight ahead, hoping that concentrating on the bustling traffic would keep my attention off my inner struggle. It didn't.

After I was silent for a while, Baxter said gently, "I know you told me you were okay. But are you really okay?"

I blew out a long breath. "Not exactly... I could use a meeting right now."

"Then that's what we'll do. Tell me where."

"There's one starting soon at the Methodist church near the station. I can walk over."

At eleven-thirty P.M. on Wednesdays and Fridays, there was a small AA group that met in Noblesville. I liked the fact that the meetings were always short and sweet, and the group members seemed to be a little more down-to-earth than at other places. The only downside was that I wasn't often awake at this late hour.

As he drove, Baxter tried his best to fill the dead air with one-sided small talk. I was too spent to make much conversation. I busied myself trying to make my appearance less of a trainwreck. I'd brought along some makeup wipes to remove the nonsense from my face and an elastic band to pull back my too-big hair. Other than my clothes, which I could cover most of by keeping my coat on, I looked presentable enough to go to an AA meeting.

Baxter passed the station and pulled into the church parking lot.

I said, "Oh, you're dropping me off? Thanks."

"Well, I don't know if you've heard, but there's a killer on the loose, preying on women running around alone."

I laughed. "Is that so?"

He parked his vehicle and turned off the engine. "That aside, do you think I'd just dump you here by yourself after what went on tonight?"

I stared at him. "Well, you're not coming in with me."

He smiled. "I'd like to see you try to stop me."

I had a feeling I'd end up breaking down during this meeting, and I didn't want him to see that. "You know all anyone does here is bitch and moan about their lives, right? These meetings can be a real downer."

"That's not true. I've been to AA meetings with friends and family members before. I know exactly what I'm walking into."

"Don't you have a report to file or something?"

"Quit trying to get rid of me, Ellie. I'm not going anywhere."

"Not even if I ask nicely?"

He turned to face me. "I get it—you're embarrassed. Don't be."

I bowed my head, my cheeks flaming. "How can I *not* be? The moment I walk through that door, I'm nothing more than another sad drunk," I muttered, my tone bitter.

He grasped my hand. "That is absolutely not true. The mere fact that you're here proves you're *not* a sad drunk. I never want to cause you to feel embarrassed in front of me. All I want to do is support you." His hand tightened around mine. "I'm in awe of the amazing turnaround you've made. Don't you know that by now?"

I didn't have enough restraint to keep my emotions in check if he held my hand much longer. I pulled away. "I guess you have a better marker than anyone to measure my progress. You're the one who saw me at my worst."

"And even that didn't scare me away."

"I know. And I appreciate that. Um..." I shook my head. "Okay, I'm just going to say it. A big part of the reason I don't drink anymore is...you." When his eyebrows shot up, I held up my hands. "Don't worry—it's not because I'm trying to please you."

"Good."

"It's because..." I sighed. "The look on your face when you realized I was an alcoholic absolutely killed me. I never want to see you look at me that way again." Tears stung my eyes as I recalled the evening when Baxter had given me a one-man intervention.

His face fell. "Did you think I was disappointed in you?"

"You *were* disappointed in me. And you weren't wrong."

"Ellie, I wasn't disappointed. I was terrified. Terrified something would happen to you and...I'd lose you forever."

No man had ever cared about me the way Nick Baxter did. I didn't have enough control left to keep the tears from leaking out. I brushed them away quickly, but not before he noticed.

He sighed. "Sorry. Did I get a little deep for tonight?"

"Not any more than I did."

We locked eyes, but after a moment we both looked away.

Clearing his throat, he said, "We should probably go on in."

Baxter sat by my side throughout the meeting. When my turn to share came around and I hesitated, he whispered words of encouragement in my ear. While I opened up to the group about my struggles tonight, he listened to my every word as if he were hearing the story for the first time. When I choked up, he put his arm around me for support. I was thankful he was too stubborn—too caring—to allow me to push him away.

We didn't speak until we got to the station's parking lot. It was midnight, the start of our mandatory eight-hour sleep break. Even though we'd spent the last half hour off the clock, if we set foot inside the station past our designated hours, Jayne wouldn't hesitate to have us physically removed.

I said, "Thanks for staying. It means more than you could ever know."

He smiled. "Thanks for letting me."

28

The next morning, the first order of business was yet another meeting, which I wasn't looking forward to at all. Baxter and I would have to give a full report on our fact-finding mission last night. We wouldn't take the time to play the recording, but everyone would want to know word-for-word what was said and dissect every nuance of my conversations with the two juiceheads. I knew Baxter would do everything in his power to be discreet about my personal issues surrounding the incident—most of them unspoken and luckily not captured on tape. But I still worried that basically having to relive it could undo the positive steps I'd made during my meeting and my heart-to-heart with Baxter.

As I got out of my car, Vic approached me and came in for a kiss. At the last second, I turned my head. His lips landed on my cheek.

I didn't know why I did it. It just seemed like the thing to do.

To cover, I joked, "No PDA at work, Agent Manetti."

He smiled, not seeming to have taken offense at my brush-off. "You're no fun, Ms. Matthews." We began walking together toward the station. "How did last night go?"

I yawned. "Didn't get as much sleep as I might have. Nate woke up, so I went and hung with him until he fell back asleep."

He frowned. "Isn't that Rachel's job? Your priority on your sleep break is to sleep."

Something about his reaction rubbed me the wrong way. "My priority is my family, Vic. It doesn't matter what time it is."

He rubbed his eyes. "I wasn't trying to start anything. I was asking how your undercover mission went."

My mind immediately went to the moment when Baxter had his arms around me, telling me he didn't doubt me for a second. I cleared my throat. "Oh. Um...it was interesting."

"And successful, considering you found us a brand-new person of interest. Not bad for your first undercover op."

"Maybe, but from now on I think I'll leave the undercover ops to you professionals. It's really not that fun to pretend to be someone you're not." Okay, now I was even starting to sound like Baxter. I had to get him out of my head.

Not an easy task considering I ended up sitting next to him in our meeting.

"Hey," he said as I took the last available seat. "Get any sleep?"

I was relieved he wasn't acting differently toward me. I hoped I could manage to do the same. "Sort of. Nate woke up crying at two. Nightmare. Rachel sleeps like the dead, so I got up and settled him back down."

"Even if it meant you losing some sleep, I'm sure it made his day to get to see you. He's told me on more than one occasion that he doesn't like it when I make you work late. Next time I see him, I expect I'll get an earful and get put in some sort of wrestling hold. According to him, Auntie Ellie hung the moon."

Much different reaction than Vic's. I couldn't help grinning. "Oh, that kid. When I hear things like that, I want to chuck it all and be a full-time stay-at-home aunt."

We didn't get a chance to continue our conversation, because Griffin told us all to sit down and start shutting up. But I did happen to notice the shy smile growing on Baxter's face as we spoke. So much for not acting differently.

Griffin smirked at Baxter and me. "Well, Dream Team. It's about damn time. Let's hear all about this new person of interest you found. I think we have a promising lead, here."

Baxter nodded. "Michael Hopkins is Skyler Marx's 'best bro,' by his own admission. They've known each other since they were teens and have quite a history, evidently."

Jayne chuckled. "That's an understatement. Hopkins has a ridiculous list of misdemeanors to his name, and every one of them matches up with one on Skyler Marx's record. But we'll get to that later."

Baxter continued, "He told Ellie that Marx's relationship with Shawna Meehan wasn't going well and that Marx had plans to break things off with her."

Sterling said, "That doesn't jive with what Marx told us. Who's lying?"

Shrugging, Baxter replied, "I'd lean toward Marx. He was trying to cover his ass for murder, so he wouldn't want to tell us his relationship with the victim was on the rocks. According to Hopkins, she was being possessive and demanding to know where Marx was and who he was with at all times. Aside from pissing off Marx, this was a bone of contention between her and Hopkins as well. Hopkins said she didn't like him and that the feeling was mutual. Not only were they competing for Marx's time, but they were also competitors in all the area races."

Griffin frowned. "Another connection with the racing scene."

I said, "And another connection with Rip Barbell Club. Michael Hopkins is the worker who went home sick from there the night Shawna was killed, which caused James Lorenz to have to stay. What if he faked it to force Lorenz to stand Shawna up so she'd be alone and easy pickings? The only real symptom of being sick that Hopkins exhibited was throwing up, right? Big deal. Making yourself vomit is the oldest trick in the book to get your boss to send you home from work. He's in this mix somehow."

Smiling at me, Vic nodded. "Good insight. I'll follow up on that."

Baxter went on, "From the way Hopkins talked, there was a good deal of jealousy between the him and Shawna, especially on his side. He couldn't beat her at running, and she'd throw it in his face. When he and Ellie started discussing Shawna's death and Ellie suggested Shawna may have had it coming, he said, and I quote, 'I know, right? Couldn't have worked out better for me. There's nothing like getting rid of your competition.'

While that's no admission of guilt, it's enough to haul him in and question the hell out of him."

I noticed Vic's expression go dark when Baxter got to the part about me saying Shawna had it coming. Surely he realized I was only playing a part.

Baxter continued, "With Marx being on stage most of the evening, Ellie didn't have the time to strike up more than a superficial conversation with him." Hesitating, he threw me an apologetic glance. "However, she left things well enough with both Marx and Hopkins that she could easily meet up with either of them again and talk more." I shook my head, but that didn't deter him from adding, "It might be especially helpful for her to be a shoulder to cry on after we question Hopkins."

Sterling rolled his eyes. "Matthews, how did you manage to strike up a rapport and get so much info so fast out of the guy?" Giving me a knowing look, he added, "You took him to the men's room to loosen him up, didn't you?"

Vic pushed out of his chair so violently it slammed against the nearby wall and toppled over. He yelled across the table at Sterling, "You shut your damn mouth—"

I held up a hand calmly. "No, no. Sit down. I got this." I lasered a glare at Sterling, but kept my tone even. "No, I did not make the *second* biggest mistake of my life, you misogynistic bastard. The man simply needed someone who'd actually listen to him and show a little interest in what he had to say. That's all I did. It really wasn't that difficult."

Griffin's voice was like steel. "All three of you shut this shit down. Now. I will not have this kind of disrespect on my team."

Vic righted his chair and sat down. Staring daggers at Sterling, he said, "It won't happen again." His words were as much a threat to Sterling as a reply to Griffin.

Jayne, whose only tell that she was perturbed was a slight flare to her nostrils, said, "Moving on, Michael Hopkins's misdemeanors include several instances of drunk and disorderly, trespassing, criminal mischief, and that sort of thing. Nothing violent, but any priors in this case are worth our concern. He's done hundreds of hours of community service and even a couple of thirty-day stints in county. Ellie, when you do meet with him today, it won't be alone."

I nodded, my hopes of never going undercover again—and never crossing paths with the juiceheads again—dashed. Instead of concentrating on what was said during the rest of the meeting, I fretted over having to hang out with a possible killer or two again.

I did manage to rouse from my stupor to hear Griffin drop a total shit bomb on us. He'd gone on television last night to make a public plea for people to call into our tip line with any information they might have regarding Shawna Meehan and Angela Meadows' deaths. It took all I had not to curse out loud. In my opinion, the tip line was the single worst police tool ever invented. It seemed like a great idea, and on rare occasions when we got an actual tip, I admit it did indeed save the day. But there was a horrible downside to the tip line, one that civilians never knew about. A public call for tips was like opening the floodgates for the crazies. There would be dozens of wild goose chases we'd either have to research or physically go on before one measly tip panned out in the slightest. In short, it was a nightmare.

When the meeting ended, Griffin approached me. "Since the detectives will be busy for a while interrogating your new friend Mike Hopkins, I thought you could use your time this morning vetting tips from the tip line."

And there it was. I pasted on a smile. "I'll get right on that."

Baxter, who was gathering up his notes next to me, was trying his best not to burst out laughing at my misfortune.

The moment Griffin was out of earshot, I murmured, "Laugh it up, Detective. You know our afternoon is going to be running down the tips I vet."

His mirth vanished. "Oh. Well, hell."

"Yeah."

After going through the transcripts of the tip line calls from last night, I'd lost what little hope I had in humanity. Some calls had me laughing at their sheer ridiculousness, some had me sincerely worried for the callers' mental state, and a couple had me feeling the need for a shower. There were none I thought were even remotely useful regarding our investigation. I was sitting at Baxter's desk using his computer, and as I leaned back in his chair to take a break, I saw Vic storm from the direction of the interrogation rooms, down the hall, and out the door. The man was pissed about something, but I felt it best to let him walk it off by himself.

Several minutes later, Baxter came up and leaned against the cubicle wall behind me. "So...how's the tip line vetting coming along?"

"Suckish."

He nodded. "That's normal. Tip line's usually my job, because Sterling thinks he's above it. I'm happy to pass the baton along to you."

Holding my hands up, I said, "Don't you be passing me anything—unless it's some gossip about why Vic flew out of interrogation like a bat out of hell."

Baxter grinned. "Your boyfriends went at it in there."

"Did you mean for that to sound dirty?"

He rolled his eyes. "They got into a verbal altercation."

"That's no good."

"Nope. We listened to the tape from last night before we interrogated Hopkins, so Manetti was already boiling from some of the things that were said to you."

I winced. "Good thing there was no video to go with the audio."

"No kidding. Then Hopkins got smug with Manetti once he figured out who he was. Manetti's on Skyler Marx's shit list for his role in helping Shawna Meehan file her restraining order. Things got heated in there, and Griffin kicked Manetti out. But Hopkins' lawyer was already all offended and said the interview was over. To add insult to injury, Hopkins didn't give up enough during interrogation for us to hold him."

"How about the fact that he's a borderline psycho and has no alibi for a murder that knocked off his competition both on and off the track?"

"We need more. He said he wouldn't talk until his attorney—who is Marx's slimy attorney, by the way—got here. And then he still wouldn't talk, except for the expletives he yelled at Manetti. Major fail."

"Ouch. I didn't think Mike was that smart. Now what?"

Baxter grinned at me. "He's going to be pretty shook over getting hauled into the police station. He needs a good listener with a friendly face."

I scowled. "No one has ever accused me of having a friendly face."

"He likes you. I bet he'd tell you his deepest, darkest secrets if you asked."

"Maybe, but I don't want to hear them."

"Seriously, you're our only hope."

"Would you stop saying that?"

He shrugged. "It's either that or tip line duty."

"Tip line duty."

While Baxter wrote his report on Mike's interrogation, I slogged through this morning's tip line nonsense and surprisingly got two tips worth looking into. Baxter and I headed out to do the first interview, where we met a woman who turned out to be a nursing home resident of advanced age. She'd sounded knowledgeable and lucid over the phone, but in person, it was clear that she had no idea who Shawna was, even though she'd assured me earlier that she'd spoken to her just last week.

As we left the facility, I said, "Sorry about that. She sounded great over the phone."

Baxter chuckled. "It happens. On to the next."

"Are you sure you trust me after that one?"

"Always."

I felt a smile tugging at my lips, but it died when I got out my phone and read the text Jayne had just sent: *We need some damage control done ASAP with Hopkins. Manetti followed him to his gym and continued the argument they started in interrogation. Manetti crossed a line and Hopkins is crying police brutality.*

"Something wrong?" Baxter asked.

I hadn't realized I'd stopped dead in my tracks in the middle of the parking lot. Wordlessly, I handed my phone to him.

He read the text and shook his head. "What the hell was he thinking?"

"He wasn't."

29

How could Vic have been so stupid? He came unglued because of what he heard on the surveillance tape, and then he didn't like the way Mike's interrogation went, so he decided to go beat a confession out of him? If he didn't get removed from the task force for this, then Griffin wasn't doing his job.

Even though Vic had promised me he would work on his attitude and had showed signs of improvement, he hadn't made any real change. His single-minded focus was still on finding a way to nail Skyler Marx, and possibly even Mike by association. We still had no real evidence against either of them, and assaulting Mike today was about the worst thing Vic could have done.

If there was one thing I'd learned over the last couple of months, it was that people didn't change their ways unless they wanted to. Nothing anyone else could say or do would make a damn bit of difference if the person didn't want to do the work. I wanted to quit drinking and eat healthier, so I did. I didn't want to go on Vic's crazy diet and exercise regimen, so I pretended. Vic didn't want to take my advice about not being such a psycho over avenging Shawna's death, so he pretended. It was time we quit pretending with each other.

In the meantime, I had to clean up his mess. That meant having to go home and change into some less professory clothes and heading to Rip

Barbell Club to go undercover again, which I didn't want to do. Baxter wired me up just like last night, and he sat in the parking lot to listen while I headed inside to...I didn't really know what I was supposed to do. Use my feminine charm to distract Mike from filing a complaint against Vic?

As if Baxter were reading my mind like he always did, he said in my ear, "Don't worry about doing damage control for Manetti. If he did cross a line, then he deserves what's coming. Just get Hopkins talking. You were great at it last night."

"Okay. Thanks." I pushed the front door open, hoping no one who knew me as Ellie Matthews, criminalist, was here. I breathed a sigh of relief when I saw a young woman at the front desk instead of James Lorenz.

"Hi...can I help you?" she asked, eyeing the jeans I was wearing.

"Yeah. I, um...didn't come here to work out, obviously. I came to see Mike Hopkins. Is he working today?" Remembering my stupid groupie persona, I forced out a giggle. "I didn't get his number when we met last night, so I had to track him down the old-fashioned way. Feels kind of stalk-ery, but we hit things off and I really want to see him again. So here I am."

She evidently bought my story, because she smiled and said, "I totally understand. Dating is hard. Mike's in the office." She pointed toward a hallway near the back of the room. "Down that hall, last door on the left." Lowering her voice, she added, "He's not feeling so great. He could use some cheering up."

I put on a concerned face. "Oh, no. I'll be sure to do that. Thanks."

Ducking my head so my hair fell across my face, I hurried toward the back, hoping none of the gym rats got a good look at me. I was playing with fire being here.

I knocked on the door marked "office" and called, "Mike? Are you in there? It's Ellie from last night."

A strained voice said, "Ellie?"

I opened the door to find Mike lying on a threadbare couch in the cramped office. I'd forgotten all about the bar brawl from last night. He had bruising on his nose and around both eyes. He was holding one hand over his upper chest and wincing as if he were in pain.

Rushing to his side, I cried, "Mike! Holy shit. Are you okay?"

He smiled, but it looked like it hurt him to do so. "I am now. How did you find me?"

"You told me you worked here."

"Oh, right. Last night's kind of a blur."

I took his hand. "I'm so sorry I bailed on you. Bar fights freak me out. There's so much chaos. I panicked and ran."

"It's okay. You'd have probably gotten hurt if you'd stayed. I'm just happy you wanted to see me again."

Subdued and weak from his injuries, Mike didn't scare me in the slightest. The problem was, I had to get him keyed up in order to make him start running his mouth. It wasn't going to be easy, because I was pretty sure he'd taken some kind of painkiller. He seemed overly mellow. I hoped he hadn't taken a drink with it—it was dangerous enough for an addict to ingest any kind of mood-altering substance.

"Of course I did." Gathering my courage, I reached over and brushed a lock of hair back from his forehead. "Did Skyler do all of this to you? Are you guys speaking to each other still?"

"Yeah, we'll be fine. It takes him about a day to cool off." He rubbed his chest and frowned. "I had a visitor this morning who I think did a lot more damage to me than Skyler ever has."

I went for a surprised look. "What do you mean?"

He looked away. I was afraid he was going to clam up on me, but he finally said, "Some guy barged in here this morning while I was lifting and tried to start something with me. Asshole pinned me with my own barbell. I had three hundred sixty-five pounds sitting on my chest, plus however much pressure he was adding." He rubbed the spot. "I think I may have a cracked rib."

I cringed, hoping Vic's poor decision hadn't in fact injured Mike's sternum. Even if it didn't, it was going to leave one mother of a bruise. I had an idea. "What have you done to take care of yourself?"

"I've been resting, but it's not helping much. And I have to get back to work soon. Can't lie around all day."

"Let me help. Take your shirt off."

Mike raised one eyebrow. "I like where this is going."

Baxter said in my ear, "How exactly is him getting naked going to help with a cracked rib?"

I had to bite back a smile. To Mike, I said, "Slow your roll, there, gimpy. Where do you keep your compression bandages?"

He gestured to a cabinet on the opposite wall. "Top shelf."

I got out a couple of bandages, helped Mike into a sitting position, and helped him out of his shirt. Damn, but if he didn't have a sick body underneath it. I wrapped the bandages tight around the angry red stripe on his chest and secured them in place.

"Better?" I asked.

Mike rubbed his chest again. "Actually, yeah."

"Good. You'll need to ice the area a few times today, too. That should help even more. And rest when you can. No more lifting today."

"Yes, ma'am." He grinned at me. "I know what else might make me feel better."

Baxter said, "If he lays a finger on you, do not hesitate to slug him in the chest. Make it hurt."

I handed Mike his shirt. "Honey, you couldn't handle me in a weakened state."

Mike's eyes grew big, but he said nothing as he put his shirt back on.

I asked, "Are you in some kind of trouble, Mike? People don't generally run around pinning other people under barbells without a reason." I was afraid my question came out a little on the accusatory side, so I added, "Do I need to get my crowbar out and persuade this guy to leave my new man alone?"

Mike cast his eyes down. "Better not. He's FBI."

"I'm sorry, did you say *FBI*? An officer of the law did this to you? What the hell did you do to him? Steal his wife? Run over his dog?"

A ghost of a smile passed over Mike's face. "I shut down his witch hunt for Skyler."

"I don't understand."

"I got hauled in this morning by the cops and got interrogated about that girl Shawna we were talking about last night. They were trying to get me to admit I helped Skyler kill her. Don't they know I'd never roll on my boy?"

Baxter said, "The way he said that makes it sound like he's hiding something. Keep going."

I said to Mike, "Wait. Are they trying to—"

The door opened, and the woman from the front desk poked her head in. "I'm sorry to interrupt, but Jackie is here for her session with you. Do I need to reschedule her, or are you feeling better?"

Mike smiled at me. "I'm better. Tell her I'll be out in a couple of minutes." When she closed the door, he took my hands. "I have to go back to work, but I want to hang out with you some more. I get off at five. Can I see you then?"

Damn. I'd thought this would be my last undercover op, but we didn't have enough time for a deep conversation. He was beginning to open up to me. It would be a waste to abandon the foundation I'd laid.

"Yeah, I'd like that."

Baxter said, "Don't let him pick you up. Offer to meet somewhere for dinner. How about Mabel's Diner? There should be plenty of people there at five."

Mike asked me, "What do you want to do?"

"How about dinner? I've been craving a Mabel's Diner cheeseburger all week. I can meet you there a little after five."

"Works for me."

I sensed he was going to lean in, so I hopped up from where I'd been kneeling next to him before he could get to me. "Don't forget to ice that sexy chest."

"Will do. Thanks, Ellie."

I had to hold back from running to the safety of Baxter's SUV. I got in and slumped down in the seat, exhausted.

Baxter said, "Again, great performance. He likes you. If you don't get interrupted tonight, I'm confident he'll tell you everything we need to know."

I let out a pent-up breath. "At least this time I get food out of the deal."

He laughed. "Priorities."

As we pulled into the station parking lot, I spotted Vic sitting alone in his vehicle.

Baxter evidently saw him, too. "Looks like Manetti's out here hanging with all his friends."

He wasn't wrong. I had a feeling everyone was pissed at Vic about the crap he pulled earlier.

I said, "I'll meet you inside in a few."

"I know that face. Are you going to go kick him while he's down?"

"He needs a good bitch-slapping. And I'm just the bitch for the job."

Baxter shook his head. "Sometimes I think you enjoy picking fights."

I gave him a mock punch on the arm. "You want next?"

"No thank you."

"Coward," I tossed over my shoulder as I hopped out of the SUV.

I approached Vic's car and tapped on the window. He looked up, but didn't appear too happy to see me. He was in a mood. But so was I.

He opened the door and got out of his car. "You look like you've got something to say."

I snapped, "You're damn right I do. What the hell were you thinking assaulting the best lead we have? He's never going to talk willingly now, so he's become my problem. I had to go meet with him to try to worm any information I could out of him. We got interrupted, so I had to make a dinner date with him tonight to finish our conversation. So, yeah. I'm not exactly happy with you. Not what I wanted to do with my evening."

"You sounded plenty happy flirting with him last night."

My mouth dropped open. "Oh, no way. Tell me you're not jealous about the things I said to those two morons during my *undercover work*."

His frown deepened. "All I'm saying is that I saw a side of you I didn't know existed and I frankly didn't like. You're awfully good at making people think you like them."

After staring at him for a moment, I replied, "Well, Vic, you're awfully bad at it." Knowing the next thing out of either of our mouths would be even more hurtful, I decided the best thing to do would be to walk away.

30

Needing a break from the crazy, I called Rachel. Thursday was her early day—she had no classes after noon, so she usually went home unless she ended up staying to do some studying with her classmates. She thought it was weird when I called instead of texting her, but something about hearing her voice always grounded me. She and Nate had just gotten home, so I told her I'd pick up lunch for us.

When I opened my front door, Nate and Trixie both launched themselves at me. I kneeled down to greet them and got inundated with little boy and doggie kisses.

"How come I never get a welcome like that?" Rachel joked, a genuine smile on her face.

I picked up Nate. "Because you don't abandon this family for days on end. I'm sorry I haven't been around this week, Rach. No one wants this case wrapped up faster than I do."

She gave me a one-armed hug and ruffled Nate's hair. "Someone tells me you were around last night when it counted. Thanks for getting up with him. I heard nothing."

"It was my pleasure. We had a good time, didn't we, buddy?"

Nate let go of my neck long enough to nod his head. Then he put the vise grip back on me. I didn't mind a bit.

I held up the bag of takeout I'd brought. "I say we have a picnic on the living room floor. I'm too tired to sit up straight to eat at the kitchen table."

"Ooh, cool!" Nate chirped. He wiggled to get down from my arms. Indoor picnics evidently trumped welcome home hugs.

Nate babbled all through lunch about his little friends at day care. I'd missed the daily updates. Once he was done eating and went to his room to play, Rachel brought me up to speed on how her classes were going. Her grades had been better last semester, but I wasn't going to say a word. At least she was going to class and trying to fit back in.

She said, "I guess your slutty groupie thing went okay last night since you got home in one piece."

I smiled. "Sort of. I caused a bar fight."

Her eyes grew wide. "You were in a fight? Did you get hurt?"

"No, no, no," I said hastily. "I *incited* the fight. Two guys started duking it out over me, and the whole bar decided to join. Nick got me out of there, though."

"Oh. Whew." She laughed with relief. "Well...congratulations, I guess. Not everyone can say they've started a bar fight."

"Our white trash roots are good for something."

"You can take the girl out of the trailer park..."

Rachel had never said anything to me about how she was handling the misunderstanding on Valentine's Day. Since this was the first decent conversation we'd had lately, I finally got the nerve to ask her. "Speaking of Nick, are you doing okay with what happened Monday?"

Her face fell. "He told you."

"No, I answered the door and figured it out."

She put her head in her hands. "He must think I'm so stupid."

I moved so I could sit next to her and put my arm around her. "He doesn't think you're stupid."

"I'm still mortified. And going bowling with him that night was excruciating. I don't know how I can ever face him again."

"Rach, don't put this on yourself. It was his fault as much or more than yours. It was a simple misunderstanding."

"That makes me look like a moron with a schoolgirl crush."

I shook my head. "It absolutely does not. It could have happened to anyone." When she didn't say anything, I ventured, "Do you...have feelings for him? Is that what's making this so hard to get over?"

Rubbing her forehead, she said, "I don't know."

"Please don't let it ruin your friendship. You need him in your life. Nate needs him, too."

She thought for a moment. "Why are you defending him? You two have avoided each other every time he's come over here since Christmas. Don't think I haven't noticed the looks that pass between you two. It gets all kinds of awkward when you guys are in a room together."

I honestly thought she'd been so out of it the past couple of months that she hadn't noticed. I cleared my throat. "We had some issues, but we've worked through them. We're good now."

Eyeing me, she said, "Issues... Wait. Did you guys hook up back in December? Is that what all the angst was about?"

"No."

The kiss Nick and I had shared was way more intimate and meaningful than any sexual encounter I'd ever had. If I let her keep guessing, it wouldn't take her long to figure out why there was so much tension between us. And given the fact that the sting over the misunderstanding about Valentine's Day still hadn't eased for her, finding out the truth could hurt her even worse.

I made a show of looking at the clock on the wall and getting up from the couch. "I need to get back to work."

"I can tell something's still up with you. What are you keeping from me, Ellie?"

"It's nothing. Really."

Nothing except yet another reason why I had to keep my true feelings for Nick Baxter locked away.

Baxter wasn't in his cubicle when I returned to the station, so I took over his desk and continued to slog through the tip line transcripts. After a while, they all started sounding alike, and I needed a break. I went to the break-room for some coffee.

Baxter found me sitting there alone. "Guess who used to date Skyler Marx way back in the day and has been suddenly showing up at his gigs lately?"

I rubbed my temples. I was going to have to find some Advil before returning to tip line duty. "Could you narrow it down a little? He gets around."

"Someone connected to the case."

"Hmm. Eve? She seems like she gets around, too."

He shook his head. "Guess again."

"Mateo's fake wife?"

"Nope. Let me give you a hint. They dated before she became a mild-mannered wife and mom."

"I don't..." My jaw dropped. "Oh! *No.*" I shook my head, not wanting to think what I was thinking.

He grinned. "Oh, yeah."

"Wait. Where did you get this information, and how do we know it's not bogus?"

"The sheriff's been running down Skyler Marx's friends and acquaintances. She vetted the info herself."

"But Skyler Marx is *so* not Rebecca Caldwell's type."

"I think he's every woman's type, judging from the comment his buddy Hopkins threw out last night about the amount of tail he gets."

"Eww."

He held out his hands. "Hey, his words, not mine."

I frowned. "Maybe before Rebecca settled down, she decided to have one last fling and Skyler happened to be the first guy she saw."

"One of their previous addresses matches up. They lived together for six months. Not a fling."

Grimacing, I said, "Ugh. What was she thinking?"

He shrugged. "I might have been able to look past the previous relationship if she hadn't been sniffing around him again during the last couple of months."

"The fact that she showed up to hear his band a few times doesn't mean they're doing it again. Maybe she simply enjoys his music."

"She came alone, and they were seen leaving together."

I had no rebuttal for that.

He went on, "So...you understand this paints her in a bad light—ex-girl-friend back in his life with no alibi for his current girlfriend's murder. For my money, she's looking better than Mike Hopkins right now."

I stared at him. "Please tell me you're not going to charge her with murder."

He frowned. "I will if the evidence lines up against her. I realize your gut says she's innocent—"

"As do the giant shoeprints at the second scene."

"Not necessarily. She could have talked her husband into doing the deed or even hired someone. We can't give her a pass because you think she's a nice lady."

This conversation was compounding my headache, and it felt like it was headed toward argument territory. Baxter seemed pretty adamant about this one, but Rebecca's involvement still didn't add up for me, supposed affair or not. I got up from the table and refilled my coffee cup. He walked over and got himself a cup of coffee and then leaned against the counter, only about a foot away from me. With my conversation with Rachel still zinging around in my brain, I couldn't be this close to him and remain coherent.

I walked as nonchalantly as I could over to the other side of the room. "Is a happily married woman going to risk losing her home, her marriage, and her child to knock off some rando who years later starts dating her loser ex?"

Baxter shook his head. "Except Shawna's not just some rando. She's also a competitor and kind of an enemy to Rebecca."

"Sort of, but it's not like Shawna stole Skyler away from Rebecca. She's just the latest in a long line of 'tail,' as you so politely put it."

"I don't think you're looking at this objectively because of your feelings toward Rebecca. What if she wanted to leave her husband for Marx, and Shawna was standing in her way?"

I made a face. "Why in the hell would she want that? Skyler is one of the worst people I've ever met. And he's not even that good a kisser."

Baxter's jaw clenched. "Shut up, Ellie," he muttered.

My eyebrows shot up. "Shut up? What's with the attitude all of a sudden? It's not like I compared him to you." I could have kicked myself for blurting that out. Then again, a Freudian slip might have been inevitable—I hadn't been able to get the mental image of our kiss out of my head since I'd thought about it earlier.

He wiped a hand down his face. "Just...stop talking. Please."

A voice growled behind me, "You kissed Skyler Marx? *And* your partner?"

Wincing, I wheeled around to find Vic standing at the door, fury evident in his entire being. Baxter wasn't trying to pick a fight with me—he was trying to save me. I should have known.

I said in as calm a tone as I could manage, "Skyler Marx kissed *me*. It was a surprise attack."

Vic glared over my head at Baxter. "And Captain America here...was that also a 'surprise attack'?"

"No. But it's none of your business, because it happened before you and I ever went out."

"You made a huge deal out of telling me about your tryst with Detective Sterling, but made no mention of this. Why hide it? Is there something more going on between the two of you that you don't want me to know about?"

Out of the corner of my eye, I saw Baxter flinch, but he kept quiet. I hated that he was trapped in here to watch while Vic and I went at each other.

"I don't have to tell you about every guy I've kissed."

Vic rolled his eyes. "Right, because that would probably take all day."

I stared him down. "Would you like to rephrase that?"

He shrugged. "Okay, I'll rephrase. Who *haven't* you been intimate with around here?"

Vic could get nasty in a fight, which I'd known since I'd met him. But I could give as good as I got.

I barked out a snide laugh. "Ooh, wrong answer, pal. I don't have to take this shit from you. We're done."

His eyes widened in shock, but only for a moment. His expression hardening, he spat out, "Fine by me," and then turned and stormed out of the room.

"Fine," I griped at his retreating back.

Baxter said quietly, "Ellie, I—"

I held up a hand. "No. This is over, and I'm not wasting another moment of my life on it. Besides, we've got a job to do."

Sighing, he replied, "Okay."

It would have been great not to waste another moment of my life stewing about my epic fight and subsequent breakup with Vic, but that wasn't how I was wired. This was when I would have reached for a drink before. Now, chocolate would have to suffice. After eating two candy bars on the drive to Rebecca Caldwell's work, I felt ill and still had a craving for a drink. Although a technical victory, I felt like the incident at the bar last night had been a major setback to my overall sobriety. I didn't want to get drunk, exactly, but I couldn't get the taste of vodka out of my head.

Baxter began, "After what went down earlier between you and Manetti—"

"You mean when I kicked his sorry ass to the curb?" I said a little louder than I intended.

"Yes, that. I wondered if you'd want to take a little time for yourself this afternoon. You need to be at a hundred percent for your dinner with Hopkins tonight. No distractions."

I nodded. "I need a meeting."

He glanced over at me, his face full of worry. "Because of what happened today or because of last night?"

"Yes."

"We can stop and find one now if you can't wait."

"No, it's fine. We need to get this mess with Rebecca figured out first."

"Could you at least call your sponsor in the meantime?"

I rolled my eyes. "I've got to bite the bullet and get a new sponsor. She left me a ten-minute voicemail this morning detailing her trip to a new supermarket, in which she had to forego picking up her weekly loaf of bread because the bread was located in the same aisle as the beer. Seriously? She should be way past that by now if she's trying to mentor someone else."

"Maybe that could be how you spend your break—finding a new sponsor you can actually talk to."

"And where might I find one of those? You saw the people at the meeting last night. They're all whiny and petty and self-involved, like my sponsor. No matter what meeting I attend, I find the same type of people and hear the same things. If they aren't bemoaning the fact that their neglectful or abusive significant other is being mean and making them want to drink again, then they're complaining that their enabling friends are pressuring them to go out and party. Or my personal favorite—that they're stuck in a crappy dead-end job because that's all they could get when they were drunk all the time. Problems that could have been corrected in the time it took to bitch about them."

He grinned. "You just don't like people."

"Guilty. But when I try to share what makes me want to drink, like violent crime scenes I can't unsee and dealing with the aftermath of Rachel's kidnapping, they don't get it. They all just stare at me like I'm some kind of freak."

"Joking aside, I see what you mean. I agree that you didn't fit in with the people last night."

"So you think I'm a freak, too?"

"No, not at all. I think you haven't found the right group yet. One of our deputies goes to AA meetings specifically geared toward first responders. I'm betting there are similar ones for other types of law enforcement personnel. I think he has to drive down to Indy, but it might be worth it for you to be around people who are fighting similar battles. He's on duty today. We can run him down when we get back, if you want."

I smiled. "That sounds perfect."

31

Rebecca Caldwell worked in one of the high-rise office buildings near the Fashion Mall. My belly full of chocolate did not appreciate the straight shot to the twentieth floor on the powerful elevator.

"Ugh," I grunted, clutching my stomach as the elevator screeched to a halt and bobbed into place.

Baxter nudged my shoulder. "Puking is my thing. Nobody likes a copycat."

I managed a sarcastic, "Ha, ha," under my breath, but appreciated his dumb joke to lighten my mood.

We were directed to Rebecca's office by the receptionist. Judging by the woman's surprised yet offputtingly gleeful expression, I assumed her next order of business would be to sprint to the water cooler to gossip about why there was a detective here to see Rebecca.

Rebecca's office door was open. When Baxter knocked on it, Rebecca popped her head up and instantly went green.

"What...what are you doing here...at my work?" she choked out.

"We'd like to speak to you again," Baxter replied.

She nodded, and Baxter closed the door behind us. He and I took the two chairs facing her desk.

He got right to the point. "You told us you didn't really know Skyler Marx. That's not quite true, is it?"

Eyes growing wide, she breathed, "I...used to know him."

"You used to live with him."

Her voice wavered. "That was a long time ago."

"True. But what concerns me is that you've been seen with him lately. And you seem to want to keep that quiet—enough that you've lied to us about it twice now."

Tears spilled down her cheeks as she let out quiet sobs.

I turned to Baxter, a pleading look on my face. He shook his head. He wasn't backing down.

He said, "Mrs. Caldwell, we need you to tell us the truth about where you were on Friday night after you left Agent Manetti's house and also where you were Monday night."

She blubbered, "I was at home with my family. Both times. I swear. You have to believe me."

"Give me a reason to. Come clean about your relationship with Skyler Marx."

I said gently, "Look, Rebecca, if you're worried about this getting back to Jonathan, don't be." When Baxter sent me a warning glance, I added, "Unless your relationship with Skyler has a direct bearing on the case, what you tell us will be completely confidential."

She put her head in her hands. "It doesn't matter. Jonathan knows."

Now I was a little worried. "Um...if you're not trying to hide your affair from your husband, then what exactly are you hiding?"

Raising her head, she admitted, "I'm pregnant. A couple of months ago, Jonathan and I went through a rough patch. I went out one night and happened to run into Skyler. We had a few drinks, and...I made a stupid mistake." She shook her head sadly. "And then he sucked me in and I kept making the same stupid mistake over and over again. Then I found out I was pregnant. When I told Skyler it could be his, he said he wanted no part of it. Being with that jackass made me come to my senses and realize what a good thing I have with my husband. I told Jonathan everything, and by some miracle we reconciled. We have an ultrasound next week to find out exactly how far along I am..." She let out a heavy sigh. "And then we'll know who the father is."

My heart ached for her. Her personal drama was crazy enough, only to have murder become entangled in the whole mess. Add pregnancy hormones and morning sickness, and this poor woman must have been at her wit's end.

"I can't even imagine what you must be going through right now, Rebecca."

Before I could say any more, Baxter cut in. "Has your husband confronted Skyler Marx about your situation?"

Training her gaze on her desk, she said, "Yes."

"When?"

"A few weeks ago."

"Did he get any satisfaction out of that confrontation?"

"Not much. Skyler was...his usual self. He laughed at Jonathan for not being able to hold onto me."

I could see Baxter forming a terrible suspicion. I didn't like where this was going.

He asked, "How did your husband respond?"

She let out a shuddering breath. "He hit Skyler in the face."

Baxter's jaw clenched. "Is that all your husband did to him? Did he also maybe threaten Marx about what might happen if he got near you again?"

I sucked in a breath. "Could you excuse us, Rebecca? And is there an empty room we could use for a few minutes?"

She pointed wearily to her left. "Two doors down."

I hopped up and gestured for Baxter to come with me. Once we were inside the tiny conference room and he'd shut the door, I hissed, "You are going loose cannon on this. You're drawing all sorts of conclusions that aren't even remotely connected. It's not like you."

Baxter's expression was stony. He approached me, stopping only inches away. He growled, "You feel sorry for her. You're letting your emotions rule your view of the facts. That's not like you."

Despite his close proximity, I stood my ground. "The fact that Skyler knocked up Rebecca isn't grounds for her husband to go on a killing spree."

"Are you hearing yourself? It totally is."

"If and only if the victims had been Skyler and Rebecca. Otherwise your theory makes no sense."

"Nothing in this case makes sense, in case you hadn't noticed. We're not going to solve this unless we start thinking outside the box."

I griped, "You're so far outside the box on this one, you're in the next county."

He ran a hand through his hair. I hadn't realized how frustrated he'd become. I felt bad for bashing his idea.

I smiled up at him and softened my tone. "But maybe that's because we're literally in the next county right now. Maybe your detective powers only work within the confines of Hamilton County." We were just south of Ninety-Sixth Street, which served as the county line between Hamilton and Marion counties.

He squinted. "What?"

"I'm making a bad Nick Baxter joke to ease the tension. Keep up."

His expression relaxed. "A joke. Is that what that was?"

I shrugged. "It was bush-league, I know. I don't have your level of expertise with bad jokes."

Smiling, he said, "I appreciate the effort."

Sensing that the type of tension radiating between us had changed, I took a step back. "Okay. So...for the sake of argument, I'll jump on your crazy train. What if we revisit our original idea about someone trying to make Skyler look guilty by using a guitar string as the garroting wire? I could get behind that theory fitting Jonathan—or, I hate to say this... Rebecca—trying to get back at Skyler."

"Exactly."

"But I'd like it better if one of them had a real reason to want to end Shawna's life."

"Her hatefulness toward Rebecca isn't enough? What if Shawna knew Skyler was cheating on her with Rebecca and had something to say about it? What if she went after Rebecca and threatened her? The Caldwells could have motive coming out their ears."

"I agree it's possible, but that's a lot of ifs. Isn't it kind of a stretch to kill Shawna only to frame Skyler—and not even do a good enough job to make the charge stick? Why not kill Skyler and be done with the rat bastard once and for all?"

He gave me a mock frown. "I thought you were going to go with my theory, not shoot holes in it."

"But isn't that why you keep me around? Because I can think like a delinquent?"

A smile pulled at the corner of his mouth. "That's not why. So are you on board with me bringing the Caldwells in for formal questioning?"

I hesitated, but then said, "I will support whatever decision you make, because I trust your judgment."

He eyed me. "But you don't agree."

I shrugged. "A round of formal questioning or even a night in jail is not tantamount to a guilty verdict. If you decide not to charge them, then I guess there's no real harm to be done." I couldn't resist adding, "Except for the emotional scarring, of course."

Smiling, he said, "I'll take full responsibility for that."

"Deal."

Baxter called Sterling and had him go pick up Jonathan at his work. Then we had to inform a pregnant woman that she was going to have to report to the station for more questioning. Baxter took pity on her and told her he'd give her time to pull herself together and leave on her own so her coworkers would be none the wiser about where she was headed.

True to his word, the moment we got back to the station, Baxter ran down the deputy he'd mentioned who attended the first responder AA meetings. The two of us sat in the breakroom and talked, which really helped. He said he'd make some calls to get me set up with a new sponsor and find a meeting that would suit my needs.

As I was exiting the breakroom, Agent Griffin happened to be walking past. Without slowing down, he said, "Wow. Three new promising leads in under twenty-four hours. Now that's how a Dream Team is supposed to do it."

I forced a smile and tried not to feel so guilty about what the poor Caldwells must have been going through at the moment.

I had to rush home and change and then rush back to the station to meet Baxter, only to rush over to Mabel's Diner to get in position and test our surveillance equipment before Mike arrived. Once we had everything working, Baxter and I sat down in a booth inside and he gave me a last-minute pep talk, sort of.

Studying me from across the table, he asked, "Are you nervous?"

"Not really."

"This guy is one of the best leads we have. He might even have some inside information on the Caldwells."

I frowned at him. "Don't push it."

"Sorry, couldn't resist."

"Are they being treated nicely?"

"Yes. In fact, the sheriff herself is questioning them, because she's the one who's been doing the most digging into their backgrounds."

I nodded. "Good." Jayne was fair and kind. She was definitely the best person for the job.

"Focus up. We can't forget the fact that Mike Hopkins could be dangerous. I'm still not such a fan of you hanging out with him."

"I know, Dad. I'll be fine." I pointed to Baxter's vehicle, which was parked outside the window by our booth. "You're only going to be a few feet away, watching and listening in."

"Yeah, but still. If something happens, it'll take me a few seconds to get to you."

I waved a hand in dismissal. "I've been out joyriding all alone with a serial killer before. I survived."

He glared at me. Grabbing my hand to hold my arm still, he shoved back my sleeve to reveal the scar from the knife wound I'd received when I'd pissed off said serial killer during that joyride. "Barely."

His touch sent a shiver through me that left me trembling. Baxter mistook my reaction for residual trauma from getting cut. He gently pulled my sleeve back into place.

Tightening his grip on my hand, he said, "I didn't mean to upset you. I'm worried about your safety, that's all."

"I know." I squeezed his hand. "The real reason I'm not nervous is because I never have to worry about my safety when you're around."

The corner of his mouth curved up slightly, and he let go of my hand. "Well, don't let that be an incentive to do something reckless."

Sighing, I complained, "I do one reckless thing one time, and now you don't trust me."

"Considering I thought for a good thirty minutes I'd lost you to a maniacal serial killer, I'd say I'm justified."

"Fair point. But really, how reckless can I get inside Mabel's Diner?"

He grinned. "I'm not answering that question because I'm afraid you'll take it as a challenge."

I gave him a mock frown. "It's like you don't know me at all."

"Oh, I know you better than you think."

That much was true.

I glanced at my watch. "He should be here any second. Time for you to get lost."

He took my hand again, sending another tingle through me. "Be careful. If you get spooked or anything happens you don't like, tell him you're going to the restroom. I'll meet you at the back door and get you out of here."

I couldn't resist one last retort. "What if I actually have to use the restroom?"

He let go of my hand and stood. "Then hold it, smartass."

I smiled to myself as I watched him leave the restaurant.

A waitress came up and said, "Sorry I didn't get here sooner. We've been slammed."

"No problem," I replied. "I'm waiting for someone, anyway."

She gestured to the door. "Detective Baxter, right? Is he coming back?" she asked, a hopeful smile on her face.

"No, I'm waiting for someone else." Her reaction piqued my interest, so I added, "How do you know the detective?"

She blushed slightly. "He was so kind to me a while back. I had a problem with my ex coming in here and harassing me. Detective Baxter took care of it."

I smiled. "I'm not surprised. He's a good man."

"And good-looking. The other girls who work here swoon every time he comes through the door."

I wondered if Baxter was listening in on my mic yet. He'd get a kick out of hearing this. "They think he's pretty hot, huh?"

"Big time. You're a lucky woman."

My eyebrows shot up. "Me?"

"Well, yeah. I've seen you here with him before. You're what—his wife?"

Now it was my turn to blush. I shook my head. "His work wife, maybe. That's all."

She eyed me skeptically. "You sure about that? You two were just sitting here holding hands."

"It was nothing."

A slow smile spread across her face. "You keep telling yourself that. I saw the way you were looking at him, especially the way you were checking out his butt as he walked away. Not that I blame you."

My jaw dropped open in horror. The worst part was that she wasn't wrong about where my gaze had landed as he walked away. If he was listening, I was going to die of embarrassment. In case he was, I said, "We're undercover. It was all for show."

She wouldn't let it go. "Right. And the way he looked at you... Damn. No man's ever looked at me like that."

Truth be told, no man had ever looked at me the way Baxter did, either.

I glimpsed Mike pulling up outside and getting out of his car. I had to end this horrendous conversation, so I said hastily to the waitress, "All that aside, I seriously am here undercover. Can I count on you not to say anything to the guy I'm about to have dinner with? Detective Baxter and I need for this meeting to go well."

She was suddenly all business. "Absolutely. Anything for Detective Baxter."

"Thanks."

Mike was taking his dear sweet time getting in the door, so as soon as the waitress was out of earshot, I cleared my throat and asked Baxter, "How much of that did you hear?"

"How much of what?" Just as I was about to breathe a sigh of relief, he added, "So how's my ass? Above average, I hope."

Holy hell. "I wasn't—" Mike was finally walking this way, so I put my hand over my mouth and hissed, "Damn it, Baxter. Not a word."

"For now. Later we're going to have lots of words about this."

32

I put on a smile and waved to get Mike's attention, thankful for something to take my mind off the situation, even if it meant sharing a meal with a possible murder suspect. As strange as it sounded, there was something I liked about Mike—he reminded me of a sad little boy. But there was also something I feared about him, which I purposely hadn't mentioned to Baxter. When Mike had gone dark during our conversation last night, his eyes had changed. They'd become almost lifeless, devoid of humanity. While I wasn't thrilled at the thought of having to see that again, if I didn't get him somewhat agitated and talking about any reasons he might have had to kill someone, this meeting was going to be for nothing.

Mike waved back and approached me. He laid a hand on my shoulder and came in for a kiss, which I managed to deflect onto my cheek with a slight turn of my head.

"How are you feeling now?" I asked, filling my voice with concern as I reached across the table to take Mike's hand as he sat down. "Are you still in a lot of pain?"

"Hell, yeah. Skyler says I should sue that asshole Agent Manetti *and* the FBI. We've got witnesses. He could get what's coming to him."

Since Vic had been instrumental in getting Shawna's restraining order against Skyler, I was sure Skyler would love nothing more than turning the tables on Vic.

"What in the world did he want with you, anyway?"

"Can I get you guys something to drink besides water?" a cheerful voice asked.

Shit. Nosy waitress was back. She'd better be cool.

So much for cool. She plunked down two overflowing glasses of water on the table between us, sloshing water on our intertwined hands. Mike pulled away from me to wipe his hand on a napkin.

The waitress giggled nervously. If she blew my cover and screwed this up for me, I was going to throttle her. "Oh, sorry."

Mike glared at her in response.

She looked at us expectantly. "So...drinks?"

"Coffee, please. Black," I replied, trying to keep a neutral expression on my face.

"Same," Mike said.

Worried there were going to be multiple interruptions dogging our conversation, I said, "Can we just go ahead and order? I'd like a cheese-burger and fries."

Mike said, "Steak and salad."

Baxter said in my ear. "That's a mistake. Mabel's steaks suck. They pre-cook them so they can get them out fast."

She left our table, but Mike didn't jump back into the conversation.

I prodded him, "So what did the FBI guy want with you? You'd already been questioned and released, right?"

Mike scowled. "Yeah, but he had it out for me from the start. I didn't give up anything, and that pissed him off. He had the balls to come to my gym, where he proceeded to hold down my barbell while he tried to force me to confess to helping Skyler kill Shawna. The guy was off his nut."

"No way. I mean, wasn't Skyler found innocent already?"

"Sort of. They didn't have enough to keep him in jail, so they had to cut him loose. But now they supposedly found new information about him hitting her again."

I wasn't supposed to know anything about this, so I said, "Again? Was he abusive? Is that why he was a suspect in the first place?"

"Yeah. They used to get in epic fights. But it's not like she didn't hit back."

"Well, he still had a hundred pounds on her. Not really a fair fight."

"True, but he did stop. He hasn't laid a finger on her in six months. After he got slapped with that restraining order, he realized he'd been way too violent with her. He saw himself turning into his dad and didn't want to be like that anymore."

Baxter said, "Stay with that. It doesn't line up with what Tracy told us about Shawna's recent injuries."

I reached over and gently took hold of Mike's chin, tilting his head down so I could take a better look at the cut on the bridge of his nose. "For someone who doesn't want to be violent anymore, he really did a number on you."

Mike grinned. "Bar fights don't count. We have to blow off steam somehow."

"So did he start beating you up instead of Shawna?"

The grin fell from his face. It was replaced by an angry frown. "Why are you dissing my boy Skyler? You barely know him."

"Back off. Don't lose him," Baxter said.

Pursing my lips into the best pout I could muster, I said, "I like you, Mike. I'm only worried about how you're doing."

"Still, leave Skyler out of this," he growled.

"What is his deal with protecting that loser?" Baxter griped.

I said, "Fine. I will. So—"

"Here you all go," the waitress said, appearing at our table and setting our plates in front of us. "Can I do anything else for you?"

Mike snapped, "You could remember the coffee we ordered."

Her smile faded. "Right. I'm so sorry. I'll be right back."

"Your date's a real dick," Baxter said.

I stuffed a couple of French fries in my mouth to give myself a moment to think. The waitress returned with our coffee, but said nothing except a quiet apology. Hopefully Mike's asshole routine, while totally uncalled for, would work in my favor and make her want to stay away. I'd been wondering if his little episodes of going to the dark side were legitimate anger issues or were merely symptoms of withdrawal. I wasn't the nicest person to be around when my cravings got out of control, so I found myself starting to cut Mike some slack for his occasional disturbing behavior.

I said, "So are you afraid the police are going to come after Skyler again? Or try to trick you into giving him up or even try to bring you down with him?"

He shrugged and cut into his steak. "No matter what, they won't be getting anything out of me. I know Manetti is trying to get me to narc on Skyler, but that's never going to happen." He took a big bite of meat and chewed it before he added, "Besides, that son of a bitch tried to steal Shawna away from him. Does he actually think I'm going to help him after all that?"

"No kidding. So did Shawna cheat on Skyler with him, then?"

"No. Her and Skyler were broken up when her and Manetti hooked up. Manetti pulled some kind of knight in shining armor bullshit and convinced her to get the restraining order."

"What's his beef with Skyler? It sounds like he's looking for reasons to get the poor guy in trouble with the law. And you by association."

He took another bite of steak and mumbled, "Tell me about it."

Now for a tough question. I cleared my throat. "But there's no way they can pin either of these murders on you, right? Like, if you have an alibi, you're good."

His brow furrowed. "That's the problem—I don't have a good alibi for the night Shawna died. Skyler doesn't either."

I faked a concerned expression. "Ooh, that's not good. Where were you?"

"At home, puking my guts up. Alone."

"Can you...I don't know...prove you had food poisoning or the stomach flu or something? I mean, if you were that sick, you couldn't have murdered anyone."

He turned his attention to his salad, chewing as he thought for a moment. "I don't think I had either of those. I hadn't eaten anything for hours, so it wasn't food poisoning. And it didn't really last long enough to be the stomach flu. It kind of reminded me of how I get if I eat shrimp."

Baxter said, "He sounds pretty sincere. Try to gauge his expression. Keep going with this."

I gave Mike a sympathetic smile. "Are you allergic? I totally understand. I break out in hives if I have even one bite of shellfish. You throw up instead?"

Nodding, Mike replied, "Yeah. It's like clockwork. Thirty minutes after I eat anything with shrimp, I'm projectile vomiting. Every time."

"Whoa," Baxter said. "He might not have eaten anything before he got sick, but I bet he drank something, especially if he worked out before his shift started. Find out."

I made a face. "Eww. I think I prefer hives."

He chuckled. "Hives would be a lot less messy."

"You know, sometimes they use shellfish in things you wouldn't expect. Is it possible you drank something that might have had a fishy additive in it?"

He joked, "Not unless they've changed the formula for Gatorade."

"Or someone tampered with his Gatorade," Baxter said.

I nodded. Between my anxiety over being undercover again and the thought of someone essentially poisoning Mike's drink, I wasn't hungry anymore. I pushed my untouched burger away. "Hmm. Weird. So back to your alibi—do you need one? Can I say I was with you?"

He reached over and took my hand. "That's nice of you, Ellie. But I've already gone on record saying I was home alone. If I change my story now, they'll think I'm lying."

"Oh, that sucks. So how are you going to stay out of trouble? Are they going to try to throw you in jail like they did Skyler?" I asked, trying to go for a worried expression.

He released his grip on my hand and slumped in his seat, eyes cast down. "I don't know. I mean, I didn't kill her, so it's not like they're going to be able to find any evidence against me. But yeah, they could do the same thing to me that they did to Skyler, just because I had the bad luck of getting sick that night instead of working." He looked up at me, that sad little boy peeking out again. "I don't want to go to jail, even for a couple of days. I've been there before, and I don't think I can handle it again."

Relief had washed over me when he made it clear that he didn't kill Shawna. I replied, "I've been there, too. It's scary." I paused for a moment, trying to find the right words. I leaned across the table and lowered my voice. "Do you think the police would leave you alone if you rolled on someone else?"

His face went dark again.

I held out my hands. "I'm not talking about Skyler. I'm just saying that..." I blew out a breath and left my side of the booth so I could slide in next to Mike. He still looked pissed, but he made room for me. "Skyler knew Shawna better than anyone, right?"

"I guess."

"So it makes sense that he should know if someone was out to get her. I mean, if she was scared, she would have gone to him, wouldn't she?"

"Yeah, probably."

"Has he ever talked to you about who he thinks could have killed her?"

Mike hesitated, glancing around the diner before he murmured, "He thinks it was Manetti."

I had to fight to keep from rolling my eyes. It was becoming evident that Skyler and Vic had a permanent pissing contest going on. "Why does he think that?"

"From all the times the guy has come after him over Shawna. Because he used to call her all the time when she was with Skyler, asking to her to go running with him or out for coffee. Basically trying to date her under Skyler's nose. Oh, and she was at his house right before she died. Skyler thinks he followed her out there and killed her because she refused to dump Skyler and be with him."

The more he talked, the more I realized how Vic's actions to protect Shawna could have been taken another way, especially by the guy on the receiving end. It was no secret to anyone that Vic had it out for Skyler. He and his quick temper could easily have come off as confrontational and violent instead of heroic.

When I went quiet, Baxter said, "Shake this off, Ellie. This is just one loser's opinion, and it's clouded by the situation and probably a toxic amount of alcohol."

I cleared my throat. "Did Skyler tell any of this to the police?"

Mike shook his head. "He was afraid to. He figured if he even breathed Manetti's name, the cops would turn on him and he'd get locked up forever."

His fears weren't completely unfounded. Not that the department would have turned on him and trumped up charges or falsified evidence, but he probably would have been treated less kindly if he'd gone in there pointing the finger at one of our own.

"I don't blame him for that. I would have done the same thing." I put my hand on Mike's shoulder. "But that still leaves the problem that neither one of you have an alibi for the night Shawna died. I don't want to see either of you in jail for someone else's crime." Letting out a breath, I said, "For the sake of argument, let's say it's not the FBI guy. Is there anyone else Skyler talked about who was acting strangely toward Shawna? It doesn't even have to be lately. It could have been an incident from...a couple of months ago."

Even though I'd laid the foundation with my arbitrary two-month time-frame, I was really hoping Mike didn't bring up the Caldwells. What he did bring up was even worse.

Cocking his head to the side, he said, "You sound like a lawyer or a cop or something. You barely know us. Why are you so interested in all this?"

Baxter said, "It's okay. He hasn't made you. Stay calm, and he won't. I hate to say this, but you're going to have to flirt your ass off."

My heart racing, I leaned in. "Why am I interested?" I asked, letting out a little giggle that nearly gagged me. "I guess I've played it too cool." Putting my lips near his ear, I whispered, "I have a *huge* crush on you."

He leaned back so he could look at me. His mouth curved up in a smile. "Me? Really?"

Oh, this poor guy was so easy to fool.

I smiled. "Yes, really. I know we only met last night. But between your sexy muscles and your adorable smile and the fact that you stood up for me to your best friend...I'm into you." I slid my hand up his shoulder and wrapped it around the back of his neck. "I'm not leaving your side. Even if I have to move heaven and earth, I won't let you go to jail. We're going to go talk to Skyler right now and figure out someone else to pin this on. I don't care if they're guilty or not, as long as it's not you. You know I'll lie to the cops for you. Whatever it takes to keep you out of jail. The only handcuffs you're going to wear are the ones in my bedside table."

"I said flirt with him, not proposition him," Baxter griped.

While I'd expected a reaction like that out of Baxter, I hadn't expected the one I got from Mike.

His eyes shone with tears. "You'd do all that for me? You barely know me."

"I know you're special, Mike Hopkins."

Baxter groaned.

Mike grabbed my face and kissed me. Even though I wasn't into it, I found that Mike wasn't a terrible kisser. Much better than his supposed lady-killer friend Skyler. Baxter of course was telling me to "abort, abort," but I had Mike right where I wanted him, and I was not going to let my efforts be in vain. He was going to walk back into the station and talk openly with Baxter if it was the last thing I did. And if I could somehow convince Skyler to go with him, all the better.

Mike set his forehead against mine and whispered, "You're special, Ellie Collins. No one has ever stood up for me like that."

I smiled. "Well, get used to it. Now let's go clear your name."

33

Amid frantic objections from Baxter, I got in Mike's car and rode the short distance to Skyler's apartment. Baxter followed us, cursing and griping in my ear the whole way.

Mike grabbed my hand as we walked up the sidewalk, his expression full of hope and happiness. I felt bad for leading the poor guy on, but if things went well, I would in fact be helping him stay out of jail. As for my other promises...he was going to be sorely disappointed.

Mike rapped on one of the first floor doors. It only took a moment for Skyler to answer. He looked happy enough to see Mike, but when his gaze fell on our intertwined hands, his expression turned sour.

Mike said, "We came over to talk."

Skyler leveled a glare at him. "I thought we settled this last night, *bro*. I won. You lost."

Mike held out one hand. "Look, man. Ellie and I really like each other. Right, Ellie?"

I said to Skyler, "He's right; we do." When he didn't quit his glaring, I decided to stroke his ego a little. "It's nothing against you. I think you're great, but...Mike and I are so much alike. We get each other. But the last thing I want to do is come between the two of you. You can hate me all you want, but please, Skyler, don't hold this against him."

He studied us for a minute, then gestured to me and asked Mike, "You hit that behind my back?"

Baxter said, "If you want to clock him, you have my blessing. I'll turn my head."

Mike shook his head. "No. I swear. We only went to dinner."

Skyler looked me up and down and shrugged. "Whatever. She's a borderline grenade, anyway. You can have her."

Baxter said, "On second thought, don't waste your time clocking that assclown. Move a smidge to the left, and I'll shoot him."

Mike leaned over and whispered in my other ear, "He didn't mean that. He's just mad. You're beautiful."

I smiled at both men's attempts to make me feel better. Skyler made a move to shut the door, so I gestured to Mike.

Mike said, "Hold on. The real reason we came over here is because Ellie wants to help us stay out of jail."

Skyler grunted, "She a lawyer?"

"No, but she's got some good ideas. Come on, man. We've got nothing to lose."

"Fine," Skyler said, rolling his eyes as he let us into his apartment.

The apartment complex was okay from the outside, a little dated but kept up well enough. Skyler's apartment, however, was trashed. If he didn't have mice and roaches running amok, I'd be shocked. I couldn't imagine stuck-up Shawna setting foot in here.

I said, "I'll get right down to it. Mike says neither of you guys has an alibi for the night Shawna was killed. You've both been questioned, so the police believe you could be involved in some way. What we need is to find a new suspect for the police to harass. You take your information to the cops as a peace offering. If you're truthful with them and can convince them that you're genuinely trying to help find Shawna's killer, they'll start giving you the benefit of the doubt."

Skyler was shaking his head before I even got done with my speech. "No way. The cops are never going to give me the benefit of the doubt. Screw them. I'm not helping."

Mike said, "Come on, man. The point of this is to help ourselves. We've got a shit ton of strikes against us already. At this point, I'll try anything to make sure I never spend another minute in jail."

Skyler stared at us, saying nothing. This was going to be a hard sell.

I sighed. "Mike already told me you think that FBI guy...um..." I turned to Mike. "What was his name?"

"Nice touch," Baxter murmured. "You're not so shabby at this under-cover work."

Mike said, "Manetti."

I nodded. "Right, Manetti. You're thinking he could have killed Shawna, but you were afraid to say anything to the cops because he's one of them."

Skyler raked his hands through his hair and sat down heavily on his couch. "Mike, you dumb son of a bitch. Can you not keep your damn mouth shut just once?"

I said, "I agree that you shouldn't go around accusing FBI agents of murder, whether you have a leg to stand on or not. I'm talking about someone else—anyone who might have had a decent reason to kill Shawna. Was there ever anyone who came at her or tried to hurt her or anything like that? Even if it happened a while ago. Maybe even an old girl-friend of yours? We just need a little something to work with to throw the heat off you guys."

Mike chimed in, "She says all we need is someone to pin it on. It doesn't matter if we think they did it or not."

I said, "It would be ideal if there were a concrete reason that this person could be guilty. For instance, did Shawna ever get into a public fight with anyone?"

After perusing the collection of opened beer bottles littering his coffee table, Skyler found a half-empty one and took a swig. "I don't know. I wasn't around her twenty-four/seven."

Mike stared at his friend, looking like he was going to be sick. "Is that left over from yesterday afternoon?"

Skyler glanced at the bottle he was holding. "Yeah, so?"

"How in the hell can you stomach Natty Ice flat *and* warm? It's barely drinkable ice cold and fresh."

We were getting off track here. I said, "Skyler, surely you and Shawna talked about life stuff, though. Who did she complain about? Who did she hate?"

Skyler barked out a laugh. "Fat people."

This fool was getting on my nerves. "Right, but everyone has enemies of some kind. From what Mike told me, Shawna never passed up the opportunity to be a bitch."

Skyler raised his bottle in the air. "True that."

"So?"

"So what?"

"Look, dude. Either help us, or I'm going to the cops and telling them you did it. I won't think twice about throwing your bitch ass under the bus to protect Mike."

Standing to his full height, Skyler came my way to tower over me. "That would be a big mistake."

I crossed my arms and stood my ground. "If this is your attempt at intimidating me, it's not working."

Baxter's voice was wary. "Don't push him. Something tells me he won't think twice about hurting you."

Mike stepped between us. "Come on, you guys. We gotta stick together on this."

In a less confrontational tone, I said, "Skyler, you're the person who knew her best. I feel like you're the key to this, even if you don't think you have the answer. The only thing we know for sure is that there's someone out there she pissed off enough to kill her."

Skyler sank back down on the couch. "Yeah. His name's Manetti."

I sighed. "Again, we can't go with that angle. Let's try another—obviously you and Manetti were fighting over Shawna. If she was such a catch, then was there some other guy out there who also wanted her but couldn't have her?"

"Lots of guys wanted her."

"Why?"

"She was gorgeous."

Sure, she was pretty, but nothing out of the ordinary. "And?"

Skyler smirked at me. "And she knew her way around a dick."

"Oh, I can't unhear that," Baxter said.

I shook my head to clear it. "Start naming names."

Skyler said, "The dorky manager at my gym."

Mike furrowed his brow. "James?"

"Yeah. He always looked at her weird when I'd bring her to the gym with me."

Mike said, "He has a lazy eye. He looks at everyone weird."

James had an alibi for that night, but they couldn't know that I knew that. "What's his last name?"

"Lorenz," Mike said.

I got out my phone and made a note. "Who else?"

Skyler replied, "Her trainer. For a while I thought they had a thing on the side."

"What's his name?"

"Devin King."

He at least had an alibi for Angela's murder. "Keep going."

Skyler trotted out his trademark smirk again. I wanted so badly to slap it off his face. "This butch chick, Tracy, who goes to my gym. I think she has a thing for both of us."

Alibi again. "Last name?"

"Uh..." He looked at Mike for help.

"Greer," Mike said.

I frowned. "Isn't there anyone shadier than Mike's boss, a personal trainer, and some girl from your gym? Dig deep, Skyler. Was there no one in Shawna's life she thought was a creeper?"

He actually seemed to be thinking about this one. He found another half-drunk bottle of beer and gulped it down. Nodding, he said, "Yeah. I don't remember his name, but there was this guy...an old coach from high school or something. He used to date her friend—you know, the other one who died? Angela? Sometime last spring...he kept calling Shawna, wanting to talk. Shawna always hated him for something he did to Angela back in high school, so she wouldn't speak to him. Then one day he kept showing up everywhere Shawna went, trying to get her to talk in person. Completely freaked her out. But then he quit calling, and as far as I know she never heard from him again."

Baxter said, "That sounds promising. And not for nothing, but he sounds like a much better suspect than either of the Caldwells. I'll shoot this to Sterling and have him figure out who this guy is. Amazing job, Ellie. Now make up an excuse so you can get out of there."

I couldn't help but smile. Finally a suspect that actually made sense for both murders. "An ex of Angela's who stalked Shawna? That's the perfect suspect. Plus if he was a coach of theirs from high school, that makes him skeevy as hell."

"We don't know his name, though," Mike said.

"Let the police figure it out. It's their job. I say we go make you some permanent 'get out of jail free' cards. Let the finger-pointing begin, boys!"

Even though he had a new and improved suspect, Baxter was still not happy about me riding to the station with Mike and Skyler.

His voice was tight with apprehension. "Keep an eye on them. They're still dangerous, regardless of the fact that we have a seemingly better suspect now."

I was trying to tune him out, worrying over how I was going to get these two knuckleheads through the station without blowing my cover. I knew practically everyone in there by name. All it would take was one person saying, "Hey, Ellie, how's the case going?" and I'd be made. These guys were pretty stupid, but not that stupid.

Finally, Baxter had something constructive to say. "Hey, why don't you suggest they call me so I can meet you guys outside and take you in through the side door? Tell them it'll avoid having to go through all the nonsense at the front desk. I gave your new boyfriend my card earlier. Maybe he still has it. I'll zoom around you and be waiting for you when you get there."

I said to Mike, "Hey, is there a certain detective you've been talking to? If you call and give them a heads up that you're coming in, then maybe you can avoid having to explain what you're doing to the moron at the front desk. Might make this whole thing easier. And quicker."

"Um...I guess..." Mike said, digging into his pocket. When Baxter, who had been behind us, chirped his siren and passed us, Mike panicked. He very nearly swerved into a car parked on the side of the road.

Baxter said, "Would you tell that idiot to keep his eyes on the road? And by the way, very early in my career, I spent a couple of months being the 'moron at the front desk.' It's a thankless job, especially because of people like you, who clearly don't appreciate what we front-desk morons have to put up with."

I had to hide a smile. I loved Baxter's stories of his time as a cop before becoming a detective. He certainly paid his dues before getting the big promotion.

Mike got Baxter's card out and handed it to me. "You're still going in with us, right? I don't know if I can do this without you."

"I told you I'd be there for you. I mean, if they let me. I may not be allowed in the room with you while you give your statement." I got my phone out and dialed Baxter's number.

"Detective Nick Baxter," he said in a put-on growly voice. There was an annoying split-second delay between the earpiece and my phone.

"Yeah, hi. I'm calling in for some friends, Mike Hopkins and Skyler Marx. They said they talked to you before, and they have some new information for you regarding that murder you falsely accused both of them of."

"Is that so?" Baxter asked, not bothering to keep the chuckle out of his voice. "You tell those juiceheads I said—"

Afraid they might overhear, I cut him off. "So you'll meet us at the side door of the building? On the north side? We're like five minutes out."

"I'll be there with bells on, ma'am."

When I hung up, Skyler leaned forward from the back seat until his head was between Mike's and mine. "What if this doesn't work?" he demanded. "What if they think we're lying and throw us in jail for...you know, purgatory?"

I rolled my eyes. "I think you only have to worry about purgatory if you're Catholic."

"What?"

"Never mind. This is going to work. Just tell them what you told me about that Angela girl's creepy old boyfriend. If they ask more questions, *answer them. Truthfully.* I know you're not exactly pals with the cops after your arrest. But the more open you are with them, the more they'll help you."

"You know, you're starting to sound like a cop now. What's your deal?"

"Just hang on a couple more minutes," Baxter said.

I blew out a breath. "If you must know, I sound like my PO. I did a little time a while back, and I had a really rough stint in lockup." I rolled up my sleeve. "See this? That's just one of the places I got cut. If I'm coming on a little strong..." I reached over and placed my hand on Mike's thigh. "It's because I don't want anyone I care about to have to go through something like that."

Mike smiled and grasped my hand. "You're so sweet. I can't see you in lockup."

I was never so happy to see the station. The moment Mike parked the car, I was out of it and ordering the two of them to stay put while I made arrangements to get them inside.

I breathed a sigh of relief when I saw Baxter appear at the side door. I had to hold myself back from hurrying to approach him. I couldn't keep the smile from my face, though. Since he was facing the parking lot, where Mike and Skyler could see him, he had to keep his expression passive.

He stuck out his hand to me, and we shook hands as if meeting for the first time. "I still can't believe you managed to get Marx to come to the station willingly."

I chuckled. "I promised there'd be beer."

The corner of his mouth turned up a fraction. "I'd believe it if I hadn't been witness to all the masterful manipulation you dished out. Now I'm not sure whether to believe what you say to me or not."

"You don't need to worry. I'm retiring my evil powers effective immediately." I waved at Mike and Skyler to come our way. Turning back to Baxter, I added ominously, "Or maybe I'll use them one more time to force you to buy me an expensive dinner and an assload of dessert later."

"Done. You earned it."

Mike and Skyler approached us, both of them with a wary look in their eyes.

Skyler said, "If we talk, you can't arrest us, right?"

Baxter shrugged. "As long as you don't admit to any crimes."

"What do you think we are, stupid?"

As I worked to keep from laughing out loud, I noticed Baxter clenching his jaw and making sure not to look in my direction.

He shook his head. "Not at all. Let's talk."

34

For Mike and Skyler's benefit, Baxter escorted me toward the conference room, where I'd supposedly wait for them. A couple of deputies took Mike and Skyler and put them in separate interrogation rooms, setting them up with coffee and leftover donuts from the breakroom as a gesture of good faith. When Baxter and I got to the conference room, the task force was assembled there waiting for us. We gave them a quick debriefing on what we'd managed to find out.

After congratulating us on a job well done, everyone got up to head over to listen in on Baxter's interviews with Mike and Skyler. Once I thought I was alone, I let myself relax, lowering my tired, achy head onto the table to rest. I didn't realize that one person had hung back.

"What the hell were you thinking?"

I raised my head. "Huh?"

Vic barked, "Going to that sleazebag Marx's apartment? Riding around in a vehicle with not one but two murder suspects—"

"*Former* murder suspects," I corrected him.

He glared at me. "Don't get cute. I could have Detective Baxter's badge for this. Putting a civilian in danger like that."

"First, I'm hardly an unsuspecting civilian. Second, it was my decision. I went against Baxter's strict instructions not to get in Mike's vehicle. Twice. He followed us both times and kept our coms open. I was never in danger."

"I guess by now it shouldn't surprise me that you refuse to learn from your past mistakes."

Too exhausted to consider the consequences of my words, I fired back the first thing that came to mind. "What, like you?"

His expression went hard. "It was certainly my mistake to care about someone like you." He stalked out of the room and slammed the door.

Ouch. I hadn't meant to get nasty with him yet again today. Being at odds with Vic tended to bring out the worst in me, and vice versa. I thought about sending him a text to apologize, but it should probably be said face-to-face to have any effect. Regardless, I knew no apology would be well-received until he had some time to cool off.

I went home to change and shower, which I felt like I needed after all the nonsense with Mike and Skyler, especially since a mere ten minutes in his gross apartment left my hair smelling like I'd slept over at a frat house. When I returned to the station, I read through several more tip line transcripts (all useless) while I waited for Baxter to finish up with Mike and Skyler.

I finally got a text from Baxter: *If you're at the station, hide somewhere away from the back hall. I'm escorting the juiceheads out. By the way, I let your boyfriend down easy for you. I won't lie—he cried like a little bitch.*

I couldn't help cracking a smile at Baxter's rude remark, but I honestly felt bad about leading Mike on. The poor guy needed someone in his life who'd listen to him and stand up for him. But even under normal circumstances, I wouldn't have wanted the job.

Not long after, Baxter found me at his desk. "All set?"

"Yes. I'm starving." As we made our way out of the station, I asked, "How did it go? Were they as talkative with you as they were with me?"

"Very nearly. Marx was standoffish, but who can blame him? We've locked him up once this week for murder. I imagine he was worried it could happen again if he said the wrong thing."

"So I take it he didn't try to convince you that Manetti is our killer."

Baxter held the door open for me. "No, he kept that to himself. But Hopkins had a lot to say about him. Only when I told him Manetti had his service pistol taken away and is on a probation of sorts, he seemed satisfied enough to shut up about it."

My jaw dropped. "Probation? When did that happen?"

"It's not a full probation. He's still on the task force, but he's not allowed to interview anyone alone. Sterling has to babysit him, which neither of them is thrilled about. Griffin laid the hammer down while you were at lunch."

I slapped my forehead. "Right before I dumped him."

He had to fight a grin. "Yeah. Rotten timing on your part."

Frowning at him, I griped, "Why didn't you tell me?"

"We've had a lot going on today. And Manetti is never at the top of my list of discussion topics."

"Still."

Once we were settled into his SUV, he said, "Not that I'm counting, but that's two breakups in one day for you. Must be some kind of record."

"For you too, right? Both were your fault."

His eyes grew wide. "The Manetti thing was a long time coming."

He was right, but I couldn't help needling him. "You keep telling yourself that."

He frowned and started his vehicle. I suddenly noticed how exhausted the poor guy looked.

I put my hand on his arm. "Hey, hang on a second. I mean this in the kindest way possible, but you look like hell. Let's postpone dinner. You need a nap."

"You're willing to give up the expensive dinner and assload of dessert I've agreed to buy you so I can get some rest? That's true friendship."

"I said postpone, not cancel. You're still on the hook for it, just not tonight."

He grinned. "No way I'm postponing. We have a lot to talk about, remember? Let's start with my ass—scale of one to ten."

I spent the rest of the ride to the restaurant deflecting Baxter's attempts to embarrass me over the ass incident, thankful it was dark enough inside his vehicle to hide the heat I knew was coloring my cheeks.

He finally decided to behave once we were seated at our table. I managed to get him to agree not to talk about any subjects relating to the investigation, any of the people connected to it, and especially not his ass. We instead talked about the beginnings of our careers. He told me about his time as a front desk clerk, which was actually quite uneventful. I told him the story of my first homicide case, where I'd thrown up everywhere. He thought that was pretty funny, considering his puking problem. I made sure to stress that I hadn't vomited because of my reaction to the carnage, but because of the stomach flu I'd come down with that morning and had foolishly tried to hide because I didn't want to miss out on my first case. Then our conversation turned to our college exploits. I never would have guessed my straight-shooting partner had been a wild child in college. I hadn't had such a good time in months.

As we were finishing gorging ourselves on dessert, his phone beeped. "Sorry, I'll just be a second." He studied his phone for a moment and then handed it to me. "Have a look at this."

While Baxter settled up the bill with the waiter, I read the email Sterling had sent him with a rundown of what he'd found out about Shawna and Angela's high school cross-country coach. Evan Thompson had been young at the time, in his early twenties. He was let go from his job for being caught snuggling up to one of his team members—and even though her name wasn't mentioned in any reports because she was underage at the time, it wasn't difficult to figure out who it had been. He hadn't been formally charged for his misconduct with Angela, but not long after, he managed to rack up a couple of assault charges. He'd evidently kept in touch with Angela over the years. And most damning of all, she'd received a slew of calls and texts from him lately—he'd called her several times in the last couple of weeks, and their text messages showed they'd made plans to meet a couple of times. Sterling was in the process of tracking him down to haul him in for questioning.

"Who would have thought that my two idiot friends would provide us with our best lead yet?" I said as I returned Baxter's phone to him.

We donned our coats and gloves, preparing for the several-block trek down Carmel's quaint Main Street to where his vehicle was parked.

As we walked, he said, "If we're lucky and Evan Thompson is our guy, today could be the last day of the investigation. Your life can go back to normal." Baxter smiled. "At this point, you're probably ready for a break from me."

His words hit me. If the investigation ended, I wouldn't be spending every waking moment with him anymore. I didn't like the thought of it.

Chuckling, he said, "What's with the frown? This is a good thing."

"Right. I do want to get back to teaching. But...I don't want a break from you."

He stopped in the middle of the sidewalk and caught my arm. "I... We can still hang out."

I nodded, trying to recover from blurting out something I hadn't meant to. I took a step back from him, just out of his reach. "Sure. That's what I meant."

He started walking again and changed the subject. "Where did you run off to at lunchtime?"

I fell back into step next to him. "Home. I needed some time with the fam. Oh, and I'm under strict orders from Nate to give Detective Nick a high five. So here you go." I held up my hand.

Smiling, Baxter hit my hand with his. "Tell him I'll be by soon to get one in person." His smile fading, he added, "How's Rachel doing? She barely returns my texts and won't return my calls."

"She's doing okay. Probably better than you think. If you want my opinion, you two need to sit down in person and talk it out. I don't want to be the middle man or overstep here, but I don't think it's as complicated as you're both making it."

He stopped walking again, and I turned to face him. That same wounded look from before we'd reconciled resurfaced in his eyes. "Feeling rejected is pretty complicated, especially on Valentine's Day of all days."

Between his expression and his loaded words, I was taken aback. I said quietly, "Are we still talking about Rachel?"

He took a step toward me. "What if we're not?"

I thought for a moment before I spoke. I couldn't keep pretending anymore. It was driving me crazy, and he deserved to know the truth.

"Then I'd say anyone who'd reject someone who's smart, nice, and humble, who's always on her side and accepts her the way she is and is always there for her...is monumentally stupid." I lowered my head. "When I saw you standing at my door on Valentine's Day, I realized you were the one I wanted to spend my evening with. I lost it when I thought you were there to take my sister out instead. Not my finest moment."

"Ellie."

I raised my gaze to meet his.

"It's about damn time you figured it out."

I smiled even though my eyes were threatening tears. "We still can't—"

"I know. Now isn't the time for us, for a lot of reasons. But that's not going to stop me from doing this."

Baxter reached for me and leaned in, but just as his lips brushed mine, both of our text tones chimed at the same time. He got to his phone first, and I knew something was wrong from the way his expression clouded over. I fumbled to get to my phone and read the text from Agent Griffin: *911. Task force to pinned location ASAP. Agent Manetti assaulted.*

My body went numb. "Assaulted?" I breathed.

Baxter put his arm around my waist to usher me the final few steps to his SUV. "Don't assume the worst."

I blinked back tears as I climbed into his vehicle and turned my attention to studying the pinned map location Griffin had sent. It was at a point along the White River Greenway. Vic must have been out jogging when he was attacked. Just like Shawna and Angela. I used everything I had not to let my mind go where it was inevitably headed as Baxter sped to our destination, lights flashing and siren wailing. He spoke to me along the way, but I didn't register any of his words. Once I'd convinced myself not to dwell on what we might find when we got there, all I could think about was the last thing I'd said to Vic.

When we arrived, there were already two squad cars, two FBI vehicles and an ambulance on the scene. Baxter put his hand on my shoulder and steered me toward a knot of people congregated near the open doors of the ambulance. My breath hitched as I saw Vic lying still on a gurney with an oxygen mask covering his face and blood smeared all over his forehead. But a wave of relief surged through me when I saw his hand reach up and rip the mask away so he could speak to Agent Griffin.

I broke away from Baxter and hurried to Vic's side. "Are you okay? What happened?" I choked out, tears spilling onto my cheeks.

Vic stared back at me, clearly unimpressed by my show of emotion. He looked even worse up close. There was a gash over his left eye, and he had a fat lip. His left arm was held in place by a splint, and his clothes were wet and muddy and torn. The knuckles on his right hand were angry and red, but that was probably a good thing—it meant he at least got in a shot or two at his attacker.

He grunted, "Don't bother worrying about me," and put his oxygen mask back in place.

Griffin pulled me back so the EMTs could wheel Vic's gurney toward the waiting ambulance.

"Wait!" I cried. "We need to swab his hands for DNA."

Griffin said, "Already done. I've put an FBI team on this assault case."

"Are you sure this was an assault, not..." I took a moment to steady my voice. "Are you sure this isn't an attempted murder case the task force should take because it's related to our investigation?"

Griffin's expression softened, which I wasn't expecting. "Yes, this is related, but not as much as you might think. Although the attacker was wearing a ski mask, Agent Manetti believes it was Michael Hopkins, in retaliation for the incident earlier today."

"Oh." I blew out a sigh. It put my mind more at ease that this didn't seem to have been an attempt on Vic's life. But I couldn't help being disappointed in Mike for lashing out. And in my powers of positive persuasion. Baxter's, too. We thought we had him subdued.

Griffin clapped me on the shoulder. "Don't worry yourself too much, Ms. Matthews. He's a tough old goat. He'll be fine."

Griffin left me to go confer with his fellow FBI agents. I watched as the ambulance drove away.

Baxter appeared beside me. "Nothing we can do here. You want to follow him to the hospital?"

I nodded. "Yeah. Drop me at the station so I can get my car."

"Okay." As we started walking back to his vehicle, he said, "I heard what you said to Griffin about wondering if this was more than a simple assault. The more I think about it, I think I'd like to speak to Manetti and get the whole story straight from the horse's mouth. Mind if I follow you over?"

My heart seized. "You think my assumption has merit?"

"Unfortunately, yes. Especially since Sterling can't find Evan Thompson anywhere."

35

After picking up my car at the station, I drove to the hospital with Baxter right behind me the whole way.

I knocked on the open door of Vic's room in the ER. "Hey," I said quietly.

They'd replaced the splint on his arm with a sling, but they hadn't gotten around to fixing his face yet. His eyes were closed. "Go away."

Baxter said, "I know this isn't the best time, but we'd like to ask you some questions about what happened to you tonight."

Vic opened his eyes so he could give us a disdainful glance. "Oh, you're here too? Of course you are. You know the Bureau is on this, right? They're probably arresting my attacker as we speak. You two need to stay out of it."

I approached his bed. "Point noted, but...we think there's a possibility it wasn't Mike Hopkins who attacked you. Evan Thompson is looking pretty shady right about now, especially since Sterling can't find him. Maybe Thompson saw an opportunity to strike at one of the members of the task force and took it."

Vic closed his eyes again. "That's a stupid theory. Besides, I don't even know this Evan Thompson guy. Why target me?"

I took a deep breath and reminded myself he had to be in a lot of pain.

Plus, he was probably still mad as hell at both of us. "We're only trying to help, here."

"Maybe I don't want your help."

Baxter said, "Just give us a few minutes. You've got the time to spare."

Vic looked up at us and frowned. "Fine. Anything to get you two the hell out of here."

Baxter kept his cool, ignoring the jab. "I'd like you to walk us through this from the beginning. Since you assumed you got jumped by Hopkins, you believe your attacker was a man, correct?"

"Yeah."

"Did you get a good look at what he was wearing?"

"No."

"Griffin mentioned you said he was wearing a ski mask."

"Yeah, so?"

"So you didn't see his face."

"That was probably the point of the ski mask."

"Did he say anything to you?"

"No."

"From struggling with him, would you say he had a similar build as Hopkins?"

"Yes. He was strong. Muscular."

"Good. How about his height? Was he shorter or taller than you?"

Vic snapped, "You think I let a little man jack me up?"

Baxter flicked a frustrated glance at me. "So he was big and tall, then. Wearing a ski mask. That's all you know, yet for some reason you're positive it was Mike Hopkins."

A glare was Vic's only reply.

Finally, I couldn't take it anymore. "You are the worst victim ever. Will you quit being such a baby about getting your ass kicked and answer the man's questions?"

Vic turned his glare on me. "Fine, but I want you out of here." His mouth turning up in a smirk, he added, "Essential personnel only."

I left the ER and headed to the cafeteria to get some decaf coffee, hoping to settle my frayed nerves. I might have been done with Vic, and I was pissed about the way he threw my own words in my face to dismiss me, but the last thing I wanted was to see him hurt.

As much as I believed they were barking up the wrong tree, I was glad the FBI had taken over investigating the assault case. It would be best for the task force to not have to split our focus or our time. However, if it was in fact the killer who'd come after him, it would help if we were at least somewhat involved. Then again, if Baxter and I were wrong and it was Mike—or even Skyler, who had a much bigger beef with Vic than Mike—it wasn't worth wasting task force time and resources.

Baxter found me several minutes later. "That was painful."

I gave him a half-hearted smile. "I'm not at all surprised. Did you get anything else out of him?"

"Not much. His nurse interrupted us to take him to X-ray. But before he left, he mentioned that if for some reason the Mike Hopkins angle doesn't pan out, he's planning to randomly accuse Skyler Marx next."

Saw that one coming. "Great. So if Vic's attacker and the killer are one and the same, the only positive thing that came out of Vic's assault is confirmation that the killer is tall and strong. No new news."

"That's correct."

I groaned. "I hate this case."

"Same. But on a lighter note, the Caldwells were still being detained while Manetti was getting roughed up, so we know it wasn't either of them."

"Which means they're no longer suspects?"

"After questioning them, the sheriff feels like they can go back to being persons of interest. They're not out of the woods yet, but at least they don't have to spend the night in jail."

I let out a sigh of relief. "That's one bit of good news in this mess." I leaned back in my chair and took a long sip of my coffee.

"I take it you're staying here until Manetti gets released?"

"I think I owe him a solid after today."

Baxter smiled. "Take your time. I'll see you tomorrow."

It took a good hour to gather my courage to go back to Vic's room. I knew there was no rush, because it would take him a while to get X-rayed. When I saw him there in his bed, I noticed they'd done more work on his injuries. His face had been cleaned and there was a bandage covering his left eyebrow. I hated to think how vicious and out of nowhere the attack had been if Vic of all people had been unable to better defend himself.

"Will you let me back in to apologize?" I asked from the doorway.

"Knock yourself out." His voice had lost its edge from earlier. He sounded exhausted.

"I'm sorry I called you a baby. I—" I sighed. "It upset me to see you all beat up, and more than anything I want to nail this guy to the wall. What you saw was my frustration over the fact that whoever did this to you also made for damn sure that you had no way of recognizing him."

"Thank you for the apology."

"Can I take you home and get you settled?"

"No."

"Can I get you something to eat or pick up a prescription for you?"

"No."

"Is there anything I can do for you?"

He sighed. "You've done enough to me today."

Before I could reply, Tracy Greer rushed into the room and went straight for Vic. She clearly wasn't mad at him anymore.

She threw her arms around him and breathed, "Vic! Holy shit, are you okay?"

"Tracy, hi. Please don't squeeze," he said, his voice becoming strained.

"Oh, sorry." She let out an uncharacteristic giggle and straightened up. Undeterred, she grabbed his hand that wasn't in the sling. "I was so worried when I heard about what happened. I tried to call you, but you didn't answer. I came straight over as soon as I figured out what hospital you'd been taken to."

He frowned. "How did you hear?"

"I was at the gym just now when two FBI agents barged in and arrested Mike for assaulting you. They dragged him out of there kicking and screaming. I couldn't believe it. More importantly, though, I wanted to make sure you were okay."

He halfway smiled. "I appreciate your concern, but I'm fine."

"Well, you don't look fine. But don't worry. I'm going to take you home and take care of you."

It seemed to me like she'd forgotten all about their conversation yesterday and was trying yet again to ensnare him. I let out an inadvertent snort.

Tracy turned to me, her disdain for me written all over her face. "Why are *you* here?"

Vic said, "She was just leaving." He smirked at me. "I'd rather have Tracy take me home."

Tracy's face lit up.

I saw where this was going. Vic was playing with fire. Using Tracy to get back at me wasn't like him, but then again, he'd been doing a lot of crazy stuff lately. This was going to come back and bite him in the ass. I assumed Tracy had no problem with being used if it got her a free ticket into Vic's house alone with him. However, when the evening didn't turn into the romantic Florence Nightingale scene she'd clearly imagined, there'd be hell to pay. Vic was in for some serious drama. But that was his problem, not mine.

I nodded. "He's right. I was just leaving. You two have a nice night together."

The next morning, I got a call from Baxter as I was pulling out of my driveway at one minute after eight.

"I'm on my way. I'll be a few minutes late," I grumbled, not bothering with pleasantries. I got no sleep, tossing and turning all night worrying about Vic.

He said, "I take it no one called you, either."

"Called me about what?"

"Another death."

I groaned. "Anyone we know?"

He hesitated. "Yes."

My stomach clenched. "Don't keep me in suspense."

"Mike Hopkins."

My breath caught in my throat. "What?" I croaked. "What happened?"

"We're not entirely sure. Get over to Rip Barbell Club and help me figure it out."

36

I drove to the gym trying to hold it together. I didn't want to see Mike dead. Through all the nonsense of the investigation and even thinking for a time that he could be the killer, I didn't dislike him as a person. His personality, even with its quirks, had grown on me. I was honestly sad that he was gone.

By the time I got there, the gym's parking lot was already packed with law enforcement vehicles. I weaved my way through them, clamping my hood down over my head to guard against the biting wind.

Jayne came out of the building and stopped me before I could enter. "I need to speak to you, Ellie."

"Can we do it inside?" I asked. "I'm freezing."

"No, this can't wait." She frowned. "I'm not removing you from the task force, but—"

"I already don't like where this is going."

"Look, I hadn't intended for you to be out here this morning, but Detective Baxter informed me that you were already on your way. I can't let you process this scene and have your name all over it. You're too close for a number of reasons. I'll let you have a look so you and Detective Baxter can stay in the loop of this investigation, but other than that you have to stay away. Amanda and Beck have already started working inside, and Chief

Esparza and Detective Sterling will run point on this one." She added under her breath, "Unless the Feds come and yank it out from under us."

"Okay."

Her eyebrows shot up. "Okay? You usually fight me on things like this."

I shrugged. "I think you're right. I admit I'm a little shook up over Mike's death. I'd prefer to sit this one out."

"I'm not worried about your dealings with the victim. I'm pulling you because of Agent Manetti's possible link. Michael Hopkins' death could be an accident. But if we determine it to be...*not* an accident, we're questioning Manetti first."

My jaw dropped. "What?"

"I'm sorry to be the bearer of bad news."

I thought for a moment. "Wait. When did Mike die?"

"Between midnight and two this morning."

"Then what you're saying doesn't even make sense. If Mike's time of death was between twelve and two, Vic had nothing to do with it. He was out of commission way before then."

Her brow furrowed. "Not completely out of commission, from what I hear."

I had to fight to keep from rolling my eyes. "The man only has one working arm."

"Do you know where he was between midnight and two?"

"No, but I'm sure he wasn't here snuffing out Mike Hopkins."

"I'd like to believe that, but after what Manetti did to him yesterday..." She shook her head. "I'll let you see for yourself how damning this situation looks for your boyfriend."

"So you know, we called it quits yesterday."

She eyed me. "Did you break up or did he?"

"I did."

"And do you feel like he was acting particularly angry afterward?"

I frowned. "Don't do that."

As I stepped around her and opened the front door of the gym, she called, "Don't even think about tipping him off, Ellie."

When I entered the gym, I had to take a moment to steady myself. At least I'd missed the coroner collecting Mike's body, which I was thankful for. Once I was mentally ready to approach the scene, I headed toward where Baxter was conferring with Sterling.

Sterling saw me first. "Nice of you to finally show up, Matthews."

I was so not in the mood for him this morning. My tone came out even sharper than I intended when I barked, "Don't talk to me. I haven't had coffee yet." I turned to Baxter and struggled to bring my emotions down a notch. "What the hell's going on? I heard Mike got arrested last night, and now he's..." I cleared my throat, a sudden lump making it impossible to finish my sentence.

Baxter's worried eyes fell on me as he replied, "He wasn't arrested, only hauled in for questioning. He was here with quite a few witnesses during the time Manetti was assaulted, so he got off the hook pretty quickly."

While he spoke, I watched Amanda tape-lift fingerprints from a nearby weight bench. A barbell fitted with easily over three hundred pounds of weight sat near the bench with an evidence marker next to it. There were a couple more evidence markers on the floor, which I assumed went with some already collected evidence contained in a couple of tagged and sealed paper bags in a bin off to the side. There was no blood anywhere that I could see.

Baxter had continued talking, but there was no way I could give my full attention to anything besides wondering about what had happened to poor Mike. Baxter said something about the gym closing at midnight and Mike being in here after hours, but that was all I gleaned.

I snapped out of it when I heard, "What's your take on whether or not the alcohol was a factor, Ellie?"

"Alcohol?" I asked.

Sterling snorted. "Keep up, Matthews."

Baxter was kinder. "It's okay. I know this scene has you off your game. We can't tell just from looking at the scene if Hopkins' death was an accident or not. There's a half-empty beer bottle on the desk in the office, so that's a consideration."

I closed my eyes. "I feel like you're dancing around the bad news. Tell me how he died."

He hesitated for a moment and then said quietly, "Based on the way he was found...it looks like got trapped with a barbell across his throat and asphyxiated."

I felt like the bottom dropped out of me.

Sterling was rude enough to voice my deepest fears. "Ring any bells? Like exactly what Manetti did to him yesterday? We all know the G-man's a hothead, but this is a little excessive."

Baxter griped at him, "Shut up, man."

I tried not to focus on Sterling's comment. "What else do we know?"

Baxter said, "The worker who came in and found Hopkins this morning said James Lorenz and one of their new trainers closed down the place last night. Chief's on his way to see each of them to break the news about Hopkins and find out what he can."

Shaking my head, I said, "I find it fishy that Mike was lifting yesterday at all. He was in enough pain that it would have been impossible for him to bench that kind of weight."

Sterling replied, "Not if he juiced up beforehand, which is a real possibility. Becky pawed through the trash in the office and found a couple of syringes. Even injured, if Hopkins dosed before his workout, he probably thought he was Superman and could bench anything."

Amanda came over to where we were standing. "Hey, stranger."

I tried to smile but couldn't. "Hi. I'm bummed you got pulled off the task force to do your real job, but I guess this means you're back."

"Sort of. It's not the same, though."

She rolled her eyes and head-nodded toward Beck, who was heading this way from the direction of the gym's office. He stopped before he got to us and retrieved some red evidence tape and several paper bags from his open kit on the floor.

I said, "Well, I guess he's good for something. Sterling said Beck took trash duty."

Smiling, she said, "We flipped for it." She winked at Sterling and lowered her voice to a whisper. "I think someone rigged the coin toss in my favor."

He shrugged. "I know you prefer decomp over trash. Besides, Becky gets his panties in a bunch when he has to do something he doesn't want to do. No-brainer."

She wiggled her eyebrows at him. "And you like it when I owe you one."

I didn't especially want to stand around and watch the two of them flirting, so I said, "I'm going to have a look at the office."

Beck was already back in the office working when I arrived at the door. He frowned at me. "I thought you were off this case because your boyfriend did the dirty deed."

"The jury's still out on that one. And he's not my boyfriend."

I stepped into the room and swept my gaze from one side to the other. I got a stabbing pain in my heart when my eyes landed on the couch. It hadn't even been twenty-four hours since I'd been sitting there commiserating with Mike about Vic's visit. I wiped a hand down my face and gathered all the strength I could to push my emotions down and lock them away. I was going to be useless unless I got hold of myself.

I focused my attention on what I remembered about the room from yesterday. Nothing much was different in here, aside from the mess strewn all over a tarp Beck had put on the floor to examine the trashcan's contents, which included something that looked and smelled like rotten tuna salad, two empty beer bottles, two empty Gatorade bottles, and two syringes. The half-empty beer bottle Baxter had mentioned was still on the desk.

"Make sure you take those beer bottles into evidence, Beck," I said. "They should all be fingerprinted."

He griped, "I know what I'm doing."

I left the office and found Baxter speaking with Jayne near the bench where Amanda was still working.

I approached them, half-expecting Jayne to throw me out immediately.

And it happened. She said, "Okay, you two. Back to task force duty. We've got this covered."

Baxter managed to keep his face passive. After all, Jayne was his boss. "Yes, Sheriff."

To me, she said, "Did you see everything you needed to see?"

And more. "Sure did."

Baxter and I left the gym. The minute we got outside, he murmured to me, "You know something. Spill it."

"Skyler Marx was here last night."

His eyebrows shot up. "What tipped you off to that?"

"Remember yesterday when I was at Skyler's place? Skyler was drinking Natural Ice beer, and Mike was telling him how disgusting it was."

"I vaguely remember. So?"

"So, the beer bottles in the office, which you all assumed were Mike's, are all Natural Ice. I don't believe he'd blow his new sobriety on a drink he couldn't stomach. I'm not saying he wasn't high on something else, like painkillers and steroids, but I am saying that Skyler was there last night, and he was drinking. And I'm betting it went on after closing, because I'm not seeing James Lorenz putting up with drunk lifting in his gym, nor am I seeing him leaving without cleaning off the desk in the office and emptying the stinky trash."

He nodded. "Nice catch. It sounds like you're leaning toward thinking it was an accident. That those idiots were under some sort of influence and messing around with weights that were too heavy for them, and things got out of control. If that's true, then Marx may have bailed on his bro when the going got tough. Him being at the scene during the time of death window and not calling for help is enough for Sterling to try to slap some charges on him."

"That's why I didn't say anything. I know Sterling would run in guns blazing and take Skyler down, which would make Skyler lawyer up. We'll never find out what really happened unless we get to him first. You're the one cop he'll talk to."

"But we're not on this case."

"Technically no, but considering the timing, I don't think it's possible for Mike's death to be its own unrelated incident." I studied his face for a moment. "And I think you think the same thing."

Shrugging, he said, "I agree it's a little too convenient for this to have been an accident, especially one that so closely mirrors what a ton of people saw Manetti do to Mike Hopkins yesterday."

I frowned. "Exactly. And that's a real problem."

His brow furrowed. "Just so we're on the same page—you're not thinking Manetti had something to do with it, are you?"

"Of course not. You and I both know he wouldn't kill Mike."

"Right. He would only assault him."

I sighed. "He screwed up...there's no getting around that. But I don't believe he deserves the shitstorm I'm afraid is headed his way. I can't sit by and watch his career—and his life—implode. As angry as I am about how stupid he's been through all of this, I have to do something to try to keep him out of trouble. Will you help me help him?" I pleaded.

"We're kind of on a time frame, here, with two murders to investigate."

"I firmly believe this is all connected, and finding out what happened here last night is going to ultimately help our investigation. If switching gears to help Vic starts getting in the way, I promise I'll back off."

He hesitated for so long I thought he was going to say no. "Okay, fine."

37

We pulled up to Skyler's apartment and headed for the door. While Baxter knocked, I peeked into the window through a missing slat in the blinds. There was no movement inside, not that I expected any at this early hour. If Skyler had been out drinking after midnight, I doubted he was awake yet.

"You see anything in there?" Baxter asked, continuing to pound on the door.

"No." It took some real restraint for me not to bust the window and go throttle Skyler until he gave me the answers I wanted.

Baxter took out his phone and made a call. After waiting for a moment, he hung up. "He's not answering. Went straight to voicemail." Turning to survey the parking lot, he added, "I don't see his vehicle. He could be sleeping off a bender somewhere else. Maybe he got a booty call last night and left the gym before Hopkins died."

"That's plausible." I frowned. "And I guess I hope it's the case. Either that, or I hope Mike was murdered."

Baxter gave me a questioning look. "That's kind of morbid."

I snapped, "Not as morbid as it's going to get if I find out Skyler was there and did nothing to help Mike, and didn't even call nine-one-one. I'll kill him."

"Simmer down, tiger. There have been enough murders this week."

Giving me an apologetic smile, he added, "You know we have to tell Sterling about your theory on Skyler's involvement now, right?"

"I know."

He said, "I guess we could spare a little time to sit on this place and see if he comes back, unless you want to get to the station."

As we started walking back toward his vehicle, I replied, "Stakeout versus tip line duty? I feel like you should know my preference by now."

"I do, but it's going to be chilly, and I know you don't like the cold."

I smiled. He did know me. I wished the remedy for a frigid stakeout would be that we huddled together for warmth, but after our conversation last night, broadening our relationship was on a near-permanent hold. I'd tried to put our almost-kiss out of my mind, but it kept creeping back.

Being cooped up in a small space inches away from him was not a good choice. As we sat there keeping an eye on Skyler's front door, Baxter made small talk about the weather forecast for the week while I focused all my energy on squelching any thoughts that weren't about the case and trying not to worry about Vic being blamed for Mike's death. When it became apparent that I was unable to add anything to the conversation, it got oppressively quiet.

"So, did you take Manetti home last night?" he blurted out suddenly.

That loaded question got my attention, totally derailing my attempt at professionalism. "Ugh. No. Tracy Greer showed up and Manetti decided to be a dick—excuse me, *more* of a dick—and told me to get lost so she could take him home."

"Why?"

"I suppose in some weird way he was trying to make me jealous."

Baxter asked uneasily, "Did it work?"

"Of course not. Besides, she's no competition."

He let out a bark of laughter. "Humble much?"

"Oh, come on. We're all well aware of where we fit into the global pecking order." I put my hand low, near my lap. Tracy is here." I raised my hand about twelve inches. "I'm here." I raised it another twelve inches. "And Eve is here."

Baxter shook his head. "I disagree."

"According to Skyler, I'm a borderline grenade."

"Skyler is a—" He stopped and glanced at his phone. "Let's change the subject to something more positive. They've got Evan Thompson."

We abandoned our stakeout and sped to the station. Once there, we headed straight for the interrogation room where Evan Thompson was being held. Agent Griffin and Sterling were already in there questioning him, so we went next door to the observation room to watch their interaction. Jayne greeted us with a head nod when we walked in, but didn't take her attention off the two-way glass.

Thompson was fidgety and jumpy, eyeing the two men across the table from him as if they were snakes ready to strike.

Griffin said, "You left out some key details about your relationship with the victim, Mr. Thompson. We know you were let go from your coaching job for having an inappropriate relationship with Angela Meadows when she was in high school. We also know you've kept in contact with her since then, especially in the past week or so. Did you think we hadn't done our homework and you could snow us?"

Thompson was nearly in tears. "No. I'm not trying to snow you."

"Then why omit the fact that you had plans to meet her twice in the last five days?"

He put his head in his hands. "I didn't want my girlfriend to find out."

Sterling said, "Because you were cheating on her with Angela?"

Thompson snapped his head up. Eyes bulging, he cried, "No! We never... It's not like that—I swear!"

"What's it like, then?"

Thompson paused, I assumed to either come up with a good lie or to figure out how to frame the ugly truth. His overgrown mustache twitched as he finally said, "I was... Angela called me and said she had some races coming up and knew her competition was gaining on her. When I was her coach...I had a hookup to get some..." He let out a sigh. "Performance enhancers. Ones that...aren't on the market in the U.S., if you know what I mean. She would take them every once in a while to get ahead."

Sterling nodded. "Ah. You were her dealer, not her lover. But you let people believe you were a pervert rather than ruin your business. In my mind, this makes you an even better murder suspect."

Thompson let out a whimper. "What?"

He pressed, "So does this mean your motive for killing Angela Meadows was about drug money instead of relationship issues? What about Shawna Meehan? Were you her supplier as well? Did she not pay up or something and you had to end her, too?"

Classic Sterling, going for the throat early in an interrogation. I noticed Griffin's shoulders stiffen and Jayne's jaw clench. Baxter wiped a hand down his face. No one seemed to like his tactic, but it worked, sort of.

Thompson's jaw hit the floor. "I didn't kill Angela!" he choked out, his face draining of all color except green. "Or Shawna! I didn't kill *anyone!*" He broke down and began blubbering incoherently between body-racking sobs.

Griffin wordlessly turned his head toward Sterling. His profile exuded contempt.

Sterling shrugged, unfazed by Griffin's ire.

Over Thompson's crying, Griffin said, "Mr. Thompson, pull yourself together. This is a time-sensitive issue. We need to better understand the nature of your relationship with both victims, and we need to know where you were between six-thirty and seven P.M. on February—"

Thompson suddenly leaned over and vomited on the floor, causing both Sterling and Griffin to jump out of their chairs to avoid the splatter.

Jayne shook her head, grumbling, "And that's why I shouldn't have allowed two alphas to run an interrogation with a clearly nervous suspect." To Baxter, she said, "We'll have Mr. Thompson transferred to a different room and let you take over for a while, Detective. Ellie, I need you to run his prints."

Baxter and I went our respective ways. Happy to have something to concentrate on besides my thoughts, I spent forty-five minutes alone in the lab office plotting Evan Thompson's fingerprints and running them through the AFIS computer. There was nothing tied to his prints, including the two assault charges on his record from years ago. Either the Podunk police department in rural northern Indiana hadn't felt the need to fingerprint him at the time of his arrest, or they hadn't bothered to file the prints properly.

I headed to the conference room and dropped off my report to a still pissed off looking Agent Griffin. I didn't stick around to chat. I wandered down the hall and found Baxter sitting at his desk.

"That was quick," I said, not expecting him to be done with questioning Thompson so soon.

He spun in his chair to face me. "There wasn't much to discuss."

I gave him a puzzled look. "The man is a murder suspect."

"*Was* a murder suspect."

"Seriously? I can't take much more of this," I complained, collapsing into the chair by his desk.

"I take it his prints were clean."

"They were. He didn't even pop up on the possible top twenty matches of any cases in AFIS."

Baxter nodded. "I figured as much."

I wasn't ready to give up a perfectly good suspect. "Maybe he's very careful to always wear gloves while committing crimes."

"I hate to burst your bubble, but his alibis check out for both murders and for Manetti's assault. During the Shawna Meehan murder, he was coaching his girlfriend's kid's basketball team with dozens of people watching. During Angela Meadows' murder, he was at a Narcotics Anonymous meeting. The group leader, no less. Last night he left work and went straight to his girlfriend's house for the night. His girlfriend, his phone, and his vehicle's GPS confirmed."

I frowned. "Sounds like a real stand-up guy, except what about him stalking Shawna? That's a pretty big deal, and there's no way it's a coincidence."

"Maybe it is. According to Thompson, he quit the drug scene years ago. When Angela contacted him about getting some drugs, he said he freaked out. He didn't tell his girlfriend for fear that she'd think he was back in the game. He met with Angela to try to talk some sense into her, but she wouldn't listen. So he went to Shawna for help, who wouldn't ever engage him in conversation long enough for him to tell her why he wanted to talk to her."

"It makes a great story, but I'm still not convinced. Don't forget he has priors for assault."

"That was ten years ago, and both were just bar fights."

I rolled my eyes. "*Just* bar fights. Why do men never think bar fights count?"

Baxter grinned at me. "I feel like there's no right answer to that question. In this case, Thompson said the second time he was all coked up on some kind of homebrewed 'roid cocktail and beat the shit out of one of his friends. Supposedly it was his wake-up call, and after that he left his bad behavior in the past."

"*Supposedly.* Did no one here think to drug test him when they hauled him in? He was super jumpy earlier. Twitchy, even."

"Wouldn't you be if you were cooped up in a tiny room with Sterling and Griffin?"

I frowned at him. "Whose side are you on?"

"The side with the facts."

"Fine. Are you *sure* you feel like he's telling the truth?"

He gave me a mock wounded look. "I thought you always trusted my gut."

"I do…"

"But?"

"But there are so many red flags. Was there *nothing* that seemed fishy to you about him?"

Chuckling, he replied, "Only his pornstache."

I let out a bark of laughter. "That thing was definitely fishy."

Baxter's face turned a shade paler. "Especially since it had a couple of chunks of vomit still clinging to it during our interview."

"Sick."

"And yet I couldn't look away."

I sighed. "So Pornstache is out of the running."

"I'm afraid so. His alibis are solid, his financials are clean, and there are no texts on his phone that would lead us to believe he's doing anything shady. We're still checking emails and social media, but I say he's not our guy."

I trusted Baxter's gut, plus the facts were pretty overwhelming. "Boo. He was such a perfect suspect otherwise."

"I know. I guess this means you're on the case for a while longer."

Even though it meant a lot more work and late hours, and even though

I'd had a rough morning that was likely to turn into a horrible day, I could feel my lips pulling into a smile at the thought. "I guess I am."

I needed to not neglect my actual job, but at least we were coming up on a weekend. If we were lucky, we'd have this wrapped up soon and I could go back to work as usual on Monday. More importantly, though, we needed to find the killer before anyone else got hurt. With that in mind, I prepared myself for a lot of crazy and dove into the list of tip line calls.

I hadn't been at it long when Baxter appeared next to me. "I've got some news you're not going to like."

Looking up from my screen, I muttered, "Story of my life."

"Manetti has been brought in for formal questioning."

Deep down I knew it was inevitable, but hearing the words out loud was a jolt to my system. I felt all my nerves frazzle as I struggled to keep my voice steady. "Okay."

"Griffin's in a meeting with the FBI brass, so they're icing Manetti for a while. I thought we could go talk to him. If you want."

I nodded and stood, then followed him down the hall.

We found Vic in one of the interrogation rooms, pacing. I stared at him for a moment through the tiny window before going inside. His poor face was even more bruised than it had been last night; his left eye now nearly swelled shut. He was unshaven, which never happened. His salt and pepper stubble advertised his age too much for his liking. His left arm hung in a sling, although I imagined his pride hurt more than his dislocated shoulder. With all that plus the uncharacteristic slump to his broad shoulders, he was a shadow of his normal self.

I opened the door. "Vic?"

When he turned around, the expression on his face told me his anger toward me hadn't dissipated even a little. "I'm already having a shitty day. Can we not do this?"

I entered the room anyway, with Baxter right behind me. "We're not here to upset you. We want to go over a few things. I know we're not assigned to your assault case or to your...other case. But we could use your help."

He stared at us for a so long, the tension in the room began to get unbearable. "Fine. Let's get this over with."

I blew out a breath. "Do you have an alibi for last night between midnight and two?"

"I was asleep."

"Alone?"

"Does it make a difference to you?" he snapped.

I impressed myself by not letting his remark ruffle me. "No, but it makes a difference to your alibi."

"Tracy left around eleven-thirty." He hesitated, then said under his breath, "I had to insist."

I bit my lip to keep from cracking a smile. I would have loved to lay down a big "I told you so," but now was not the time. "Are you planning to have a lawyer present?"

"Do you *want* me to look guilty?"

Baxter changed the subject, but not to an any less difficult one. "If you hadn't heard, Evan Thompson is no longer a suspect. Everything about him checks out."

Vic's jaw clenched. Losing our most promising suspect only meant more heat on him. Unable to stand still any longer, he went back to pacing.

Baxter added, "Also, the Caldwells are back to 'persons of interest' status."

Vic said, "So you've got nothing."

Glancing at me, Baxter replied, "We have a lead on some possible information."

His voice dripping with even more sarcasm, Vic said, "So, to recap, you've got nothing."

I said, "Not necessarily. We've got someone who had an up-close-and-personal confrontation with the killer."

"Who?"

"You."

Vic rolled his eyes.

I held up my hands. "Hear me out. I think it makes more sense that the killer came after you than anyone else."

Frowning, he said, "Are we back to this again? If you're so sure it was the killer who attacked me, then why didn't he kill me when he had the chance?"

"Because discrediting you by trying to implicate you in Mike Hopkins' death would inflict so much more mayhem on our investigation. Killing you would only serve to make him a cop killer and you a martyr."

"And no one would want that," Baxter added under his breath.

Vic either didn't hear him or chose to ignore him. "I was interviewed on the five o'clock news last night. Maybe someone I'd made an enemy of years ago happened to see it and decided to come after me. I don't think I'd be here right now if it was the killer."

I said, "I find it hard to believe some random enemy from back in the day decided to exact his revenge on you on that particular day at that particular moment. It's too much of a coincidence."

Vic still wasn't convinced. "It was risky to attack me out in the open. That's not our killer's signature."

Baxter shook his head. "His signature is about spectacle and perhaps even punishment. Kicking your ass checked both those boxes."

As Vic stared daggers at Baxter, I griped, "Guys, you're proving my point that this whole situation is having exactly his intended effect. This was a carefully crafted attack by someone intent on causing chaos."

Vic decided to turn his anger on me. "Need I remind you that you're neither a profiler nor a detective, Ellie? You're wasting my time."

I gestured around the room. "Time? You're being held for questioning as a homicide suspect by your own team. You've got nothing *but* time. You might as well spend it letting us help you instead of sulking like a child."

He only growled at me in response.

Baxter stepped in. "You know, Manetti, Ellie is the only person in this county who believes a hundred percent in your innocence. There was never a question in her mind that you could be guilty. You sure as hell can't say that about your own colleagues."

Vic's face became stony, as it always did when he was masking his feelings for the sake of his job. I could tell it was killing him to hear this, but he needed it. After a few moments he sat down wearily and said, "Fine. Let's explore the theory that the killer planned to frame me for Michael Hopkins' death."

Baxter and I both took seats across from him at the table.

He continued, "Our killer isn't some all-knowing entity. It wasn't public knowledge that I went to Rip Barbell Club and had a chat with Hopkins yesterday. If I were working the case, the first thing I'd do is find out who witnessed our altercation."

Finally he was using his brilliant mind for good. I said, "Well, you were there. Did you see anyone you knew who already has a connection to this mess?"

Casting his eyes down, he admitted, "I was in full rage mode. I honestly wasn't paying attention."

Baxter got out his phone. "I'll have one of the deputies work on getting a list of the gym's check-ins during that timeframe."

I said, "We might want to look at the whole day. Due to his injuries, including the ones from the bar fight the night before, Mike wasn't himself. Anyone who knew him would have noticed. If they'd taken the time to ask him if he was okay, it's a decent possibility he blurted out the whole story. Having a big tale to tell would have got him all kinds of attention, which we know he craved."

Vic grimaced. "It's going to take time to comb through all those people."

I thought about how this would be infinitely easier if we could just talk to Skyler Marx, and a lightbulb went off. I didn't know why I didn't think of asking Vic. "Where do you think Skyler Marx would be right now?"

He only stared at me in reply.

I explained, "We need to talk to him, and we can't find him."

"What's it to me?"

"It could mean an alibi for you. We think he was at the gym with Mike last night."

Vic snorted. "Like he'd alibi me."

Baxter said, "You never know 'til you ask."

Vic's face grew dark. "I'm not asking him for shit."

I said, "Well, I will. Do you know where we might find him?"

"Why would I know that?"

I shook my head. "Oh, come on. Don't try to tell me you didn't tail him until you knew his daily routine by heart back when he was making trouble for Shawna."

He shrugged. "I didn't."

"Liar. You surveilled him, waiting for him to screw up so you could arrest him. What's his morning schedule?"

Glaring at me, he finally relented. "You might find him at the music store on the square in the mornings. He's one of those tryhards who pretends to test drive a new guitar but is actually getting his jollies by showing off his skills."

Baxter made a face. "Does he play 'Stairway to Heaven'?"

"It's about that bad. If he's not there, he might be at the bar a couple blocks south of there. They're open twenty-four hours and serve a decent breakfast."

I struggled to keep a straight face as I said, "So you really have stalked him, then."

As Vic was muttering something under his breath, the door opened. "Why are you two in here?" Agent Griffin demanded, his tone sharp. "I know you're both well aware you're off the Michael Hopkins case."

Baxter replied, "We know. We're trying to come at finding the killer from another—"

Griffin ignored him and lasered his gaze on me. "I don't give a shit what you're doing. This conversation—and your relationship with Agent Manetti —ends now."

Vic grumbled, "She's already seen to that."

Griffin went on, "Let me be clear, Ms. Matthews and Detective Baxter— neither of you are to have any contact with Agent Manetti until we get this cluster sorted out. Your jobs depend on it."

I frowned. "Why does it matter if we're not on the case he's being held for?"

His jaw clenched. "It matters because my boss, your boss, and the media are all breathing down my neck about how we're handling Agent Manetti as a possible suspect. I'm not letting anyone, especially you, muddy the waters more than they already are. Get out. Now."

38

"Griffin was kind of harsh in there," I complained once the door to the interrogation room was safely shut.

"Are you surprised, though?" Baxter asked. "He's in a tough spot. He allowed Manetti to be part of the task force knowing the guy was too close from the start. I wouldn't want to be him right now. His ass is on the line as much as Manetti's."

"Except the threat of becoming a convicted murderer and going prison, of course."

He chuckled. "Okay, I'll admit Manetti's got it worse."

"Which means we need those names ASAP, and we need to look for Skyler downtown."

"The list is in the works, and I'll send a deputy to round up Skyler. While we're waiting, I think we should take a break and grab an early lunch. Today has been plenty angsty, and it's not even noon."

I trained my gaze straight ahead as we walked down the hall. Angsty was an understatement. My thoughts had drifted to alcohol more times than I'd have liked, and I'd done my best to try to pretend even to myself that it hadn't happened. If I was going to be at my best, I needed a meeting a lot more than I needed lunch.

"I'll have to take a raincheck."

"Meeting?"

I nodded.

"Want company?"

I shook my head. It was all well and good for Baxter to have gone with me the one time, but I didn't want it to become a common occurrence. I leaned on him for so many things; I didn't want my sobriety to be one of them. I hoped he didn't take my response the wrong way. He gave me a quiet "Okay," and headed for his desk.

There wasn't a meeting close by for another thirty minutes, so I had time to kill. After talking with Vic, I needed a breather. I grabbed a cup of coffee and wandered to the lab, hoping it would still be empty and quiet. It wasn't.

Beck looked up from the evidence bag he was opening to greet me with a sneer. "You can't be in here."

Amanda, who was standing behind him, rolled her eyes. "She can be in here. She just can't handle any evidence from the Hopkins case."

Evidently feeling the need to assert his authority, he said, "Don't even look at it, Ellie. Steer clear of my evidence."

She shook her head. "Don't listen to him. You can look all you want. We have a lot to process, and I'm not sure where to start. I could use another set of eyes."

His voice cracked as he cried, "*I'm* your other set of eyes!"

We both ignored Beck's pouting as Amanda walked me over to two transport bins full of evidence bags.

She said, "We have a couple dozen fingerprints I lifted from the barbell, AKA the possible murder weapon. We have a few items from the area where the victim was found. We also have the garbage from the office and a bunch of fingerprints from random places. I was going to start with the fingerprints on the possible murder weapon unless you have any other ideas."

I said, "The beer bottle found on the desk would be my number one. It's less likely to have been smudged than the ones in the trash can."

She turned to Beck with a smile, which surprised me until I registered that it was fake. "Beck, would you get the bar and the weights out of evidence and do the second pass on them? Those weights are way too heavy for me to carry. "

Beck puffed out his tiny chest. "Sure, I can handle it. No sweat."

Once he'd strutted out the door, she said, "That should keep him busy for a bit. I finally figured something out about him. Even though he's 'the boss,' I can run the show if I stroke his ego every once in a while. When I can stomach it, of course." She laughed.

I chuckled. "Impressive. I don't know if I'd ever be able to stomach stroking anything of Beck's."

"Eww, I didn't need that visual." Amanda began rooting through the bins of evidence. "Jason said you had a hunch that Skyler Marx had been at the scene last night solely based on the brand of beer we found."

I shrugged. "Not a lot of people drink Natty Ice, right?"

"Fair enough. He must have thought your hunch had merit, because he arranged for a deputy to watch Marx's apartment and put a BOLO out for him and his vehicle. No luck so far."

It surprised me that Sterling had taken my idea and run with it. As strangely as this case was playing out, instead of being annoyed, I was beginning to worry that they hadn't found Skyler yet. I also had a feeling Skyler wasn't going to be simply hanging out in a music store or a local bar after what went on at the gym last night. Something didn't feel right.

She went on, "We know the garbage in the office arrived there after closing, so it's all decent evidence. Jason said the trainer who helped close the place emptied all the trash cans prior to locking up." She plucked a grocery-sized paper bag from one of the boxes. "This is the bottle in question."

After cutting through the red evidence tape sealing the bag, she carefully removed a cardboard box from inside. From that box, she lifted out a Natural Ice brand beer bottle fitted with a makeshift lid. It still had liquid inside.

"Nice transport. No spillage," I said.

She replied, "I was a little concerned. We didn't have a proper container to transfer the beer to at the scene, so we did the best we could. I swabbed the rim of the bottle for DNA before capping it up."

I watched as she set the bottle down on her worktable and took several photos. She removed the lid and took more photos, then went to the storage cabinet and retrieved a glass jar. "Now to get the beer out so I can process this thing."

She carefully began pouring the beer from the bottle to the evidence container. We both gasped when the last bit of liquid dribbled out, thick with a white residue.

"Who crushes up drugs in his own beer?" I asked, my voice trembling.

"No one," she breathed.

I said, "We need to check the Gatorade bottles, too. For my money, those were Mike's drinks."

Amanda put the beer bottle down and grabbed two other bags from the bin. She went to a different table and began opening the bags and removing the Gatorade bottles.

While she worked, I called Baxter. Without even bothering with pleasantries, I said, "Grab Sterling and come to the lab," and then hung up.

Holding the bottles up to a bright light and sloshing around the bit of liquid left in each bottle, Amanda said, "I'm not seeing any of the same residue here. Just plain Gatorade. We can send it to the state lab to be sure, but for now, I think the beer bottle is the one to focus on."

I nodded. "I agree."

She hurried over to a cabinet to gather fingerprint powder, brushes, and tape lifts. She changed her gloves and began examining the Natural Ice bottle under the bench magnifier. Snapping a few quick photos under the bright light, she then brushed black fingerprint dust over a section of glass and pressed a fingerprint lift onto it. After carefully peeling it off and securing the tape to its backing, she raced into the office to plot the fingerprint and run it through AFIS.

Baxter and Sterling entered the lab, and I beckoned them to come to the office so we could talk while Amanda worked.

I said, "There's a white residue in the bottom of the beer bottle from the desk in the gym. We believe someone got drugged last night."

Sterling cursed under his breath.

Baxter wiped a hand down his face. "That sounds like good old premeditation."

Amanda was concentrating on the computer screen, but managed to murmur, "I've got a near-perfect print. Give me two minutes and I'll know whose it is."

I asked the detectives, "Anyone find Skyler?"

Shaking his head, Sterling replied, "He was supposed to show up at work at eleven, but hasn't yet. According to his manager, he's well aware that one more screw-up and he's fired. We've also been trying to locate his phone. It hasn't pinged a cell tower since last night around midnight near the gym."

My uneasy feeling grew. "Skyler is late to work even under the threat of being fired. We don't think he went home last night. And he hasn't used his phone in nearly twelve hours, nor have any of his apps updated or anything. Considering the circumstances, he's either on the run or dead in a ditch somewhere."

Baxter said, "It's equally possible his phone is dead and he's still sleeping off whatever he drank last night."

"What does your gut say?"

Amanda turned her computer screen to face us. "Forget your gut. This print says Skyler Marx had his hands on that beer bottle last night. He either dosed it or drank it. I'm going to tape lift all the prints from the bottle and find out if there are any others besides Marx's." She left the office.

Sterling mused, "If Marx dosed it and Hopkins drank it, that could account for his death being an accident of sorts. We could still nail Marx's ass to the wall for manslaughter."

I said, "I'm sticking with my original idea that Mike wouldn't touch Natty Ice, even if he was still drinking. I say Skyler drank it. But then who dosed it? Not Mike."

"Why not?"

Baxter said, "Because he worships the ground Marx walks on. She's right. There was someone else there with them last night. And now I'm kind of worried about Marx's safety. If he was drugged, he had probably fifteen to thirty minutes before he was out of commission. Even if he'd gotten into his vehicle immediately, that leaves us with a fairly small radius of where he could have ended up. He couldn't have got past the county line."

Sterling said, "Aside from a couple of fender benders, there were no accidents reported last night in Hamilton County, either. Unless he drove his car into the White River or one of the reservoirs unnoticed, we'd know about it."

My jaw dropped. "Are you saying we have a missing persons situation here? That someone took Skyler and his vehicle?"

Baxter nodded his head slowly. "It's a very real possibility."

"Damn, this case just got a lot more interesting," Sterling said, chuckling.

"And horrifying," I snapped. "Who knew these two were going to be there alone after hours and knew that Mike had got accosted by Manetti earlier in the day? What about the guys who closed down the gym? What did they have to say?"

Sterling replied, "James Lorenz, the manager, and Sam Berry, the new trainer, both told the chief independently that Hopkins and Marx were the only people in the gym when they locked up a few minutes after midnight. They said those two hang out in there after hours all the time."

"Well there you go. I'm sure they heard all about how Mike's day went. One of them could have camped out in the parking lot long enough for the other one to leave and then headed back inside. What about them—did the chief say if either of them acted squirrely?"

"He said Lorenz was crying like a little girl, which sounds pretty normal based on my experience with him. His report didn't note any behavioral red flags for Berry."

"So what's your next move?"

He frowned. "I don't have to run it by you."

I snorted. "Spoken like a man who doesn't know what his next move is."

Baxter cut in, "I'll run with the list of gym check-ins as soon as we get it. It may point us to someone who has a beef with Manetti and wants him under suspicion for Hopkins' death."

Sterling stared at him. "How are you going to pare down that list? Everybody who knows Manetti hates Manetti. He's a dick."

Baxter changed the subject again. "Is there no task force meeting today?"

"No time. Griffin doesn't know if he's coming or going." Sterling chuckled. "Dude is not having a good day. The FBI is all over his ass. It fell to him to round Manetti up, formally dismiss him from the task force, and put him on suspension from the Bureau. He had to take Manetti's badge and gun right before he started questioning him. Talk about awkward. Oh, and in case you didn't hear, Griffin has the clout to slap the same punishment on the rest of us if we even talk to the guy. It almost makes me feel bad for Manetti."

I looked at the clock in the office. My meeting was scheduled to start in ten minutes. "As much as I'm enjoying this conversation, I've got stuff to do." Without any more explanation, I marched out of the lab and headed for my car.

After sitting through my meeting and even finding the strength to participate, I felt better. But as I walked out into the parking lot and noticed a familiar vehicle, I knew my improved mood wouldn't last. I tried to keep my face passive as Vic got out of his car and headed my way.

"What are you doing here?" I asked, at a loss as to why he would have sought me out.

"I need to talk to you."

"Wait. I guess what I'm more interested in is why you're not in custody. I mean, I'm glad you're not, but—"

"They have nothing to hold me."

"That's good. So how did you know where to find me?" No way Baxter would have facilitated a meetup between us, and he was the only one who knew where I was going.

He shrugged. "You and Detective Baxter are usually joined at the hip. He was alone at his desk when I got escorted out, and your vehicle was gone. I figured you were either at home getting some family time or you hit a meeting." His eyes became hopeful and sincere, which wasn't the norm for Vic Manetti. "I know I'm putting you in a tight spot, but I think I have an idea about the killer."

I felt for him, and I was sure everyone he knew was icing him out at this point. But Griffin had some serious power, and he wasn't afraid to use it.

Even though this was only a side consulting gig, I'd grown to like it and didn't want to jeopardize it.

I said gently, "I really shouldn't—"

"Look, I know you probably don't want to talk to me about anything at this point. And I don't want to get you into trouble, but...I have an off-the-wall idea, and I need a sounding board before trying to take it to Griffin. That is, if he'll even listen to me at all."

I didn't think his chances were going to be too great. With all the craziness Vic had been involved in during the last twenty-four hours, Griffin was ready to throttle him. I couldn't see Griffin sitting down with him and being able to have a productive conversation. I didn't want to further spoil Vic's day by telling him that, though.

He continued, "If I'm coming off crazy, well..." He shrugged, his shoulders slumping. "Your opinion of me is already shit, so if my theory sounds stupid, I won't have far to fall."

My heart twinged. I'd hurt him deeply. "Vic, that's not true. I know I've called you out lately over your methods, but I still think you're a damn good investigator. And even though you and I aren't in the best place right now, no personal feelings I might have will ever change my opinion about that."

He nodded, but seemed to be off in his own little world. "What if it's two people?"

"What if what's two people?"

"The killer. What if the reason we haven't been able to find one perfect suspect is that there are two killers?"

My eyebrows shot up. "Wow. That idea would definitely put an interesting spin on the investigation." Even though I was intrigued by what he'd said, I was still going against orders here. I shook my head. "Wait. Vic, I'm sorry. I can't. Griffin will have my head if—"

"I'm not asking for any new information. Just listen and pick apart my theory."

"That seems like a slippery slope."

"What's more important? Rules or justice?"

I smiled. "Have I rubbed off on you? That sounds like something I'd say."

He ignored my attempt at light-heartedness. "Well? What's it going to be?"

Sighing, I said, "Okay, fine. If there are in fact two killers, that would mean there'd have to be two people with no alibi for either of the first two murders. We don't have—" I frowned. "Oh. We do have two people like that, but it's the Caldwells. Please don't say you think it's them."

He shook his head. "I'm thinking more along the lines that one person killed Shawna and another person killed Angela so they'd both have at least one alibi."

"What, like in *Strangers on a Train*?"

"Not exactly. In this case they didn't need to swap victims. By making the murders look like they were committed by the same person, they were trying to force us to find one suspect who fit both crimes."

I nodded, contemplating how many new possibilities this could open up for us. "That's kind of brilliant."

"Thank you."

"I was talking about the killers."

He frowned.

I laughed. "I'm kidding. You're brilliant, too."

Clearly not in the mood for jokes, he went on, "The saliva found on Angela Meadows' body has been nagging at me. It strikes me as out of character for a killer to have been so meticulous and serial-minded about both crimes, leaving what he wanted us to find and taking what might implicate him, only to give himself away by leaving his DNA all over Angela's face. I think the person who killed Angela was in love with her."

"I'll buy that. But it doesn't prove there are two killers."

"Maybe it doesn't prove it, but it could explain a lot of the roadblocks we keep running into. If there's been only one lunatic doing all this, I believe we would have found saliva on Shawna's body as well. Serial killers generally follow a pattern, and kissing Angela was a big deviation from the signature established with Shawna."

"You can't write it off as escalating or getting cocky?"

"Not since the action was non-violent. If he'd raped Angela, then I'd absolutely say he was escalating. Or if he'd done some sort of post-mortem mutilation. On the flip side of that, if we'd determined that he'd also kissed

Shawna, I would have said it was part of his ritual. But by only doing it to Angela, he exhibited impulsiveness and emotion. Maybe even some regret and remorse. And that's not consistent with being a card-carrying serial killer, which I think is what whoever is doing all this is trying to emulate."

"Oh. I never thought of it that way. In that case, I think your two killer theory sounds valid. I wouldn't call it stupid or crazy."

He nodded, still seeming somewhat unconvinced. "Thanks for listening."

As he made a move to leave, I put my hand on his arm to stop him. "Vic, I'm happy to listen anytime. About anything. As far as I'm concerned, the past is behind us. I don't want to be your enemy."

Seeming to contemplate my offer, Vic stared at me for a moment. "Okay." Without another word, he left.

39

My mind was reeling from my conversation with Vic. Two killers? I drove immediately back to the station to bounce the idea off Baxter. He was at his desk, going over a list of people who'd been at the gym during Vic's assault on Mike.

I said, "Can we go somewhere private?"

Baxter turned to face me, eyebrows raised. "Private? Sure. Where?"

I lowered my voice. "Somewhere no one can overhear us."

A smile played at his lips as he leaned closer and murmured, "What do you have in mind?"

He'd made a couple of flirty comments lately. I figured I could join in. "An afternoon delight, of course."

He turned bright red from his neck to the tips of his ears. Oh, damn. I'd gone too far with him, forgetting he'd be way too easily embarrassed by my normal brand of flirting.

"I'm joking, Baxter. It's about the case."

"Right. I knew that."

He followed me into the office supply closet, which was a little close for two people. Even on the heels of our uncomfortable exchange, neither of us seemed to mind.

I said, "I had a visitor waiting for me after my meeting. For starters, I can't believe they let Manetti out so fast."

Baxter grunted. "For all his bravado about not lawyering up, he did ask for his FBI Agents' Association rep to be present during the interrogation. She had him out of there in under an hour. Griffin was not pleased. But let's face it—we know he's not guilty, at least of killing Mike Hopkins, so it's a good thing someone was on his side."

I was relieved to hear that. "Yeah. Anyway, he wanted an opinion from a neutral party on a semi-crazy theory he came up with."

"So he chose you?"

"Okay, so he wanted an opinion from a hostile party who he knew wouldn't sugarcoat her response."

Chuckling, he said, "That tracks."

"He's thinking there could be two killers."

Baxter stared down at me for a moment, pondering my bombshell before saying anything. "Working as a unit? There wasn't evidence of that at the Woodland Gardens scene."

"No, working separately. That way each killer has an alibi for the other murder."

"What about Hopkins?"

"He didn't even bring Mike into the mix. His sticking point is the saliva on Angela. He doesn't think the same person killed both her and Shawna. I think his idea is valid, and it opens up several possibilities."

Nodding slowly, he said, "Especially if we take the gym check-in list I'm working on and cross-reference it against our persons of interest. We should also revisit anyone without a solid alibi for Shawna's murder. If you remember, we let a few people have a pass if they had an airtight one for Angela's. We could easily come up with more suspects than we know what to do with."

"Sounds like the Dream Team is back in business." I raised a hand, and we high-fived.

But then I did a crazy thing. I pressed my hand against his and inter-twined our fingers. I looked up at him, hoping I hadn't overstepped. Judging by the intense yet sweet expression on his face, I hadn't.

I said, "I know we said it isn't the right time for us." I blew out a breath.

"But I've got to be honest, Nick. I haven't been able to get you out of my head since last night." I felt a light sweat break out as I continued to bare my soul. "I mean, not just since last night. You haven't been off my mind for any significant amount of time since..."

He let go of my hand to wrap his arms around my waist. "Since we met?"

Letting out a soft huff of laughter, I replied, "Okay, I'll admit it. Since we met."

He smiled. "I always knew you were into me."

"Is that so?"

"Yes, it's been painfully obvious how massive a crush you have on me. I honestly feel bad for you."

I ran my hands up his chest and clasped them around his neck. "So this is you taking pity on me, then."

"Absolutely."

He leaned toward me, and this time, with nothing to interrupt us, we shared a long, lusty kiss.

Once we finally pulled apart, I was at the same time euphoric and heartsick. "What do we do now?"

Baxter sighed. "We go back to work, like we're supposed to."

"And forget this ever happened?"

He stroked my cheek. "Never. We'll figure this out. I promise." Pulling me into a tight hug, he added, "In the meantime, game face. This was a long time coming for us, but no one else will see it that way."

"I know. But we're pros at repressing our feelings, right?"

Leaning back to grin at me, he said, "You, not so much."

I gave him a mock frown. "What if you don't count my angry outbursts?"

"Oh, if we're not counting those, then you're...slightly above average."

"Your confidence in me is overwhelming."

Baxter and I couldn't speak freely at his desk about what we planned to research this afternoon, and we sure as hell couldn't breathe a word in the conference room designated for the task force. We managed to talk Amanda into letting us use the lab office (and into keeping Beck occupied and out of our hair) for a while.

Baxter said, "Let's start by weeding out anyone with alibis for both murders. That would be…Mateo Padilla, Eve Shelton, Tracy Greer, and Evan Thompson."

I crossed their names off our persons of interest list. "Can we also cross off Mike, since we think his death could be the work of the killer or killers?"

He thought for a moment. "I'm going to say no, because if it is in fact two people working together, Hopkins could have been one of those two people and pissed off his partner enough to end him."

My shoulders slumped. "Oh."

"I know you had a soft spot for him, but he still has to be on our radar."

"Okay, fine. Let's start at the top and start making matches. Chris Bruner. Not a great suspect in my mind, but he has no alibi for Shawna's TOD. He could have partnered with…" I trailed off as I searched the list for someone with no alibi for Angela's murder. It was a short list. "Are you freaking kidding me? The only people with no alibi for Angela's murder are Jonathan and Rebecca Caldwell? That can't be right."

Frowning, Baxter said, "Ooh. That doesn't look so good for the mild-mannered Caldwells."

I threw the clipboard with our list on the desk in disgust. "Damn it, Baxter. Are we back to them again? The sheriff herself cleared them after her interrogation."

Unfazed by my angry outburst, he picked up the clipboard and started perusing the list. "No, she only demoted them from suspects to persons of interest. Unless we can find something else, your new theory may put them back in the hot seat."

"*My* new theory? This is Manetti's fault."

"It's also our best lead right now. We didn't finish talking about Chris Bruner. How do you feel about him being half of our dynamic duo?"

Shrugging, I replied, "If Eve had been one of the victims, I'd say maybe. Chris didn't seem to like Shawna like that and had no beef with her."

"So he said. He knew both victims. He also lied to us a lot."

"Yes, but it was painfully obvious when he was lying, and the way he tried to cover his tracks was pathetic. Whoever killed those women is so much sharper than Chris could ever hope to be."

He conceded, "That's true. But what if someone else was the brain and he was the brawn?"

I snorted. "The man cried over eating mashed potatoes. You really think he garroted Shawna's neck nearly in half?"

Baxter groaned. "I don't need that mental picture so soon after lunch."

"Yes, you do. Don't forget that the person we're trying to pin this on has a serious violent streak and a much stronger stomach than you. Chris doesn't fit that profile."

"I suppose not, but you never know when a mild-mannered suburbanite is going to snap."

"If you say 'like the Caldwells,' I'm quitting."

He grinned. "Then I won't say it, I'll just think it."

"Moving on," I said, taking the list back from him. Scanning down it, I said, "Here's someone we didn't do a whole lot of research on—Devin King, Shawna's trainer. He's got a rock-solid alibi for Angela's death, which is why we initially tossed him aside, but no alibi for Shawna's. Why would a trainer kill one of his clients, though? Where's his motive?"

"You said Shawna could be a difficult person. Maybe he got fed up with her."

"Then quit being her trainer. Problem solved." I frowned. "But wait, Skyler did say that he thought she and her trainer might have had a relationship on the side. That's definite motive. And not for nothing, but he also mentioned he thought James Lorenz might have had a thing for her."

Baxter nodded. "And Tracy Greer, too. Rebecca Caldwell also brought up Tracy's girl crush on Shawna—although her take on it could have been a result of gossipy pillow talk with Skyler."

Making a face, I said, "Rebecca and Skyler's pillow talk. Now that's a mental picture *I* don't need."

"We're even, then."

I kept reading down the list. "Speaking of James Lorenz, we never logged an alibi for him for Angela's TOD. He had such a solid alibi for Shawna's TOD that we'd already ruled him out before Angela was found."

He nodded again. "Oh, yeah. He wasn't connected in any way with

Angela. At least not that we know about. I say we rule him back in until we nail down his alibi." He stood. "We've got two possibilities. Let's get to it. We can discuss the rest of these clowns on the way."

We hurried to Baxter's SUV and headed for James Lorenz's house.

I loved the way Baxter came alive when he had a new idea to bat around. His blue eyes full of fire, he said, "What about the pairing of Devin King and James Lorenz? They're both trainers in the area, so they're probably at least acquaintances. They've each got a missing alibi. They're both strong and could overpower someone half their size. And either one could kick Manetti's ass into next week."

"I don't hate it, except Mike would be a sticking point. James was 'crying like a little girl,' as the chief put it, over Mike's passing. They were close."

Baxter shrugged. "Maybe Devin went rogue and did the deed behind James's back."

"I could get behind that. But why would Devin kill Mike and drug Skyler?"

"Let's say he put the drugs in the beer to take out Skyler...but then Mike became collateral damage in a legit accident once Skyler became too incapacitated to spot him. Or there's always our original idea that Mike's death was the easiest way to screw with Manetti and the investigation."

I thought for a moment. "It sucks that Mike was probably nothing more than a pawn in all this. But why kidnap and/or kill Skyler?"

"Skyler Marx is a dick move waiting to happen. It's safe to assume he's done something unforgivable to one or both of them at some point."

"Like beating up their friend Shawna?"

"Seems like a good enough reason."

I let out a bark of laughter. "Yeah, it's a good reason for those two guys to come after Skyler. But if they cared so much about Shawna's safety, they would never join forces to become a murdery duo to kill her."

Frowning, he replied, "Maybe they would if they both loved her and she kept going back to Skyler."

"Then why was Angela the only victim someone made out with? No one corpse-licked Shawna. Where's the love?"

It didn't take us long to get to James Lorenz's house, which was a little over a mile south of the station. Baxter pulled to a stop at the curb and turned his frown on me. "I thought we agreed not to use any combination of the words 'corpse' and 'lick' again."

"I never agreed to that."

"More importantly, I feel like you're enjoying shooting holes in my theory."

I grinned at him. "Only because I think you're on track for a break-through. One of your legendary strokes of genius is about to happen. I can feel it."

Baxter's eyebrows shot up, and he smiled. "Genius, huh?"

"Yes, and you're pretty, too. Let's do this."

We got out of the vehicle and walked to James Lorenz's front door. Baxter pounded on it. "Hamilton County Sheriff's Department."

We heard footfalls inside the house, slow and heavy. James Lorenz opened the door, looking pale and sickly. "Can I...can I help you?"

Baxter said, "Sorry to bother you, Mr. Lorenz, but we're tying up some loose ends on our investigation. First, I want to say that I'm sorry for the loss of your coworker, Mike Hopkins."

James got even paler, if that was possible. His breath hitched. "Thank you. He was my friend."

I felt bad for the guy. I barely knew Mike, and I missed him.

Baxter continued, "We realized we didn't have a record of where you were on February fourteenth from six-thirty to seven P.M. Can you help us out?"

James cleared his throat. "Was that when Angela Meadows was killed? I was...I was eating dinner...out."

The man was a mess. I asked gently, "Where did you go for dinner?"

"Skyline Chili."

Baxter said, "Skyline Chili? All the way down on Eighty-Second?"

"Yes."

"By yourself?"

"Yes." James brightened. "But I have my credit card receipt, if that will help." He disappeared into his house, only to come back after a few seconds with a crisp, new-looking receipt from Skyline Chili with a timestamp of 6:42 P.M. on February fourteenth.

Nodding, Baxter said, "Right smack in the middle of our window. Looks like this puts you in the clear." He tapped the receipt and chuckled. "Sky-line Chili for one. Kind of a shitty Valentine's Day, huh?"

I was shocked to hear that come out of Baxter's mouth, but I managed to keep my face passive. It was unlike him to be so snide, but like I'd said, I knew he was on the verge of figuring something out.

James gave us a small one-shouldered shrug. "You could say that. I didn't have anyone special to spend the evening with."

Baxter pasted on a fake smile and said sympathetically, "Hey, I feel you, buddy. Same for me."

I clamped my jaw shut so I wouldn't react. This exchange was getting weirder by the minute.

Baxter continued, "I hope you're going to take some time off for your mental health. First your friend Shawna, and now your friend Mike. I can't imagine what you're going through. It's going to be difficult for you to go back to work. I've lost colleagues before, and I won't lie—there'll be a void in the gym without him. He seemed like a good guy. Senseless death. Abso-lutely senseless. Never should have happened."

I had expected Baxter's invasive prodding to reduce James to a puddle of tears at our feet, but it had quite the opposite effect. His eyes became steely, and the sinews in his neck strained against his skin. Dude was pissed.

Baxter kept up his monologue. "Skyline Chili on Eighty-Second. Now you've got me craving chili." Turning to me, he said, "We were near there a few days ago, right? When we went to Ashley Sporting Goods to speak to Tracy Greer about Shawna Meehan." Without waiting for me to respond, he zeroed back in on James. "You ever shop there? They have some nice equipment. I guess you probably know that since you're friends with Tracy. She ever get you a good discount?"

The color had returned to James's face, and now it was mottled with red. He snapped, "Turns out we're not as good of friends as I'd thought." Pausing for a moment, he twisted his lips into a smirk and added, "As a matter of fact, she, uh...she told me to come by the store that night...that she'd slip me her employee discount for some expensive running shoes I've had my eye on. After I drove all the way down there, I found out she wasn't even scheduled to work that night. Nice *friend*."

Baxter shook his head. "That sucks. But, hey, at least you got some chili out of the deal. We'll get out of your hair now. Keep your chin up, man."

I forced a smile and said, "Bye, James. Thanks for your time."

I followed Baxter to his vehicle. He didn't say a word or make eye contact with me until he'd pulled away from the curb. He then very calmly said, "You're right, I am in fact a genius."

40

"Yeah, yeah. You totally forced James to crack and out his partner. Absolute genius. But why in the hell didn't you arrest him, *genius*?" I demanded.

Baxter turned at the first cross street and parked out of sight of James's house. Taking out his phone and dialing the station, he said, "First and foremost, I'm not arresting a killer and putting him in a vehicle with you."

I narrowed my eyes at him. "Because you think you're supposed to be my protector now or something?"

"No, because the sheriff would straight up kill me."

He shifted his attention to his phone and ordered for a crew to come out and take James Lorenz into custody for further questioning. He ordered another crew to find Tracy Greer and wait for us at her location.

After hanging up, he pulled away from the curb and began circling the block. "Second, I now have a rapport with this fool. Me arresting him would ruin that, so I'm going to let our deputies play bad cop." He came to a stop half a block from James's home, where we could keep an eye on both the front door and James's vehicle parked in the driveway. Smiling, he asked, "You want to know how I figured it all out?"

I'd figured part of it out, but he deserved this. "Please enlighten me."

"It finally dawned on me that James Lorenz set the whole thing in motion. He's the reason Shawna was running alone in the middle of nowhere. He's the one who sent Mike home when he mysteriously got sick at the gym. He's the one who stepped in to cover Mike's shift to give himself a solid alibi. Now let's talk about Manetti's assault. He said his attacker was strong, muscular, and tall. James Lorenz might come off as kind of a wuss, but the guy is jacked. But here's the real tipping point—the knuckles on his right hand were bright red, very likely from his fist slamming repeatedly into Manetti's face. He kept that hand hidden while we were talking, but when he gave me the credit card receipt, I saw it up close and personal."

I rolled my eyes. "Way to bury the lead. You could have started with the red knuckles."

He bit back a smile. "So you didn't notice."

"No," I growled. I wouldn't admit it, but I'd been more focused on him than on James Lorenz during their discussion. Yet another downside to mixing personal and professional relationships.

"Speaking of the credit card receipt, did you see this thing?" He held it up. "It's pristine. It clearly hasn't been in his wallet or pocket or anywhere a normal person puts receipts. And the timestamp? A little on the nose, don't you think? Three minutes before Angela was killed?"

"So that means Tracy ran over from work and used his credit card at Skyline while he was killing Angela."

Grinning, he said, "Exactly. Much like he clocked her in and out at the gym and used her credit card to pay for her membership while she was killing Shawna."

"These two sure do love their 'paper trails.'" I frowned. "So what I don't get is why he lied and said Tracy wasn't at work the night Angela was killed. We talked to her boss, and it didn't seem like he was lying to us."

"I think Tracy killed Mike, and that pissed James off. He threw her under the bus for Angela's murder to screw her and to cover his own ass."

Two sheriff's department cruisers pulled up in front of James's house. We hung around only long enough to watch the four deputies take James into custody before we headed south to Tracy's home in Fishers. She'd called in sick to her day job today, which was a serious red flag.

I had to admit, I was nervous about this one. I'd always thought Tracy had a screw loose. It was one thing to question James before we'd come to the conclusion that he was one of the killers. This time I didn't know if I could play along with our "tying up loose ends" routine while face-to-face with Tracy. She was scary on a good day.

I felt Baxter's hand come to rest on mine. "You know I'm not letting you out of the vehicle on this one."

My jaw dropped, and I snatched my hand away. "The hell you're not."

"Ellie, this is not up for debate. I wasn't sure about James until we started talking to him, and I made sure to keep the conversation as light as I possibly could so he had no idea we'd made him. I can't guarantee this conversation will go the same way. Tracy Greer is a hothead, and she hates you."

He had a point. I could see Tracy throat-punching me for looking at her funny.

I sighed. "Okay, fine. I'll sit in the car like a child."

"Like a *civilian*." He changed the subject, sort of. "James Lorenz and Tracy Greer are not the duo I would have expected. Why would they partner up? What do they have in common?"

Still feeling petulant, I said, "They're both ugly AF."

He laughed. "I don't think we can use that in our official report. Try again."

"As for the weird partnership, I don't know. But what I do know is that Tracy was jealous of Shawna's ultramarathoning, she had some sort of girl crush on her, and she wanted her boyfriend. She fits the profile, too. She's early thirties, knows both women, is strong and fast, judgmental, intelligent, arrogant, and violent. Other than not being a dude, she's a perfect match."

Baxter nodded. "Okay, good enough. What beef do we think Tracy has with Skyler? Or Mike, for that matter?"

"She was very opinionated about Skyler being guilty of killing Shawna and us letting him go in time to kill Angela. I mean, clearly that was to throw us off, as was the fact that she was the only person who told us Shawna had been beat up lately. Manetti didn't notice any bruising—and I'd like to think he would, especially considering his ongoing quest to rescue her from Skyler. No one else said a word about it, either. Would Tracy lie in order to try to implicate Skyler, even though she supposedly likes him?"

Baxter thought about it for a moment. "You said Manetti has to fight off her advances on a regular basis. What if Skyler at one point had to do the same thing and was a monumental ass to her?"

Shrugging, I said, "I could see that. A woman scorned is enough motive for pretty much any crime imaginable. But Mike...I don't know what she'd have against him. I'm also not clear on why anyone wanted Angela dead."

He pulled up to a stop at a house at the end of a cul-de-sac in an older neighborhood south of downtown Fishers. Two cruisers who'd been parked several houses away pulled in behind us.

Before he got out, Baxter reached out and placed his hand on my arm. "You know I'm not being a macho man, here. I'm following protocol."

I smiled. "I know. Be safe."

He nodded and got out, leading four deputies toward Tracy's home. I watched nervously as he knocked on the door and announced his presence. A minute went by, but Tracy didn't come to the door.

I saw Baxter place one hand on his gun and knock again. After waiting another minute or so, the five of them fanned out in different directions around the house, pausing to peer into the windows. I lost sight of them when they all disappeared behind the house. The seconds ticked by so slowly. Baxter had taken the keys with him, so I couldn't roll down the window to try to hear anything going on. I opened the door a crack and heard a muffled whining sound, but nothing else. It sounded like a dog. Moments later, I heard a loud crack, as if something broke. After another nerve-wracking minute, I nearly leapt out of my skin when my phone rang. It was Baxter.

"Did you find her?" I asked.

He let out an uneasy laugh. "No, but what we did find is... Well, you just need to see for yourself. Come around back."

I flew out of the SUV and to the back door of the house, its doorframe splintered from being kicked in. Baxter was standing in a hallway looking ill.

"Dead body?" I asked, noticing a sharp smell in the air. It wasn't quite decomp, but it was pretty nasty.

He shook his head and gestured to an open door with steps leading down to an unfinished basement. The foul odor was coming from down there. I hustled down the stairs and damned if I didn't find Skyler Marx, alive and well. Sort of. One arm was handcuffed to a support pole in the center of the room, and one of the deputies had just freed him from a ball gag normally used for bondage play.

The moment Skyler's eyes came to rest on me, he cried, "You bitch. You lied to me to get me to go talk to the cops."

I stared at him. "You're chained up and gagged in someone's basement, and this is what you lead with?"

"You set me up!"

"To be fair, you were stupid enough to fall for it."

Baxter, who'd followed me down the stairs, said, "Can we talk about the situation at hand? What the hell are you doing tied up in Tracy Greer's basement? Is this a sex thing gone wrong?"

Skyler glared at him. "You think I'd hit that on purpose? She brought me here and made me her...her sex slave."

Baxter and I shared a look.

Baxter asked, "Where's Tracy now?"

Skyler shrugged. "Hell if I know. As long as she's leaving me alone, I don't give a shit."

"We need you to tell us exactly what happened while we figure out how to get you free. I don't suppose she keeps the key to these handcuffs around here anywhere?"

Skyler shook his head. "She takes it with her. Don't you cops all have a universal handcuff key?"

"Not for this type of cuff," Baxter replied. The cuffs were sturdy, but judging from the leather straps woven through the long chain, they were made to be bondage gear.

Baxter began poking around the room, looking for a tool to break Skyler's chain.

I said to Skyler, "Can you start with how you got here? Were you and Tracy hanging out and things got weird or what?"

Skyler rubbed his eyes with his free hand. "No, I remember being at the gym, and then suddenly I was here."

Baxter glanced over at me and grimaced.

I said, "How do you think that happened?"

"No friggin' clue. Me and Mike were there lifting after closing, like we always do, and then that hag Tracy starts banging on the door and wouldn't stop until we let her in. She wrecked our bro time. Dumb bitch."

Figuring I knew the answer, I asked anyway, "Were you so drunk you blacked out?"

"No, I'd only had a couple. I don't know what the hell happened. It kind of felt like a bad drug trip, though, for a while."

There it was.

"What did Tracy do when she was at the gym with you? Was she acting strangely?"

"No more than usual. She was being annoying and begging to work out with us. I thought she was still pissed at me from last week."

"What happened last week?"

"She asked me if Shawna and I would be down for a three-way with her."

Baxter and I shared yet another glance.

I asked Skyler, "What was your answer?"

He looked at me like I was crazy. "I told her hell no."

"How did she respond to that?"

"She asked why, and I said it's because I only nail hot chicks and wouldn't touch her ugly ass if she was the last woman on earth."

My eyebrows shot up. "Well, at least then she knew where she stood with you. Why do you think she was so interested in hanging out with you and Mike last night after you were so awful to her?"

Shrugging, he said, "I figured she wanted a free session with Mike. She's always asking him for help but never wants to pay for it."

"Did she seem angry last night?" I asked.

"Yeah, but no more than usual. She's got bad 'roid rage."

"Speaking of steroids, did Mike take something last night? With his injury, I'm amazed he was able to lift with you."

"He was only spotting me at first, not that I need it. But then Tracy came in and was, like, practically bullying him into lifting. She even gave him one of her doses. I don't know what all it had in it, but he was feeling no pain and lifting as much as I was in no time."

I sighed. Maybe Mike's untimely death had in fact been an accident, or at least not completely intentional. If Tracy dosed Mike to keep him busy while she whisked Skyler away to her creepy sex basement, Mike could have kept lifting alone and got in over his head. While I was stewing over that, Baxter brought over an old shovel he'd found to use to free Skyler.

He said, "Scoot as far away from the pole as you can." Before taking a swing, he paused and looked down at Skyler with disdain. "Did you piss yourself?"

Skyler snapped, "I've been tied up all night!"

He gestured to an empty plastic bucket a few feet away. "Yeah, but there's a bucket within reach, dipshit. Surely you could have figured that one out in all your free time."

"Hey, I've been tortured here, you assholes!"

There wasn't a scratch on him. I asked, "What exactly did she do to torture you?"

"She made me have sex with her."

"Is that it?"

"That's rape. Isn't that enough?"

I shook my head. "I'm sorry, I didn't mean to downplay what's happened to you, Skyler. Yes, that's more than enough. I wondered if she threatened you or abused you as well."

"Other than making me call her Shawna and tell her she was pretty, no. Oh, and she wore dirty clothes while we did it, as if she's not gross enough."

Baxter, who'd lifted the shovel to break the chain, stopped mid-swing. "Whoa. Did she say why?"

Skyler shuddered. "Shit got weird, and I didn't ask questions. I closed my eyes and powered through it."

Baxter started hacking at the chain with the edge of the shovel head. After several tries, a link finally broke and Skyler scrambled to a standing position, free of his bondage.

"I'm out of here," he said, heading for the stairs.

Baxter stopped him. "We need to put you in protective custody until we find Tracy."

Skyler shoved him aside. "The hell you will. I can take care of myself."

I scoffed, "Like you did last night? If I were you, I'd take him up on it. Tracy's more dangerous than you've given her credit for."

He wheeled around to face me with a menacing frown. "So am I."

Baxter stepped between us. To Skyler, he barked, "Back off. We at least need to take you to the station for a formal interview."

Skyler seemed uneasy. "I don't want to talk about this anymore. Ever."

Baxter didn't have time to continue the conversation, because a crew of law enforcement officers, led by Agent Griffin, charged downstairs and took over the scene. They whisked Skyler away and pushed Baxter and me to the perimeter of the room.

Griffin headed toward us. "Ms. Matthews, Detective Baxter. Looks like you found a big piece of the puzzle, here. Ms. Matthews, I'm going to have you lead the team to process this house. Start here in the basement." After looking around and sneering at the sheer dirtiness, he added, "Hope you don't have plans this evening...or tonight, or tomorrow."

I forced a smile, knowing this task would effectively cut off my partnership with Baxter for a while. "Lucky me."

Baxter said, "Not to tell you what to do, Agent, but you might want to have a look at something in one of the bedrooms upstairs before deciding where to start. You too, Ellie."

Griffin frowned, but followed Baxter and me up the stairs. There was a knot of FBI agents crowded in the hallway of the house. They all seemed uneasy as we trooped past them and stopped at the entrance to the bedroom.

"Oh, shit," I breathed as I zeroed in on the bed.

Two brightly-colored exercise outfits lay neatly atop a snowy white duvet. The off-putting part was that one of them looked like a bucket of blood had been poured down the wearer. The other outfit had several holes in the shirt, each ringed with an alarming amount of blood.

Baxter said, "If I had to guess, those would be the 'dirty clothes' Skyler Marx told us Tracy dressed in during their, um..."

"Late night rapey roleplay," I supplied.

He winced. "Yeah."

Griffin stared at the clothes in horror. "Okay, new plan. Start in this room. Collect the clothing and get with the coroner to see if we can get a match to our two victims' wounds. Swab the blood, and I'll get the DNA testing fast-tracked through the Bureau." He turned to his team. "You guys find Tracy Greer. Now."

Once the agents had vacated the hallway, Griffin turned to Baxter and me. "I have to hand it to you two. This is a big find. I hear you had James Lorenz taken in for questioning as well. How does he fit in with all this?"

Baxter replied, "We believe Lorenz and Tracy Greer are working together. They covered for each other so they'd both have solid alibis for the murders. James Lorenz also has wounds consistent with having assaulted Agent Manetti."

"I don't know how you figured this out, but I'm damn relieved that you did."

I felt the need to do whatever I could to repair the damage to Manetti's reputation with the Bureau. "Detective Baxter put most of it together, but we have to give credit to Agent Manetti. He was the one who came up with the theory of there being two killers working together. It's the reason we took another look at James Lorenz."

Griffin's eyes narrowed. "I got a text from Manetti earlier about that. When was it that you two spoke to him?"

I suddenly felt like I'd stepped into a trap. Baxter started to say something, but I cut him off. "I spoke to him a couple of hours ago. Alone. Once he told me his idea, I brought it to Detective Baxter to see if he thought it had any merit."

Baxter, who I knew had seen this coming as well, cut in, "We'd hit a wall, so there was no reason not to look into—"

Griffin exploded. "You two violated a *direct order*. You're both dismissed from the task force effective immediately. And don't think I won't be taking this blatant act of insubordination to your sheriff for review."

I wasn't letting Baxter's career get tarnished because of me. I got in Griffin's face. "No. *I* did this. Only me. I made the decision to talk to Manetti on my lunch break. Detective Baxter was not there, nor did he have any knowledge of what I was doing. He violated no order. I did. Dismiss me."

The agent's nostrils flared. "Fine. Get out. Detective Baxter, you can stick around, but you'll be riding the bench on this one. Another toe out of line, and you're done."

Baxter muttered, "Yes, sir."

Baxter and I both left the house, neither of us uttering a word until we got to the curb, out of earshot of the swarm of law enforcement personnel milling around the property.

Around the lump in my throat, I said, "Nick, I'm so sorry. If I'd kept my damn mouth shut—"

He shook his head. "Don't worry about it. We figured out who the killers are, and that's all that matters. Now someone else has to do all the grunt work, and if we're lucky, most of the paperwork. Griffin's just jealous he didn't get to swoop in and solve the case himself."

I smiled. "You're way too forgiving with me. Especially when I nearly wreck your career."

"I'm more worried about your career. I know Sheriff Walsh is like family to you, but she's going to have to come down on you for this in one way or another."

Looking down, I said, "I know. I didn't intend to put her in a tough spot, either. Maybe it would be best if I cooled my heels for a while. I'll take my questionable judgement back to my day job where I can use it to shape young minds."

He let out a chuckle. "I'm sure any disciplinary action against you will only be a temporary thing. You want to use some of your newfound spare time tonight to meet me for dinner? Sounds like my services aren't going to be in high demand this evening."

"Are you sure you don't need a break from me?"

"Never."

41

Jayne's disappointed expression could have said it all, but she didn't pull any punches during my disciplinary meeting. "Damn it, Ellie, why am I even having this conversation with you? I told you *this morning* not to talk to him. And what do you do? You run straight to him. Have you lost your mind? How is it that the fallout from yet another of your unhealthy romantic relationships managed to make its way into your work again? Agent Griffin is demanding I make an example of you. I'm at my wit's end here."

I hung my head. The last time Jayne had come down on me this hard, she'd stuck my shoplifting teenage ass in a jail cell with a couple of crack whores. And although it might not have felt like it in the last forty-eight hours, my relationship with Vic was one of the healthier ones I've ever had. However, I had disobeyed orders, and it didn't matter the reason or the circumstances, or even the outcome.

I gave no rebuttal, only murmuring, "I'm sorry, Jayne. I'll take whatever's coming to me with no objections."

"You sure as hell will." She shook her head and griped, "Luckily you're a contractor and not an employee. I can let you go quietly instead of having to publicly fire you. At least I won't be handing the media something else to talk about."

The local news was already having a field day with the fact that Manetti got dismissed and then questioned in a homicide case related to the ones he'd been investigating. I didn't envy him having to claw his way back into good standing in the Bureau and in the community. I was thankful I wasn't about to meet a similar fate. Being in the spotlight after Rachel's abduction had been bad enough. I couldn't handle any more public attention, and neither could my family.

Even worse, if my firing stuck and I was no longer allowed to consult for the department, I wouldn't get to work with Baxter again. And that would be heartbreaking. Granted, I did have the potential of seeing him in my personal life, but would there be the same amount of fire and excitement between us without the thrill of the job? It distressed me to wonder about it.

Jayne exhaled a heavy sigh. "Get your things together and go."

I stood and blinked back tears on my way to her door.

As I opened it, she said quietly, "You did good work out there, finding us some solid suspects and evidence. I'm even more proud of you for standing by a friend, even though it cost you."

On my way home, I swung past Walgreens and bought out what was left of their discounted Valentine's Day chocolates. I needed something to take the edge off. Today had been hellish enough that if there were ever a time to reach for the bottle, this was it. I knew I was walking on shaky ground.

The first heart-shaped box I reached for was fairly small and emptied in the six minutes it took me to get home. Thank goodness it was Rachel's late day at school, so she and Nate wouldn't be there to witness my bingeing. Trixie, on the other hand, wanted nothing more than to help me eat the second box I cracked into, so I gave her a handful of dog treats to keep her busy while I gorged on the candy no one thought was good enough to give to their special someone on Valentine's Day. By the third box, I had to stop for fear of vomiting everywhere, but at least my stomach was too full to even consider drinking anything. Problem solved, sort of.

After a much-needed nap brought on by my sugar coma, I felt better. But nothing compared to the feeling that rushed over me when I saw Baxter's smiling face as I approached him outside the restaurant where we'd agreed to meet.

"Hey," I said, a sudden flutter in my gut. I'd gone out to eat with Baxter countless times, but this time felt strangely like a date. Our professional ties were broken indefinitely, so this was one hundred percent personal.

"You doing ok?" he asked.

I shrugged. "Jayne fired me, and then I fell asleep partway through my third box of crappy Valentine's candy."

His face fell. "I'm so sorry, Ellie." He pulled me into a hug.

My cheek against his chest, I smiled. "I'm good now, though. How was your afternoon?"

He let me go and held the door open for me to enter the restaurant ahead of him. "Griffin wasn't exaggerating when he said I'd be riding the bench. He put me on scene entry log duty."

I stared at him. "You're joking, right?"

"Not even a little."

"What a waste. He's such an ass."

Baxter got us on the list for a table, a fifteen-minute wait, which wasn't bad for this restaurant. The entryway was packed with other patrons, so we went and stood outside to be able to speak more openly. Two more couples had the same idea, so he lowered his voice and said, "It was only for a couple of hours. I did get to interview our suspect, at least."

I replied, "That's great. What did she say? Or are you allowed to talk about that with me?"

"As far as I'm concerned, you did the work and you deserve to know the outcome. I was talking about James Lorenz. Tracy Greer is still out there."

He'd leaned in when he said their names, so close that his beard brushed my ear. I had to force myself to concentrate on his words. "I bet Griffin's not happy about that."

"That's an understatement. I think she must have come back home, saw the circus at her house, and bailed. We know she ditched her brand-new car and bought an old junker with no GPS a couple of hours ago in West-field. At this point, she could be in the next state by now. Any of the four of them, actually."

"Ooh. That's no good."

"Especially since we've got Lorenz singing like a bird. He says he had no idea Tracy was going to kill Mike, and once she did, he came to his senses and was trying to work up the courage to turn himself in. When we showed up at his door, he was in the middle of getting his affairs in order and evidently needed more time, so he lied to us. I don't know how many times he apologized for it."

I wrinkled my nose. "He apologized for lying to us?" I lowered my voice to a whisper and added, "Did he apologize for stabbing Angela Meadows to death?"

"Oh, yeah. Once he started talking about her, he lost it and started banging his forehead on the table. I had to wrestle him to the ground to get him to stop, and then we had to sedate him. I'll get another crack at him once his meds wear off."

My jaw dropped. "Damn. I can't believe I missed that."

He grinned. "Definitely one of my weirder interrogations. Turns out, James and Tracy have been buddies since childhood. They stuck together through some pretty tough bullying and a lot of dating rejection—the latest and most heartbreaking being his rejection by Shawna and Angela and hers by Shawna, Skyler, and Manetti. Tracy convinced him it was time they quit being victims and fought back. According to him, she cooked up the whole plan and ran the show. He was supposedly only along for the ride. He mentioned them having some kind of longstanding pact to have each other's backs."

I murmured, "Only along for the ride? This wasn't a trip to the mall. This was two highly premeditated serial killery slaughters and an ass-whipping of epic proportions. Does he really expect us to buy his pathetic excuse?"

"Doesn't matter, because his house is full of evidence that he killed Angela, and he told us exactly where to find it all. We got the murder weapon, his bloodstained clothing and boots, and the photos of the scene he saved on his computer."

I shook my head. "Wow. Slam dunk. That is, if you can find Tracy."

He rubbed his eyes. He looked tired. "She'll turn up. It's hard to fly under the radar for too long."

My text tone chimed. I glanced at my phone out of habit, forgetting I was no longer on duty. After reading the text on the screen, I let out a quiet grunt.

"What's up?" Baxter asked.

I frowned. "This text from Manetti: *My shoulder is so stiff I can't move it. Can you come over and help me get my shirt off? I have it stuck halfway.*"

His eyes grew dark. "Sounds like a pity-themed booty call."

"That's kind of what I was thinking."

"You said you guys buried the hatchet. Maybe he read too much into it."

"That, or he's high on painkillers."

I'd told Vic earlier that I'd listen anytime he needed to talk, but it was a little much to ask me to come over and help him take his clothes off. Another slippery slope.

Rather than going straight for the hard no, I replied, *Are you sure you meant to text this to me?*

After a moment, I received another text, which I read aloud to get Baxter's take on it: "*I know this is awkward for both of us, but it would be weird to ask one of my guy friends for this kind of help.*" I shook my head. "And it's not weird to ask me? I think I should pass on this one. I don't want to appear interested in revisiting our relationship."

His brow furrowing, Baxter grumbled, "As much as I hate to say it, he's got a point. It's less weird to ask your ex than to ask another guy. Anyway, this place takes forever, and Manetti's house is, what, five minutes away? You could get this over with and be back before we get the text that our table's ready. I'll drive you over if you want."

I smiled. "So you can protect my virtue in case he tries to seduce me?"

He looked away. "No."

"Lying doesn't suit you, Detective."

His expression softened. "And refusing someone who needs help doesn't suit you. Only hours ago you threw away your job to stand up for the guy. Why stop now?"

I let out an exaggerated sigh. "Fine. I'll go do my second good deed for the day. My reward will be seeing his reaction when I tell him in person what a psycho his friend Tracy is."

"He probably already knows. Plus, I don't think that's how good deeds are supposed to work."

"Close enough. You stay here and don't let our table get away."

"Okay, but don't hang around for too long. I'm sure he's lonely, but that's not your problem to solve."

I smiled. "You sound jealous."

"If you're not back here in eleven minutes—"

"I know. You'll drive over and come barging in to protect my virtue."

"Damn straight."

I got to Vic's place in exactly five minutes and rushed to the door. I wanted to get in, get out, and get back to my dinner with Baxter. He didn't answer, and I was about to ring the doorbell again, but I got a text from him saying, *It's open.*

The troubling thought crossed my mind that he was in his bedroom and was going to insist I go up there. That kind of game really wasn't like him, though, so I put it out of my head. Upon entering his house, I heard a chair scraping to my left.

"Vic?"

No answer.

I entered his living room, which was an open concept with a dining area and kitchen. It was dark, but he had candles lit on the dining table. My heart sank. Not a good sign. He was sitting in one of the chairs with his back to me and was not in fact stuck halfway in his shirt.

I approached him and griped, "What the hell was that text about? Your shirt is fine."

He didn't reply, other than shaking his head and grunting.

Irritated, I marched the rest of the way over to stand facing him. When I got there, I sucked in a breath. He was duct taped to the chair by his wrists and ankles, and his mouth was taped shut. His eyes were wide with fright. I reached out to remove the tape from his mouth, but stopped short when I heard a familiar voice.

"Keep your hands to yourself, princess."

I looked over my shoulder to find Tracy Greer stepping out of the shadows of the kitchen, holding two heaping plates of food. I inadvertently let out a gasp, but willed myself to stay calm. I didn't know if she knew that I knew all of her secrets. Granted, it was no secret that something was off based on the fact that she had Manetti bound and gagged at his own dinner table. By candlelight, I couldn't see whether or not she had a weapon on her, but it stood to reason that Vic wouldn't have agreed to any of this without a fight. Theoretically, I could have lunged at her while her hands were full, but I wouldn't have put it past her to break both of those plates over my head and stab me with the shards.

The only way this situation could end in my favor would require me to keep her occupied for ten minutes—five for me not to show back up to dinner on time and five for Baxter to drive over here and make good on his promise to not let Vic try to suck me back into a relationship.

I said in the brightest tone I could muster, "Tracy, hey. You startled me. How's it going?"

She replied in a grim tone, "Not so good. Someone ruined my plans."

"Oh. That's too bad. I hate it when good plans get ruined. Are you guys just sitting down to dinner? I came over to check on Vic, but he seems to be in good hands. I'll leave the two of you alone."

As I made a move to try to get the hell out of there, she came my way and backed me up toward the table. "Nonsense. You're staying to have dinner with us. Right, Vic?"

Vic was straining against his restraints, but to no avail. It looked to me like she'd used a whole roll of duct tape on him. He was going nowhere unless he managed to break that chair into pieces.

Tracy set the two plates down on the table. In a single swoop, she removed a hunting knife from the back waistband of her jeans and had it at my throat. She repeated, "Princess is staying to have dinner with us. *Right, Vic?*"

Vic stopped struggling, his broad shoulders slumping in defeat. He nodded, his eyes anguished as they stayed trained on me.

I could feel the tip of the knife pricking my skin, but I managed to stay sane by clinging to the hope that it would only be nine more minutes before Baxter came to rescue us. Only nine minutes.

Tracy stuffed her free hand into my front pants pocket and snatched my phone. She launched it across the room. It smashed into the wall and clattered to the floor. "You won't be needing that tonight. We'll be much too busy."

I hoped she'd broken my phone, because if Baxter sent a text to me that didn't show as delivered or he called and it went straight to voicemail, he'd immediately know something was up. I cleared my throat, careful not to make any sudden movements that would drive the blade into my neck. "Dinner looks great. I'm starving."

She sneered. "I bet you are, fatty."

Still? "You know, body shaming is hurtful, Tracy. And it's no way to speak to your dinner guest."

Not the time to make a point about her behavior. She grabbed me by the hair and shoved me down into the nearest chair. "Shut up, bitch. Now hold still while I tape you up, too."

I scanned everything within reach for an object I could grab to use as a weapon. There was nothing nearby I could use to bludgeon her, so I would have to come up with something creative to at least divert her attention. For now, I'd have to talk my way out of being bound to my chair.

I waved a hand, "Oh, taping me up isn't necessary. We both know I can't outrun you."

Her face twisted into a smirk. "That's for damn sure." Suddenly her eyes got a nasty glint, made even more sinister by the flickering candlelight. "Oh, wait. I almost forgot. What's a dinner party without entertainment?"

A shiver ran down my spine. "Dinner is more than enough. I'm fine without any entertainment."

"Not a chance." She picked up an empty highball glass from the table and thrust it into my hand. "Go pour yourself a drink. Be a good princess and fill it all the way to the top. I'll even let you pick your poison."

Oh shit. *I* was the entertainment. She was going to push me off the wagon and then run me over with it.

42

I shook my head, remembering how I came unglued over merely the taste of a couple of drops of vodka. A glass full of liquor would send me so far over the edge I might never claw my way back. "Seriously, I can't. I...I won't. I've worked too hard. You can't make me drink."

"I can't make you drink?" Tracy laughed. "We'll see about that." She went straight for Vic and drove her knife blade into his upper arm, directly into the bicep.

"No!" I screamed, coming up out of my chair.

She pulled the bloody blade out and pointed it at me. "Fill your glass, or he gets one to the gut."

I froze, my eyes glued to the wound coursing blood down Vic's arm. He was groaning in pain.

"Do it *now*," Tracy barked.

I obediently went over to Vic's bar cart. He had a decent but small assortment of alcohol, and the cart doubled as his station for making his health nut drinks. Tracy had said for me to pick my poison, which couldn't have been a better term for it in my case, but it was also an indicator that she knew little about alcohol. The coconut-flavored rum had roughly half the alcohol content of the vodka or bourbon, which would work in my favor. I could do this. My confidence got another slight boost as I noticed a canister of one of the many powdered energy drink mixes Manetti had made me try on the cart's lower shelf. It was nothing more than glorified cornstarch, intended to be a source of sugar-free, clean carbs for energy during a workout. As I was pouring my drink, I nudged the canister off the cart with my foot and gave it a tap it so it rolled to a stop next to my chair.

The odor of the rum, which I'd always thought to be pleasant, was like a knife to my nose. Once my glass was sickeningly full, I returned to the table and set it in front of me. Unlike last time when I'd had a drink within reach, I wanted nothing to do with this one.

Raising my eyes to meet Vic's, I said, "Vic, I'm so sorry. I didn't know she was going to—"

Tracy cut me off. "Drink."

I couldn't stall any longer. My throat tightened and tears prickled my eyes. I had to do whatever I could to keep my wits about me. But between wrestling with the shame of my impending loss of sobriety and the very real possibility of getting blackout drunk, I feared my mind would be rendered useless all too soon.

I said, "Tracy, please—"

She poised her knife at Vic's abdomen. "I said, *drink*."

Blowing out a shaky breath, I reached for the glass. I put it to my lips and hesitated. Tracy wasn't going to let me out of this, and she wasn't afraid to hack up Vic to force me to be her puppet. I took a sip and winced as it burned its way down my throat.

"More," she ordered.

I took a bigger sip, which seemed to satisfy her. Smiling, she left Vic's side and walked toward the kitchen. While her back was turned, I swiped the utility lighter sitting next to the candles on the table. I shoved it under my legs and gave Vic an encouraging nod.

Tracy retrieved a roll of duct tape from the kitchen counter and threw it overhand at my face. I caught it an inch from my nose. "Wrap up your ankles. Tight. If I don't like how you do it, I give Vic another poke."

If I did this right, I could waste a lot of time with the tape. Unfortunately, I could already feel that alcohol working. My edge was gone, and I was on the way to feeling warm and fuzzy. For the first time in my life, I fought that feeling. I tore off a piece of tape and wrapped it around my right ankle and one of the chair legs.

She snapped, "That's not nearly enough tape. And it's not tight enough."

I held my hands out. "Sorry, I realize that now. Bear with me; I've never done this before."

I took my time ripping more of the tape away from the roll. If she was going to make me use the same amount of tape she'd used on Vic, I didn't think there was a way to affix it so I could get out of it later, even if I managed to wrap it loosely.

While I was wrapping my ankle, I decided to try to slow things down even further by striking up a conversation. "I saw Skyler earlier. Surprisingly, he did not say to tell you hi."

"Like I care. I'm done with him, anyway."

I nodded. "Oh, that's right. I heard he told you how he really felt about you. It's one thing to be turned down as potential girlfriend material. It must have been rough to be written off as a candidate for a threesome. I mean, theoretically, you don't need to like the person or even be attracted to them as long as they're down with being the kinky third wheel. Is that why you made the garrote you used to kill Shawna out of guitar string? To implicate Skyler because you were pissed at him?"

Tracy said nothing.

I continued, "I'll take your lack of denial as a yes. Too bad for you the charge on him didn't stick. But I guess you showed him in the end. Speaking of that, a little friendly advice—you might do better with men if you don't hold them against their will. Some people enjoy bondage, but I think you may be doing it wrong."

Snorting, she replied, "I'm sure you'd know. Vic tells me you're quite the skanky ho."

I stopped taping to pop my head up and look at Vic. He closed his eyes and shook his head. Thinking fast, I said to Tracy, "Is that so? Maybe you should take the tape off his mouth so he can say that to my face like a man."

If I could force Vic into a corner, he might come out swinging—or at least figure out what I was doing and play along. One of our knock-down-drag-out fights could distract anyone, even a psycho like Tracy.

Tracy shook her head. "I'll decide when and if the tape comes off. Take another drink and get back to work."

I took a big mouthful of rum and bent over, pretending to quickly "get back to work." Once my head was down past my knees, I discreetly spat the liquor out on Vic's rug. If I could continue to spit instead of swallow, I might be able to keep my mind sharp enough to prevent Vic and myself from becoming Tracy's next victims.

Not for nothing, my liquid courage at least helped me keep a running conversation. "Vic's just mad because Skyler came onto me and I kissed him." I glanced up to catch her reaction.

Her expression darkened. "You and *Skyler*? You managed to get your claws in him, too? What are the odds? And you cheated on Vic with him?"

"I was trying to get information out of Skyler, so it didn't count." This was actually going well, aside from Vic's stab wound. It had to be less than seven minutes by now. I turned my attention back to my second ankle.

"It counts, you whore."

I didn't see it coming, but felt an explosive blow to the back of my head that brought tears to my eyes. I heard Vic growl and Tracy laugh. Stunned and disoriented, I raised up slowly to find her with one arm draped around his shoulder. Everything looked blurry and dark, except the candlelight, which seemed way too bright all of a sudden.

Hugging Vic's head against her chest, she said, "Why, when you have such a catch here, would you throw him away? He really cares about you. He told me so." She let go of his head to slap him on the cheek. "Didn't you Vic?"

He nodded. That was when I noticed a big goose egg on the side of his head. Now I understood how he got himself in this predicament. She'd managed to knock him out.

Tracy continued, "He told me back in December that he'd found someone he thought he could see a future with."

I flicked my gaze at Vic, which made the backs of my eyes throb. He wouldn't look at me.

She raised her voice. "Why don't you want him, Ellie? Are you stupid or what? He's handsome and smart and kind. He was invested in your relationship, and you didn't give a shit. You don't deserve him."

After she'd bashed me over the head, I'd taken a break from taping myself up. She'd gotten so incensed that she hadn't noticed. Even better, she was no longer paying any attention to how I was wrapping my ankles. I got smart, and on my second ankle, I used plenty of duct tape on both my ankle and the chair leg, but I neglected to tape one to the other. If I could keep her attention elsewhere, my plan to get us out of here might just work.

My head pounding with each word, I said, "Maybe I don't deserve him. But do you? You had your goon, James, beat him up. You orchestrated Mike's death so he'd take the fall or at least be accused of it. And now you've tied him up in his own home and shanked him. Where's the love?"

She shrugged. "Like Skyler, I felt Vic needed to be punished for rejecting me."

"What is wrong with you that you can't take a little rejection?"

"A little rejection? My whole life has been nothing *but* rejection."

"Could it be because you're always going for men who are out of your league? There's always someone out there who won't reject you if you're willing to lower your standards."

Her expression turned stony. "Is that what Vic did with you? Lowered his standards? I still don't understand why he turned me down multiple times for you, an alcoholic loser. Speaking of which, I want to see you chug that drink like the drunk you are."

Her focus was fully on me, and I couldn't think of a way to distract her. Chugging rum was going to get me very drunk very fast, but there was nothing else I could do. As I tipped my glass, Vic started struggling and making noise. Tracy glanced down at him, and when she did, I used the opportunity to slosh some of the rum onto my jacket sleeve. It absorbed quickly and invisibly into the dark brown wool, and I got the much-emptier glass up to my lips again before she turned back to me and continued her tirade. I made a big show of wiping my mouth and pretending to feel the burn of my drink.

"He did so much for you, you ungrateful bitch. He trained you and showed you how to eat right—not that you took his advice—and he made you stay sober. You owe him your *life*. But what do you do? You kick him to the curb over one little misunderstanding."

I bristled. Nobody "made" me stay sober but me. "Yes, he saved me from getting shot back in December. I'm grateful to him for that. And he helped me through a difficult time, but I put in the work. We didn't end things over one little misunderstanding—it was a series of big, fundamental disagreements that impacted our personal and professional relationships." I wondered if what she'd said was the story Vic had told her or if her warped mind had twisted the information. Right now, it didn't matter, and I needed to get a grip on my emotions.

She stared daggers at me. "You're just like Shawna. Too full of yourself to see your shortcomings. It's not fair that you both had these men at your feet and then...and then *stomped* on them."

Grabbing Vic by the hair, she wrenched his head around so he was face-to-face with her. It was all the opening I needed to place my hand over the cloth napkin at the table setting in front of me and pull it onto my lap. I had my tools in place now, but I still needed a little more time.

She screamed at Vic, "I would have been the perfect girlfriend, but no! You didn't want me! Even after Shawna died and Ellie dumped you, you still didn't want me. *Nobody* wanted me after Shawna died!"

Tracy seemed to be struggling between love and hatred for Vic. I couldn't help but think if he could convince her that she had a chance with him, she'd stop this madness. The tape would have to come off his mouth first.

Fearing she was contemplating turning her knife on him again, I cried, "Tracy! It's not that he didn't want *you*. Please understand that. I'm sure if you gave him the chance to explain—like now, if you'd take the tape off his mouth—he'd tell you that he has too much baggage to start a new relationship with you or anyone right now." She seemed to loosen her grip on him as she listened to me, so I went on, "He and I were bonded over the traumatic experience we shared back in December. I can't even begin to put into words what we went through together. That's why our relationship was so strong and so volatile at the same time. You—or anyone in the world, for that matter—merely flirting with him and trying to lure him away could never sever that bond. I'm sorry that his actions toward you might have seemed like a brush-off, but he couldn't just flip a switch and be done with our relationship. Plus Shawna had just died, and he's still not dealing with it very well."

Tracy let go of him, and I breathed a sigh of relief. To my surprise and delight, she ripped the tape off his mouth. A smile beaming on her face, she said, "Is that true, Vic? Is our timing just wrong?"

Had she not had us both bound and at knifepoint, I might have felt sorry for her. It seemed like all she wanted was someone to love her and tell her she was special. Wasn't that what we all wanted?

Of course Vic being Vic, he couldn't simply play along. He had to try to take control of the situation and be the hero. "Tracy, let Ellie go. This is between you and me. Trust me, if you lay a finger on her, every law enforcement officer in this county will be lining up to—"

As I noticed Tracy getting angrier with each word he said, I cut him off. "Vic, answer the woman's question. It's hard for people who haven't had life-and-death experiences to understand how going through a trauma can draw two people together—romantically or otherwise. Please explain how the timing for you and Tracy just isn't right. It's too soon." I gave him a pleading look and hoped he got the underlying message.

He couldn't have sounded less encouraging as he said in a flat tone, "Um...sure. Tracy, it's not the right time for us to start a relationship."

Would it have killed him to flirt with her a little? It was like he wasn't even trying to talk his way out of this. He was much better in a hostage situation when he had the upper hand. And a gun. If we could stay on this track of conversation and keep her happy, we might buy enough time for Baxter to get here and break this party up before anyone else got hurt. Where was he, anyway?

Tracy didn't seem to notice Vic's lack of enthusiasm. Turning to me with a triumphant smirk, she said, "I might have doubted him, but I knew he could come around. He's too good a man to enter into a relationship with me before he's ready. You, on the other hand, seem to have been able to flip that switch and be over it. Maybe it's because you have no soul."

"Maybe it's because she was never really into me in the first place," Vic said, his tone rough and pained.

My jaw dropped. Was this his attempt at picking a fake fight with me? If so, it was a terrible one. I hoped this was the head injury talking. He was being way too real for this type of situation, and unfortunately he wasn't wrong. I never knew he'd picked up on that.

Before I could say anything, Tracy broke into a huge smile. "Ooh, tell me more. Ellie, is this true? It sounds like you led poor Vic on, and for what? Free meals? Free training? Or was it to further your career? Take another drink before you answer. I've always found liquor to be something of a truth serum."

I took another sip and held it in my mouth for a moment. Her gaze was again dead on me, and Vic made no move to distract her this time. After swallowing, I said, "It was the sex. The sex was amazing."

She nodded. "I've always imagined that would be true. So you are in fact nothing more than a skanky ho." She let out a condescending little chuckle.

I could handle a little verbal abuse from Tracy, and I was holding my liquor decently so far. Vic, on the other hand, wasn't looking so good. He was sweating and murmuring to himself, and the bloodstain on his sleeve was growing. I was beginning to wonder if that bump on his head was more serious than it looked. That, coupled with the sheer stress of the situation and the loss of blood could cause all kinds of trouble.

He confirmed my suspicions when he raised his voice and slurred, "How stupid was I not to see that you were in love with him all along?"

Tracy's good mood vanished. She turned on me. "In love? You're in love with Skyler? What, were you using Vic as a *placeholder* until Skyler was in the clear? How could you do that to another person?"

I realized I couldn't count on Vic's help with this situation; what was coming out of his mouth was way too unpredictable. I needed to keep Tracy's attention on me. If he said something that made her want to hurt him again, I didn't know if he could take it.

I snorted. "If we're judging sins, I don't think we're comparing apples to apples. At least I never killed anyone."

Okay, so maybe I wasn't holding my liquor as well as I thought. That comment came out before I had a chance to weigh how much it might piss Tracy off.

She bellowed, "You killed my chance with Vic! Now he's heartbroken, and *I'm* the one who's paying the price for it. Who knows how long I'm going to have to wait for him to be ready!"

I needed to change the subject away from our little love triangle, and fast. It had to be only a few more minutes before Baxter would get here...I hoped. A nagging voice in the back of my mind kept saying, *What if he doesn't come to get me like he said he would?* I did my best to push my fear aside. I couldn't think like that. This was Nick Baxter we were talking about. He always came through.

I opened my mouth to try to steer the conversation to a less volatile topic, but Vic in a sudden moment of clarity snapped at her, "*You* killed your chance with me by killing Shawna. I cared about her. Plus, an FBI agent of all people is not going to be interested in a relationship with a criminal."

Tracy seemed genuinely taken aback. "Vic, I did what was necessary for some people, including you, to see the error of their ways. I'm not a criminal."

He sneered at her, nostrils flaring. "Tell that to Shawna. They're going to lock you up and throw away the key for what you've done. Silver lining, though—your love life might actually improve. I'm sure there are all kinds of psychos out there who'd jump at the chance to join you for a conjugal visit while you're rotting in prison for the rest of your life."

Even though I was shocked and appalled that he'd chosen to go at her like that, I inadvertently giggled at the mental image. I never giggled. The liquor was definitely getting to me. My glass was nearly empty, and I'd consumed a considerable amount of it.

Tracy's face fell. Her tone filled with hurt, she said, "I don't want a bunch of one-night stands. I want..." She trailed off, staring at Vic with tears in her eyes.

After his outburst, Vic was looking incredibly pale. The man was about to pass out. While her gaze was trained on him, I reached down and quietly unscrewed the lid from the drink mix canister.

I did not like the look she was giving Vic. It was different, and it scared me. Maybe some good old frenemy bashing would do the trick to distract her from whatever she was thinking. "I feel like we've beaten this horse to death, Tracy. Speaking of beatdowns, let's talk about Shawna. I would love to know why you killed her. I mean, she was kind of a bitch, and I'm sure she had it coming, but she had no real personality. What was the point of going to the trouble to end someone like that? I'm honestly interested in your reasoning."

She ripped her eyes away from Vic to give me a strange look. "You don't understand why I wanted to kill her?"

"Not at all. In the grand scheme of life, she was a total nobody."

Her jaw dropped. "A nobody? Are you insane? She had everything. Everyone wanted to be her friend."

"Not everyone. But you clearly did. Did she turn down your offer for friendship?"

She said quietly, "She said she didn't have the time for friends."

"That's a crappy thing to say. So because of all that...you decided to punish her by taking away what she had? Is that it?"

For the first time tonight, Tracy looked uncomfortable. "Not exactly."

I pressed on, even though I could hear my words beginning to slur together. "Or...wait. You wanted to *become* her."

She looked down and didn't respond.

"That's why you took her clothes and made Skyler call you by her name. But why become Shawna Meehan? Why not somebody cool?"

Snapping her head up, she seethed, "You think you're so smart. Shawna *was* cool. She was beautiful and tiny and in perfect shape. She had two insanely hot men fighting over her. I want that. I *deserve* that."

I could feel my body starting to shift to slow motion. My stomach was boiling with acid, and I felt a dull ache in my head that I didn't believe was a product of the wallop Tracy had given me. How did I used to be drunk all the time and still manage to function? And why did I do it for so long when it made me feel this terrible?

I said, "So...make it happen for yourself. Is it that impossible for you to get a date? You're not much in the personality department, but you're smart. That has to count for something. And don't forget that Skyler and Vic are not the only 'insanely hot men' in the greater Indianapolis area."

She barked, "Someone like you would never get it."

Digging my fingernails hard into my palms to try to snap myself out of my stupor, I replied, "Enlighten me. And while you're at it, explain how crazy you have to be to have wanted these guys so much, but then after getting rejected by them, jumped to framing them for murder and physically and mentally assaulting both of them. I'm pretty sure Skyler is going to need some heavy therapy after what happened in your basement. He was in a bad place when we went in there and found him earlier."

Vic started muttering nonsensically, "I wish just once you'd look at me the way you look at him... The way you trust him without question... Your little inside jokes.... The way you two communicate through a look..."

I wished Vic would shut up or just pass out. He was clearly talking about Baxter instead of Skyler, but based on the anger radiating from Tracy, she'd again misunderstood. I had to be careful how I handled this conversation, because I'd be damned if I let her find out how much I cared about Baxter. I'd never put a target on his back like that.

Incensed, she screamed at me, "How long have you been with Skyler? Long enough to have inside jokes and communicate without talking? How long? Weeks? Months?" She grabbed one of the plates of food and launched it at my head. I managed to duck to the right, but I felt it make contact with my ear.

My heart thudding and my ear searing with pain, I said as evenly as I could, "I'm not with Skyler. He's an idiot. And Vic's not making any sense. I'm pretty positive he has a concussion." When she didn't look convinced, I added, "Call Skyler and ask him what he thinks of me. Trust me—he hates my guts."

She shook off her uncertainty and went back into beast mode. Eyes wide with rage, she fired back, "Why should I trust you or believe anything you say? You're *worse* than Shawna. Just as condescending, but with nothing to back it up. You're a loser and a drunk. You need to be put in your place. You need to suffer like everyone else who's caused me pain. As much as I'd love to watch the life drain from your eyes like Shawna's did..."

Without another word, Tracy plunged her knife into Vic's gut. He cried out in agony. My cries died on my lips. I couldn't get a breath.

I sat there helplessly as Tracy stood over Vic. My heart seized as he went limp, his head dropping and lolling against his chest. She turned to me with a sinister smile as she slid the knife out slowly. A bloodstain bloomed on his shirt, growing bigger by the second.

Numb with shock, I wrenched my eyes away from him to stare at her. "Why? Why did you..." I choked on a sob. "Why not me?"

Tracy cackled manically. "Because this hurts you so much more. You get to watch him bleed out and know it's all your fault. And when you go run off and try to have your happily ever after with your new boyfriend, every time you look at him all you're going to think about is how Vic died because of the two of you."

A white-hot spark of anger engulfed my chest. This woman did *not* get to decide my fate. I put my hands under the table, flicked the lighter to life, and lit the edge of the cloth napkin on fire, my head clearer than it had been all night.

Tracy went to the bar cart and poured herself a drink. "Now let's drink a toast to our dearly departed Vic." Coming over to me, she raised her glass. "To Vic. Raise your glass, bitch."

I raised my glass, but instead of drinking, I splashed the remaining rum on her shirt. While she was distracted for a moment, I brought up the now flaming napkin, held it in front of her, and tossed part of the drink mix toward the flames, aiming it all right at Tracy's face. A ball of fire burst toward her when the starchy powder hit the flame. Startled, she screamed and stumbled back. I kept tossing more and more of the mix in her direction, creating flash after flash of fire. Dragging my chair with me, I forced her back toward the wall. I threw the flaming napkin and the empty tub at her face and picked up a full bottle of liquor from the bar cart. With all the strength I had, I swung it at her head like a baseball bat. It made full contact with her temple, and she dropped to the floor, motionless. My anger still raging, I stomped out the fire from the napkin that had fallen at my feet and raised the bottle again to rain down another blow to Tracy's head. But catching a glimpse of Vic out of the corner of my eye, I hesitated. He wouldn't have wanted me to avenge him, even though finishing her was the one thing I wanted to do more than anything. I began to sob, letting the bottle slip harmlessly from my hands to the floor.

A minute or so later, I heard my name being called. When I looked up, Baxter was rushing toward me, his face ashen as he took in the grisly scene.

"Ellie, what happened? Are you hurt?"

I shook my head and pointed at Vic, choking out, "You're too late."

43

Baxter's attention turned to Vic. Placing two fingers on Vic's neck, he paused for a moment and then drew in a sharp breath. "His pulse is weak, but it's there."

My legs gave way, and I sat down on my chair, stunned. In a matter of seconds, Baxter had his phone out calling for help, had Vic laid down on the floor, and had begun putting pressure on both of Vic's wounds to stop the bleeding.

He said sharply, "Ellie, snap out of it. Tell me what happened here. Is Tracy dead?"

My words all ran together. "I...I dunno. I only hit her once."

He said, "Come here and take over for me. I need to make sure she's subdued."

I made no move to get up. Everything had gone fuzzy again.

Baxter snapped, "Ellie!"

I jumped. If I didn't get my shit together, Vic would suffer even more. The idea of that spurred me to shuffle myself and the chair around, wrenching my still-taped leg to get myself down on the floor next to him. I placed my hands on his two wounds and pressed with everything I had left.

The next few hours were a blur. First responders converged on Vic's house and carted us all outside. Vic got taken directly to the hospital. Tracy's burns were minimal, so she was unceremoniously awakened and then arrested by two stone-faced FBI agents. She disappeared in an FBI vehicle, on her way to what was sure to be the worst night of her life. She'd get no mercy at the hands of Vic's fellow agents, not that she deserved it.

After being examined by the EMTs and enduring the shame of having my blood drawn to determine my blood alcohol concentration, I was then checked over, photographed, and swabbed by the FBI's criminalists. Unfortunately, I wasn't so drunk that I didn't want to die of embarrassment. Once that torture was over, I was whisked away to the sheriff's station by Jayne herself, who was hovering over me worse than Baxter was. When I wasn't being forced to regurgitate my story over and over again for the many investigators involved in the case, I spent the night holed up in Jayne's office, sitting on her couch and trying not to break down over the fact that Vic was in surgery, fighting for his life. He'd lost a lot of blood and had suffered a severe concussion and a substantial amount of internal damage. Baxter and Jayne took turns sitting quietly with me and holding my hand.

The worst part of my night was when Griffin and a couple of FBI agents I didn't know came to the station to interrogate me. While the rest of the investigators I'd spoken with had handled me with kid gloves, these guys pulled no punches. About ten minutes in was when my alcohol buzz decided to wear off, and I thought my head was going to split open. Griffin ended our agonizing conversation by congratulating me on apprehending Tracy and saving Vic, and then he apologized for taking me off the case. He said he'd make sure my dismissal from the task force would be expunged from my record and that I'd be reinstated with the sheriff's department immediately. He even said he could use someone like me at the Bureau. I had to bite my tongue to not blurt out that there was no chance in hell I'd ever work with him again.

Vic had been in surgery for hours. It had been touch-and-go for a while, but they were able to stabilize him. We finally got word that he was out of surgery and in recovery. After I heard he was awake and in stable condition, I felt like I was able to breathe again.

After having told my story so many times to so many people, I was exhausted and grouchy and felt like I needed to sleep for days. Once I was allowed to leave, Baxter ushered me straight to his vehicle.

As he pulled out of the parking lot, he said quietly, "Ellie, I wanted to ask you about something you said to me at Manetti's house."

I rubbed my forehead. "I'm kind of tired of talking about what happened at Manetti's house, if it's all the same to you."

He blew out a breath. "I need to know if you're angry that I didn't get there sooner."

"Huh?"

"You said, 'you're too late.' "

I did remember saying that, and it had been gnawing at me ever since I'd said it. I wasn't mad a Baxter, and I didn't mean to imply that he was in the wrong in any way. I was furious with myself for giving up on Vic and assuming he was dead just because Tracy said so, and I'd misplaced my feelings.

When I didn't respond, he said, "I'm so sorry. I had no idea you were in that situation. You know that if I'd known I would have been there immediately. When you didn't come back, I texted you and called, and that's when I got concerned. I know we said ten minutes, but I thought we were joking. I hope you weren't sitting there counting the minutes until I—"

He didn't need the stress of knowing I was literally sitting there counting the minutes until he showed up to save me. "I know. And I wasn't blaming you, Nick. I didn't mean it like it sounded. I was devastated. When Tracy stabbed Vic, he went lifeless. Then she started talking about him like he was dead, and I didn't question it. I shouldn't have been so easily swayed. I should have moved heaven and earth to try to revive him, even if I thought it was a lost cause."

"You did nothing wrong. I listened in from the next room while you were debriefing the FBI on all the details. It sounded to me like you fought smart and kept Tracy occupied as long as you possibly could."

"Not long enough."

"You stopped a serial killer and saved Manetti's life."

"*You* saved Manetti's life. I stood there and cried like a little bitch, ignoring him while he was bleeding out." My breath hitched in a sob.

He reached over and took my hand. "Do not blame yourself for that.

You were being tortured, and you had a head injury. You weren't thinking clearly."

"I was drunk. That was the real problem."

"None of that was your fault."

A tear spilled over and ran down my cheek. "If I wasn't such a raging alcoholic, Tracy wouldn't have decided to break me by forcing me to drink."

"Maybe not, but she would have figured out another way to hurt you. Ellie, what you did was nothing short of amazing. You shouldn't fixate on the one thing you think you did wrong."

I pulled my hand away from his to wipe my eyes. "Tell that to the guy at the hospital who had to fight all night to stay alive because I was too busy having a pity party to help him."

Baxter pulled his vehicle to a stop. "Tell him yourself."

I looked out the window and noticed we weren't in fact at my house. "I thought you were taking me home."

"I figured you'd spend about two minutes there and then insist on going to the hospital to see for yourself that Manetti is still kicking. Plus I'm betting you won't sleep until you apologize and clear your conscience."

"It's super creepy how well you know me."

He smiled, but it quickly faded. His eyes became so sad it hurt me to look at him. "On that note...since I'm still on the task force and you're now a victim who will have to testify in Tracy Greer's case as a civilian..."

I let out a heavy sigh and tried to swallow the lump in my throat. I knew this moment was coming, but that didn't prepare me for the heartache gnawing and raging inside me. "We can't be together until the trial is over."

"Yeah."

That could be a damn long time, especially since the Feds were involved.

I nodded and tried for a flippant response. It came out as a growl. "Well, this day just keeps getting better and better. I guess now we don't have to worry about how to tell Rachel about us."

"Ellie—"

"I shouldn't have brought that up. Not the time. Never mind."

The potential fallout of me ending up with Baxter so soon after the Valentine's Day incident was no longer an issue. However, I didn't even want to think about how learning of my ordeal tonight would affect my sister. It could very likely set back the progress she'd worked so hard to make. I dreaded the task of having to break the news to her when I got home. I didn't know how I was going to keep myself together if she spiraled downward again because of me.

It was as if I could feel my heart breaking. If I didn't put some distance between Baxter and myself, I was going to start ugly crying again and never stop. I opened the door. "Thanks for the ride."

"You don't want any company?"

I so very desperately wanted his company. I wanted his company more than anything I'd ever wanted in my life, and it was the one thing I couldn't have.

I cleared my throat. "Thank you for the kind offer, Detective Baxter, but that's not necessary since we're nothing more than work colleagues."

He let out a sad huff of laughter. "Oh, right. Of course, Ms. Matthews. Good night."

"Good night."

Hospital visiting hours were over, but a select few of us had been granted special permission to see Vic after his surgery. It took me a while to regroup after my conversation with Baxter and gather my courage to go up to Vic's room. There were so many things I needed to say, but I wasn't sure he'd want to hear them. And then there was the worry that between the injuries from his assault the day before and the ones from tonight, he might not be of sound enough mind to understand much at all. Concussions were tricky and unpredictable, out of anyone's control.

I met Griffin of all people in the hallway as I approached Vic's room. I intended to only nod politely and walk past, but he pulled me aside. "Ms. Matthews, I'm glad you're here. Vic could really use someone like you in his corner right now. Regardless of what happened to him tonight, he's still in some hot water with the Bureau for some of his earlier actions."

My jaw dropped. Between the trauma of tonight, the pain of having to shelve my relationship with Baxter, my worry over Rachel, and the apprehension I felt about talking to Vic, I had no filter left. "Seriously? You falsely accuse the guy of murder, won't listen to his theory—his *correct* theory—about the fact that there are two killers, offer him no protection whatsoever after being attacked by one of the killers, and take his gun so he's unarmed when the *other* killer comes after him...and yet *he's* the one who's 'still in some hot water'? Maybe *you* should be the one in hot water, *Steve.*"

His expression darkened. "I did my job."

I gave him a fake smile. "Oh, okay. Well, maybe the press would like to know just how well you did your job."

"You go to the press about this, and you'll never work in law enforcement again."

In for a penny, in for a pound. I didn't even blink as I said, "You fully reinstate him with no black marks on his record, and I won't go to the press."

He hesitated a good five seconds, staring daggers at me. "Fine."

"Fine."

Griffin flicked his eyes downward. "Vic's my friend, too, you know. It damn near killed me to have to remove him from my task force, and interrogating him for a homicide was even worse."

"Then act like it. You don't have to be a robotic G-man all the time. Have a heart. Vic certainly does."

"His heart gets him into trouble."

I sighed. "It certainly does."

I couldn't put off talking to Vic any longer, so I pushed past Griffin and went into his darkened room. He was sleeping, but I couldn't resist touching him and making sure he was indeed alive.

As I reached for his hand, his eyes fluttered open. "Ellie. I hoped you'd come."

Ooh. That sounded like the head injury talking.

I said quietly, "I wasn't sure you'd want to see me."

"Why wouldn't I want to? You're the reason I'm alive."

I frowned. "That's not entirely accurate."

"Several people have been here, and they all said the same thing—you knocked Tracy out and saved the day. And there was something about fire?

I don't know. What I do know is that I owe you my life." He shifted in the bed and winced.

I said, "Let me do the talking here. You don't seem like you're feeling so good."

He gestured at the IV bag near his bed. "I'm okay. I've got some good drugs."

That at least explained his interest in seeing me. Maybe Vic on drugs would be more receptive to my apologies.

I smiled. "That's good news. But about me saving you...the main reason I came here is to apologize."

"I should be apologizing to you for bringing you into that situation."

"I know you never would have sent that text to me, luring me to your house so Tracy could torture me. When I saw that goose egg on your head, I knew she'd set up the whole thing."

He frowned. "She knocked me out when I refused to play along with her game. She must have taken my phone at that point. I woke up bound to a chair."

"Right. So anyway...while I will take credit for stopping Tracy...I feel responsible for your colossal blood loss and the fact that you were unconscious for so long. I could have done numerous things to try to help you, but..." I looked away, unable to face him. "I thought you'd died, and I lost it. I should have kept it together and tried to do something, but I—"

"Ellie, stop. I was lucid for long enough to know what Tracy did to you. What was going on inside your head was written all over your face while she was forcing you to drink. That had to be nearly impossible for you to do, and I know you did it only so she wouldn't keep hacking me up. So don't apologize for being human."

"If you say so. But...there's something else I did to you that's maybe even worse." I hung my head. "Tracy was right. I did use you. It was wrong, and it wasn't fair to you that I went into our relationship essentially intending for it to go nowhere. I didn't think about your feelings. I know I hurt you, and I'm so sorry. I don't expect you to forgive me for that."

He stared at me for a moment. "Do you think I'm stupid?"

His reply threw me. "No, absolutely not."

"Then why did you think you could fool me? About anything?"

"I..." I shut my mouth and thought about it. "I wasn't trying to fool you... I was..." I frowned and paused another moment.

Vic's dry sense of humor was still intact at least. "You got this one. I'll wait."

I said uncertainly, "Trying to fool myself?"

"There it is."

"Well if you knew that, why didn't you call me on it? You never hesitated to call me on any of my other crap."

He flicked his eyes away. "I was hoping maybe you'd eventually succeed at fooling yourself and decide you like me better than him."

"Oh."

"But I know now that's not going to happen."

I sighed. "Well, if it makes you feel any better, romantically speaking, we can't get within ten feet of each other for at least the next year. I'm now both a victim of a suspect he'd been investigating as well as a witness to an attempted murder of an FBI agent perpetrated by said suspect."

He grinned. "Wow, that really sucks for you guys."

I smiled. "Why do I feel like your words are less than sincere?"

"Ellie, it's fine. As much as it pains me to say it, there's no denying you two are perfect for each other. Sickeningly so."

Shooting him a dubious look, I said, "Thank you?"

"Let's talk about something more fun—like how you knew that throwing drink mix on a flame would make a fireball."

I shrugged. "Being a former delinquent has its perks. The degenerates I hung out with in high school liked to play with fire. They were always tossing something on a bonfire and making it flame up or explode or something. Cornstarch is cheap, and it makes a big, flashy show. Your favorite chalky energy drink is like ninety-nine percent cornstarch, so it's a fireball waiting to happen."

"Good to know." His demeanor turned serious as he studied me for a moment. "I also heard you lost your job because of me."

Smiling, I said, "Only for a couple of hours. Griffin made sure I got reinstated, but I think I'm going to take a break for a while. If I don't pay some serious attention to my real job, I'm going to get fired from it, too. Oh, and if you were wondering about the status of your job, don't. You'll be reinstated with no tarnish on your record."

Eyeing me, he said, "What did you do? Threaten to set Griffin on fire?"

"Just his reputation."

He groaned. "Damn it, Ellie..."

I snickered. "I think the proper response is 'thank you, Ellie.' "

"Thank you, Ellie. Now will you please keep your nose out of my career?"

"Same to you."

"I guess I deserved that."

"You did." I headed for the door. Turning back, I added, "I'm glad you're not dead."

The corner of Vic's mouth curved up. "Me, too."

"Anything else I can do for you?"

"Now that you mention it, while I'm recovering, I'll need a workout partner with a painfully slow pace who won't mind if we have to cut runs short when I get tired. Know anyone like that?"

I smiled. "I know just the girl for the job."

PARTED BY DEATH
Book #4 of the Ellie Matthews Novels

The case seemed open and shut. But there are secrets below the surface that somebody will kill to protect...

When an unidentifiable body turns up at an abandoned water park, expert criminalist Ellie Matthews is recruited to once again step into a puzzling investigation that has "cold case" written all over it. Still nursing old wounds as she navigates a tense relationship with her former partner, and frustrated over a dead-end investigation, Ellie finds solace in her close friend, Vic Manetti.

Ellie barely has time to regroup before a beloved local reporter is found dead in an apparent murder-suicide. Paired up with a lively out-of-town detective and tasked with unraveling a complex network of leads, Ellie begins to retrace the explosive stories that the late journalist had been working on—only to uncover heinous secrets that somebody is willing to kill to protect.

The closer she looks, the more tangled the case becomes. With the media ready to condemn the reporter's husband as a monster, Ellie and her new partner must put their lives on the line to expose the sinister truth behind the murders—and to avoid becoming victims themselves.

Get your copy today at
severnriverbooks.com/series/ellie-matthews

ACKNOWLEDGMENTS

Thank you to the amazing team of people who have worked so hard with me to create this story—my editor, Julia Henderson, my publicist, Laura McKeighen, my cover designer, Kim Killion, and my many beta/ARC readers!

Thank you to my family, friends, fellow writers, and loyal readers for encouraging me to finish this novel, which was on hold for a couple of years while I dabbled in the coffeehouse business.

Thank you to my "Name-a-Victim" contest winner Melissa Hopkins for naming one of our poor victims, Michael Hopkins. He's named after her husband, but it's all in good fun, I assure you.

ABOUT THE AUTHOR

Caroline Fardig is the *USA Today* bestselling author of over a dozen mystery novels. She worked as a schoolteacher, church organist, insurance agent, banking trust specialist, funeral parlor associate, stay-at-home mom, and coffeehouse owner before she realized that she wanted to be a writer when she grew up. When she's not writing, she likes to travel, lift weights, play pickleball, and join in on vocals, piano, or guitar with any band who'll have her. She's also the host of a lively podcast for Gen Xers called *Wrong Side of 40*. Born and raised in a small town in Indiana, Fardig still lives in that same town with an understanding husband, two sweet kids, and three exhaustingly energetic dogs.

Sign up for Caroline Fardig's reader list at
severnriverbooks.com/authors/caroline-fardig

Printed in the United States
by Baker & Taylor Publisher Services